THE CONSEQUENCE OF WAR

BRIAN OLDHAM

The Consequence of War

ISBN: 978-0-9994748-1-5 [print]
ISBN: 978-0-9994748-0-8 [ebook]

First edition, 2017
Printed in the United States of America

Cover design by Alan Gilliland

For more information or to contact the author, please go to
www.BrianOldhamBooks.com

For Michelle.
She listened to my story.

CONTENTS

1. The Fight   1
2. The List   12
3. The Brother   20
4. The Job   24
5. Providing Cover   28
6. OCPD   32
7. The Biker   34
8. The Abyss   38
9. Dinner   44
10. The Safe House   54
11. The Secret   58
12. Solace   59
13. Watched   64
14. The Friendship   70
15. The First Strike   78
16. The Foundry   85
17. The Contract   91
18. The Condo   95
19. Fog Lifters   102
20. A Family Dinner   107
21. The Pier   111
22. The Trend   121
23. The Session   125
24. Omelet for One   132
25. The Clubhouse   135
26. The Talk   138
27. The File   143
28. The Tea Dance   149
29. The Recon   155
30. The Check-In   161
31. The Cross-Check   164
32. Closing Arguments   167
33. The Walk   170
34. The Ride   175

35. Juno's House   181
36. The Interrogation   185
37. Juno's Friend   188
38. The Man without Limits   191
39. The Confession   194
40. B. A. Lamb   201
41. The Shower   207
42. The Surveillance   212
43. Meet Rick Vargas   215
44. An Exchange of Trust   221
45. Informant   224
46. The Truth   228
47. Misericord   231
48. The Partnership   239
49. The Task Force   244
50. The Vow   248
51. The Mastiff and the Fat Boy   256
52. The Bottom   263
53. The Hospital   266
54. The Debriefing   270
55. Exit Strategy   275
56. A Slender Thread   280
57. The Coffee Shop   286
58. Final Briefing   292
59. Operation Fuck the World   297
60. Organ Concert   303
61. The Nest   310
62. Acorn Industrial Area   316
63. Elijah Moves   321
64. The Rush   323
65. The Gate   330
66. Finding Culver   336
67. Absent without Leave   339
68. The Release   341
69. Epilogue   348

Acknowledgments   351
About the Author   353

1

THE FIGHT

Elijah woke with a start, labored breathing chilling the sweat that clung to his chest. It was the same dream, the one he had most nights now, it seemed. He pushed himself up to a sitting position, listening. He was alone, as usual, but he felt a powerful presence in the room. He could vaguely make out the faint industrial sounds of the warehouse district, gearing up for a new day. Truck engines, trailers bumping along, dumpsters being opened and closed.

He was home.

Elijah ran a shaky hand through his hair, kept in the same short fashion from his military days. A habit, and a comfort. The darkness seemed especially thick around him as the dream clung to his mind. He was hyper aware—had been since he came back two years ago—and pushed himself into the focus of a soldier.

This has to stop. Needs to stop.

The dreams started differently, but always ended up with the same haunting end. With him, trapped inside the chest cavity of a dying man. He wasn't sure how he knew what a chest cavity looked like from the inside. All he knew was that it wasn't his own. It was tight, and hot, with no space between the inner chest walls and the organs. The lungs moved a lot, but the heart was firmly planted, cycling its chambers in its nest of veins and arteries. The diaphragm was moving, thick and tightly stretched across the bottom of the cavity, secured to the ribs. Was that even accurate? He needed to Google a dissection, someday. But it felt so *real*. Trapped in darkness, the scent of fresh blood thick within the damp, red walls. He was familiar with that smell. With blood.

Then it would happen the same way. The heart would speed up, the lungs and diaphragm inhaling in the damp warmth. He was trapped, amongst the clavicles holding the shoulders apart, the inner sternum, the ribs outlined against the linings. Then, with an explosive *thud*, the sternum would crack and smash inward. The strong bone breaking—no, *tearing*—the lining, swinging in to puncture the top of the heart. The bottom half of the now-broken bone would be pushed to the side, tearing a lung and ripping open blood vessels.

The blood would start to flow. An unthinkable amount of blood, gushing over the deflated lungs, past the squeezed heart like an abalone being hit to relax it before eating. A choking sound would thunder from above, and Elijah knew how this would all end. The owner of this chest was already dead, even though it would take almost eight hours for the body to be officially dead at the cellular level.

It wasn't the blood or the organs that terrified him in these dreams. It was himself. He *knew* it was himself who delivered the punch that broke the sternum. He had killed this unknown man.

Elijah had delivered this blow many times in his waking hours, and it always had the same terminal effect. It was usually part of a combination of blows to an opponent, the enemy of the day. Anticipate the movement of your opponent and step right into its path, using the advancing energy of the man to magnify the force delivered. Elijah could almost feel it, the accumulating forces from his planted foot through his limbs, up his bending torso and down his arm into the hardened, open hand where the palm would connect with the doomed sternum.

Elijah had delivered many of these blows; he couldn't say how many deaths he'd caused this way.

He hated himself for it.

He was out of the US-declared war zone, discharged now from the military. But the world was at war; a war against evil, against one another. Everyone was a soldier, some just weren't aware of it. Elijah had come to accept that there would be blood and there would be death, even as a civilian. Everyone died.

He was just moving that infinite sentence from his people to an aggressor.

Elijah pushed himself out of bed. He wasn't going to be able to go back to sleep. He lived in a safe house crafted in the quiet end of a warehouse not far from the waterfront. Juno, an old friend from the military, owned the building and had helped Elijah create the hideaway. Together they had walled off the last twenty feet of the depth of the warehouse and all across the sixty-foot width. No one knew there was an extra twelve hundred square feet in the back, let alone that someone lived there.

It was what he wanted. He felt the ache of loneliness, but in the two years since returning from Afghanistan he just couldn't . . . feel things. Not the way he used to. Connecting with people was hard, trusting them even harder. A secret home away from ignorant civilians was the best thing for him, for now.

He dressed in all black, invisible. This could be part of the reason he was alone all the time. There were small cameras installed in the grooves of the building, their displays on a monitor by the door. He peered into the dim screen. No one was crouching in front of the door. Why would anyone be there? He was an unknown, with no power or influence. A nobody.

Through the camera's eye, he could see along the side of the warehouse and around the nearest corner. All was clear. He waited for a full minute, then hit the button on his fob and quietly stepped out. There was a foggy mist coupled with the predawn darkness that he found comforting.

Elijah stood and bathed in the darkness.

There was a freestanding shed on the corner of the warehouse property where Juno and Elijah stored their bicycles and an electric plug-in car—complete with charging port. The car belonged to Elijah. Juno had a house and a family in the Adams Point neighborhood.

Elijah grabbed his bike and took off down the street. The sun wouldn't be coming up for almost another hour. At least he'd be able to get a good seat in Buster's. The coffee shop was open most hours and was a short two-mile ride from home.

Buster's had been a coffee shop down in the port for over forty years. It was a square, stand-alone building with white wood siding and two big windows in the front. There was a small porch with a round light that illuminated the hand-painted "Buster's" sign in the dark and thick fog.

Once he was parked, he folded his Montague Paratrooper bike and locked it to a wall in sight of the coffee shop. He was ready for his first caffeine download of the day. Just before he got to the door, however, he heard a definite thump, or maybe a thud. Turning around, he could make out the heads of three men behind a dumpster down and across the street, jostling around something unseen.

They were laughing and yelling to one another, but the sound was muffled by the dumpsters and the fog. Elijah crept down the street until he could see the men behind the dumpster clearly. A fourth man was crumpled on the ground, cowering as his attackers beat him.

Elijah's heart pulsed with rage against his chest. The man on the ground was slim, young—clearly not a fighter. Elijah crept closer.

"Faggot!" One of the men jeered, stomping on the kid.

Another attacker laughed, murmured something Elijah couldn't make out.

Elijah balled his fists. They were weak bastards, beating up a defenseless person in the still-dark morning whom they had determined to be gay, somehow, and deserved a beat down.

I bet none of them would have the courage to do this without his buddies.

Even from this distance, Elijah could see the beating was getting out of control. His breathing deepened and he felt the waves of battle wash over him, fueling him.

These three were now the enemy, and he was the executioner.

Elijah strode over to the group. He didn't care where they were or who would see. Without a word, he slid his arm over the shoulder of the first man in reach and placed him in a choke hold. The man struggled, grabbing at Elijah's arm for release. But after a short moment, he went down to his knees, semi-conscious.

A second man looked up from the beating. His eyes widened at the sight of Elijah, but his shock was quickly covered by anger. "Hey, fuck head! What the hell do you think you're doing?"

The third man had noticed the newcomer, but he took a step back, uncertain. Elijah knew his face said death.

Elijah dropped the man from his choke hold and pushed him to the side. That enemy was finished. He had a new opponent to face.

The second man's face twisted in a snarl. "I'm going to fuck you up, you son of a bitch."

He lunged toward Elijah. Elijah took two calculated steps toward the attacker, right arm pulled back, then exploded into the man's chest. The combined speed and force of the two men amplified the impact. Elijah heard—and felt—the sternum snap into the chest cavity. The aggressor slid to his knees and fell forward, with no attempt to soften the fall. He was either already dead or in shock and soon-to-be dead.

Elijah stared at his hand, then the body on the ground. *Just like my dream.* His stomach twisted at the thought.

There was still one more. Elijah turned to face the last attacker, but the man had turned and was hauling ass out of the vicinity. The choked man lay near the corpse (or soon-to-be corpse), but he was still alive. He'd survive. Elijah almost smiled, but didn't. It was a job well done, but he walked a dangerous line. One he feared that crossing could be a point of no return.

Elijah stepped closer to the beaten man still cowering on the ground. He was in his twenties, dressed in what were once nice business clothes but were now torn and stained with dirt and blood. The man looked pretty beat up, but it looked like Elijah had gotten to him before any lasting damage was done.

Elijah crouched next to him. "The fight's over, man. You OK?"

The young man groaned and rolled over. He had a black eye blooming across his left cheek.

"Should I call for help?"

The man gave a small shake of the head. "No. I just need . . . I should get out of here."

Elijah extended a hand and helped the stranger to his feet.

"Why'd you help me?"

Elijah looked at his hands, specifically his right one. His murderous one. "They were assholes. You were defenseless. I can't just walk away from that." He shrugged. "Feel your ribs. Everything intact? Does it hurt to breathe?"

The stranger patted his sides and took a deep breath. "I'm OK." He stood at an odd angle, a clear indication that his back hurt. There were blood stains on his shirt sleeves, and he was bleeding from his nose and lip. He would be sore for at least a week, longer depending on how badly he bruised.

The man took a small step and winced, taking his weight off one leg. "Damn. Could you . . . ?" He gestured at his leg, a little sheepish.

Elijah glanced wistfully down the street at Buster's, then made a decision. "Sure. Let's go get some breakfast." He laughed to himself about that. He never went to breakfast with anyone. It took saving a man's life to get a breakfast buddy.

The stranger smiled. "I'm Phillip. Phillip Statham. Thanks so much, you're being very gallant."

Elijah recoiled at that, but helped Phillip walk the short distance to Buster's. He'd saved people before, it was part of being a redeemer, but he rarely had any contact with those people. It was his habit to just fight and then move on, letting the victim decide on their own what to do next.

Buster's was a small joint, with a small staff consisting of one chef and one other person to manage the diners and keep an eye on the cash register. Most regulars were quiet, respecting one another's privacy. It's what had attracted Elijah to the shop in the first place. That, and it was close to work. Elijah was friends with most of the regulars, though they all only knew each other's first names.

When Elijah walked through the front doors with a beat-up stranger hanging on his arm, he attracted some curious glances. But no one bothered them.

The manager, Elroy, greeted Elijah with a familiar smile that disappeared when he noticed Phillip. With a concerned look, Elroy grabbed a key from behind the counter and handed it to the newcomer. "Why don't you go wash up? You look like shit."

Phillip thanked him and limped off to the restroom, key in hand.

When he had left, Elroy raised an eyebrow at Elijah. "Really? You're bringing them in now?"

Buster, the café's owner, made a point of giving people a second chance in life. One of the main beneficiaries of that was Elroy Peters, who had done fifteen years for bank jobs. Once he was out of prison, he had decided he was never going back. He found Buster after that and had been working at the restaurant with him ever since. He knew his regulars, including Elijah, and was the human news source for them all.

Elijah kept his face neutral. Anything he revealed could be added to Elroy's news network. "It was three to one."

Elroy nodded knowingly. "They must not be from around here, or they would've heard about the masked avenger."

"Yeah, without the mask."

Elroy smiled. "You should think about getting one." He glanced outside and his smile faded. "There're cameras all around this area, you know. You should be more careful."

A few minutes later, Phillip joined Elijah at his table. Each table had a flag stand that looked like a mast; the diners could raise their flags when then needed help. Elroy had already poured two cups of nice, hot coffee and left a menu for Phillip.

Breakfast passed in silence, which suited Elijah just fine. They each had oatmeal with berries and honey and crushed almonds along with a thick piece of toasted seed bread. At one point, Phillip made a comment that it was unusual food for a diner like this, and Elijah had nodded at their fellow patrons around the room. "Most guys here are either bodybuilders or just healthy eaters. You feed your audience." Men in this part of town were warehouse workers, dockworkers, truck drivers, and such. There were some who were drunks or dope heads, and some were just straight, honest laborers. But a lot of the men, at least the ones Elijah ran into, were solitary men who took pride in their physical health and used a health-conscious lifestyle to keep them out of trouble.

It worked for him, most times.

Phillip played with the table flag, his fingers idly running along the mast. In a quiet voice, he asked, "Did you kill those two men?"

Elijah didn't say anything. No one in the café was listening to them, or would say anything if they were. Some suspected what Elijah did in his spare time.

"They weren't moving," Phillip continued. "I'm not even sure they were breathing. Are they dead?"

Elijah took a sip of coffee. "Only one. He stepped toward me to hit me and I put up my hand to protect myself. I don't even know what really happened myself, but he must've had a weak heart."

Part of him wasn't sure if that was entirely true. There had been other ways he could've protected himself. Wasn't there?

Phillip dropped his hand from the mast. He was shaking. "Oh god. And it all happened so fast . . ." He swallowed and glanced out the window toward the dumpster, out of view. "It could have been me."

"But it wasn't. So calm down. They were going to kill you. It was a real fight and I did what I was trained to do."

Elijah frowned. He had been involved in many fights over the last two years, some of them with similar results to that morning. If he kept on like this, he was afraid he was going to disappear into the darkness. The frustrating part was he reveled in his competency. It wasn't fair that he was so talented as a soldier and that it didn't mean anything now that he was home.

"Trained? Trained for what—"

Red and blue lights flashed outside the café. The wail of an ambulance was in the distance, not far behind the cruisers.

Elroy came over to the table and tapped Phillip on the shoulder and motioned for him to follow. Phillip threw a worried glance at Elijah, who nodded for him to go. There was a false wall in the pantry for private goods, large enough for Phillip to stand behind. Phillip had done a good enough job cleaning up, but you couldn't hide the blood stains and bruises from a cop with too many questions.

Elroy came back out and stood next to the cash register, reading the paper. An officer came in asking if anyone had seen or heard anything about a fight down the block. Elijah shifted in his seat, careful to make only the appropriate amount of eye contact with the officer. Too little, you were suspicious. Too much, and you were guilty.

There was little surprise when no one could come up with any information. The officer motioned for Elroy to get him a coffee to go.

"We're dealing with a *homicide*, people." The officer stood in the doorway. "This makes it a problem for everyone." He looked around the room to see if that got any reaction at all, but no one stirred. "The manager's got my card, in case any of you suddenly remember something."

The officer left with his coffee in hand. Once he was gone, Elijah felt a few side glances thrown his way, but no one made any trouble. No one would.

Elroy retrieved Phillip a while later, once the cops had collected their photos and left the scene.

Phillip sat with a heavy thud. "Everything OK?"

Elijah nodded. "Trying to keep you from getting involved with that mess."

Phillip released a sigh and ran a hand through his hair. "Thank you. You've done so much for me, and I don't even know your name."

"That's right."

Elroy refilled their coffee mugs. "How'd you get into this in the first place?"

"I left early this morning to go to the train and they picked me up. Next thing I know, I'm over here trying to get away from them." He gave a shaky laugh. "I can't believe I was almost a martyr for the gay community. In Oakland!"

Elroy exchanged a glance with Elijah. *Gay?* it seemed to ask. Elijah just shrugged.

"I have some money," Phillip said. "Let me pay for breakfast. As a thank you." He took a twenty and ten and handed them to Elroy. "No change, please."

Elroy smiled and said to Elijah, "I like him." He walked off toward the cash register.

"Do they know where you live now?" Elijah asked.

Phillip nodded. "They saw me leave my condo. Is there any way you could walk me home to grab a few things? I'm going to clear out for a few days, especially if one of those guys is out there right now. Is it too much to ask for you to come with me? It will only take a half hour—max."

Elijah took a deep breath and let it out. This was not how a redeemer's day went. But he surprised himself when he turned to Phillip and said, "I've got a bit before work starts. Sure."

They left through the front door, Phillip still leaning on Elijah. "You're not some kind of serial killer or something, are you?"

"No." Elijah stared ahead as they walked. "I'm a soldier."

2

THE LIST

Elijah smiled when he saw that their destination was one of the new high-end condos built in the waterfront district, an attempt to attract the more adventurous urban dwellers into the area. Phillip led the way into the building's lobby, Elijah following behind as he walked his bike. They rode the elevator up to the third floor to Phillip's place, just two doors down the hall.

The apartment was surprisingly European in style, with soft lighting and mid-century modern furniture, the kind Elijah usually only saw in storefront windows.

Phillip dropped his keys on a table and took a deep breath. "I really appreciate all that you've done today. Do you want some cold water or juice or anything?"

"I can find it. You just pack. Is that OK?"

"Sure. You can figure out the kitchen." Phillip went into his bedroom.

Elijah found the glasses in an elm wood cabinet by the sink. While he waited for the fridge dispenser to fill the glasses, he examined the modern, expensive-looking appliances. Whatever

Phillip did for a living, he wasn't bad at it. Even the floors were beautiful.

He found Phillip packing a duffel bag in the master bedroom. It was clean, sparse yet intentionally decorated with the same style of furniture from the living room and kitchen. "All this European?" he asked, handing the man a full glass.

Phillip took the water with a nod of thanks. "Danish. I know, stereotypical of a gay man, right?"

Elijah shook his head. "It's nice."

Phillip smiled. "These days it's hard to predict how people will react. Thank you."

Elijah shrugged, a little embarrassed. "I understand not being mainstream."

Phillip pulled a white button-down shirt from the closet and began folding it carefully. "You know, most parents can tell early on if their child's going to be gay. Fathers usually have a hard time with it, what with not passing on the macho gene and all. But not my dad." He placed the shirt in the duffel bag and reached for another, this one pastel orange. Elijah stood quietly by the door-frame. He wasn't sure why Phillip was telling him this.

"My father was really involved in my childhood," Phillip continued. "He saw it before Mom did. He never tried to 'fix' me, he was just there for me. He's a great listener."

Elijah walked back out to the living room, glass in hand. "Not your mom so much?"

Phillip laughed. "Hell no. Mom confronted me one day when I was in high school. We're getting dinner on and she asked over her shoulder if I'm gay. I said yeah, I was, and she just froze. Iced me out the rest of the meal."

Elijah ran a finger over the rim of a crystal vase. He was interested, for some reason, in Phillip's story. Maybe it was because he'd just saved the guy's life. He asked, "And your dad?" The condo wasn't so big that they couldn't talk from separate rooms.

"When I told my mom, Dad was sitting at the table. He gave

me a little nod and a smile. He'd known all along. We've had a great relationship ever since. It's the kind of relationship where we can be together and not have to talk, you know?"

Elijah nodded, though Phillip wasn't there to see it. That's how it was with Juno. Elijah now stood by the sliding balcony door, watching the waterfront district below. "How long did it take for your mom to come around?"

"Ten years and counting." Phillip strode into the living room, searching for something. "She never told anyone I was gay, and to this day tries to cover it up if anyone suggests it." He pulled a laptop charger from a wall plug and returned to the bedroom, calling over his shoulder, "She's always been disappointed in me. No number of scholarships seemed to fix it."

The sound of sliding drawers and padded thumps came from the closet.

Elijah poked his head into the second bedroom, examining the big closets and airy bathroom. It was all very homey and comfortable. He liked this place, the way it was decorated, and he found himself liking Phillip. Wait, did he just think about decorations?

Elijah said, "You seem confident in yourself now."

Phillip walked back into the living room, the big duffel bag and a backpack slung over his shoulders. "I guess because of my dad. I dress how I like, but I'm pretty calm in public. I'm very comfortable just being me."

Elijah smiled and shook his head, remembering how Phillip had called him *gallant* right after Elijah had killed a man. He was impressed with Phillip's confidence, but there was more to it than that. Phillip was very aware of his self, of who he was and what purpose he served. He was an outcast in society, but he still *fit*. Elijah envied him.

"What?" Phillip asked.

"Nothing. It's Elijah, by the way. Elijah McCoy."

Phillip grinned and extended a hand. "Nice to finally meet you, Elijah."

Phillip had a firm handshake. That was good. Elijah nodded toward the door. "If you're ready, let's get moving. Maybe we can each actually work today."

Elijah walked Phillip down to his Scion iQ in the underground lot. They exchanged numbers and parted ways. The fight had taken place just before six. It was only seven thirty. If he hurried, Elijah could still make the eight o'clock roll call.

The office for Longshoremen's Union Local 10 was an old brick building down by the Oakland Docks, not too far from Buster's. When Elijah arrived at the foreman's shed, there was still a long line of workers waiting to sign in for the day. There was almost always work to do in this busy port, but Elijah didn't always feel up to working. Some days, he just didn't feel like being around people, even tough dockworkers. But today, he wanted to work. Hell, he *needed* to work today—and for the next couple of days too, loading and unloading trucks and ships. He needed to get his mind off his dreams, the bodies, both real and remembered.

He liked to work with men and out in the open doing honest labor (mostly). He got himself on the work list and waited for the call. When a ship was ready to unload, there'd be a call for salaried workers and extra casual workers. Once you accepted a job, you stuck with it until it was finished. It was possible to unload some container ships in fifteen hours. The pay was just over twenty-four dollars an hour, and Elijah figured the average guy here was making around forty-five grand a year. Being part of a union had its perks. By paying monthly dues, he got contract negotiations, safety protection, and lots of benefits. Elijah had managed to work enough over the past few years to make around fifty grand, just from dock work.

Elijah usually worked about three days a week. He paid no rent to Juno and never would. He had tried, they'd almost come to blows a few times about it, but Juno wasn't having it, period. As a result, Elijah was able to keep most of his hard-earned, honest money.

He also made quite a bit of money in less honorable ways.

Sten Ekbridge was the foreman on the docks where Elijah most often worked. Sten was a good friend of Juno's, aware of his and Elijah's six-year tour in Afghanistan and Iraq. He made sure Elijah was picked early any day he showed up. Whether as a favor to Juno or out of respect to veterans, Elijah wasn't sure. But one favor Sten did directly for Elijah was to keep the other men away from him. He let the word *executioner* slip one day and that pretty much took care of it. Elijah preferred the term *redeemer*, but he didn't care what Sten said so long as it got the message across. It did.

"Don't fuck with him," Elijah had overheard on more than one occasion, from more than one man. Sten wasn't protecting Elijah, but the others.

When Elijah got out on a job, he'd just go to work. He avoided the card games, the drug sales, and the lazy bastards who were just there for an easy paycheck. If anyone asked about him (they rarely did), he'd just shrug. They didn't care about the silent veteran. They realized he wasn't going out with them for after-hours drinks or to a game on the weekend. He was there to work, no more.

That evening, Elijah came down from the ship for his dinner break to find Juno waiting for him, holding a small Tupperware that was sure to be full of Gabija's tasty cooking. It always made Elijah smile that, even though Juno was Lithuanian, his friend's coffee-colored skin blended in with many of the longshoremen moving around on the dock.

Juno was a giant of a man, towering over Elijah at six foot four and probably weighing over two hundred and thirty hard-packed pounds. He had been a real chore to pull out of the line of fire. That had been in the hundred-hour battle they fought in back in Afghanistan. Elijah had pulled a wounded Juno into a protected position during the battle before gathering the weapons of fallen soldiers and fighting off the enemy's attempts to capture or kill them. He'd defended his injured friend for over four hours before relief finally came. Elijah had taken the lives of many enemies that day. Juno was the only person that saw Elijah as a human being with value, and he wasn't going to let anyone harm him. It was amazing to Juno, and the man was forever grateful.

Elijah joined his old friend on the docks and shared a meal.

Juno handed Elijah a napkin. "I went to Buster's for coffee this morning. Elroy had an interesting story for me. What the fuck happened, man?"

Elijah shrugged, feeling sheepish. "You know I can't just walk away from bullies beating up a helpless person."

"Bullies, sure." Juno took a bite of kugelis. "You killed a man, bud. You went too far, and you know it. Worst of it is, it looks like a revenge killing, or a gang thing. Nothing missing, body undisturbed. Cold murder, man. The police *have* to look into this. You could have at least taken his wallet or something."

Elijah smiled. "Or marked him in some way. Written a hate message with his blood or something like that."

Juno fought to conceal a smile, but Elijah knew him too well. "You fuck. OK. Who was it this time? Some little kid, a charity worker, Mother Theresa?"

Elijah swallowed his bite and shook his head. "Grown man. Gay. It was a hate crime, and it would've turned into murder if I hadn't stepped in."

"It still turned into murder."

"It got to me, alright? I just like to remind people that there's another world out there, one where they're held accountable. Where you get what you give."

"So, then what would *you* get in this world of yours?" Juno sighed, setting his empty Tupperware down beside him. "It sounds like you're trying to justify what you did. Look, I get the desire to interfere with that kind of a weak-ass bullshit, but did you have to kill the asshole? Was he carrying some kind of weapon? Did he threaten to cut you up? Shoot you?"

Elijah didn't answer. Across the dock, a seagull cried.

Juno sighed again. "I thought you were trying to stop being so violent."

Elijah looked down, examining the grime caked under his fingernails. "I am. The second guy attacked and I just . . . snapped. I didn't decide to kill him, it just took hold of me. And when I did . . . I enjoyed it." He swallowed. His throat was dry. "I knew he was dead the moment he went down. But for the first time, I stopped to talk to the victim and ended up taking him to breakfast."

He wasn't sure why he mentioned talking to Phillip, as if the small act of kindness would forgive his greater sin.

"I know, that's what Elroy said. You're going to get shot by the police one of these days. They won't bother arresting you."

Elijah nodded, still looking down. He knew this.

"So take it easy. Stop this shit." Juno's eyes were hard and he was his soldier self. "You've got a good job, a nice home. A friend." Juno nudged him. "You're turning it around, and Gabija and I really want you to come out of this. *I* want you to come out of this. It's been over two years since we got back, Elijah. I don't like watching you slowly embrace your inner hermit—or worse."

Elijah looked at Juno. "Something's after me. I keep having that same dream."

"The one with the chest?"

"Yeah. I didn't go out looking for trouble this morning, but I can't just walk away from bullshit. We killed so many people, Juno. How does coming home change that? How can we be encouraged to be so cruel overseas and then just expect us to be, what? We were vicious, man. Great soldiers. It's just not as easy for me as it was for you. I wish it was."

Juno leaned forward, propping his elbows on his lap as he stared across the shipyard. In the dying light, he didn't look like a man in his early thirties. He looked older, tired. "I was lucky enough to have the love of a good woman who gave me children to love. My family reminds me every day who I am, who I want to be, and what I have to do. Gabija gave me that. It's time for you to find someone to care about."

Elijah snorted. "Easy enough."

"Let me connect you with my therapist. No, I'm serious. Talking to her really helped me. She's the one who diagnosed me with PTSD—you probably have it too. You've just gotta talk it out, man. You're a good guy. A good friend. Let Selma remind you of that."

Elijah nodded his head. "You know, I don't think I've ever been in love. Fucked up, right? I feel so fucking lonely." He let out a breath, more of a frustrated huff than a sigh. "Fine. Think she'd want to talk to me?"

Juno grinned, his weariness vanishing in smile wrinkles. He clasped Elijah's shoulder and shook him. "Yeah, I think she will."

Together, they watched the sun dip below the horizon, the shipyard a silhouette against a bloody sky.

3

THE BROTHER

Phillip left work early that day. Despite his best efforts, he couldn't completely conceal the cuts and bruises on his face, and the attention was more than he could bear. He loved his job, but it was hard enough being the only gay man in the office. Showing up looking like a poster child for a social program didn't help. That would be another benefit to staying at Rick's house. Rick understood. They'd been best friends for years, and Rick was one of Phillip's greatest inspirations when it came to emotional strength and endurance. The way he'd handled what happened to Jason . . . it was moving.

Rick lived in the Hoover-Foster neighborhood not far from the waterfront. It was an up-and-coming area with lots of urban amenities. The two-story home, a restored Victorian, had a long stairway up to the front door. It looked like something right out of a Southern romantic comedy, but in the heart of Northern California. The diversity in this neighborhood was part of what had attracted Rick to the area. There were more women, a low white population, and an open-minded friendliness that made the Brazilian businessman feel safe and at home. Phillip had to agree.

If it was closer to his work, he'd want to live here too, but he had his emotional connection to the Produce District.

Phillip pulled up at Rick's home and knocked on the front door. Rick answered a moment later and stepped out to hug Phillip.

"Oh my god, you look worse than I imagined," Rick said, examining Phillip's face. "Your hair is a tragedy. Come in. I want to hear everything—did you go to work this way?"

Phillip followed Rick into the living room. "I had no choice. I couldn't force myself to heal faster. I was tempted to buy concealer on my way in, but I was already running late."

"I don't think makeup would cover that bruise." Rick shook his head. "Water? Gin and tonic?"

"Yes, that one." Phillip dropped his duffel bag and collapsed on the couch. The soft seat was a comfort. "I had an awful day. I've taken a lot of verbal abuse over the years for being gay, but I never thought people would act like animals. First the men in the alley, then the guys at work. The only decent human being I've interacted with today was the man who rescued me, and I'm pretty sure he'll be in jail by the end of the night."

Rick returned from the kitchen and handed him a crystal glass with the gin and tonic. There were crushed limes at the bottom, just as Phillip liked it.

"Why do you say that?"

"Because he killed one of the men beating me."

Rick gasped. "He what? Phillip! You didn't tell me that part."

A sob escaped Phillip. He couldn't help it. There had been so much that had happened, so much violence and confusion. So much pain. "I think he had to. It was that or die. I thought—I thought I was going to die today. It was awful, knowing that these guys could do anything to me and I couldn't fight back. But this guy came along and saved me. He knocked one guy out, killed another—it happened so fast!"

Phillip took a sip of his drink. Cool on his lips, the tickling warmth in his belly helped calm him.

"Who was this guy?" Rick asked. "Did he hurt you?"

Phillip shook his head. "No, he was so helpful. He's a veteran named Elijah. He took me to breakfast—but I paid, as the gentleman I am—and escorted me home to pack. He had this air of danger around him, you know? Like he could kick your ass with a glare."

"Sounds hot."

Phillip gave a weak smile. "You think everyone is hot. But he kind of was, yeah. He didn't shout, or make a bit fuss to scare off the thugs. He just walked in and took over. I felt safe around him."

"Sounds like he took care of it."

"No. One guy ran off and the other one will be out of the hospital soon, I'm sure. Oh god. What if they come back for me?" Phillip put his face in his hands and took a deep breath. *Don't cry. Not now, don't cry.*

Rick scooted closer to him and put an arm around his shoulder. "I don't know how smart these guys are, but I would think they'd be afraid that this Elijah guy would kill them if he ever saw them again. But you can stay here as long as you want. I worry about you living down in the mean old docks. You should be more aware. I don't want any more martyrs for the gay world to mourn. Besides." Rick smiled and gave him a shake. "It'll be fun living together for a while. Like a long slumber party."

"Thanks. I don't know how long it takes for haters like those to get over the idea of killing me. I just can't stop thinking about the man who saved me. He killed a man for me today. That freaks me out. I don't want killing in my life—it's horrible."

"Me either," Rick said. "I'm glad he saved you but wish it didn't take killing someone. How did he act after all that? Did he seem any kind of normal when he was in your condo?"

"Yeah—totally relaxed!" Phillip sat up. Rick handed him his glass to drink. He was definitely starting to feel better. "I mean, I guess it makes a little sense. He's been to war, I'm sure this wasn't his first time. He was really kind to me, actually. He listened to my coming out story."

"You shared that?"

"Yeah, and he *listened*. When we were leaving, he gave me his name and we exchanged phone numbers. He didn't seem to want to be left alone, but he didn't invite me to contact him, either."

Rick looked thoughtful for a moment. "A dangerous hunk saving men in the slums of the city . . . it's like a comic book. Well, let's keep an eye on the local news. I'm sure the homicide is being covered. Now." Rick turned his body to face Phillip, a wicked smile on his face. "Tell me exactly what he looked like—in detail."

Phillip shook his head. "You're sick, Rick."

4

THE JOB

The next morning, Elijah sat in a Peet's Coffee Shop sipping an Americano and browsing the Internet on his laptop. After what had happened yesterday, it was best he stayed away from Buster's for a while. He always enjoyed the atmosphere at Peet's. The heavy aroma of coffee and pastries was so good, and the people were usually in a pretty good mood, too.

He had decided to take a break from dock work. Normally, he could power through his problems by working hard and collecting sweat and honest muscle. But not this time. The thug's death weighed heavily on his mind to the point where it was too great a distraction for him to work safely. So instead he found a Peet's and spent the morning scrolling through the news and doing a little research on PTSD. So far, what he had found seemed to describe him fairly well: social isolation, hostility, hyper vigilance, nightmares.

By the time Elijah had arrived home last night, Juno had left him a message saying he'd set up an appointment with Dr. Selma Greenfeld next Monday. All Elijah had to do was confirm. She worked for an agency, or maybe her own business, called Solace. It couldn't hurt to go see her. If anything, it'd be interesting just to see the person who'd been talking to Juno for the past couple of years.

Someone tapped his shoulder.

He jumped, jerking around to see a beautiful Latina woman standing behind him. His reaction had startled her. He could see it in her soft brown eyes.

"I'm sorry," she said. "I didn't mean to scare you. My name is Roxanna. I'm Hector Ramirez's sister—he works with you on the docks? He said that I could ask you for help. Is this an OK time? Or maybe another time . . ."

Roxanna's hair tumbled over her shoulders in long silky curls, black and shiny. She was wearing a soft tan sweater that zipped down a little in the front, and she wore tight jeans and had a Coach purse slung over her shoulder. She must have been in her late twenties, not too much younger than Elijah.

She smelled good.

Elijah stood and pulled out the chair next to him. "Sit down, please. What's up, Roxanna? Hector OK?"

Roxanna let out a deep breath, a little more emphatically than Elijah thought necessary. Her words tumbled out. "Hector's fine. I've been watching you for ten minutes. I was trying to get my courage up to come over here. I just—Hector said you would know what to do."

Elijah nodded slowly. His stomach tightened as he saw where this was going. There was really only one reason why people ever came to talk to him, and they were always referred by others.

"Just take it easy," he said. "We're talking. Can I get you a cup of something? A pastry?"

She shook her head. "No, thank you."

"Alright. I like Hector, you know. Strong guy, great worker. And he's pretty funny too, I'm sure you know." He smiled, trying to lighten the mood.

Roxanna returned the smile, hers a little smaller. "He's always been a great storyteller." She swallowed. When Elijah didn't say more, she went straight to the point. "I've been having a problem with a man following me around and bothering me constantly. I've asked him to stop and leave me alone. He's convinced I'll go out with him, but when I say no he gets mad." She gripped her purse in her lap. "He scares me."

The ambient sounds of the café faded as Elijah focused on her words. "A stalker, huh? Can you describe him for me?"

"His name is Penny Garlitz. He's a big, scary-looking guy and has a goatee and tattoos on his neck and arm. Horrible ones, about death and stuff. He could be a recruiting officer for a local bike gang. No manners and a foul mouth. I can't get rid of him."

Elijah took a sip of his coffee. There were bike gangs in Oakland, her jest could be not far off. "How did this all start?"

"I went to a club with my girlfriends about three weeks ago. We were having a good time. Most of us came straight from work for the happy hour. This guy—Penny—was sitting at the bar staring at me. He tried to buy me a drink but I wouldn't let the bartender set it down next to us. I was being clear."

Elijah nodded. He felt his good moral resolve slipping. He knew what this man needed and he was able to deliver that. It was why people came to talk to him. "Then what happened?"

Roxanna glanced around, as if afraid she'd find Penny standing at the cashier. She put her hand on Elijah's arm. He flinched. "He came over to talk to me and we all pushed him away. We were laughing at him. I know that sounds bad, but I didn't think much of it at the time. When I got home that night, I saw him on the corner sitting on a motorcycle from my apartment window. He was trying to figure out what apartment I was in, I know it. He's outside my building all the time now. He shouts at me on my way to my car, telling me to go out with him, to have some fun, that I'm a hot dancer. It's embarrassing and frightening."

"And how exactly do you want me to help?" Elijah put his coffee down. "Don't be vague. Tell me what you want."

Roxanna looked around the room again and scooted her chair a little closer to Elijah. They leaned toward each other. She was close enough for him to feel her soft breath on his face. "Hector says that you can scare anyone. I don't want you to hurt him or kill him, but I want this to stop." She looked down at her lap, took out an envelope, and put it under his backpack on the chair. "He's going to hurt me. Please, help."

Elijah touched his backpack to acknowledge the transfer. "I don't think talking to him is going to stop him," he said slowly. "From what you're saying, sounds like it would just get him going. I can hurt him. Talking isn't going to do anything but get him mad."

Roxanna shuddered. "If you attack him, one of you might end up dead."

"What if that's what it takes to make him go away?"

Roxanna grabbed Elijah's wrist. Her eyes were focused, full of fear. "Please promise you can do this without killing him. I won't get any help from the legal system 'til he harms me. I need your help."

Elijah considered this. He'd heard of what crazy stalkers were capable of. Serious injury, rape, abductions, even forced prostitution. There was nothing to say to a person like that, no threat that could stop them from getting what they wanted. If Penny was anything like Roxanna described, she could be in serious danger. And from the way she gripped his wrist, she knew it.

"I'll help you," he said. "Here's what we can do."

5

PROVIDING COVER

J uno's office was in the front of the warehouse. He liked being close to the heart of his business, overseeing the warehouse operations and stopping by the Port to connect with those handling his imports and exports. Juno started Ranger PX just after returning from war. It had been an odd opportunity, the idea of starting a trade business with civilians he'd met in the Middle East. Elijah had been opposed to the idea at first, but Juno didn't believe there were as many enemies in the world as his friend did. He wanted to provide the food products that would allow those who'd served to eat the cuisine they'd learned to love while on tour.

Over the past two years, Ranger PX had boomed. He imported ethnic specialty foods like teas, spices, curries, and tahini from the Durand Line through the mountains that served as a negotiated border between the countries involved. In return, he also exported tools—from quality hammers to Sawzalls—all over the Middle East, from Saudi Arabia across Iran and up into the Hindu Kush and through Afghanistan and Pakistan. It felt good, working with the poor people he met on the other side of the world. In a way, it was like an absolution for the horrors he had caused in war. They were good people. Whenever his trading partners were in the US, he had them come visit him in Oakland City, if possible. He took very good care of them. After all, they had taken care of him, once before.

Needless to say, Juno was a busy man. The son of a Lithuanian immigrant, Juno was raised to believe that hard work was one of the greatest virtues a man could possess. He'd worked hard all his life, helping his father with the family store, studying through business school, and then fighting for his country. It hadn't been easy, coming home. After experiencing the things he had in combat, it was difficult to find the motivation to work. But since he had Gabija, he had purpose. Something to work hard for, someone to provide for. Especially with their children.

Not everyone would think running a trade company could be satisfying, but for Juno his business was like another child. There was great joy to be found in its growth, and some growing pains. He made frequent trips to his accountant's office and his attorney's office for paperwork, the ultimate pain.

He was sitting in his attorney's office, writing a contract for a new vendor, when his phone vibrated.

Juno and Elijah had a deal that when one of them called, the other would answer or text within a few minutes. So when Juno looked down and saw that he had a call coming in from his friend, he excused himself and stepped out of his attorney's office.

"Hey, buddy, what's up?"

There was the faint sound of traffic coming from Elijah's end. "I'm down in the alley behind your attorney's office. I saw your Leaf. Can you come down and talk for a minute?"

Juno frowned. The alley? What was so important that Elijah had hunted him down to talk in person? "I'll be down in five."

Alleys in this part of town were nothing like the movies. This one was clean, sunny, and provided a nice quiet place to talk. Elijah leaned against the brick wall of the attorney's building, his hands stuffed in his pockets. He was alert, as usual, his face set in a serious, almost aggressive frown. It broke Juno's heart. Elijah may be in jeans and a T-shirt, but he had never taken off the soldier's heavy uniform, and its weight was tearing his old friend down.

Elijah grabbed Juno's hand and gave a shoulder bump, a familiar greeting. "I accepted a job today, and after what we talked about last night, I thought you'd want to know."

Juno suppressed a groan. *Is this another redeemer job?* "Do I get to be an accountability partner or something?"

"Just a voice of reason."

"I thought this voice of reason told you to walk away."

"I know, I'm working on it. I confirmed with Selma. I really want out of all this."

Juno nodded. "That's a great start." He paused, trying to search Elijah's unreadable face. "But you're still taking the job?"

"You know Hector Ramirez?"

That took Juno by surprise. What would Hector want with a redeemer?

"Yeah?"

"I talked to his sister. She's having a problem with a stalker, of the biker variety. She's tried everything to get rid of him, but it's only escalating. She came to me for help."

"What does she want you to do?" Juno's frown deepened. Stalkers, bikers—none of this sounded good.

"That's what I wanted to talk about. Whatever I do has to be serious enough that he can't come back on her or me after a twelve-week physical therapy course, right?"

Juno grimaced. "You and I both know that if he's still alive when you walk away, he'll plan your murder for the rest of his life."

Elijah stared at his feet, silent. Juno sighed. "When are we finding him?"

Elijah looked up, excited. "You're coming with me?"

"To keep you out of trouble, if nothing else. I'm willing to put my body where my mouth is. I'll help."

Elijah grinned. "Thanks, man."

"We'll just beat the shit out of him and see if he comes back. Got it? If he does, we'll beat the shit out of him again, but no more. Does Roxanna know what you're going to do?"

"Yeah, we made a plan. Tonight, six thirty. I'll pick you up." Elijah clasped a hand on Juno's shoulder. "Thank you. Really."

Juno watched as his friend rode away, out of the alley and back toward the warehouse. When he was out of sight, Juno turned and kicked a nearby trash can. This wasn't what turning your life around looked like. It was a tough situation, for sure. Roxanna was in real danger, and it didn't feel like she had many options.

I've got a wife, and kids. I'm too old to be doing stuff like this.

But his friend needed him there, whether he knew it or not. Elijah had had death in his eyes—always a dangerous sign. Maybe this was why Elijah was so deadly where Juno was not.

Death might be his purpose.

6

OCPD

Officer Shana Thomas sat at her desk working on reports from the previous day's shift. She'd been excited about a lot of her new duties when she joined the force, but she didn't realize how much she'd love writing up the reports. It was every criminology major's dream—all the details, research, and follow ups were an exciting challenge to her. All relevant information was important in prosecuting a case. Besides, it'd really help her career to be seen as overly detailed.

Sergeant Jamel Marks walked into the station. Shana could feel his eyes on her before he spoke. "Thomas, why are you always here so early?"

"Lots to do," she said, not looking up from her typing. "Criminals to catch, reports to file."

Shana had been a full-time student athlete while in college, dedicating forty-plus hours a week to basketball while juggling a full load of classes. Working late and arriving on time, if not early, was second nature to her by now. Working at the station felt to her a lot like her college days, only now instead of dribbling a ball down the court she was hustling perps into court. She was determined to be the best cop in the department before she hit thirty.

Marks huffed. "Enjoy all that."

She waved him on as he walked past her desk in the bullpen and into Lieutenant Culver's office.

Shana had just poured herself a second cup of coffee when Marks emerged from the lieutenant's office.

"Hey Thomas!" he called.

"What?" Shana looked up in surprise when Marks dropped a file on her desk.

"The lieutenant wants me to follow up on a death near Buster's Café this morning. I asked if I could use you to work this. You free?"

Shana raised an eyebrow. "Why me?"

Marks smiled. "Because I hate paperwork. Check it out."

Shana opened the file and scanned its contents. The victim was found before sunrise by a dumpster near the docks. Units were on scene within ten minutes after an anonymous call. Preliminary evaluation of the deceased was that he was hit once in the sternum, crushing it. The deceased had his wallet, keys, and cell phone on him. No money was missing, ID still in the wallet—as was his pocketknife.

"It doesn't look like the attacker took anything," she said, closing the file.

"Not that we can tell. He had an employee's ID around his neck. It looks like he works for a trucking line in the port. The lieutenant wants us out and talking to people this afternoon to construct a timeline. How fast can you finish your current reports?"

Shana took a large gulp of her coffee. "Pretty fast."

7

THE BIKER

That evening, Elijah picked Juno up in the Focus plug-in and drove over to Roxanna's office.

People might have thought it odd to see two tough-looking men riding in an electric car, but after fighting in the Middle East they had both decided that they hated oil and petrochemical fuels. Neither of them wanted to spend a dime on something that would fund the enemy that had killed so many of their friends. Both agreed that the majority of US citizens were under some kind of mass hypnosis—why else would everyone own gas-powered cars and drive them all the time, then complain about the terrorist empire abroad? It was insanity. That was also why Elijah and Juno had bikes and walked whenever they could, if they weren't using public transit.

For nights like this, however, it was good to be in a car.

Elijah parked next to the opening of the employee parking lot, waiting. He texted Roxanna and told her they were there, ready to go. Her navy-blue Dodge Charger pulled out of the lot twenty minutes later. They followed her, at a reasonable but vigilant distance. Elijah and Juno exchanged a short smile. They were thinking the same thing, that this reminded them of sitting in the helicopter on the way to a mission.

Roxanna led them to an apartment building a few miles inland from her office. She lived far enough from the bay that it was often sunny in her neighborhood, but the salty tang of the ocean still lingered in the air. The whole city smelled of salt water.

Roxanna turned left from the main road and drove through the small lot for visitors and into the apartment's gated parking lot. Elijah drove past, continuing down the main road and intending to make a U-turn. "Keep your eyes peeled for this biker piece of shit."

They parked the car two spaces back from the entrance to the apartments, in the visitor's lot. Elijah pulled up the emergency break and was about to step out when Juno grabbed his arm. "We're here just to beat the shit out of him, right? No more?"

"Yeah, no more."

Juno's grip tightened. "Promise me?"

Elijah shook off his grip. "Sure. Come on."

Roxanna had parked just inside the opening to the lot. She stepped out of her Charger and slowly pulled out her various bags from the backseat, giving the men a chance to get closer. She had her gym bag, lunch bag, and a leather briefcase. Elijah and Juno had had plenty of time to quietly get out and move toward the lot by the time she'd arranged everything on her arms. When Roxanna saw their stealthy approach, she clicked the gate open once more and began walking toward her building.

A large, tattooed man stepped out from between an SUV and pickup truck near the building's entrance. Penny Garlitz smiled broadly at Roxanna as she approached. "Hey little girl."

Elijah and Juno were striding across the lot, Elijah keenly aware of Juno's vigilant gaze on him, assessing him.

"Your ass looked real fine bending over those bags. Damn. That was all for me, wasn't it? Why don't you come on over here and let me have a better look."

Roxanna stiffened but didn't look at him, instead altering her course toward the door. Garlitz blocked her way. "I'm getting real tired of this bullshit, honey. Let's train you proper, right now."

Roxanna turned around, heading toward another entrance door. All the while, she pretended she couldn't see or hear the man before her. Garlitz grabbed the straps of her bags and pulled her close to him. She tried to pull away, but the heel to one of her stiletto boots snapped off and she lost her balance. Garlitz ripped the bags from her shoulder and grabbed her by the throat, lifting her up off the ground. Roxanna clawed frantically at his hand, gasping for air.

Elijah and Juno were running. The distance quickly closed between the soldiers and the stalker.

Juno shouted. "Drop the woman and step back."

Garlitz looked over in surprise at the newcomers. He dropped Roxanna, who slumped to her knees in front of him, coughing. The biker pulled out a switchblade and bent over to place the point on Roxanna's throat.

That was his first mistake.

When he looked up, he found Elijah standing over him. Elijah pushed Garlitz's forehead back, exposing his throat, and reached in and clamped his other hand around the man's trachea. He crushed it. Garlitz's knife dropped from his open hand, bouncing harmlessly off the asphalt. He fell on his back, his mouth working to draw in air through his collapsed trachea.

Juno arrived, ducking down to check that Roxanna was OK. "Elijah, don't—"

But it was finished.

Elijah turned back to Roxanna, his vision blurred with battle fever. "Are you OK?"

"I will be." Roxanna kept her eyes on Juno and Elijah, avoiding, Elijah noticed, any glance toward her fallen stalker.

Juno examined Garlitz's motionless body, then spun around to confront Elijah. "What the fuck, man?"

"I did him a favor."

"What happened to our plan?"

"Is he still alive?" Roxanna sounded afraid.

Juno ignored her. "You could've broken his nose and that would've made him drop the knife and step back. But no. Instead you immediately go for the kill. Don't you want to change your life?"

Elijah's head spun. A sudden chill overcame him. The sun had only just started to set, but his peripherals pulsed with oncoming night, distorting Juno's face and blurring his thoughts. It had been right, he thought, to kill that man. He didn't know why, but it was. An easy target, one less piece of evil on this earth.

"Elijah, focus." Juno gave him a shove. "You're in serious trouble—really serious. I didn't come here to kill a man. I came to help you."

Roxanna covered her mouth and gasped. "He's dead?"

Elijah shoved Juno back. "I don't know what came over me, OK?"

"Bullshit, man. You're just as much in control of what you do as any of the rest of us. Do you want to lose everything just because you have no control? Be a man and fight it!"

The wail of a police siren echoed from around the block. Juno looked back at the parking lot entrance. "You need to get out of here."

"What about you?"

"I saw an assault, I stepped in. I'm a respected man in this city. I'll figure it out and call you in a few days."

"Juno—"

"Go."

Elijah fled the scene.

8

THE ABYSS

Elijah arrived back at his safe house several hours later. He cleared the house—his usual custom coming home—then plopped down on his sofa. What do you do for an evening after killing a man while your only friend talks to the police?

He grabbed his laptop to put on some music.

Tonight he thought he'd listen to some sitar music, mixed with some tar music from Iran. The local music had been one of his few sources of comfort while on tour. Hopefully, it would serve to calm him down now.

His little home didn't have much in the way of material things, but he was proud of what he did own. The Bluetooth speakers were a good purchase, he thought, as was the Apple TV. Documentaries were his favorite, and he had access to the warehouse's Wi-Fi network. He had a little kitchen and living area, but his pride and joy was the king-sized bed on a platform in the back of his home. He really didn't need that big of a bed, but he had slept in some really uncomfortable places and situations in his life and dammit, he deserved to luxuriate in this beautiful bed. Maybe one day he'd share it. Probably not.

He did have an eight-foot-long black hardwood table and two library style hardwood chairs, so Juno had a place to sit when he came to visit. Juno was the only other person who had ever been inside his home.

Elijah opened Safari and navigated to the CNN homepage. He'd relax and look at some news, spend some time on his journal (a habit formed from Juno's encouragement) and then get to bed early. He wasn't going to work in the morning so he could sleep in. He'd call Juno's house in the afternoon to see if he was home yet or not.

Scrolling through an article covering a local election, he saw an ad for Facebook. He laughed to himself. Could you have an account that had no friends? *I could just post to myself. I wonder if Juno's on Facebook.*

He clicked away from the ad.

Elijah was on his third article when he heard a clunk from the kitchen. His internal alert system locked in the on position. He heard it again and scanned the kitchen, the dining area, his bed on the platform. He didn't have problems with rodents, had never had any animal get in.

Maybe I just put something in a cupboard wrong and it shifted.

He heard it again.

He sprang to his feet, poised for an attack. When nothing jumped out, he sidled toward the kitchen. There was a kind of darkness moving across the kitchen floor. He frowned. The kitchen light was on, but it wasn't hitting the floor right.

The darkness moved from the floor into the kitchen air, pulsing slightly. Elijah approached it. Was there something blocking the light? No, the light came from above, but then disappeared in dark mass three feet from the floor. The kitchen was silent.

"Make yourself known." Elijah's voice was strong, assertive. "Step out. Now."

There was no response.

The three canisters lining the back of the counter moved toward the sink, as if sliding on magnets. One fell in.

Elijah frowned, now uncertain. He stepped through into the strange darkness, which could be felt, to the sink and picked up the fallen canister. He went to place it back on the counter when the darkness closed around him. It was thick, stifling, constricting, almost like water, or soft fabric—malleable, but confining. The canister fell from his hands and shattered on the floor. He tried to stand taller, to pull his arms up to an offensive position. He at least felt well balanced; he could work with that.

A deep, resonant laugh filled the safe house.

A familiar chill went down his spine. Something squeezed Elijah's chest, making it difficult for him to breathe. He tried to move away from the dark. What the hell was going on?

Elijah struggled to move his feet, but it felt like he was lifting a hundred pounds in addition to his weight. Suddenly, he stumbled backwards and fell to the floor. The darkness came to hover over him.

The laugh returned, a terse sort of chuckle. Derisive and threatening, it was the laugh of one who liked to attack the weak when they were down and broken.

I am not weak. I am not finished.

Elijah rolled over to his stomach and pushed himself up into a low crouch. "Come out of hiding, coward."

The laugh this time was accompanied by a disembodied voice. "How does it feel to have a superior force push you down? Does it frighten you?"

Sweat covered Elijah's hands, his heart running wild. "No."

As he stood up, a violent thump struck Elijah in the chest. It nearly knocked him off balance.

"You like to break the sternum of your enemies. That can be so effective if you know how to do it." The darkness almost seemed to pulse with the words. "Curious, what a little bit of power can do. It can turn an irritating push into a bone-crushing, devastating end.

And you do it so beautifully. Tell me, Elijah, have you been enjoying the view from the inside of the chest cavity? Have *you* ever thought what it would be like to be crushed?"

Elijah was conflicted. He was *not* going to start talking to disembodied voices. He didn't feel totally sane on his best day, but he knew that this was going too far.

He put his hand in a blocking position to protect his sternum and scanned the room. There were ways to broadcast a sound, a voice, but he wasn't sure how one would project a punch. The technology was surely being developed, somewhere. But in the meantime, how can you protect yourself from something you can't see?

Almost as if in answer, the darkness contracted to a ball the size of his chest about three feet from him. Then another one appeared to the right, then one to the left. This was not a situation he could understand. If he were to be attacked, he had no defense. He'd have to take the brunt of it and fight back with whatever he had. *If* he could fight back.

The spheres started to hum with a low, electronic sound. They seemed to grow darker, or denser. With each touch against his skin, Elijah turned involuntarily, until he was slowly spinning in place. He tried to fix a focal point so that he wouldn't get dizzy but it wasn't working. His feet were light and he was having trouble staying upright, like he could fall over at any moment.

It had been a long time since he felt this afraid.

The spheres pulled back and he stopped spinning, but the world did not. It was all he could do to focus on staying upright.

The spheres convolved back into the single large mass of darkness. The voice said, "I smell your fear, Elijah. You are the cause of fear. You are what people fear in the dark. You are a soldier of darkness, a destructive, delectable force."

The world had stopped spinning, finally. Elijah growled. "I'm my own man, and no one's soldier. Get the fuck out of my house."

It laughed. This time, it sounded genuinely amused. "Give

yourself to your nature, Elijah. You did not become a soldier, you just discovered you were a soldier. That will never change. *You* will never change. People can't stop you, you're too powerful. So relax. Go out and take what you want. Why deny your appetite? *Feast.*"

Elijah balled his fists. How dare someone break into his home and tell him what to do. "Who are you, you evil bastard? I'm not talking to anyone not brave enough to show himself."

There was a flash, but it wasn't a flash of light. Whatever it was, it left the negative imprint on his eyes like a flash of lightning. From the flash, Elijah saw a man, bigger and stronger than anyone he had ever encountered. It was there for an instant, then it was gone. Elijah blinked, trying to orient himself. The flash had burned the image of that man into his mind forever. The man seemed almost inhuman in strength, with a dead smile and a palpable aura of evil streaming off him. There was a smell of the herb anise in the air.

"Careful, Elijah. You are not my equal. You are a servant who will learn to serve me. I will crush you if you don't. There is no goodness in you anymore, Elijah. Become my willing servant, and you will have all the power you desire."

Elijah felt an icy grip on his heart, like his life was beginning to drain out of him. He tried to push the sphere of darkness away from himself. He tried to kick it. The darkness pushed back.

No, no I won't let this beat me. "I'm not going to serve you. You can't crush me, but if you can you better do it now before I kill you first."

The sphere suddenly grew to fill the kitchen, enveloping Elijah and plummeting that end of the safe house in a deep darkness. In the darkness a door opened, revealing a vast abyss. "You are mine to play with. I have much work for you to do. Say you'll be my servant."

"I won't! I don't care if you crush me or kill me, I am not going to serve you. I serve no one. Get the fuck out!"

The darkness evaporated in an instant.

It was gone. No wall of darkness, no sphere. No door. No voice. The only lingering evidence was a sense of nausea and a sharp pain in his heart. He was shaking. He could still smell the faint anise.

What the hell was that?

9

DINNER

Juno wasn't home yet the next afternoon. Elijah had spent the night in Juno's warehouse office, jerking awake from a light doze at every scrape and rustle from the outside street. A vigorous dawn bike ride and workout in the gym hadn't calmed him. What the hell had been in his safe house? His *safe* house, violated.

Maybe he was going crazy. Juno said he could have PTSD—were visits from dark masters part of that?

Juno's right. The violence is getting to me. If the police didn't shoot him first, where was he going to end up? A slave to a possible hallucination—or worse? And there was the other dead man, too. The one who tried to kill Phillip.

Phillip.

The young man was confident, brave, and had said he wanted to help Elijah. Well, Phillip may not believe him about dark beings in his kitchen, but maybe he could help in other ways.

Elijah phoned Phillip and was connected on the third ring. "Hey, Phillip. It's Elijah. What are you doing for dinner tonight?"

The lava-orange Scion IQ spun to a stop a few yards from the bench where Elijah sat watching the sunset. He smiled at the two energetic men waving at him from the car. Just seeing Phillip and his friend lifted his spirits. And that car—if they were lesbians they would've shown up in a pickup truck at least, but not these gay guys. *Lava orange, good God.*

Phillip's bruises were fading, though Elijah had a sneaking suspicion that some form of concealer was involved. His blond hair was different too, let down in a styled, asymmetric bob. It had been combed back and gelled the day they'd met. The casual suit from before was replaced with black linen pants and a white shirt. Elijah thought it looked good on his swimmer-esque body.

The friend jogged over to Elijah and extended a hand. "Hi, I'm Rick," he said in a lightly accented voice. "Phillip's been living with me the past couple days, after what happened. Thanks for saving him. I've heard a lot about you."

Phillip had mentioned on the phone that he was staying with his Brazilian friend, and that he'd be coming to dinner with them. Rick had big, soft brown eyes that contrasted nicely with his hard body. It looked like he worked out with weights. Elijah was surprised at himself for noticing all that. Rick was wearing tight black jeans with a snug, gray long-sleeved shirt.

Elijah shook Rick's hand and asked, "So you're the badass friend?"

"Badass? Me?" Rick looked between Phillip and Elijah, a hesitant smile pulling at his lips. "Did Phillip tell you that I'm a badass?"

Phillip held his hands up in protest. "I plead the fifth."

Rick looked at Phillip like he was wrongly accused. Phillip smiled back at him.

"Come on," Elijah said. "I've got reservations."

The Fish Garden was a sixty-year-old restaurant overlooking the bay. It had plenty of outdoor seating and great views of the water from inside. The staff all wore blue jeans and V-neck Fish

Garden T-shirts with a picture of the building on the front. The men were seated inside in a back-corner booth where they could look out and see the marina and the working port beyond. It was a pleasant evening, but a fog was rolling in on a chilly breeze.

A few moments passed in amicable silence as the three men watched the lights of the port through the windows and the other diners.

Rick spoke first. "Phillip says you were a soldier. Thanks for your service."

Elijah smiled, an empty smile for an often-empty statement. "You know, veterans are the most thanked and talked about group in this country, while, at the same time, the most reviled and ignored."

Rick frowned and exchanged a glance with Phillip. "What do you mean?"

"Do you know about the life of a soldier?" Elijah asked. "It's horrible. Mostly boredom, interspersed with soul-crushing violence and death. We all worked really hard to learn complex skills that have absolutely no value back here at home—with the possible exception of discipline and mental endurance. And after all we go through, we come home to the people we love who no longer understand us, don't like the way we behave, and who're uncomfortable with us around."

Elijah took a drink of water. His own family had hardly spoken to him over the past few years. The glass thudded on the table as he set it down. "The same government who underpaid us while in the service now finds us repellant and can't cough up a decent support package—even though active duty military and veterans make up only one percent of the population. People say thank you left and right, thinking it's enough, when what we really need is support. But, you're welcome."

Rick was sitting with his mouth open, a faint blush creeping up his face. "I'm so sorry. I didn't realize—I was just trying to say that

I respect you for fighting and that I'm glad you came back. Do you have a support group right now helping you heal?"

Rick looked at Phillip, who was staring intently at Elijah. "I think that a chance at a normal life is something everyone at this table can understand."

Elijah met Rick's earnest eyes and felt a twist of guilt in his stomach. He shouldn't have snapped at him like that. Unwilling to drop eye contact, he leaned over and put a hesitant hand on Rick's shoulder. "I'm not mad at you, Rick. I just think it's important to not let people off the hook too easily when they engage with veterans. If people really want to help, they can try by helping us with our benefits, trying to understand us, and giving more opportunities for the men and women a little too old to be starting out in the domestic world. I usually can't even express this frustration and anger. For some reason, you two seem to give me the confidence to be able to talk like this."

Elijah surprised himself with his words. He'd never really voiced these things before, even though he'd thought them for a while. Maybe all that PTSD research was already starting to help.

Phillip nodded. "That sounds fair."

Rick hesitated, as if torn by something—a nuance Elijah wouldn't have picked up on if he hadn't already been studying the man's face. Finally, Rick nodded as well and said, "I'll find a veteran support group to join. No one should have to face that alone. Can Phillip and I do anything for you in particular?"

There's something dark in my safe house I need help evicting. No, Elijah wouldn't tell them about that—they'd think he was crazy. There were a lot of things he could tell them that'd have the same effect. Overwhelmed, Elijah dropped his hand and looked at the table.

Rick leaned forward. "I work in an engineering firm here in town. We produce urban transportation interfaces between bike share, busses, rail, and the new trolleys that are going to start running here next year. We have an internship program where we take in two people and train them in our specialty for two years while they go to college at our expense. No age limit, no prior experience needed. We also give them an additional monthly stipend of thirty-five hundred dollars. Can I put your name in for this program?"

Phillip's eyes were wide. "Rick . . ."

Rick glanced at Phillip. "I know, uncharacteristic of me. But Elijah, I want to do this for you."

Elijah didn't know what to say.

Rick continued. "At the end of the internship, you'll be offered a permanent position with the company. Our new engineers start at sixty-five thousand dollars a year, with health care and a pension. I'm on the recruiting committee for this program. Any recommendation from me is an almost-guaranteed acceptance. What do you think? Is this something you're interested in?"

Elijah blinked, taken aback. An engineering firm? A career . . . one without violence, away from the lowlifes of the docks. He was only thirty-two, maybe it wasn't too late to start a new career. But why offer this to *him*? He'd just killed a man, not twenty hours ago. He took a deep breath, trying to regain control.

"All this just because I helped Phillip?"

Rick took Phillip's hand. "You saved his life. Let us help give you a new one."

Elijah felt a shudder up and down his spine. No one had ever noticed him the way Phillip had, and now Rick. A paid education and a career . . .

I could be like Juno. No longer alone, just trying to survive. He could work every day, go home to a family. Have friends. *No, best not get ahead of myself.*

"Will you let me think about this for a few days? I really appreciate this."

Rick smiled. "Of course, take some time. But I'm serious about this. I'll be your personal sponsor."

Phillip grinned. "Always the generous one, this guy. First letting me stay with him, then offering you a job—I knew I kept him around for a reason."

Rick gave Phillip a playful shove in the booth.

"I don't have any fancy jobs to offer," Phillip said. His voice grew somber. "But, if I can say this, you seem to be withdrawn and not really a part of society—kind of like you're living in the closet. We certainly know all about that. Can we help you come out? Our friends would be happy to include you when we do social things."

Rick nodded. "Oh yes, we have lots of fun."

"We go dancing at bars, to concerts, parties—we shop and take hikes and go on bike rides, too. You can join us for anything that fits your fancy. You've been around a rough crowd for a long time. Why not try hanging out with a group of fun, gentle people? And for times when you don't feel like having fun, let me be someone you could talk to."

The server came and took their orders. While Phillip described the exact modifications he wanted to his burger, Elijah thought about the two men's offers. He could go and spend time with Phillip and Rick's friends. He'd probably like that. They were fun, open, honest, and a good distraction from the memories that plagued him. But that was the problem with friends. Eventually, he'd have to talk—talk about the war—and he wasn't sure if his new friends would like what he had to say.

The server left, and all eyes returned to Elijah. He cleared his throat, nervous. "I'd love to join you guys sometimes. It's just that, well, I don't know if you really want to hear the kind of things I keep inside. I've done some bad things. People tend to cut you off when they hear any details, waving it away with an 'Oh, that was in a war.' Well, yeah. But it still happened."

"What kind of things?" Rick whispered.

Elijah took a breath. This would come out eventually. Might as well scare them off now before he gets to know them any better.

"I was in the Seventy-Fifth Ranger Regiment. It's part of the special forces. We have over sixty-thousand guys trained to do a number of valuable things—take over an area, drive people out of an area, destroy an area, and so on."

Elijah paused, but Phillip motioned for him to continue. "A lot of the work we did was covert, which meant we had to be quiet so we wouldn't be reported or known. When you have to be quiet, there's nothing like a knife. It's not a matter of letting an enemy get close; it's about getting close to them on purpose."

As he spoke, Elijah's surroundings began to fade, and in his mind he was back on a mission. He was approaching a village in the dead of night, filled with cold determination. "One of the jobs I had was to go into an area and instill fear in the local residents. Shake them up by entering the homes at night of important men and slitting the throats of some of their household. In the morning, everyone'd wake up and see what we'd done—terror successful. It sent a message. This could happen to them anytime, anywhere."

"Weren't you afraid of getting caught?" Phillip asked.

"Every time. You've got to get in town and in the house undetected. If you wake anyone up, you'd ruin the surprise. The point was to instill fear. You get the most fear by waking up to a finished attack, not engaging in one. If anyone saw you, they'd shout an alarm or attack you with a gun or some other weapon. If you have to shoot them back, that'd cause enough noise to wake the whole village. You'd be in a huge firefight before you could move. If that were to happen, a quick death would be your prayer, but in reality they'd probably torture you first."

Phillip had scooted closer to Rick, whose gaze was leveled intently on Elijah. Elijah shivered. It was like the man was trying to read his soul.

Memories clouded Elijah's vision, scenes of the past overtaking his present. Killing a sleeping man was easier than most opponents, but they rarely died sound asleep. Elijah remembered entering many houses, his equipment secured tight on his body so nothing would rattle. Targets usually slept on the floor, on some kind of pad or bed. It had to be done in a few seconds. Elijah would plant one leg firmly on the floor and one knee pushed deep and hard into center of the chest so they couldn't thrash. A side sleeper just needed to be rolled over to get at the throat. One hand covered the nose and mouth, to prevent noise and air flow. This clamp could be dislodged by a struggle, so he'd put his thumb along the jaw bone to anchor the grip, pulling it up tight as he pressed down hard. Knee and hand, placed at exactly the same time. The victims always woke instantly, a rapid flow of emotions glittering in their moonlit eyes. First confusion, then recognition, then fear, anger, and finally acceptance and deep sorrow. Throat slits gushed and pulsed and always left blood on his uniform.

"Killing a man isn't like the movies. You don't slit a throat and walk away from a corpse. They thrash a lot, and the gurgling sound from the cut throat is horrible. It never leaves you. It can take up to five minutes sometimes for the blood volume to reduce enough for the blood vessels to collapse and stop circulation. The whole time, you're just crouched there, watching."

Phillip broke the silence. "That's horrible."

"It's a horrible experience, watching a man die—especially if you're the cause of it. And then to get up and move on to the next victim, the next house . . . all for a terror message. It's messy, smelly, and disturbing." Elijah had spent hours doing this, halfway across the world. By the end of a night, he had little strength to leave. His muscles would ache, his breath labored, and visions of the deaths fresh in his mind.

Elijah's gaze dropped to his hands clenched beneath the table. Fresh shame washed over him at the memories. Why had he accepted these missions? Why did he, of all people, succeed in this special training?

The words from the darkness returned to him. *You do it so beautifully, Elijah . . .*

Minutes passed in a heavy, delicate silence. Phillip and Rick were pale, Phillip even a little green. Elijah saw this and scolded himself. *You said too much. They'll never want to see you again.* He could say more, about the smell of blood and bowels, of the heat, the stench of fear . . .

Instead, he said, "So you see, it's hard finding people to talk to about these things. I got to the point where I was a preferred combatant for our team. I did this and things like it, and now I have a problem believing that anybody who knows this about me could ever feel comfortable around me. But it's part of me now. I saw every combatant as a human being, but when it was me or them, I made sure I always prevailed. There was a human life ended. I don't know what to do with that data."

Rick reached over and put his hand on Elijah's arm. Elijah flinched but didn't move away. He felt warmth running up his arm.

Rick's words were gentle and kind. "Oh, Elijah, it wasn't your fault. You were in a position where you had to kill, or die. I'm so sorry you had to have this experience. I'm not even sure what to say right now." He looked to Phillip for support.

"So . . . now you think you've changed into something that normal people would reject?" Phillip asked.

Elijah nodded. "I lived through it, but sometimes I wonder if I survived. Or how much of me survived. Or did I survive, but am now dead inside? Shit."

Rick squeezed Elijah's arm. "I'm not going to reject you, Elijah. I want to be here for you. I had a partner die from AIDS, not too long ago. It was a slow decay and very tough to watch." His voice cracked. "Toward the end, it was messy. I think I saw what you saw, but in slow motion."

Phillip interrupted. "But you didn't cause Jason's condition."

"No." Rick sighed. "I was just there to help. That's the difference between the soldier and the paramedic. I guess I was more like the paramedic."

The server was standing behind Phillip with a big tray of food, uncertain if he should interrupt. Rick noticed and motioned for him to approach. The table was silent as server passed around the food. When he was finished, he left in a hurry.

Rick touched Phillip on the shoulder and looked at Elijah. "It seems to me—and I can't say why—that you're still in the battle-field. Let us help you come home again. If that's the kind of thing you have trapped inside you, you've got to let it out. If you keep stuffing it all down inside, one day you'll boil over. I don't want to see that happen to you."

Phillip nodded. "Me neither. We're in, Elijah, and I mean that we are totally committed to helping you—if you'll let us."

Elijah had a tear in the corner of his eye. He wiped it away. "I think you already are."

10

THE SAFE HOUSE

The office light popped on. Elijah sat up from the couch, smiling sleepily at the figure standing in the doorway. "Welcome back, Juno. I thought you wouldn't be in for another hour."

Juno walked over to his desk by the window and powered up his computer. "I've been out of the office for three days. There's a lot of pile up I need to work on."

"Did you get your phone back?"

"Yeah, they gave it back to me when I was released. It was dead, though. Had to wait until I was home to charge it. You can imagine the earful I got from Gabija on the ride home."

Elijah flipped his legs over the edge of the couch, placing his feet on the floor. He leaned forward, resting his chin on balled fists. "Was she angry?"

"Hell yes. She understands why I was with you that night, but she's still mad I got myself involved in a *murder*." Juno gave him a pointed look.

Elijah nodded. He got the message. "I'm sorry they held you for so long."

"Eh." Juno shrugged out of his coat and looped it over his chair. "Cells don't scare me."

"I know, but I'm still sorry you had to do that for me. I'm a pain in the ass for you, man."

"You're my brother, and that's that." Juno settled behind his desk. "It was the right thing, getting you out of the way before the cops showed. By the time I left, the police were pretty confident I was really just trying to protect a woman from an attacker. It surprised them that I knew of Roxanna, but I told them that I drive by her apartment when I'm in that part of town, just to show Hector some support. I convinced them that I feel like everyone's father."

"You are, you know." Elijah crossed the room and turned on the coffee maker. After a short silence, he said, "I did miss you. Welcome back."

Juno eyed Elijah's disheveled clothes, an eyebrow rising in suspicion. "Been here long?"

Elijah tried to smooth his shirt, but the wrinkles were set. "Actually, I've been sleeping here for the last couple nights. I had a scary visit from something the other night, and I haven't been back to the safe house since."

The wrinkles in his shirt were set, alright. They'd been set for some time by now.

"What in the world could scare you?" Juno asked. "Are you OK?"

"The only thing that broke was my brain. I think I'm going crazy."

Juno studied Elijah, his dark eyes searching for something in his face. "You look like we did out in the field—like shit. What happened?"

Elijah told Juno everything that had happened since the fight. The darkness, the strange voice, the deep abyss, and the compulsion to serve something he could not see. Listening to himself talk, it all sounded so unbelievable.

"So, I think I'm going crazy," he concluded. "I'm positive I was alone but at the same time . . . I've been sleeping here on the couch ever since. It's just that that evil felt so *real*. This could just be another level of my PTSD, right?"

Juno leaned forward at his desk, his mouth a grim line. "When you were telling me the details, I had a very clear vision of what happened. I can't tell you where this came from, but I can tell you that I did see and hear it."

"What?"

"You had a visit from the evil one."

Elijah scrunched his brows together. *Was that a code name?* "What evil one?"

"Satan. He watches everyone. This isn't just some theory or superstition. You had a visit from the prince of darkness. You're still under stress from coming home, you just don't seem to be able to let it go. Your only contact with other people is often violent. I think that Satan sees you as vulnerable—and valuable—and wants to use you."

The coffee maker beeped, and the pot's gurgling eased into a still quiet. There was an uncomfortable silence in the office.

Elijah's stomach sank. "Really? You really think I had a visit from the devil? Like really, a visit from the devil in my safe house?"

Juno nodded, solemn. "I do, brother. I really believe this is the truth, and you're going to have to face it if you're going to be able to handle it. You're vulnerable. I know it's been tough, being back, but you have to *try* to find the good in you. Instead you isolate yourself, withdrawn and alone. It's not good, man. And I'm probably enabling you by building the safe house instead of putting you in an apartment building. Is today when you're supposed to see Selma?"

Elijah nodded, wondering just how much Juno was able to handle his own PTSD. He wasn't used to seeing his role model resort to fantasy.

"It is," he said.

Juno stood from his desk and walked over to the coffee maker, pouring them each a mug. "Good. Let's start to really make changes in your life. Go see Selma and talk to her. She can take it. Spend some time with your new friends. Ask Rick for the internship—I'll help you with the discipline to actually go. You can come study at our house and eat dinners with us. The kids would love doing homework with you. There're some good things starting to happen in your life and maybe the prince of darkness sees that and wants to get to you before you change."

Elijah took the offered coffee with a nod of thanks. He did feel out of control. He hadn't meant to kill that biker, he just did. But that was the problem, wasn't it? He was just acting with violence without thought. He needed help. But what Juno was proposing . . . "I'll go to the appointment. But Juno, there's no evil spirit after me. There's no such thing. I can fix this on my own."

"Face it, Elijah. You can't control yourself, else this biker motherfucker would still be alive. The enemy we faced overseas was real. We could study them and figure out how to beat them. We did a good job over there. But that doesn't mean the enemy didn't come home with us."

"Yeah, people are bad everywhere."

"More than that." Juno settled behind his desk. "There's good and evil, darkness and light. And if you're so sure there's no such thing as demons, why have you been sleeping here?" He raised an eyebrow, a faint smile on his lips. Elijah had nothing to say to that. "The first step to conquering your demons is to show them you're not afraid. Reclaim your space and go home, Elijah."

11

THE SECRET

E lijah entered his safe house for the first time in several days. It was untouched, the broken canister still spread across the kitchen floor. He didn't feel anything unusual. Everything seemed fine and in order.

He dragged a hand across his tired face. He would've sworn that what he saw was real, but it *couldn't* have been. And even if it was, who would believe him?

There was a story he read several years back about how commercial pilots often see unexplainable things in the sky during flights. The article said that they never call them in because they don't want the reputation for seeing a UFO. They do, however, talk about it amongst themselves at bars from time to time.

I'm doing just that. He had already decided not to tell Phillip and Rick, and he knew he'd never tell anyone outside of Juno about that night. Even Juno's reaction wasn't comforting. People didn't have confrontations with the devil.

. . . Did they?

I need to go to the gym. A solid workout would pound the crazy right out of his mind.

12

SOLACE

The gym was styled after a converted warehouse with two cement walls connecting in a V toward the parking lot and blended steel beams and corrugated metal walls finishing out the square. There was even a small section near the top of one wall made of chain link fence, allowing air to circulate in and out.

Elijah changed and hit his workout. He never did cardio, because he rode so much, and instead focused on stretching and working through his muscles for strength and stamina. Today he worked on his shoulders and back a little more than usual in an attempt to relieve some of the tension built up there.

The whole time he exercised, Elijah's thoughts were consumed with what Juno had said. It was a surprise. Juno was levelheaded and quickly saw threats and knew how to handle them. It was what made him such a good partner in combat. He didn't imagine things that weren't there and was never distracted by fear. His focus had kept Elijah on task many times. But the devil? Elijah just couldn't believe that his hero would use a myth to explain something serious that had happened to him. Elijah needed a better answer to what happened. He wanted Juno to grab him and just tell him to snap out of his dark fantasy. That was what it was, right?

Yes, Elijah had been scared by the presence in the kitchen, but afterwards he had been more scared that a monster like that could be living inside him, in his mind. But the devil? It was stupid. Juno was supposed to be the strong one, the one who actually came home from the war. He had a family, a great job, and lots of friends. He wasn't supposed to be messed up like this. If his hero was this unstable, what hope did Elijah have of pulling through?

Demons in my house? Come on.

Solace was in a nice garden office in the commercial district at the bottom of the hill, close to the Hoover-Foster neighborhood where Elijah thought Rick lived. Elijah walked his bike into the central courtyard garden and folded and locked it up where he could see it from the Solace's office windows.

The receptionist gave him an intake form to fill out. Elijah sat in square fabric chair in the lobby and examined the questions.

Question Four: Address. He wrote Juno's office as his home address, as was his custom. When he was done, he returned the forms and took a seat, waiting for his name to be called.

The walls were painted soothing colors, covered with upbeat but compassionate posters. There were flowers on the counter and the temperature was a perfect sixty-five degrees—unobtrusive, so as not to distract. It was quiet. He leaned to the side to peek at the bike. It was still there.

This isn't so bad. Elijah tried picturing Juno sitting here.

The door opened and a tall, elegant woman in her sixties walked into the lobby. She was wearing a loose white silk blouse, grey wool pants, and black leather shoes. She approached Elijah where he sat and held out her hand.

"Hello. I'm Dr. Selma Greenfeld, but please call me Selma in session. Juno's told me about you. Welcome. I look forward to our time together."

She led him into her counseling office. It looked like the living room of someone's single aunt. She had a large, comfortable leather armchair for herself and a little footstool. The office had a long couch and at the other end of the room another chair that seemed to be a recliner of some sort. The coffee table was adorned with daisies and a strategic box of tissues. There were some pleasant, generic pieces of art hanging on the walls and placed on the shelves. It was quiet in this room, probably soundproof to some extent.

Selma lowered herself into her armchair, gesturing for Elijah to do the same. "I record all of my sessions so that I can take notes after we are done. We'll be able to reach back and review as we proceed over whatever period of time you want to spend with me here. We'll work in one-hour sessions and I would suggest once a week until we start to realize just what you want to discuss and how deep you can go. If you are ever uncomfortable, you can stop a session just by saying you want to do that. We can talk about anything here, Elijah. I know that you and Juno served together and that you have both been in combat. So, don't feel like you have to be careful about what you want to say. Do you have any questions?"

"No." Elijah was nervous, his palms starting to sweat. "Juno told me about how the sessions work. We just . . . talk?"

Selma draped her hands over her lap. "That's right. I'll ask some questions, but I'm here to listen."

Elijah nodded slowly, looking around the room. There was a figurine of a child playing near a pond on her desk. He had seen other children, close to the same age, gather water from ponds in the Middle East. It wasn't as serene as the porcelain made it out to be.

"I don't know where to start."

"I have a questionnaire here we can use to break the ice," Selma said. "It's something that I want to offer. This is a tool we use to help identify PTSD. If you want, we can just work through this today—it'll be a good opportunity for us to get used to talking with each other. Don't feel like you have to talk all the time. We can have periods of quiet while you think or feel. Is this something you want to do?"

Elijah gripped the couch's armrest, sitting straight and tense. "Yeah, let's do that. I'm tired of feeling stuck in the past, and I'm scared of where my future is headed."

Selma nodded. "A lot of this work is going to be designed to help you discover what you really want to do, and how you want to live your life. It can be complex to make some changes in life, but if we work together and just go step by step, you can move mountains."

She smiled.

Elijah nodded. Selma reached over and picked up her laptop from the side table and showed Elijah the screen.

"This is the worksheet. Ready?"

He nodded.

"Alright, let's get started. When did you serve and where?"

They began to construct his service experience, Selma asking straight-forward, factual questions. Most of them were yes-no questions, easy enough for Elijah to answer. He began to breathe more easily when he realized Selma wasn't going to push him any further than he wanted to go. There were a few times when a particular question would send him back, transforming the office to a den of chaos, gunfire and screaming all around him. Selma seemed to sense when this was happening and would soothe him with soft words, bringing him back to the art-filled office. "These are just words, and memories," she would say. "They can't harm you."

They finished the evaluation just as their scheduled hour ended.

Selma stood, extending her hand again. "Thank you so much

for opening up to me, Mr. McCoy. I'd like to meet with you again next Monday and keep that same time each week, if that'll work with your schedule."

Elijah blinked. He shook her hand, a little dazed. *That went by so fast.* He was kind of sorry to be done. "Yes, Mondays are fine. And you can call me Elijah."

"I will." She smiled. "I'll go over the evaluation and have your PTSD status ready for you next Monday. It will be something you can take to the VA, if you want. Do you have any questions for me?"

Elijah smiled. "Thanks, Selma. No, I don't think so." He turned to leave the office, but then a thought occurred to him and he turned back around. "If I saw something . . . strange, but vivid, could that be part of PTSD?"

Selma looked up from her desk. "What kind of things?"

Elijah swallowed. *Here goes nothing.* "Evil things."

Selma's face was carefully composed. "Yes, it perfectly fits the condition. Just remember, Mr. McCoy, Elijah, that the things in your head only have as much power as you choose to give them."

13

WATCHED

Elijah was really encouraged after his session with Selma. This wasn't going to be so bad—Why he had taken so long to start? Juno was ecstatic that it had gone well. Elijah himself was looking forward to the following Monday. He'd also made plans to go over to Rick's house Tuesday night to spend time with the boys. Elijah decided he'd ask for the internship. Juno was right, it would be a positive move for him. All he had to do was see if it worked.

The internship was a huge offer. It felt good to have Rick care enough about him to offer something like this. Elijah realized that meant they would be talking about very personal things for the next couple of years, at least. The idea felt . . . really good. Elijah could see Rick's face clearly in his mind's eye and he smiled.

On Tuesday afternoon, Elijah rode down to a Peet's about five miles from the gym. It was away from his regular café, but he didn't want a surprise run-in with Roxanna any time soon—Juno had told him that she wanted a date. He rode from the safe house past Roxanna's apartment complex to the base of the hills and found the café on Fruitvale, on the way to Joaquin Miller Park.

Elijah ordered a large coffee and a bagel. He'd spend the day in the vicinity of people and sunlight. What he loved about Peet's was the established atmosphere. This location was just like his favorite one, with all the same warmth and smells that made him feel good to be there. It was a new place, but the same routine. He liked that. It felt normal.

Elijah sat down and opened his MacBook Air to continue reading his e-book, *The Good Terrorist* by Doris Lessing. He found her to be a great observer of life, with a keen understanding on contemporary politics and people. The book discussed the idea of young people getting involved with terrorism in the name of politics. Elijah had seen this happen in his own life, in the United States. Since childhood, he had been encouraged to play the soldier.

And that had turned out so well for him.

He remembered when he first entered the war. The sheer number of casualties shocked him, man-made death, horrible, body-destroying death. He had seen each fallen soldier or civilian as a person with a life and a family, and even though he had eventually grown numb to the presence of death, came to savor the challenge and intensity of battle, he had never turned blind against life and its value.

But at the same time, life was defined by death. Death moves us in its own time and way. We can push each other toward death and into it. Elijah clicked to turn the page, starting a new chapter. Lessing was helping him examine how he had made this dramatic transition in his life, from a nerdy student to a deadly force.

He who won the war wrote the history book—what a load of one-sided bullshit.

All the good fiction writers were trying to go deep into the thoughts and emotions that led to death or its consequences. Doris Lessing was an exemplar of this effort. She wrote about the emotions of the dissenters and showed Elijah how insulated he had become from his emotions. It was first published in 1985, and all these years later was still right on point.

Elijah was pretty deep in thought when he noticed someone watching him from across the café.

A man of indeterminate age sat in the corner, watching Elijah with a steady, cold gaze. He was nicely dressed, with a pearl-grey overcoat open to show a navy V-neck sweater over a nice, crisp-white shirt and rich-looking slacks that matched the sweater perfectly. There were fancy gloves lying on the table next to a steaming mug. Elijah closed the lid of his laptop and went to confront the man.

The stranger did not look away as he approached, but stood and offered his hand. "Hello. My name is B. A. Lamb. Please." He gestured at the seat next to him. "Won't you sit down with me for a minute? Would you let me get you some tea or coffee, a refill perhaps?"

Elijah decided that sitting for a minute could be a cheap way to get the man to go away. "I don't need a drink. Why were you staring at me?"

Lamb smiled. "I have a proposition to make to you, Elijah."

"Did I tell you my name?"

"Oh, I already know you. You've been a busy solider this past week, ending two lives in this peaceful little city." He tsked, his tone sardonic.

Elijah gripped the table, steadying his heart rate. *Calm, Elijah.* He was ready to come over the top of the table and throttle the stranger. "What are you talking about, Lamb?"

"I have to say, you are a real prize—a secretive tough guy with only one friend in this world. You're employed, but just loosely."

Elijah was baffled. "How do you know so much about me? Are you having me followed or something? Are you police or from the DOD? What do you want?"

"I'm from a much larger organization than those. Those who serve me watch you almost all the time. You've come to my attention because you have ended the lives of some of the people with whom I used to work. We've been following you for almost six months now, and I must say, I am *very* impressed with your ability to just . . . disappear, even from society at large. You are quiet. Deadly. You are a valuable man, Elijah McCoy."

Elijah leaned over the table and stared deep into Lamb's gold-flecked eyes. "Don't mess with me, Lamb. Whatever you're up to, I'm not interested. If you've truly seen me when I'm violent, then you should know that I have no hesitation to—"

"Execute your enemies? I know Elijah. That's why I am here to talk to you. I think you should to do what comes naturally. I have a job to offer you."

"Not interested." The chair scraped across the hardwood as Elijah stood. "Now get the fuck away from me—stay *far* away. Don't look at me, don't talk to me, don't ask about me. Got it?"

Lamb smiled. "The job pays a hundred thousand dollars. Half up front and half when you are done. Would you like the first half now?"

"Are you deaf? Get the hell away from me. Disappear." Elijah's voice was low, as to not draw attention to their table. Attention was the last thing he wanted.

Lamb laughed. "Disappear—that's funny. I have the fifty thousand dollars, cash, in this briefcase." His eyes shifted to the brown leather briefcase laying on the table. "Let me give it to you. You *will* work with me. My boss insists."

"Not the top of your food chain then, eh?"

"Oh no, we all serve a greater power, don't we, Mr. McCoy? My boss said he *so* enjoyed speaking with you the other night. He says your little home is quite lovely."

Ice struck the pit of Elijah's stomach. His breathing increased, as did his heart rate. His vision clarified for the kill, his body temperature climbing. He could drag this sorry son of a bitch into the street and kick his ass all the way down the block.

Or I could throttle him. It'd take less time.

His anger was a slow burn. Just as he started to plan his move, Elijah noticed Lamb's musk.

Anise. Just like the darkness from the other night.

Elijah sat with a heavy thud, blood draining from his face.

"You have been a defender so far of the hopeless and the weak," said Lamb. "You have shown yourself to be very efficient at . . . *dispatching* those who don't behave well. You don't hesitate, and you don't hold back. You hurt people, Elijah. You kill people. You'll find that you can make a lot of money doing what comes so naturally to you. There's a name in the envelope along with the cash. He shouldn't live through next weekend if everything goes as planned—I'm counting on you to make that happen. I can arrange for him to have an appointment at just about any location and at about any time you want. This could be very easy. This is a large sum of money and will not be an isolated event. You will be rich and free, Elijah."

Elijah shook himself. "What the fuck are you talking about? Are you police, or just a nut case? Keep your envelope and go away. I'm going to get up and walk back to my computer. None of this ever happened. I don't want to see you sitting here by the time I get to my seat."

Elijah trudged stiffly to his table. He was having a hard time controlling his shaking hands, he was so full of rage. When he sat down, he stared at his laptop, hesitant to look up. After a deep, steadying breath, he glanced at Lamb's table.

It was empty, except for a large manila envelope with something scrawled across it in large script.

Elijah went back to the table to examine the envelope. His name. It was his name written across the paper in beautiful calligraphy. It felt embossed. He could just leave it there, but the next person who came would give it to the manager, or they would take it themselves and learn about Elijah's side jobs. The envelope looked fat enough to house fifty thousand dollars, and if someone took it, it could be something to blackmail him over.

Shit.

He grabbed the envelope and stuffed it in his backpack. *Shit.* Take it to Juno, Juno would know what to do. Elijah was on the verge of changing his life's direction, and he wasn't about to let an embossed envelope ruin it.

14

THE FRIENDSHIP

It was almost always cold in Oakland in the evenings. Elijah rode through the city to Rick's house. He loved the sounds of the city nightlife, of traffic and laughter outside bars and music drifting down from apartment parties. There was life in the city at night. He needed to remember that.

When he knocked on the door, he heard someone on the other side scrambling down a hall. Elijah smiled at the thought of someone running to greet him. There was a soft thump and then the door was thrown open.

Phillip greeted Elijah with a smile. "Wow, here you are again! Come on in." He moved to the side to allow Elijah to walk his bicycle into the entryway. "We've got a few friends over to play Pictionary. They're great guys, you'll be seeing more of them. Come on."

Elijah removed his jacket, gloves, and helmet and hung them on the bike. He set his backpack down and with a cold stab to his heart remembered what lay inside. He flushed, embarrassed. Phillip gave him an odd look—what could be so embarrassing about a backpack?—but had the grace not to say anything. Instead, Phillip led Elijah into the living room to join the party.

There were four men sitting around the couches of Rick's living room. There was Rick, wearing a black sweater and casual, relaxed jeans, and three strangers introduced as Ryan, Dillan, and Chris. In the center of the living room was a large whiteboard on an easel, featuring a crude sketch of a dog licking something off the ground.

Rick raised the marker in salute. "Elijah! Glad you could make it! Join us."

The surprising part wasn't that these gay men were playing Pictionary—it was that Elijah jumped right in to play with them.

His drawing ability wasn't the best—though he was better than Chris, who couldn't draw a stick figure to save his life—but his body language was on point, and he was a huge hit. He may have to relearn how to have friends and to be a friend, but this was a great group of guys for reintroduction.

"OK Elijah, you're up again." Dillan handed Elijah the marker, a broad smile on his face. "Good luck!"

Elijah erased Dillan's masterpiece of a horse and drew a card. *Computer.* He started to draw, sketching a large square to start.

"Box!" Rick yelled. "House!"

Elijah added another square at an angle from the first.

Chris squinted. "Lawn chair?"

"Present!" Rick shouted.

Elijah cross-hatched across the lower box for the keyboard.

Rick cocked his head. "Scottish present?"

The room erupted in laughter, Elijah joining them.

Elijah shook his head and mimed typing and sipping an invisible latte.

"Oh!" Chris stood, and pointed to the side table where Rick's laptop sat playing music. "Laptop!"

"Close enough." Elijah laughed.

As the night wore on, the game eventually ended, with Rick, Chris, and Elijah's team winning by a landslide. The evening felt like a family gathering for Elijah. He hadn't felt that way in a long time. Phillip and Rick knew him, and they accepted him as he really was. He could belong here, in this little eclectic family.

After the game, the drinks changed from cocktails to wine, and the conversations, while friendly, turned more serious as the men discussed the issues facing their community. Elijah listened quietly while they talked, following the conversation with great interest. Everyone was aware of Phillip's attack the previous week, and Elijah was surprised to learn that all of them were close with at least one other who had suffered due to their sexuality. The strength of these men astounded him. Most of them wouldn't know the difference between the butt and the muzzle of an M16, but they all had the steel mentality of hardened veterans. Life was tough, you can only control you and yours, move forward no matter what. They understood what it was like to be on the edge of society, and they just dealt with it—with an inspiring positivity. He would take a lesson from them.

The conversation turned to lighter things after a few bottles of wine, Phillip telling the guys about a new gala coming up. Rick smiled and excused himself, gathering dishes to bring to the kitchen while his guests continued to talk.

Elijah got up and followed him. "I can help."

Rick laid a stack of platters on the counter. "Oh, no need. But if you want to keep me company while I suds up, I'd more than appreciate it."

Elijah cut Rick off on his path to the sink. "I'll wash, you dry. You know where everything goes anyway."

Rick smiled. "Fine, you got me there."

Elijah turned on the hot water and poured soap onto a sponge. "I owe you guys so much. Thanks for inviting me over, I've really enjoyed your friends."

"Careful, you know how we like to move in with each other." Rick froze. "Sorry, I didn't mean to imply that you're gay. Just that it's nice to have you around. I think there's a gentle, decent man living inside that scary presence." He flashed a smile.

"Am I scary?"

Rick's smile softened. "Yes, but in a Liev Schreiber sort of way. Attractive but dangerous, you know?"

"Liev Who?"

"An actor. He's been in a ton of stuff, but recently he's been playing Ray Donovan in a series of the same name. He's a hunk, but also a family man."

Elijah thought he could picture it, but he wasn't sure. "So you think I act like that?"

"No, I think you look like him. I think there're lots of gay guys out there with posters of him hanging in their rooms."

Elijah laughed. "Hopefully grown men still don't keep posters pinned in their bedrooms."

"If there's a God," Rick said with a laugh. "Hey, thanks again for saving Phillip."

Elijah handed him a clean plate. "You've already thanked me for that."

"I know, but I think you really encouraged him. Not a lot of people stick up for the likes of us. He was really shaken up. He doesn't like to talk about it, but I've been friends with the guy for many years. He's still recovering. But you helped. You didn't have to walk him home, or listen to his stories. We all know Phillip can be a little long-winded." He smiled. "You did a good thing, Elijah."

This warmed Elijah's heart. He was doing good things. Despite all the darkness and violence in his life, he had managed to do something good.

"Can I ask you something personal, Elijah? It's a little controversial."

"More personal or controversial than me killing people?" Elijah nudged Rick with his shoulder, to show him he was being lighthearted. "Sure, go ahead."

"Well, in the gay community, we just assume everyone is gay. So . . ." He turned to face Elijah. "Are you?"

Elijah stopped washing and looked up. No one had ever asked him that before. He guessed he'd never given it much thought. Was he gay? He tried to think back on his sexual encounters. The closest he came was when he went to a whorehouse with a few soldiers while on tour, but the grime and smell of sweat and incense had creeped him out. He'd ended up waiting outside for his friends. Did that mean something?

He decided to answer honestly. "I don't know."

Rick raised his eyebrows. "How can you not know?"

"I've never dated anyone before, or hooked up or anything. My whole life has been spent in the service, it seems. Before that I was too young and innocent, maybe. I never wanted a relationship while I was enlisted. What if I was killed in action?"

"But what about since you got back?" Rick tossed the soaked hand towel toward the laundry room and retrieved a new, dry flour cloth towel from a drawer.

Elijah handed him a few wine glasses. "It's hard to have sex with people who don't know you exist." It was meant to be a joke, but Rick didn't laugh. "I guess I've just thought that if anyone got to know me, they'd be repulsed. Kind of a downer to find out after you've gotten naked."

Elijah shrugged. Why was he telling all this to Rick? These weren't the kinds of things a pretty boy struggled with. From what Phillip said, Rick never had any trouble finding partners for the night.

How do you know if you are gay?

Why was he afraid to ask that question? He knew that the atmosphere in his family home growing up had never invited any questioning of what was expected of the children as far as relationships went. The expected relationships Elijah was supposed to want didn't interest him, so it was easier just to not think about them.

Rick nodded. "I see. Why are you so open with Phillip and me?"

Elijah shrugged again. "You guys are nice. Non-threatening. You two already know my worst secrets. The dinner we had at the Fish Garden was amazing for me. I know it was heavy, but you guys took it so well. You didn't make me feel like a monster, and . . . you still wanted to be my friend."

He held his breath. He had just made a gamble, that Rick and Phillip valued him as much as he valued them.

"We really enjoy spending time with you. You're a good friend, too."

Elijah smiled to himself. But then a thought occurred to him, a truth he hadn't yet shared with Rick. "There's more to my life than you know. When not working at the docks, I have a side business of sorts. Have you ever heard of a redeemer?"

"Like a revenge hit man? Is that what you do?" Rick dropped the towel, alarm in his voice. "Elijah, that's a horrible thing to do. How can you expect to—I don't want you to go to jail."

"Not a hit man, just someone who helps the weak defend themselves."

"Oh." Rick was quiet, thinking. "It's not much better. You could still go to jail for it. When was the last time you did this?"

"Last week." Elijah told Rick about Roxanna and the biker, leaving out the more gruesome details.

Rick asked, "Is this sort of thing that has caused all the violence since you came back?"

"Yes." Elijah left it at that.

Rick leaned against the counter, arms folded in front of him. His eyes were kind, searching, not closed off or angry. A soft brown. "Why do you do this?"

"Most of the time it's just me finding a bad situation and not walking away from it. I just want to help others, and sometimes you have to hurt one to save many." Elijah let out a breath. There,

Rick knew most of his story. He was surprised that Rick was still engaged, instead of finding an excuse to leave the room.

"So, this Roxanna girl." Rick picked the rag up again and dried the silverware. "Do you have a thing for her?"

"No, but she has a thing for me, I think. At least that's what Juno says."

"Oh?"

Elijah changed out the dishwater. "Roxanna's a curvy, voluptuous woman with beautiful skin and big brown eyes. She's got long, wavy black hair and knows how to complement her shape when she dresses."

Rick took a breath. "You're making me horny—and I'm gay."

"Exactly. Juno told me she was hot for me. He's friends with her older brother. But the thing is, when he told me that, I recoiled from the image of her coming to hug me or anything else. What does that mean?"

Rick looked surprised at that. "That you don't want to give her all your money and freedom?"

Elijah laughed and took another dish to wash. "Juno thought he had some good news for me by telling me this. I don't know why, but I felt like I had to cover my reaction, so I told him I wasn't ready for family dinners and all the cultural drama that would entail. Why did I do that?"

"You know," Rick said, "coming from someone who lived in the closet for years, that excuse sounds like a pretty closeted thing to say. I'm here alone with you in the kitchen because Phillip thinks you're safe around men. Is he right?"

Is he hitting on me?

Elijah shrugged. "You're safe around me. All I'm saying is, I'll be happy to come to family dinners with you guys and whatever cultural drama is involved. That's all I can say."

"And you are wet and soapy right now."

Elijah splashed him. "You're not listening anymore. Come on let's get this done and get back out with the boys."

Rick sighed dramatically. "Fine, but I'm going to have trouble sleeping tonight."

"Rick," Elijah said, "on a serious note—can I be serious for a minute?"

Rick turned to him. The white towel was thrown over his shoulder. "Of course you can. What is it?"

"I want the internship."

Rick waved his hand. "Oh I knew that. I already put the paperwork in. Just give it about two weeks and I'll have some news. As far as I'm concerned, all we have to do is pick the partner that will go through the training with you."

Elijah was stunned. "Thank you."

Rick smiled. "Welcome." They didn't hug, but it hung in the air.

When Elijah got home that night, the warehouse was on fire.

15

THE FIRST STRIKE

Juno arrived at Ranger PX ten minutes after he had gotten the security call. Four fire trucks and a handful of cruisers filled the industrial street with red and blue lights, a tint compared to the orange inferno dancing against the bricks. He skidded his Nissan Leaf to a stop as close to the warehouse as the crowd of onlookers would allow and ran to the police barricade.

An officer held up a hand. "Sorry sir, we can't let you past this point."

Juno fumbled at his pockets. "I'm the owner. This is my warehouse." He pulled out an ID and showed it to the officer.

The officer examined it and nodded. "Mr. Valdas, this way."

He motioned for Juno to follow him to a group of officers standing around the fire truck. The scene was well-orchestrated chaos, everyone trying to put out the fire and protect the neighboring buildings from igniting.

Elijah could be in there. What if he's trapped in his safe house? Juno looked around, searching the shadowy faces of the crowd.

With a sigh of relief he found Elijah, standing to the side of the crowd, his bike held at his side. The two soldiers made eye contact and Elijah nodded, confirming he was fine.

The officer handed Juno over to a female firefighter who was shouting commands at what looked to be newly arrived firefighters. She turned to him. "I'm Suzanne England, the scene commander. This is your warehouse, then?"

Juno nodded. "It is. What do you know so far?"

She turned back to face the fire, the soot on her face absorbing the orange glow. "We've been fighting this for about twenty minutes. It'll be contained, but you'll lose about a third of the building. What kind of inventory do you have in there?"

"I sell tools and collect foodstuffs, lots of spices from the Middle East."

"Nothing going to blow up and kill us?"

Juno shook his head in the negative. "It's all pretty mundane. How did this start? Is it too early to ask that?"

England said, "We had a few workers from down the road tell us they saw about a dozen choppers over here before the fire started. It's our only lead so far. They didn't see them *do* anything, but they said their presence was unusual in this area. Is that correct?"

"Yes, we don't see many in this neighborhood."

"Mr. Valdas, do you have any feuds with the biker gangs here in town?"

Juno clenched his fists. "Yeah, I suppose I do now. I fought a biker a few days ago. He was attacking a woman, my combat training just kicked in and I attacked him. I guess his friends found out who was responsible."

"What happened to the biker in question?" England pulled out a notebook and started to write something down.

"Dead. The fight got pretty serious. The police are currently conducting an investigation. They'll have more information for you than me."

England lifted her eyebrows. "OK then. I guess we'll follow up on that biker lead. But understand it could still have been electrical, or some drunk leaning up against the wall smoking dope or any of a dozen other things."

"Or a biker." Juno's eyes were hard, steel reflected in the heat of the fire. All of his hard work, his love and passion, reduced to ash. "I look forward to finding out more."

The fire was contained and put out just before dawn. The crew was reduced to those who would tend it overnight to be sure it didn't flash back. Juno and Elijah finally left to go sleep at Juno's home. Juno lived in a quiet little neighborhood called Adams Point, full of young families and community parks.

When they pulled up to the house, Gabija was waiting for them on the front porch, clutching her robe tightly around her delicate frame. She gave Elijah a hug, and ushered him in the kitchen. "There's tea and some leftovers. Help yourself."

Elijah muttered thanks and trudged inside. Juno stood in the doorway, wordlessly staring at his wife's stricken face.

"How bad?" she whispered.

"They think up to a third gone. We'll have to see in the morning."

Gabija gasped, a hand flying to her chest. "That bad? Was it—" She peered down the hall at the kitchen, then pulled Juno after her to the bottom of the stairs. "Was this an accident? Something wrong with the building? You don't have any dangerous inventory, so what happened?"

"The Fire Captain told me that there was a report on a bike gang near the warehouse before the fire started."

Gabija narrowed her eyes. Her hair was disheveled, as if woken suddenly from sleep. Juno loved his wife's hair. "Why would a bike . . . wait a minute here, mister. Is this because of the stalker? You know, I could understand why you'd want to take the rap for Elijah. You'll get off. But dammit, Juno. I couldn't see you for a couple of days, your children had their *father* in jail, and then when you finally come home a gang sets the warehouse on fire? Are you kidding me?"

"It could still have been an accident, Gabija."

"But what if it was a biker gang? What are we going to do?" She buried her head in Juno's chest. Juno stroked her hair, breathing in her comforting scent. "I'm scared, Juno. What if they come for the house next?"

"Let the police investigate this. I'll talk to the insurance guy tomorrow and everything will be fine. I won't let this affect us any more than it has already."

Gabija pulled away from him. "Is this because you covered for Elijah? Juno, if that man should have been the one in custody—"

"Leave Elijah out of this." He lowered his voice. "I'll take care of this, love, I promise. Just let me work here."

Gabija glowered. "Please don't tell me you're putting your old army buddy above your family. Don't do this to me, Juno Valdas. I waited six long years to get you back safe, to start our family. We have two beautiful kids, and you just want to put yourself right back in danger?"

"Gabija—"

She held up a hand. "Fix this. OK?"

With that she turned and stomped up the stairs. Juno ran a hand over his face, more exhausted than he'd felt in years. *Fix this.* He'd try, all right, but where to start?

Juno joined Elijah at the kitchen island for herbal tea. They spoke quietly, the only the light on was the small one over the stove. It lent itself to their intimate conversation.

Elijah whispered, "You gonna be OK?"

Juno nodded. "It's only a building, my friend. I have good insurance, it'll be repaired in no time. No one got hurt, that's the important thing. Why weren't you home?"

Elijah told him about going over to Rick's house, and the new friends he was making. Juno smiled at this small sliver of a happy tale in his otherwise dreadful day. Elijah was making friends.

"That's great. And you got the internship?"

"I did."

Juno clasped Elijah on the shoulder. "Sounds like you had a pretty good day—well, before the fire."

"I did. But actually, there was one weird thing that happened to me before dinner."

"Oh?"

Juno's cheer slowly evaporated as he listened to Elijah's strange story about the man in Peet's.

Elijah ended with, "He said he wanted to hire me as a hit man, that I had a natural talent. He offered me fifty grand in cash, right then. But he knows everything about me, man. It scared the shit out of me."

"What the fuck? This is serious. Is he trying to blackmail you into working for him?"

"When I got back to my seat he was gone, but there was this envelope laying on his table. I've got it in my backpack."

"You took his money?" Juno growled.

"I had to! The envelope had my name on it in big script. If I had left it there . . ."

"Someone else would know too much. I get it. Is there anything else in the envelope besides cash?"

"He said it's information on the job he offered me. I haven't opened it yet, though."

"Pull it out."

Elijah rustled in his backpack. Juno rubbed his eyes. How was this stuff always happening to his friend? It was like he was a magnet for villainy.

"Here it is." Juno looked up as Elijah slapped the engraved package on the island.

They both stared at it warily, like it was a bomb about to go off.

This is ridiculous, paper can't hurt me. Juno pulled out his SWAT knife and slit the top. He dumped the contents onto the marble top.

Elijah jumped back in surprise. Juno just stood, there, staring at it. Five bundles of hundred dollar bills, casually heaped on his kitchen counter.

"That'll be the fifty grand in cash. He said it was only the half up front for this particular job."

Juno was shocked. "A hundred grand for a job? You know this money is hot—we can't touch this. I wonder if there's some kind of tracking device embedded in it. Damn it. We can't take this to the police and have a conversation about a guy who wants to hire you as a hit man. Who's the hit?"

Elijah opened the file and pulled out a stack of pictures of a man wearing a suit, taken from different angles. There was a page of information detailing the man's home, work address, and all his movements and habits. "Some Orville Forester. The guy wants him dead before next weekend is over."

Juno balled a fist. He wouldn't let his friend do that. That wasn't a path they were about to take. "We're going to burn this and bury the ashes. Did this man introduce himself?"

Elijah nodded. "Yeah, he said his name was B. A. Lamb."

Juno stiffened. A whisper flashed through his mind, as fast and powerful as a bolt of lightning.

Balaam.

Juno broke out in a cold sweat. "I . . . think you were talking to a minion of the devil."

Elijah pushed his chair back, anger in his voice. "Get the fuck out. How can I believe this shit?"

Juno shushed him, looking to the stairs. Waking his children to eavesdrop on a conversation like this was the last thing he wanted to do. "Was this guy the same as the figure you saw in your house the other night? The one in the abyss?"

Elijah shook his head from side to side and shuddered. "How can you possibly believe that? Really. That's such science fiction bullshit."

Juno leaned over the island, avoiding the money. "When will

83

you start believing me? My theory that the devil was watching you and wanted you for the dark side must be right! This has to be it, brother. I think he's moving to get you before you realize what's happening."

"Stop it, Juno."

"You've got to be really careful, Elijah. Real careful. You've got to get through this test of yours."

"Test?"

"A time of trial. This is the decision time in your life. We've *got* to burn this stuff." Juno gestured at the money and files. "I have a friend who owns a foundry. We'll go together in the morning."

"The foundry seems like overkill. There's a lighter in that drawer, isn't there?"

"If we burn it here then there'll be evidence, somehow. I feel a danger here, a serious danger. Anyone who would offer you cash like this to kill someone could just be setting you up instead. That kind of person could call in a tip to the police about you being a hit man."

"Fine. Tomorrow, then." Elijah gathered everything back into the envelope—careful to not let his skin touch the cash—and handed it to Juno. He patted his friend on the shoulder then left the kitchen, heading toward the family den where a fold-out sofa waited for him.

Juno stared at the envelope a little longer. Yes, Elijah seemed to get himself in all kinds of trouble. But he wasn't going to let the devil win.

16

THE FOUNDRY

East Side Foundry was an old brick building, but the doors and window frames all sported a fresh white coat of paint. Elijah followed Juno into the main office, where they were greeted by Niles Conklin.

Juno put his arm around Niles and said, "Elijah, Niles has been a dear friend since childhood."

Niles grinned at Elijah and extended his hand. "Nice to finally meet you. Heard so much about you. Let me know if I can help in any way. I didn't serve and have always admired the men and women who do."

Elijah nodded. Most people said something along those lines, that or, "Thank you for your service." And that one just bugged the living hell out of him.

Niles had a crisp, confident attitude about himself that matched his bodybuilder physique. He wore a brown button-down tucked into blue jeans with black dress shoes.

"I know there's a huge cost to you when you serve in a war zone," Niles continued. "I once read a book by one of the astronauts called *Return to Earth*. I think it was Buzz Aldrin who wrote it. He said that once you've been to the moon, it's almost impossible to live on the earth anymore. It just changes everything for you. He says lots of the astronauts have real trouble functioning in this world after their service. I imagine war is like that. Once you see how people act in a war, it must be hard to just walk around in a crowded city or a quiet country town. I can't imagine what goes through your mind. I can't even think of something to say to comfort you or Juno."

Elijah blinked. That was one of the most reasonable, appropriate responses he'd heard since coming home. "Thanks for not knowing. I should get that book and read it. I've also read that many police have trouble living in a world they know to be so evil."

Juno smiled, as if he knew Elijah would be impressed. "Niles was the smart one in school. He seems to get things that most people miss."

"I don't know about that." Niles brushed off the compliment. He looked between his two visitors, all business. "What can I do for you men?"

Juno held up a small paper bag that contained the envelope. "I need this to disappear into something that cannot be reassembled."

Niles laughed, as if they would soon tell him it was a joke. "The foundry might be overkill for that little bag, but . . ." He paused, and when neither Elijah nor Juno moved to stop him, continued. "But I'm always happy to help you with anything, Juno. Just don't give me the details. This way."

The building was much larger than Elijah had initially gauged. A short, padded hallway opened up to a steel catwalk above the foundry's many kilns and furnaces, large bins of metals and plastics stored along the walls. The air rang with the sounds of metal striking metal, conveyor belts whirling, and the overpowering hum of white-hot flame.

Niles shouted over the cacophony. "So I hear you're the reason Juno made it back from the war."

Elijah shouted back, "We've been through a lot together. I can't say who brought who back."

"We're pretty busy most days. The crucible and the furnaces are working almost nonstop, but we take the time to have a cigar in the afternoons. Stop by and have one with us in our lounge—both of you—whenever you're in the area."

They descended a metal staircase to the ground level and approached an open furnace. They stopped several yards from the intense heat.

"Fourteen hundred degrees," Niles said proudly. "Anything that goes into this baby will be reduced to its atoms."

The mouth of the furnace gaped wide open at them, like a hungry mouth waiting to devour them. Elijah was nervous, though he couldn't figure out why. His palms were sweating and he was struggling to breathe normally. "Do I just, go up there and stick it in?"

"No, of course not. There's a fire-retardant suit hanging up over there. You'll need to put that on."

Juno put a hand on Elijah's shoulder. "I'll do it."

Elijah watched as his friend put the bag on a long steel arm. He tentatively approached the white glow of the furnace, his silhouette shimmering in the malevolent heat. When Juno dropped the bag, Elijah watched as the heat engulfed the frail paper. There would be no trace of the bag and contents.

Juno would walk into true fire for me, and I've done nothing good for him these past few weeks. Elijah hadn't realized before that moment just how bad he was and how his violent acts damaged so many people, including ones that cared about him. *I need to change. I want to be the man who'd walk through fire for another, not throw him into the flames.*

They said their goodbyes and Juno drove Elijah back to the warehouse.

"Insurance agent will be here within the hour," Juno said as they parked. "We'll go through the inventory, and I'll be sure to skip over your home. Just make sure to check your space thoroughly for any fire damage, OK?"

Juno waited by the front office for his agent while Elijah snuck quietly around the back to assess his own quarters. When he opened his door, Elijah took a deep breath. Everything smelled of smoke, but nothing seemed to be disturbed or heavily damaged. Some of his cabling had melted together from the adjacent heat, but that was an easy replacement. He made sure the fans were on high to push air through the home. He checked out the bedroom, the living space, and the kitchen and bathroom. He went up the ladder to the attic space and did a thorough inspection. Nothing seemed to be damaged.

He descended the ladder, ready to find Juno and report back, but when he turned around he came face-to-face with Mr. Lamb sitting at his big black table. He seemed very relaxed, very patient.

Elijah strode toward the intruder. "Oh no you don't. Get out. I told you we're not gonna work together. And I don't appreciate that you left that envelope out in the open. Anyone could've picked it up."

"I know that," Lamb said with a smile. "I thought it was funny. I offered it to you in good faith. I was happy to see you pick it up. I don't think it was wise to incinerate it this morning, though. The man in the photos needs to die this coming weekend. You're expected to make that happen."

"Yeah? So you can jump me with a squad of uniforms? I don't think so."

"You are not being set up, Mr. McCoy. If I wanted you dead, I could hire someone to kill you rather than go through all the trouble of the legal system. No, this is a chance for you to be independently wealthy."

Elijah pointed at the door. "Get out."

"This man is not a good person." Lamb crossed his legs. "He hurts people for a living. Not like you, no. You hurt those who need it, to help others. This man, well, he enjoys the suffering. Not physical, no, of course not. Purely financial. He really likes it when there's a family involved, so he can watch them try to stand by their man when everything comes crashing down around him. You would be doing everyone a favor to get rid of him."

Lamb stared at Elijah, a pleasant, patient expression on his face. When Elijah didn't move, didn't answer, he sighed and pushed himself out of his chair. "I can deliver him to you. I told you that. We are talking about a minute's work for a hundred thousand dollars." He walked into the kitchen and picked up one of Elijah's remaining canisters, examining it idly. "It wouldn't be your first time *eliminating* someone, as you like to say. You could even use the money to help your friend rebuild this warehouse."

The thought of Juno's financial troubles pained Elijah, but he stood firm. "No. Got it? No."

"I have an envelope here that has ten times as much money in it. I've taken the time to reproduce the file for you." Lamb set the canister down and retrieved a folder from his briefcase. Elijah didn't need the file at this point; just going through it with Juno had stored the information into his brain.

Elijah crossed his arms. Something in his gut told him attacking this man would be a mistake, but that didn't mean he had to respond to him.

"Do this one job and I will leave you alone—it's the easiest way to get rid of me. You'll get one million dollars, and you'll never see me again. It's perfect."

"There are other people who will be happy to work with you. Why don't you go ask one of them?"

"Oh, there are people lined up to do this, and for a fraction of the price. But I want you, Elijah."

"I'm out of patience. Go."

"Or you'll do what, kill me?" Lamb gave a thin smile that didn't reach his cold, dead eyes. "Should I make a lot of noise right now and attract attention to your secret lair? You know, I'm the only reason this place wasn't destroyed in the fire. You didn't even thank me."

"Fuck off."

Lamb didn't even blink. "Mr. Orville Forester has an appointment with you this Friday evening. He will be at the end of Pier 51, alone, at 10 p.m. waiting for you. He wants to show you a file he has on someone he wants dead."

"I don't care. I'm not going to meet him."

Mr. Lamb raised an eyebrow. "But don't you want to know who he wants you to kill?"

"No."

"It's someone you know."

Elijah had a very bad feeling in his gut. He needed Lamb to leave his home, and soon.

Well, if he's not going to leave, I am.

He walked toward the door. "I have to go. Be sure to lock the door when you go." Elijah threw the door open to the chilly morning, but just as the door closed behind him he heard . . .

"It's Juno."

17

THE CONTRACT

Elijah trudged around the neighboring warehouse, the word *Juno* echoing in his head. This was outrageous. He really was in over his head. Who would want to kill Juno? Was this because of him?

How does this Lamb guy know so much about me, and how was he able to get in my safe house?

Elijah had an uncomfortable possibility in front of him. Maybe, just maybe, there was more to all this than just his mental glitches. It was unlikely that his PTSD was causing these appearances by Lamb.

Elijah had seen evil in the war zone. People were either mauling each other, planning to maul each other, or trying to recover from a mauling. People were hurt, and people were killed. Those who lived—and this included him, he knew—were permanently damaged. That was evil as he understood it. But could evil be something more? Something sentient . . . even tangible?

He rounded a corner and walked down a gravel alley. It could be an explanation for how things got so fucked up in the world. But surely it's not *real*, not in the way Juno believed. Evil was just bad people with bad ideas . . . Wasn't it? Just people who had no education in how to behave? People who just wanted to break the law?

Shit. Juno would know.

Elijah was sure the insurance guy had a copy of the police report. How would the biker death affect Juno's insurance claims? Shit. Elijah didn't have to kill Garlitz—what the fuck? This fire was just another thing on a growing list of troubles resulting from his aggression. He kicked a rock, sending it skipping down the alley.

When Elijah got back to the warehouse, Juno was nowhere to be found. *Still with the agent, then.*

Elijah pulled out his phone. CLOSE TO DONE?

Juno texted him back right away. STILL TALKING. COOL YOUR HEELS, 30 MINUTES MAX.

A black Cadillac CTS was parked outside the warehouse. That must be the insurance agent's car. Elijah paced up and down the street a few more times before settling on a big wooden crate— probably some inventory saved by the firefighters last night. He gave it a few experimental pushes and found it was sturdy enough to sit on.

Elijah sighed. He was hurting Juno. He was a loser and a troublemaker and did not deserve to have a friend like Juno. He would be doing everyone a favor if he just disappeared.

Something patted him on the back of the head. He looked around, but no one was there. He was sure that he had felt a pat. He looked up, even though he was sure that whoever had touched him couldn't be there. Fuck.

No, I can't leave Juno. He needs me right now. I've got to stay positive.

"Hey buddy!" Juno waved from the warehouse's main doors. "Over here!"

Elijah hopped off the crate and jogged over to his friend. "Everything OK with you and the insurance guy?"

"Yeah. We looked through the building and he said he'd have a claims team come out. Luckily all my computers are backed up to the cloud. Do you have time to come through with me and start a list of what we can see? I need you man."

It was like a bell went off in Elijah's head. *Juno needs my help right now.* "I'll be happy to help."

The two of them went in and got busy taking pictures with a camera the insurance broker had given Juno and making lists.

When Juno felt they had a basic idea of what the situation was, he said, "Let's go to Buster's and get a cup of coffee. I'm dead."

Elijah's stomach twisted at the words.

Juno locked the construction fence that had been put up that morning by the police. "I need to email my clients and vendors and let them know that I'm locked down for a week or two. We should be able to start sending and receiving as soon as the clean-up starts. Hopefully we can start that in a few days once the claims people are done."

Being back in Buster's again was strange for Elijah. It was virtu-ally unchanged, as if nothing had happened just yards from its doors. Elroy greeted Elijah as usual, but with less cheer than normal. He allotted Elijah more personal space, staying at least an arm's length away from him.

It's hard to believe the last time I was here I had just killed a man, and met Phillip.

Yes, this place was now marked with Elijah's memory of his new friend. Phillip was a good kid, and he had introduced Elijah to Rick, possibly an even greater man.

At the thought of Rick, Elijah felt a slight tingle. He shook it off.

"Juno, I need to tell you something."

Juno lowered the menu to give Elijah a curious—but exasper-ated—look. "More news? You've had a busy week. Wait." He leaned forward. "Did you hear from . . . you know, Mr. Lamb?"

"Hear from him? He was in my house."

"What?"

Elijah told Juno about finding Mr. Lamb in his safe house and what the man had said—with the exception of the last part. "He knows we incinerated the file and he's set up an appointment for me to meet the target this Friday. What do I do?"

Juno put up a hand. "What do you mean, what do you do? You don't talk to this guy at all. I'm telling you, he's lying. His boss is called the father of lies."

"Juno, please."

"There's probably going to be a whole team of guys at that pier waiting to kill *you* that night. That or they'll be police. Just watch, the money will be found in your safe house through an anonymous tip, and that will be shown to prove you were a drug dealer or something like that. Then I'll have to explain what a drug dealer was doing living in my warehouse. I mean this whole thing just reeks of bullshit."

Elroy set down two steaming cups of coffee. Juno picked his up and blew on it. "Just stay clear from this guy. You don't want to get involved in any of his plans."

Elijah nodded, not meeting Juno's eyes. His stomach was all in knots. Juno was right, but what if staying away from Mr. Lamb got Juno killed?

18

THE CONDO

Elijah woke the next morning at his usual time, but not in his usual place. Phillip's guest room was styled as a neutral tone seaside spa, with blue and sand walls, white furniture, and shells adorning the bookcase. It wasn't Elijah's personal taste, but he was grateful for the bed. Phillip had insisted Elijah use his condo for the next couple of weeks while the warehouse was rebuilt—it was close to his work, after all, and currently vacant. It had been Juno's idea for Elijah to ask.

"If you're not going to stay with me and the family, then I think you should stay with your new friends," Juno had said the previous day. "I don't like the idea of you out on the streets at night."

Elijah's argument had been a simple one. "I just don't think I'm a good influence on the kids."

"You're crazy, the kids love you—they think you're hilarious. And they already live with a damaged vet." Juno's voice had been almost pleading through the phone. "They know what you suffer. Besides, it's good socialization for you."

"I'm sorry, I can't do it. But I'll call Rick, see if he has a spare bedroom." Rick didn't have a spare bedroom, much to everyone's disappointment. "It's a three bedroom, but Phillip and I take up two and the third one is just crammed full of storage."

That was when Phillip had offered his own condo. "If you only need it for a few weeks, that's perfect. I'll probably move home again by next month."

So Elijah found himself that morning in Phillip's beautiful European condo near the waterfront with a bay view. From the balcony, he could see the street, a row of warehouses converted to retail, and then across the Amtrak tracks to the corner of Jack London Square right on the bay. He had his bike in the condo and his Focus Electric down in the garage where there was even a charging station. He could use his own stuff while he was here and try to be a good guest.

Elijah was watching the sunrise when his cell phone rang. He picked it up. "Hello?"

It was Juno. "Good morning brother! How's the life of the rich?"

Elijah chuckled. "I'm feeling pretty pampered up here in the clouds. What's up?"

"Sorry to call so early, but I got a call that made me laugh and I wanted to share it with you."

"Oh?"

"I got a call from Hector Ramirez. His sister—the woman from last week—"

"I know who she is, Juno."

"Right, well she wanted your number, so Hector was asking for it. Look out for a phone call coming soon."

Elijah was shocked. "You gave out my number?"

Juno sounded a little sheepish. "To a beautiful woman who wants to thank you, yeah."

"Shit, Juno."

Juno laughed. "Must be tough to be popular. I'm working from home today. I'm glad you are hanging out in the hoity-toity condo. Enjoy!"

Elijah smiled, switching the phone to his left shoulder. "Nah, hoity-toity is for people who only think they're better than everyone else—in this complex, these people *know* they are. I'm hanging with my peeps."

Elijah grabbed his bike to find a bite to eat before hitting the gym. There was a chic café, The Blue Bottle, across the street. It was filled with casually dressed but upscale, well-educated people. They all had the latest electronic gadgets and cool messenger bags. Elijah rolled his eyes at them. They were all pretending to be streetwise, but they weren't. He rode past that and looked for a neighborhood breakfast place.

He was looking for people of various races and ages going in and out. A café sign that read "The Collective" caught his eye. The tables outside were filled with his prescribed mix of people. There was even a guy sleeping at a corner table that was probably homeless. He folded and locked his bike near the entrance. A lesbian couple passed him, entering the café. One had tattoos all the way up her arm, balanced with a splash of colorful ink on her right calf.

OK, this will be fine. It was no Buster's, but it could be a fun little adventure for him. Like a mini vacation. He went in and found that they had a great bowl of oatmeal with honey, almonds, raisins, and cinnamon. Yes, this would be fine.

He finished his leisurely breakfast and got up to return his plates when a familiar face on the street caught his attention.

He ran outside. "Rick!"

Rick turned around, brows furrowed as he searched for who had yelled his name. He was in a business casual shirt and slacks and wearing rose-gold sunglasses, which complemented his bronze skin.

He found Elijah in the busy sidewalk and grinned. "Elijah! What are you doing over here?"

"Enjoying my vacation." They laughed. "But why are you here? I thought you worked uptown?"

"I do, but I'm down here talking to the bike share people. Are you leaving?"

"I was heading to the gym."

Rick eyed Elijah's arms openly, a wicked appraising look on his face. "Go to the gym often, then?"

Elijah shifted and smiled, pulling his tight T-shirt down a little over his biceps. Yeah, I go a few times a week."

He had an army friend who used to call him a "gym lizard" because he liked to work out so much. He always thought about that, whenever he went to a gym. It was Teddy who used to say that.

Teddy was dead, killed by an IED on the road to a village visit. Elijah thought about that every time he went to the gym, too.

Rick frowned. "What's wrong?"

"Huh?"

Rick took off his sunglasses. "You look sad."

"Just thinking about a passed friend. Sorry."

Rick put a hand on Elijah's arm. "Don't ever apologize for your feelings." He gave a gentle squeeze. "I've got an hour before I need to head back to the office. There's a park across the street. Want to go for a walk?"

Elijah conceded, deciding that his bike was safe. The park was a green lot between two tall white-washed warehouses. There were a few trees and a small pond with ducks. It had a nice walking loop for Rick and Elijah to absently follow as they talked.

"We used to talk about death a lot in my unit." Elijah stuffed his hands in his pocket as he walked, staring at the ground. "Hard not to, considering the circumstances. People take it real hard, you know? Everyone always asks themselves *Why them? Why not me?* We adopted the saying, 'only the good die young' to explain why we survived."

"Like the Billy Joel song?"

Elijah nodded. "None of us felt good, so it seemed right. I guess it'll always be a mystery, in a way."

"That's tough." Rick squinted up at the sun. "How'd you cope with that?"

"The best way to honor a fallen friend is to live, that's what we always said, at least."

"And what have you done to live?" Rick asked quietly.

Elijah was quiet. What *had* he done? He made more than half his money as a redeemer. He wasn't living, he was hurting. Killing.

"Nothing. I don't live, I kill."

Rick sucked in a breath. "You protect."

"Not always." Elijah balled his fists. "The frustrating thing is that I'm *good* at it. You can pull the life out of a person with a quick jerk of the hand. It's pretty easy to separate a person from their body."

"Elijah, that's horrible! You can't say things like that."

"But it's true. It's part of me." They walked in silence for a minute. There were children playing by the pond. "What do you think happens after you die, Rick?"

Rick shrugged. "I don't know. You're not your body. It's trash after you die. People are often attached to their bodies—I'm totally guilty of this too, skin care, exercise, diet—but it's not *you*. I went to Jason's funeral, after he passed."

Elijah nodded. Jason was Rick's last partner, the one who died from AIDs.

"When I looked into his casket . . ." Rick coughed, clearing his throat. "It wasn't him. Nothing about that husk was him. But someone still took the time to wash Jason, put some makeup on him and dress him in his favorite suit. I had nightmares for weeks after that. I swore that day I would never visit his grave, because that wasn't my Jason under all the dirt. But anyway. I don't know where we go, but it isn't to the ground, that's for sure."

Elijah stared at him. That was exactly what he believed about bodies after death. There was an instant separation between the person and those who loved him. The body was there, but the person was nowhere to be seen, or talked to. You could touch the body, but you could never touch the person again. So where was that person? Elijah didn't know, but he didn't think that killing a body killed the person. In his mind, he was just pulling a person out of his or her body and leaving the body behind. And once the person was separated from the body, he no longer felt threatened by that person.

"That must have been really hard for you," Elijah said. "How are you doing with all that?"

Rick sniffed, but waved a hand. "It was years ago. I'm fine now —well, mostly fine. I'll be more fine, soon." He smiled. "Have you seen that woman you saved recently? Briana?"

"Roxanna, and no, I haven't. But Juno gave her my number, so I should be expecting a call from her soon."

Rick gave a dry laugh. "What are you going to do?"

Elijah sighed. "I don't know, man. Part of me thinks I should talk to her, become her friend. But another part of me wants to pull even further into my shell, cut ties and disappear."

He could live the life of a full-time killer, if he worked with Mr. Lamb. The consequences didn't bother him. He could become totally anonymous. He might be caught and prosecuted, or he might be killed in the act of killing. But none of that bothered him. There was no personal hurt in a life like that.

Mr. Lamb was an asshole, but that didn't make him a demon. *Though I've never seen him enter or leave a room, and that's weird.* The thought gave Elijah a cold shiver down his spine.

Elijah turned, realizing that Rick had stopped walking. "Rick?"

Rick stood just outside the shade of a tree, a hand shading his eyes. A frown creased his smooth skin. "Don't disappear, Elijah. Don't do that to Juno, or Phillip . . . or me."

Something was calling to his core. Elijah wanted to be a part of society again and to have people in his life. He looked at Rick's sincere, open eyes and realized that he wanted to be a friend—and have a friend. That just seemed like a crazy idea to him at this point in his life.

"I won't. I promise." Elijah ran a hand over his short hair. "I feel so fucked up, Rick. I want the internship. I want to turn things around—but I look at all the things I'd have to change in my life to get there, and it just reminds me of how much evil I've done. How can I ever get past that? I don't think I'll ever be normal. I'll just be pretending, lying—and what happens when it all comes out?"

"What do you mean?"

"So I make friends and fall in love and get a house and everything will seem perfect, but all the time my family and friends wouldn't know the true me? I can't do that. I can't live a lie."

"I know you, and I'm still your friend. Elijah, what do you *really* want? It can't just be friends—you already have those."

Elijah paused, thinking. "Change. I want to change. But I don't know how."

Rick smiled. "Let me help you find your new self."

19

FOG LIFTERS

E lijah got a call from Roxanna the next morning. "Hey Roxanna, how are you feeling? Are you recovering OK?"

Her end had some static in the background, mixed with the sounds of traffic. It sounded like Roxanna was outside her office building. "My ankle hurts, but it's OK. I just wanted to call and thank you for helping me. I just feel so light now, not having to worry every minute about the stalker. Thank you."

"Of course. No problem."

There was a pause. "I was actually also hoping I could see you again. Are you available to meet for coffee and talk for a few minutes? Does today work?" Elijah said it did. "I work close to a coffee shop called Fog Lifters. I'll see you in an hour?"

Elijah agreed. He'd ride over.

The bike ride through city streets was pretty flat and there was a good bike lane most of the way. Parts of the city were becoming bike friendly, and for the most part people were decent drivers. A bike rider had to be aware and stay in the bike lanes where he could, but it wasn't that scary to bike in this city. Some cities were a terror to even the most experienced biker.

The fog had burned off and the day was going to be sunny and a little warmer. Elijah rolled up to the door of Fog Lifters and found a good place to lock up and went in. Roxanna was waiting for him at a small table. He smiled at her, and she beamed in return.

As he approached the table she reached up and let her ponytail loose and shook free her beautiful hair. He sat down. "Good to see you, Roxanna."

Roxanna pulled the zip of her jacket down, revealing more of her full breasts. "Hi, Elijah."

Elijah felt a jolt of surprise. This was not the kind of coffee hour he had envisioned.

"Can I . . . get you anything?" he asked.

"That's so sweet of you." She leaned forward on her folded arms, pressing her breasts even further from her jacket. "A latte and a croissant, please."

Elijah scrambled from the table to place his order. He got an African Nectar tea for himself and brought their food back.

Roxanna took a bite of her croissant. "I really want to thank you for your help, Elijah. I just feel so much safer since that horrible man is gone."

"He's gone forever. You OK with that?"

She nodded solemnly. "I am. It all happened so fast, and him choking me—it was surreal! But you were so strong and confident. I love having that kind of protection in my life. It's hard for a single mother like myself to find a man to protect her."

Elijah choked on his tea. "You have a child?"

Roxanna nodded. "Lucy will be four in May."

Elijah said, "I didn't realize that. If you don't mind me asking, where's the father?"

Roxanna's smile faded. "I was raped almost four years ago. Lucy is the product of that."

Elijah grimaced inwardly. He shouldn't have asked that. "Oh, I'm . . . I don't know what to say. I'm sorry."

"I was being followed then, just as I was now. Maybe I'm

cursed, it sure feels that way sometimes. I mean, I'm pretty, aren't I?"

Elijah nodding, crossing his arms.

"I should have an easier time than I do. When this horrible biker started stalking me, it felt just like the guy who'd been stalking me before he raped me. I was really scared—that's why I talked to Hector about it, and how I got your name."

"Whatever happened to the first guy?"

"Oh, Hector made sure that man was arrested. He'll be in prison for four more of his eight years. Then he'll be on parole. I can tell you the exact date if you want. Since he's been locked up, it's come out that he murdered two prostitutes in the year before he raped me. Hopefully he'll be convicted for those murders later this year."

"Let's hope he gets life without parole," Elijah said. "I'd like to know that you're safe going forward."

Roxanna looked at him with big eyes. "You would? You'd want to protect me and Lucy?"

Elijah leaned away from her. "Well sure. I can come over and check on your house, watch her as she grows. Like an uncle."

Roxanna's face fell, an angry glare marring her beauty. "So that's the way it's going to be? You want to be an uncle to the baby? Can you see me, Elijah? Do I look good to you at all?" She straightened in her chair, squaring her shoulders. "I'm a good person, and fun, and I can create a loving home. Don't you want that?"

Elijah squirmed in his seat. She was drawing attention to their table. "You're beautiful, Roxanna. You know that. The way you look today is almost illegal. I'm sure you're a good person and that you're a wonderful potential partner for some lucky person."

"*Man*, Elijah. Some lucky *man*. I'm a catch, damn it. Do you think I'm causing all this or something?"

Elijah was out of tea. What was he supposed to do with his hands now? "No, of course not. I think you've had bad luck in your life, but you're not a bad person. You should be married to a CEO of some big corporation based on your looks. You should be rich and comfortable and only ever worry about spa treatments."

Roxanna blushed and looked at him through her thick black eyelashes. She leaned forward and put her hand on the table, palm up. Elijah just stared at it, but made no move to take it.

She blinked and pulled her hand back. "I would be more than happy to just have a normal man who would love me and come home every night and be happy to spend time with me. I would love to be able to look pretty for a man and take care of him and go out and dance once in a while. It doesn't have to be the lifestyle of the rich and famous. And I think I could see myself that way with you."

Elijah sighed. "That's not going to happen, Roxanna. I like you. I'm happy I could help you and I would love to stay in touch, but I'm not looking for a relationship right now." He thought about Rick. *I wonder if that's true.* And it had been so easy to talk to Phillip after his attack, much easier than any conversation he'd had with Roxanna.

Roxanna's eyes widened in outrage. *"What?* Are you gay or something?"

Elijah didn't say anything for a long while. This wasn't how he had planned to spend his morning. "As far as I know, I'm asexual. There's an intimate detail I'm trusting you with. I'm so fucked up right now, I can't even imagine getting romantic with anyone."

Roxanna sat there, stunned. "Are you . . . Elijah, are you a virgin?"

Elijah flushed, embarrassed.

"Oh my god." She took a deep breath and let it out slowly. "I'm sorry for going off on you, I just get so frustrated sometimes. Forgive me."

Elijah nodded and blew out his cheeks. "It's OK. Thanks for telling me about Lucy. I know that must be hard for you to share.

You've been through a hard time, but that's going to change, I promise you."

She smiled. "And I promise to continue being your friend, no strings attached." She plopped her purse on the table and started to rummage through it. "And thanks for not blowing me off. You didn't have to ride your bike all the way out here."

"Anything for a friend." He smiled.

Roxanna pulled out her phone and started typing. When she saw Elijah's questioning look, she explained, "I'm making a reminder to get batteries for my vibrator. I'll go to Costco and get the big economy pack."

They both laughed.

20

A FAMILY DINNER

Elijah had dinner with Juno's family that Friday night. He loved family dinners at their place. Tonight, the Valdas home was making *grybas zepetins*, Lithuanian potato dumplings filled with mushrooms, carrots, and onions. Juno chopped the vegetables and prepared the ingredients as Gabija rolled, stuffed, and cooked the dumplings. Elijah sat at the bar, watching the two chefs dance around the kitchen in perfect harmony. All the steaming food smelled great; it was very comforting. Elijah found their Lithuanian culture to be rich and interesting. He himself was a castoff from a Midwestern family with no culture to claim, so he was happy to learn about theirs.

He liked the food, for sure.

Gabija had been a little cold to Elijah after the fire. He suspected she blamed him for the family's misfortunes, what with the bikers. However, tonight she seemed more relaxed, like she was actively making an effort to put the incident behind her. Elijah followed her lead. When it was time to eat, Elijah pulled the cold beet soup from the fridge. Juno's children set the table.

"So Elijah," Gabija said, passing the serving plate to him. "I hear Hector's sister has a thing for you. Have you asked her out yet?"

Elijah blushed. "Actually, I saw her yesterday morning."

Juno raised an eyebrow, a smile playing at his lips. "Is that so? How'd it go?"

Gabija leaned in, resting her chin on laced fingers. "Isn't she lovely?"

"Mama, who's lovely?" Austeja was eight, and already looked just like Gabija.

Juno shushed her, not unkindly.

"She is," Elijah agreed. "Inside and out. But we decided not to make anything of it, at least for now."

Gabija frowned. "Why? She's perfect! She's beautiful, has a daughter—she's a ready-made family. Did you even give it a shot?"

Elijah shrugged. "The timing's just not right for either of us."

Juno was looking at Elijah, thoughtful. "Gabija, don't try to mess with his love life. I'm sure he thought it through."

The children giggled. "You said *love life*," Matas snickered. He was six, a missing front tooth adding extra charm to his grin.

Juno glanced at his son. "Eat your grybas." To his wife, he said, "Elijah can take care of himself."

Gabija sighed. "I just wish I saw you with someone. Someone to take care of you." She glanced at Juno.

"I have people." Elijah looked around the table. He cherished these dinners. It was like, for one night at a time, he could pretend he lived a happy, normal life. "You know how close I feel to all of you. And I'm making new friends. I even found another vet at the gym to work out with. He's fun, in our sick kind of way." He said this t Juno, who nodded, understanding.

"But no women." Gabija didn't pose it like a question.

Elijah shook his head, stalling a moment while he chewed. When he swallowed, he said, "No, but I'm not there yet. I'm visiting with Selma, making friends. It's a process."

Juno was watching Elijah, thoughtful.

Gabija wiped her mouth, nodding. "You do seem more at ease lately. More relaxed, more talkative. I don't think I've seen you this way since you came home."

When dinner was finished, Elijah helped Gabija serve the potato pudding. It was a traditional dessert he had at first been skeptical of, but had come to love. The children hungrily eyed the treat.

Elijah served two large scoops in Matas's bowl. "So Austeja, how's school?"

Austeja groaned. "Third grade is *hard*. We're learning about ecosystems."

"What ecosystems?" Elijah asked.

"We're learning about the plants and animals of different regions, like the mountains, deserts, and rainforests."

Elijah was wide-eyed. "Listen to the big words. This should be interesting."

Austeja slouched in her chair. "Yeah, but we have to do a big report—ten pages! And we have to make a poster and it's all due next week." She scrunched her face up.

Juno smiled. "As parents we're both learning new things about all this."

"She's been filling out index cards with facts, information, and drawings to write this big report." Gabija looked proud.

Elijah widened his eyes, mimicking awe. "Impressive. You have to show me this report when you are done."

The children giggled.

"What about you?" Elijah turned to Matas. "What are you learning?"

The six-year-old beamed. "We just got computer tablets in our classroom, and we get to play fun games during center time!"

Elijah leaned over to him to give him a poke. "That doesn't sound like school to me."

"We're learning by playing games. It's fun." Matas shoveled a large spoonful of pudding into his mouth.

Elijah smiled. "You keep telling yourself that."

The dinner was a success. Juno walked Elijah and his bike out to the front curb a few hours later.

"Clean up and reconstruction on the warehouse will start Monday," he said, hands stuffed in his pockets. "It'll be good to have everything back to normal again."

"How long do you think it'll take?" Elijah buckled his helmet with a click.

"Insurance crew thought we'd be running smooth within two months." Juno looked from Elijah in his biking jacket up to the chilly night sky above. The cloud cover made the city especially dark that evening. "Do you want me to throw the bike in the van and drive you to the condo?"

Elijah hesitated. "No, no need. After all that wonderful, fattening food, I better ride back just to start circulating some blood again. Thanks man." He smiled. "Sleep in tomorrow, hang out with the family. You know how to reach me."

With that he stepped over his bike and pushed down on the pedal, propelling himself into the dark night.

21

THE PIER

E lijah rode down a couple of blocks and turned toward the bay. He worked his way down from Lake Merritt through the neighborhoods leading up to the commercial streets toward the Embarcadero. It was a five-mile ride to get down to the Embarcadero and see the harbor. As he rode, he kept an eye out for Pier 51. He made sure not to run a Google Map search to find it so there wouldn't be a record of this trip later.

It was late. No one was on the streets at this time of night, even on a Friday. He made it down to Jack London Square and then the opposite way from the condo down toward the Piers.

I'll just ride close to the Pier and see what's going on. This had become a mission when he heard Lamb say Juno's name. There was going to be a resolution tonight.

When he was a long block from Pier 51, he rode off the road. This part of the waterfront included some empty lots, working warehouses, and some shops that supported trade in the port. The road had a chain link fence along most of it with some access to the empty lots.

The bay weather was misty, but not yet a true fog. He turned off his bike lights and rolled through an empty lot onto an alley that ran behind some warehouses. He found a dark corner behind some dumpsters and pulled his spare clothes out of his backpack. Black jeans, with black bicycle boots and a black wool sweater pulled over his black T-shirt. He stuck his SWAT knife into his pocket and pulled on his black running gloves and beanie. There was already a nylon cord in his back pocket, loops tied at each end. It could be a garrote, in an emergency.

Elijah hung his bike on one of the building's metal docking bars and locked it up. It was back off the road and up from the ground and should be pretty secure. This folding bike had some real advantages. Tucked into the darkness, he listened, waiting. Minutes passed.

No sound. No motion.

I'm in a good spot. His heart was pumping with an eagerness, pushing Elijah into battle mode. He loved the dark and could move effortlessly through the night. He was at home in this environment, alone and predatory.

He slid close along the walls of the alley leading to the pier, and when there were gaps between buildings, he took care not to move anywhere a camera could potentially see him. There weren't any cameras, at least none that he could see, but he refused to look up to examine the rooftops closely. He didn't want to leave a face picture.

Elijah moved with the grace of a panther. He had seen a panther once, on a hot night in his jungle training phase long ago. It had stopped and looked at him, and he had just stood there, staring back. If was as if the panther and he shared a moment, recognizing one another as each went off to search for prey. Not brothers, but both creatures of the night.

When he got to the end of Pier 51, he stopped under a shed close to the gate. Nothing moved, only the sounds of creaking boards and lapping water filling the silent night.

The gate was never closed here. There were no vehicles parked on the pier, or even near it. If Mr. Forester was waiting for him, then he had already arrived and was well entrenched. And if there was a gang waiting for him . . .

Elijah moved quietly up the side of the pier, scouting for a good place to station himself in case there was an ambush. By the time he passed the midpoint of the pier, he had found three good places to hide. If an attack came, then he would be ready to deal with them on his way out—if he came out.

A big, old warehouse sat at the end of the pier, smiling darkly at him.

If I were going to kill someone, where would I wait? If he was inside, he'd have to have an easy access point for the victim to get in. Not too easy, but an opening nevertheless. If he was waiting outside, he would have to be in a position to move in after the victim passed through the doors.

Elijah kept his head on a swivel and sped to the side of the pier. There was nothing down the side of the warehouse, no walkway or railing to hang from the smooth wall. He dropped smoothly to his knees and peered down over the side of the pier. No space to hide between the pier and dark waters, either.

It was eerily quiet. Where were they?

Enemies could be hanging on to the other side of the warehouse, but he didn't want to expose himself by crossing in front of the building to get there.

He saw it. There, on the opposite front corner of the warehouse, a sliding door was opened about four feet. It was a thick metal door that stood about ten or so feet high and about twenty feet wide. It was on rollers top and bottom, easy to move without much effort.

That would be the victim's entry point. The attacking force would be deployed around the inside of the door, probably up above the floor, too.

Elijah surveyed the area around the front of the warehouse and didn't detect anything that could really hide a person. He used his peripherals to scan the darkness, looking for any shape or motion that wasn't a building, shed, or dumpster. Nothing.

Something light bopped him on the head. He flung himself on the ground, braced for another strike. But none came.

He knew they could be there, lying in wait, suspended inside, but unless they were going to start shooting he was in a good position. He was an executioner. If they had to move toward him to kill him, he would win. No doubt about it.

If Mr. Forester was planning on killing Juno, then he had to die. If this was a plan to eliminate Elijah, then it sure as hell had better be a good plan.

If anything Lamb had said about Forester was true, then it had been a long time since Forester had made the decision to embrace darkness. A disturbing thought occurred to Elijah. He was crouching in the darkness, at the end of a dark pier, about to enter a dark warehouse. Elijah had snuffed out the light for many men before this. He was the darkness.

This was the darkness that Lamb and Forester shared with him. Lamb's words came back to him. *You'll be doing what comes naturally to you, Elijah.*

Elijah wasn't here to check it out. *No, I'm here to kill.*

He blinked. As he was scanning the front of the warehouse, he saw a hole in the darkness—not in the wall of the building, but in the night's darkness itself. In that hole, he could have sworn he saw Mr. Lamb smiling at him, beckoning him forward. But then he had blinked, and the image was gone.

Elijah shook himself. *Get it together, man. You're seeing stuff.*

He considered sliding back down the pier and leaving. But Orville Forester was somewhere inside, waiting to hire him to kill Juno. If he didn't go in and hear that request, then Forester would find someone else. Elijah would have to move in with Juno and follow him everywhere 'til the attack came, and Gabija and the kids, too. He knew that Juno would jump into a fire to save his family, which made him vulnerable.

No, this had to be dealt with now. Tonight.

Elijah approached the sliding door, thankfully already positioned nearest the slider. Arms outstretched, he leapt up the slider, grabbing the top with his fingers. His body was already pressed close against the wall; his impact made no sound. With a great amount of control, he pulled his legs up under him so that he was in a crouch, hands clamped over the sliding door. If he had to drop off the door, he would be ready to fight.

He moved hand over hand down the long door toward the four-foot opening, careful not to shake the door or kick it with his soft shoes. From this approach, he'd be able to assess whoever was on the other side of the opening before they noticed him. He had used this surprise tactic to his advantage before. It'd afford him a couple seconds' advantage, which could make or break a battle.

He reached the end of the door and leaned over to see inside. The top of a man's head stuck out from behind some crates, about ten feet from the door. He wasn't crouched, or poised for attack. He was just sitting quietly, waiting.

There weren't any more forms hidden in the darkness, so far as Elijah could determine. Elijah sighed inwardly. *At some point, you've just gotta jump in if you're gonna act.*

Elijah grabbed the doorframe with his left hand and swung himself into the warehouse. He let his weight bring him all the way around the door's opening, so that by the time he dropped to the floor he was crouched against the inside of the door, hidden by shadows. The motion made very little noise, and was quick enough that the man behind the crates would assume it was only a rat, scurrying among the surplus.

Elijah squatted where he landed, waiting for motion, a gunshot, or whatever else he would have to face. He was on hyper alert, every rustle in the night registering within him. The man behind the crate stood. Elijah could just barely make out the man's silhouette in the darkness. He was looking intently at the door, but it was clear he didn't see Elijah squatting just to his left.

In the dark, Elijah couldn't tell if this was the man in the photographs. He was about six feet tall, probably around two hundred pounds. The man slipped to the end of the crates where he could have a better view. Elijah moved with him, keeping the crates between them.

The man stopped. "Hello? Is that Elijah?"

Elijah settled at the end of a row of crates. He kept his voice soft. "Forester?"

The man jumped. "Shit, come out where I can see you. I've been waiting for over an hour. I was about to give up."

"Stay where you are and talk to me."

Forester turned his head in the darkness, his silhouette now revealed in the faint light from the pier spilling through the door. "I want to see who I'm talking to. Are you a cop?"

Elijah didn't budge. "Talk."

Forester gave a soft chuckle. "I have a job for you, Elijah, if you are this much of a phantom. I've tried looking you up, but no one knows who you are. My contact said that you were perfect because of that—looks like he was right."

"Tell me about the job."

Forester continued to turn his head, searching for the source of Elijah's voice. "I have friends who help me with a large sector of my business. They're angry with a man who killed one of their own and want to see him pay, life for life. A man always helps his friends. If you were able to arrive here tonight without my detection, then consider yourself hired."

Elijah felt a stab of guilt in his heart. Forester was somehow in league with the bikers, and they were going to punish Juno for Elijah's mistakes. This shit had to stop, and here was as good a place as any to begin.

Forester continued. "I have a bag here with ten thousand dollars cash and a file of information on the person you would need to kill. With the endorsement of my contact for these matters, I don't care if we see each other or dance or if I just walk away and leave this bag here. I expect to hear in the next few days about the untimely death of a certain Juno Valdas. How does this sound to you, Elijah? Are you going to help me and my friends?"

Elijah moved deeper into the warehouse, among the high rows of crates. He found himself in front of a large machine that clearly had not been run in a long time. The machine was a good fifteen feet high and had panels along the front where you could access a series of levers and lights. His eyes traced the length of the machine until the end, where he realized he was looking at the toe of a boot.

So there's at least one other guy here as a backup. Elijah realized that this could still be a setup. This guy could be a cop, with his partner here hiding in the back.

Elijah raised his voice. "Are we alone here?"

Elijah slipped closer to the boot. As he approached he saw the dark shape of what could only be the barrel of a gun, about waist high.

Forester's voice was cross, either from annoyance or fear. "Move where I can see you! Of course we're alone. This isn't the kind of thing you do in a crowd. If you're not on board with the deal, I have a lot of alternatives."

Elijah shot his right hand toward the barrel of the gun. He grabbed the wrist attached to the gun with his right hand and in one smooth motion yanked the hidden man out of his hiding place. As the man lurched from beside the machine, Elijah smashed the man's knee inward with his foot, pushing on the joint until he heard the sound of breaking bone. With a low moan of pain, the gunman fired his weapon up into the rafters of the warehouse.

Elijah released the wrist and smashed his palm into the man's soft nasal tissue. The nose broke, sinking into the skull as a substantial gush of blood rose to submerge the broken tissue. In the darkness, the blood was an oily shine against the man's glistening sweat.

Elijah stepped on the broken knee as the man fell and grabbed the man's head with both hands. As the weight of the man pulled him to the floor, Elijah calculatedly drove his skull into a low brace edge next to him. The combined strength made a strong enough impact at the joint between the occipital and parietal bones, allowing the edge of the brace structure to puncture straight through to the brain.

It would only take five to seven minutes for the man to be officially dead. It had taken Elijah less than a minute to kill him.

Elijah quickly stepped back to the end of the crates, preventing Forester from having a clear shot of him, if he was so disposed.

Forester shouted. "What the fuck is going on?"

Elijah's voice was calm, even. "I just saved us from an attack by some stranger. You said we were alone, yet there was a man standing here in the shadows with a gun."

There was a loud clatter as a bag dropped, followed by the quickly receding steps of Orville Forester. Elijah stepped around the end of the crate to see Forester hauling ass to the pier exit. As Forester was running he turned to look back over his shoulder, but his foot kicked something in the dark and he tripped.

Elijah closed the distance between them in a matter of heartbeats, planting a solid knee in the middle of Forester's back, just behind his lungs. Forester was wiggling with the strength of a death struggle, trying to get an arm under him to push himself up. But Elijah was stronger. The soldier slid his right arm around Forester's neck and squeezed, using his left arm to pull his right one tighter while pulling hard backwards into the planted knee.

Forester struggled against Elijah's grip, but he was pinned to the ground. The quiet struggle took longer than the one with the gunman, but this was a slower way to go. Eventually, Forester's muscles relaxed, and Elijah knew the job was done.

Any conspiracies against Juno were now ended, at least where Forester was involved. Elijah wasn't sure what the bikers would do now without him.

Shit, I didn't even need my nylon cord.

A faint whiff of anise wafted past Elijah. There was a soft noise to his right. He scrambled to his feet, lowering himself into a balanced crouch with arms at chest level, ready to strike.

Mr. Lamb finished brushing his shoe and straightened, adjusting his cuff. "I think he tripped over my foot." He gave Elijah a pleasant, chilling smile.

A cold shiver ran down Elijah's spine, and the emptiness in the warehouse thundered in his ears. He had thought he'd seen Lamb earlier, but that was impossible . . . wasn't it?

Elijah pulled himself together. This was still business. "Are we alone now?"

"It seems so. I have to say, I truly enjoyed this whole evening. Your approach was a thing of beauty." Lamb gestured to the door. "I rarely see *that*. Have you done this before?"

Elijah balled his fists. "Fuck you, Lamb. Killing your friends— what do you want me to do now?"

Lamb shrugged, as casually as if Elijah had asked him where he wanted to go for dinner. "You can do whatever you want with the information you received tonight. Look at your hands, Elijah."

He glanced down, confused. His runner's gloves were frayed slightly at the palms, a bit of blood staining the right one.

"You're wearing gloves." Lamb smirked. "Are you cold? You came to kill tonight. That was premeditated murder. We're going to have a long, productive relationship, soldier. Do you want your payment now? You can keep the money from his bag, as well."

Remorse crashed over Elijah. He had just killed for blood money. This wasn't the new him—or was he even capable of becoming his envisioned self? *I'm a fool.*

Aloud, he growled, "Get the fuck out of my life and leave me alone. Find someone else to devour."

"Oh, I'm not the one who will devour you, but the one I serve *is* feasting these days." Lamb laughed, as if at some inside joke. "Your money is ready for you whenever you want it. I'll roll this ten grand into the other payment. Don't worry, there will be no evidence here to find, I can promise you that. I suspect that once the police realize who this is, they'll rejoice, not investigate. Until next time, Elijah."

Lamb was gone. He'd just folded into the darkness, out of sight. The anise faded away, replaced by the smells of death.

Elijah stood still for a few seconds, listening. He was sure this was a trap. His life was on the line now. He was calm and ready for slaughter, but he might be facing a crowd of what? Police? Other thugs? He walked quietly through the warehouse and found a window in the back that slid open, facing the bay. He checked that his gear was secure, then put his feet out of the window and slid down the side of the warehouse until he was hanging from his fingers. He took a deep breath and let go, pushing away from the wall and falling as noiselessly as he could into the bay.

He treaded water for a minute, scanning the shoreline and surrounding piers before swimming at an angle toward the end of the next pier. He swam under Pier 50 and worked his way in until he could put his feet down.

He made his way as stealthily as he could back to the alley with his bike, careful to avoid any cameras or curious eyes. He was cold, but he'd be OK. He put his jacket on inside out to hide the reflective surface and to get warm. After five minutes had passed without any sign of emergency vehicles or other alarms, he pulled the bike down and pedaled off toward the fancy condo. It was only about a mile.

Elijah had committed murder tonight. That's what it was. Murder. But it was necessary for him to be able to protect his friend. The police were constrained by laws and evidence. They could investigate, but had to have cause to pull someone in. Forester was going to have Juno killed, period. Well, not anymore. Elijah tried to absorb his actions and feel upset about it, but instead he was relieved.

The ride through the darkness was comforting and made him feel right at home.

22

THE TREND

The Oakland City Police facility on Edgewater near Hassler was a big, corporate-looking structure from the 1980s. It had been updated along the way, but its imposing visage remained the same. It was a heavy, solid fortress. The homicide unit was on the ground floor with a beautiful view of the parking lot. The pavement was nothing spectacular, but across the big lot Shana could see the harbor stretching out. Oakland was a working port, as unlike its cross-bay neighbor as it could be. This was the most violent city in California for its size, with over fifteen hundred violent crimes a year—five thousand if you included crimes against property. It was very busy for the police.

Shana was waiting for Sergeant Marks. It felt like she was always waiting for him. This murder case could be a big break in her career, and you couldn't work with much better than Marks, but the man was always late.

Marks rolled in fifteen past eight, his coat tossed over a shoulder and a cup of cheap coffee in hand. "Look at this," he said, gesturing to the coffee. "I had to buy this shit. With money. If I wanted coffee this bad, I could've drank some of yours." He smiled.

Shana rolled her eyes. She made the best pot of joe in the department, and he knew it. "We're late. Culver wanted us in his office ten minutes ago."

Marks pulled off his sunglasses. "What? Why didn't you say anything?"

"I texted you."

"Oh crap." Marks threw his coat on her desk, straightened his tie and spilled some coffee on his shirt in the process. "Come on."

Lieutenant Culver was not happy about their late arrival. He waved them to their seats with a solemn gesture of the hand.

Man, does that guy ever smile? Shana got being a seasoned officer and all, but the man could use a smile from time to time.

Culver pulled up a chart on a second large monitor in his office. Shana scooted closer to better read the tiny font.

"This is the data from your cases," he said, leaning back in his chair. "And this," he clicked the slide, "is the list of violent crimes in the city from the last twelve months. A hundred and twenty-seven homicides, three hundred and twenty-six forcible rapes, forty-nine hundred robberies, and fifty-six aggravated assaults. All this in a city of just under half a million."

Shana frowned. "Excuse me, sir, but what does this have to do with our case?"

Marks smiled. "Ah, rookies."

Shana scowled at him. She was pretty sure he had no idea, either.

The lieutenant cleared his throat. "Of all the homicides in the past year, four have happened in the past week, in a small area."

Marks sat up. "Four?"

"Two bodies were found down on Pier 51 this weekend. They were discovered by a group of teens looking for a place to skateboard. Do you know what makes these four murders unique?"

Shana frowned, thinking. She and Marks were assigned to the

other murder, the mysterious one from the dumpsters. A man murdered in what looked like a mugging, but with nothing stolen. The strangest thing had been the way the man was killed. "They were all killed without weapons?"

Culver nodded. "If we can solve these murders before they go cold, we could catch a break."

"But one of the murders is already solved," Marks said. He took a sip of his coffee, then dropped the cup in the trash. "A vet killed that biker in self-defense of a woman."

There was a pause as Culver allowed Marks to figure it out. Marks's eyes widened. "You think he's connected to the other three?"

"Possibly." Culver smiled. It was dry, but it did reach his eyes. Shana would count that as genuine. "I want you two to bring me that answer."

Marks crossed his arms. "All of these cases involve very precise and violent deaths. They could revolve around the biker gang or drug world."

Shana nodded, taking notes in her notebook. "What do we know about the men on the pier?"

Culver pulled out some files from his desk drawer and tossed them in front of Shana and Marks. "The last ones were a guy named Orville Forester and his bodyguard, Mateo Arias. The bodyguard had a crushed skull and Mr. Forester died of asphyxiation. No weapons used, so far as we can tell. Our informants are pretty sure they're in the drug business to some capacity, as was Garlitz. What we don't know is if the trucker was part of that world or not. Take these files and go study them. I want to know if there's a connection, and fast. We can then look for someone who might have a reason for trying to disrupt the drug business in this part of town."

Marks nodded. "You mean like someone who got into a fatal fight with a drug pusher?"

Shana looked up from her notes. "You said the biker case was a stalker killed by a veteran. All these deaths were of the type that a combat veteran could have done. Is there any reason to think that the veteran was involved in the other three?"

Culver shrugged. "Possibly. Was the Roxanna Sanchez case a stalker or a drug deal?"

Marks rubbed his jaw, thinking. "They were all killed quickly, violently, and efficiently. Almost like someone's working down a list."

Shana stared at him, an idea coming to mind. "Do you think there's an executioner in town?"

23

THE SESSION

Monday mornings were Selma's favorite. Most people dreaded coming to work after a weekend, but not Selma. She missed her patients, her office, her sense of purpose. She always took the opportunity to tidy up her office at the start of the week. She dusted the bookshelves, straightened the throw pillows. Custodial came in the evenings to clean, but there was something relaxing about the ritual of tidiness for Selma. Tidy office, tidy mind.

She only had one appointment scheduled for the morning: Juno's referral, Elijah. He was such a different man compared to his friend. Juno was a wonderful patient. He was very open during their sessions, sharing his experiences from the war and working diligently with her to understand what had happened since.

Selma loved working with veterans. She would do anything to help them better understand themselves as fully human, not just survivors. But many veterans saw themselves as guilty survivors or, worse, invisible survivors. It was her job to help them be able to share their experiences without shame and to regain contact with their full human range of emotions. She always hoped they could eventually experience "the great sadness," as she liked to call it, and finally go on with their lives.

Juno clearly saw the judgmental attitudes of the nonmilitary population. He was acutely aware of how they viewed the military, both active and retired, as the underclass in society. He talked in their sessions about how he felt he and his comrades were viewed as low-income leftovers, incapable of finding a job outside the military—an underclass. She couldn't verbally confirm this, of course, but she agreed.

Selma took the small figurine of the child and pond from her desk and ran a dust rag along its smooth surface. She loved this figurine. It reminded her of her grandmother's farm in Connecticut.

Selma always loved talking to Juno, with his humorous stories about some insensitivity he had to suffer at the hands of the people for whom he had risked his life over and over. They would have some insult for him because he was black, or because he spoke with an eastern European accent, or for some other stupid justification. He was optimistic; broken, but healing well; rejected by society, but respected as an upright citizen.

It was surprising, then, when Selma had met Elijah and discovered just how different the two friends were. He was harder than Juno, physically and emotionally. Apparently, from what Juno had told her when he initially asked if he could refer Elijah to her, this young man was a much deadlier soldier. She was determined to find out what was burning inside him. She didn't want to put out the fire—no therapist could truly do that in a person—but she did want him to be able to use the heat for creative action to build a life, to help him rediscover what it meant to be fully human.

Selma positioned the digital recorder on the table and smiled at it. It was half an inch thick and just a little bigger than a credit card. It could record for up to eight hours, had a USB connection to upload to her computer in a minute, and was sound activated.

She sighed. It was hard, sometimes, to guide people in holistic mental health without sharing her personal beliefs.

Part of being fully human was to recognize and accept that you're a sinner, imperfect, a being that made mistakes and bad judgments at times. At the same time, everyone can rise to the emotional heights of love and creativity. We can all give real love and receive it. We don't have to earn it, or be worthy of it. We are, by definition as human beings, worthy of and needy for love and acceptance. She so badly wanted her clients to see this as they continued to struggle finding themselves. She didn't see this understanding coming from organized churches anymore, but from a direct relationship with the God who made us. She realized that religion has become only the crusty, ashy shell that was left of the spiritual, transcendent love of the God who created us all.

But she had to be careful not to use that kind of language with her clients. That religious-sounding talk would just be inflammatory in this coldhearted society. It did, however, give her the strength to keep working.

There was a soft tone on the intercom. "Miss Selma, your ten thirty is here."

Selma leaned toward the inconspicuous speaker and said, "Thank you, Jeanie. I'll be right out."

Elijah settled into her Italian leather sofa with the tense posture Selma had come to expect. Back erect, eyes focused. It was an odd contrast, his meticulous attitude dressed in his laid-back jeans and T-shirt.

She settled into her chair and gave him a smile. "Nice to see you, Elijah. I have the results of the survey we took last time. It's a surprise."

Elijah returned her smile, a bit of his discomfort melting. "Really? What is it?"

"You are suffering from PTSD."

Elijah laughed, but kept his eyes locked on his clasped hands. "That's hardly a surprise, right?"

Yes, he's definitely getting more comfortable. Selma smiled. "OK, maybe not so much of a surprise. Post-traumatic stress disorder is just a long term for a form of anxiety caused by viewing, being involved in, causing, or failing to prevent something that caused serious injury or death. There are a lot of symptoms, ranging from distrust to disturbing flashbacks to suicidal or homicidal thoughts. I hope we can talk about them as we proceed."

Elijah looked up. When he spoke, it was hesitant. "It might take me a little bit to be able to talk about those things, but they're out there."

Selma nodded. "It's perfectly natural for this to take time. While veterans are the most likely to suffer from PTSD, it's not limited to military activity. But the things that happen in war are crazy. Insane. Any person who engages either goes crazy or finds another strategy to deal with what they see and do."

Elijah swallowed. "Yeah, I've had a few buddies go off the deep end."

Selma paused, giving the solider an opportunity to elaborate, but when he stayed silent, she continued. "It's common for vets to feel a deep sense of shame, but we're going to work on not letting that keep you from engaging with the people around you."

Elijah shifted in his chair. He was grim this morning. *Maybe I touched a nerve.* She made a mental note to highlight this when she typed up their session later.

"The kind of job I had in the military involved going into losing situations and turning those around with extreme violence. It wasn't something I would've done before the war."

Selma leaned forward. "How did you deal with that?"

He shrugged. "I found it more and more natural. I went from being afraid all the time to being really aggressive to be sure I survived. I became predatory."

Selma nodded slowly. "Is that you, Elijah?"

"It was me." He trailed into thought. Selma waited patiently for him to continue. "I guess it's me, but . . . there's more to me than that, I hope."

Selma stood and walked to the bookshelves. She pulled a small blue booklet from the bottom shelf and placed it on the coffee table. "Have you heard of Alexithymia before, Elijah?"

He shook his head. "No."

Selma settled back in her chair. "It's a mental phenomenon that protects soldiers from going insane during emotionally traumatic events. There are over two hundred human emotions. Alexithymia is a mechanism that cuts off your access to them so you can function when the situation is too bad to be rational. A person with this condition only feels five percent of the emotions most others feel. It's very common in veterans. It makes them feel disconnected from those around them. They can only experience a limited number of emotions and are often numb to bad things."

"I've been told I'm cold or disconnected by others. Or, if they don't say anything, I can see that they're uncomfortable with me around. I know that I don't react like other people do. So, this is the sit-in-the-back-and-hide strategy in any social situation."

Selma nodded. "And that makes you uncomfortable in return, doesn't it? Do you have a tendency to not mix with civilians so they won't notice your behavior?"

Elijah grunted an affirmative. "I go out in public with the intention of taking part, but I just don't engage with strangers and they seem to be hesitant to talk to me. So, guess I'm screwed forever."

"No! Of course not. The process recommended to deal with this condition is to recognize it and then start to work through the feelings—including the shame—so you can *express* yourself and put these things behind you. You need to be able to feel the great sadness of all you have suffered in order to feel fully human." She coughed. *Careful, Selma.* "Our end goal is to help you feel that, then get to the other side."

Elijah's voice was quiet. "I'd like that. When you said that . . . I can sense a great sadness, but I just can't express it. I'm not able to cry about what happened."

Selma smiled. "Alright then. What did you do in the service, Elijah?"

"I was in the Seventy-Fifth Ranger Regiment."

"I imagine you were asked to do some pretty tough things as a Ranger. What kind of pressure were you under not to fail?"

Elijah met her gaze with a cold steel that surprised her. "Failure would mean death. For me, Juno, and the rest of our team. When we were called in, it was usually a rapidly changing situation that had gone bad. As long as we were alive, it was considered to be an ongoing situation. If one of us was killed, it would compromise the chances of stopping a threat but it wouldn't have been a failure to the mission."

"Elijah," Selma said, "look at me and tell me if you are still fighting the war."

He swallowed. His eyes flickered between hers and his hands. Finally, speaking to his hands, he whispered, "Yes."

Selma gave him a small smile. That was a huge step for him, admitting that. "What I want us to do each week is use this space as a safe place to let you express what you're really feeling, not what you think you should be feeling. It might feel strange for you at first, but I think you may find yourself going deeper over time. You can always revise or rephrase anything you tell me when it starts to change for you."

Elijah looked up at her and gave a wan smile. It was obvious that something was bothering him. But if he didn't want to talk about it yet, that was fine. They'd go at his pace.

"I like you," he said, "but I'm not sure how to do that."

Selma settled back into her chair. "Let's start by talking about your habits and lifestyle. What type of place do you live in, and how you shop and eat? What you do with your time? How do you earn money? Little things like that. As we work through the normal issues of life, we might find ourselves talking about the attitudes that shape those habits and maybe that'll lead us to the underlying issues that are really bothering you. How does that sound?"

Elijah visibly relaxed his shoulders. "It sounds like something I can do. Were you ever in the service?"

She shook her head. "No, but I've worked with several military returnees and I think I've started to understand what your lives are like. Bear with me when I try to speak from your point of view, and help me correct any misperceptions along the way. We'll both discover something useful. If you're ready, then let's get started."

Elijah left her office at the end of the session. Selma turned off the recorder and settled in her comfortable chair, a fresh cup of herbal tea at her side. Elijah had seemed so troubled at the beginning of their session. She knew from her research that all veterans have homicidal thoughts, suicidal thoughts, and they all have problems with alcohol or drugs—and she'd wait to get to those things until she had Elijah's trust—but by the end of the session, it seemed like he was just lost, looking for someone to pull him out of himself. Whatever he was wrestling with, she was happy to see that he was still engaged.

24

OMELET FOR ONE

Elijah felt so much better when he emerged from his session with Selma. Explaining that he lived in a secret house, worked irregularly, and only really talked to Juno and his family made him realize how isolated he was.

He rode over to Eggs Cetera for an early afternoon omelet. He had spent the weekend sleeping and relaxing at Phillip's condo, but he still felt exhausted. The events from Friday consumed his mind. For the first time, he couldn't just shake it off. He had done what he had needed to do, but Lamb was right. He had gone there intending to kill Forester, not just scope it out.

I'm such an idiot. I don't even fucking know how this is going to play out now.

The cops would be investigating the murders even now, and Elijah had gotten himself entangled with some kind of crime lord.

Or the devil, as Juno thinks. Well, if Lamb's a demon, then I've crossed some kind of line and may not be able to get back. But there are no demons, right?

Since he really didn't know how to summon a demon, then he

really didn't know how to get them to leave. That would take some kind of help he didn't even know about.

His dark thoughts dried out his mouth and Elijah had trouble swallowing. His crimes were no laughing matter. He shouldn't be proud for how well he was able to do bad things. Lamb said that he should focus on being bad, that it was his natural skill. No arguments there. Lamb offered him freedom and money and power. It would be outside the law, but Elijah had certainly not been constrained by those laws over the last two years.

He had gotten so far from what he really wanted. In his heart, Elijah just wanted to love someone, be loved back, and have a sense of family in his life. Like Juno.

Elijah sipped his coffee. *What if I can't stop? Selma was right, I'm stuck in the war. But who's the enemy?*

It had been two years since he had come home, but it didn't feel that long because he was still just living the life of a soldier.

He wasn't acting rationally. He was killing people, and there were alternatives to that. He should've gone to the police right after meeting Lamb. He should've told them that he had been solicited for murder and maybe they would've used him as bait to get Forester off the streets. That would have been better.

Did he see the police as the enemy? Or did he see himself as a criminal?

When Elijah had killed the man beating up Phillip, they should've waited for the police to show up and explained what happened. But he didn't. He could've pointed Roxanna to the police for her stalker problem instead of dealing with it himself. What complicated everything was the fact that he had been living underground for so long. It'd be hard to prove who he was and what he had been doing. Well, he did work with the longshoremen. People down there knew him and could vouch for that. But he wasn't paying taxes on his other income.

What a fucking mess.

The murder of Forester and his man was the tipping point. There was no way to justify or explain those. He could've been there with the police, but now it was too late. He'd murdered troublemakers acting without any moral compass, but then, what moral compass could he claim?

25

THE CLUBHOUSE

In the southern end of the port sat a large hall that had been built for the Oakland City Seed Company in the 1950s. The Spartan building had been used as a meeting hall for the local farmers and agribusiness groups. It was a two-story red brick building with arched windows and some offices and good storage rooms in the back. It had a stage in the meeting room under which was stored racks with folding tables and chairs. The men liked to roll them out and get together to talk and drink. The Sons were a family. Their social life, business life, and personal activities all took place in the context of the club.

When the gang had bought the building, the then-leader had joked that they were bad seeds, befitting the Seed Company's old hall. As new owners, they'd installed electronic gates and surveillance cameras along the fences of the property.

Warlord Magnus Carlson sat at his desk with his feet up by the window, enjoying a midday sandwich. He was middle-aged, thickening around the waist while his hair thinned. He could have been a banker, or an accountant, as his eyes were shrewd, cruel. There was more to the man than his physique let on.

The club had leather vests and jackets, most wore Wolverine boots and the toughest jeans they could find. Black T-shirts were standard. The star of Moloch was the symbol for their gang: two triangles drawn as intricate lines interlaced into a six-pointed star. It was on the back of the vests and jackets, as well as on their helmets, jewelry, and tattoos. The crest on the chest of their colors was the figure of Moloch, a man with the head of a bull. They called to Moloch when they went out to ride, and most believed he was waiting for them in Perdition, their home of everlasting suffering and punishment.

There was a knock and Aryan appeared in the doorframe. "Hey boss. That warehouse fire only got about half of the building. Not much damage to the goods, and they're already fixin' up the place! No one hurt—it's like we did no fucking damage at all."

There was a sliver of fat in Carlson's roast beef sandwich. He chewed it for a moment before spitting it out. "Yeah, Penny is spent and now Forester's dead. Whoever he was hiring for the hit must not've liked him."

"What do we do now? Raid the warehouse?" Aryan leaned against the frame.

Carlson pulled out a black, ceramic-coated folding knife and handed it to Aryan.

Aryan tried not to take it. "I can't take that Magnus. I never went to SERE like you did."

"It's not mine, it just looks like it. Keep it clipped inside your pants in the back. You can fight your way out of anything with this. I showed you how I use it. This Valdas, and I mean ass, seems lucky. We lose Forester and now a fucking family man is breaking our balls? I don't give a fuck about the warehouse. That Valdas shitball is still walking around, acting like he can get away with killing one of our guys. Penny, no less!"

Aryan nodded and crossed his arms. "That's what we get for trusting Forester to hire someone to do a job we can do ourselves."

Carlson glared at him. "That was your call. If the job got

fucked, you're the one that done it. Find us a new vendor, alright? Keep that cash flowing."

"How's that new business going? I keep hearing about it. When you gonna tell us what it is?"

"Soon." Carlson left it at that. "How many riders we got here at home?"

"Thirty-nine men out of jail and in town. If you need more we can get them with a phone call. Everyone wants revenge. Penny was well respected, a good leader."

"Good." Carlson stood and started to walk Aryan out of his office. "We'll get it soon. Come back this afternoon and I'll give you some stuff. We're gonna hit this bastard again, just be ready to ride."

Aryan put the knife in the back of his waist. He smiled. "Yes sir."

Carlson locked the door as his drug lord left. He turned back to his desk and found Mr. Lamb sitting on his couch, smiling. "Hello, Magnus."

26

THE TALK

This was a day for the books, a day that would go down in history forever. He, Elijah McCoy, had convinced Juno to go to a gym.

"I don't think I've been here since Matas was three," Juno joked as they walked out of the locker room.

Elijah grinned. "I can't believe I got you to come."

"Well, you know me." Juno sat on the matted floor and started to stretch. "Why go to brunch when you could go sweat?"

They laughed.

"Is Gabija still upset I didn't ask out Roxanna?" Elijah slid onto a bench. Juno grabbed his ankles as he started to do sit-ups.

"A little, but she'll recover. I've got to admit, I don't understand it either. Roxanna's gorgeous, smart, funny, and seems really into you. What's your hold up?"

"You sound like her manager."

"You know what I mean. Seriously, man. What's up?"

Elijah finished his rep and sat up to hold Juno's ankles. "I'm just not dating yet. Roxanna's pretty damn perfect, but like I said, it just didn't click for us. We each have our own kind of crazy, and I sure as hell don't need to add to that."

"Everyone's got a form of crazy. I'm not the man Gabija married eleven years ago. But she's been with me the whole time, motivating me. She makes me want to get better for her and the kids. I know she gets frustrated with me, but it calls to me. You just got to find someone willing to drink your particular flavor of crazy. Get back out there, man."

They moved over to the heavy weight area to start some squats and dead lifts. Elijah began stacking weights on his bar. "No one would like me if they got to know me. It's not worth it."

Juno groaned under the weight of his bar. "This is too much. Help a brother out."

Elijah set his own bar down and hurried over to Juno. He took the bar from Juno's trembling arms and put it back on the rack.

"Thanks," Juno huffed. His dark skin glistened with sweat. "I think you're wrong, you know. I think there's someone out there who would like you, dirt and all. Even if it's for only one tousled night." He winked.

Elijah returned to his own bar and started some squats. Juno moved behind him to spot. "I just see women with their complex politics and their personal agendas and I don't think it's worth all the drama. It is always about power or money. You lucked out with Gabija."

"I did. Don't get me wrong, there's still politics, but it's easier when you're married. At least for us."

Elijah and Juno switched, this time Elijah spotting Juno's swats. They worked in silence for a while. It was good to be back in a gym with Juno, working physically as a team. It reminded Elijah of their days in the Regiment—but in the AC this time, not the desert.

"Hey Elijah?" Juno asked, setting the bar down when he had finished. "Are you attracted to anyone besides women?"

Elijah was taken aback. He laughed, but Juno's face was serious. "You fuck. You saying I want to date guys?"

"I think only you know what you want. But I've known you a long time, man. You've always had reservations and excuses for not dating women. I'm just saying, if that's something you want to try, I support you."

Dating men . . . the thought had never crossed Elijah's mind before. Rick had asked him that a few nights ago, sure, but Rick was gay. It was almost his job to ask that question. But if Juno was suggesting it . . . There must have been something good about it, for all the fuss being made over gay marriage.

"Thanks, Juno."

Juno bumped him on the shoulder. "Any time. Who knows, maybe a boyfriend will loosen you up."

Elijah frowned. "You saying I look intimidating?"

Juno started to set them up for the dead lift next. He picked up some canvas wrist straps for each of them. "Let's just say that if you were getting some, you might look a little more approachable."

Elijah laughed. "I look a little wound up, huh?"

"I've only been to this gym once, and I can already see the guys in here look at you and hope they don't get caught doing it. You need to relax. This is the gym, come on." Juno grinned. "Have some fun."

Elijah grunted, grabbing weights of his own. He brought another pair of forty-fives over to add to the bar.

"Phillip invited me to a club with his friends this Friday night," Elijah said. He had almost forgotten about it. Clubs weren't really his thing. He had planned on telling Phillip he couldn't make it.

"A gay club?"

Elijah nodded.

"Do you want to go?" Juno raised an eyebrow.

He shrugged. "I can't see me on a dance floor, can you?"

Juno stepped in front of the bar and wrapped his canvas strap around the bar, pressing the strap between his palm and the bar to lock his grip. He was panting slightly. "Go with them. If you're not having fun, then go home. But if it feels right, then see what happens. At least you get to have some fun with people, and that could loosen you up a little. Bet I'll be able to tell if you hit it."

They laughed.

"Is that how you met Gabija?" Elijah asked. "It just felt right?"

Juno smiled. "In the condensed story, yeah. I fell in love with her good heart and didn't judge how she lived or tried to control her. Now we sleep together every night. We each have our best friend to see last thing and first thing each day. It frames our days in a loving way. God's rewarded me with this good relationship. This framework gives me some hope that I might actually get over all the shit we did in the war."

Elijah looked at Juno. "It seems like a hundred years ago that I was pre-service and just a nerdy guy in school. I'm amazed at what we did in the war. It gets into you, or at least into me. Do you ever struggle with falling back into full battle mode, without remembering we're home and that there are other ways to handle trouble?"

Juno nodded. "Yeah, from time to time. People fuck with me and I think to myself, 'Do you know that I could kill you in the next twenty seconds?' I used to tell Gabija every time I thought about killing someone. All the details. Remember that time I knocked out those two guys, like a week after we got home?"

"I do." They'd all gone to a bar that night to celebrate their homecoming. A few drunken assholes had tried starting something while Elijah was in the bathroom, and when he came out the bartender was yelling for a fuming Juno to get out of his bar.

"That was when I started telling Gabija all my thoughts. She always wanted to know exactly what I'd do. Telling her relieved a lot of the stress. She'd remind me we could just walk away, call a police officer, sue if that's the sort of thing that was needed."

"Why don't you tell her anymore?"

"Honestly, I haven't needed to. My demons are quiet, brother."

Elijah thought about that. "And what about Gabija? You told

her you wanted to crush, break, slice up, and beat the shit out of people—wasn't she disgusted with you? Did she think you were a monster?"

"She should have, but we've been married a long time. She saw me go through training and we'd Skype whenever we could while I was deployed."

"I remember that."

"Yeah. She'd see me boiling when I told her some of the stuff going on around us. She really wanted me to survive and come back. She's always said that I had to do what I had to do, and that she was proud of me for being brave and tough enough to do it."

Elijah asked, "Are we animals, Juno? Are we monsters?"

Juno shook his head. "As soldiers, we're in touch with the animal that lives inside us all. But we have to remember we have another side. There's a gospel song that says, 'I'm not as good as I want to be, but I'm better than I was.' It's a daily decision for us now. Most Americans never see the compromises and disappointments of having to become an animal to survive, not the way the rest of the world does. I'm no different than people all over the second and third world. I just have to rise above this and live right."

Elijah nodded. Juno always knew what to say. His eloquence was one of the things Elijah appreciated most about his old friend. "Thanks, man."

He realized they'd just been standing there, talking in the middle of the gym. "Dead lifts and then on to back right?"

Juno let out a huff and wiped his brow. "Sure. After all this, we should be able to deadlift the Leaf."

They laughed and went back to work.

27

THE FILE

S hana sat quietly in the lieutenant's office, taking notes. Culver was holding a conference with Obed, a government man and a close friend of his, over the phone on speaker. Marks was out of the office for the day, following leads for another case.

Culver sat in his chair by the window, watching people mill around the parking lot down below. "So it looks like Valdas is our killer, huh?"

Obed's gruff voice crackled across the phone speaker. "I've looked at a lot of information on this guy and talked to a couple of my contacts in the department. If this Lithuanian immigrant is picking off criminals, he should get an award. Your city's lousy with crime, Chris." Culver grunted. "But if a jury finds him guilty of murder, well, no amount of good intention's gonna get him off."

"Marks and Thomas got a confession out of him for the stalker case last week," Culver said. "But he didn't divulge anything about the others. What I want to know is what he did in the service that would send him off the deep end like this."

"He was in the Seventy-Fifth Ranger Regiment, a group of

dangerous, violent special ops. It's headquartered in Fort Benning, Georgia."

Shana asked, "So they were like the badass regiment?"

Culver glared at her. She hadn't been invited to speak. She blushed.

Obed answered her anyway. "You could say that. They were stealthy and deadly, unidentifiable in most cases. You'll never have one of these guys write a book about what a hero he was."

Culver leaned back in his swivel chair, raising his voice as he asked, "You get a chance to look at my murder victim list yet?"

There was a sound of rustling on the other end of the line. "I did. The violence of the attacks would be consistent with the skills and techniques of one of these soldiers. These guys can become deadly in an instant."

Shana took note of that. She was trying to keep her excitement down. Her first big case, and it looked like they were dealing with an executioner after all. It was odd, though. Juno had seemed so nice when she'd spoken to him.

"Do the other Rangers have issues assimilating to civilian life?"

"Our psychological profile for these guys is geared toward choosing men who can kill quickly and efficiently, but who are considered sane. They should all be able to differentiate between an assignment in a war from civilian life. A lot of them look forward to getting back to civilization and being able to live peacefully. But it's hard to say. Shit happens over there."

Culver rubbed his temples. "Do you think Valdas did these murders?"

"He admits that he did one, and the others are very similar. Based on what we know about him, I'd be surprised if he went out intending to kill in cold blood. But if the victims initiated it, I mean . . ." Static on the line. A sigh. "He's more than capable of doing it. Valdas had always seemed better adjusted than most guys, both in the service and after. We all had high hopes for him being a poster boy for the corps when he got home."

"You think he's just defending himself against criminals targeting him?"

"But then why hasn't he come to the police for help yet?" Shana asked. She didn't look up from her notes to see if Culver was glaring at her or not. The clock ticked from its high perch on the wall.

Culver asked, "Are there more of these Rangers in the area?"

"He was always with a soldier named Elijah McCoy. They got out together and were headed to Oakland. Run him and see if he's close by. He could give you a perspective."

A known friend? Shana wrote that down, then circled it. "Do we know what happened to McCoy when he was discharged?"

Culver turned to look at her.

More rustling on the other end as Obed shuffled papers. "Negative. There's nothing here in the file about the guy post-service. They're civilians now. Your databases, not mine. If they were still enlisted, we would just ship them out of country 'til this all settles down."

"This is a good lead. Officer Thomas will look up McCoy." Culver gave a dark chuckle. "Your suggestion that some criminals are persecuting him could be true. It'd be a way out for Valdas. The fact that there's absolutely no forensic evidence to work on in these cases complicates things a bit."

"Our soldiers were good at getting in and doing a job without being detected," Obed said. "Does Valdas have an alibi for each of these?"

Culver turned to Shana, expectant. "Officer Thomas?"

Shana sat up. "Marks and I have been getting statements. Valdas said that he was still home with his family at the time of the dumpster death. It was early in the morning and he was having breakfast. Only his family can corroborate that."

"Have they?" Ober asked.

"They have. He was present for the biker death, but we already knew that. The warehouse deaths took place around midnight on

Friday. He said he had a guest that night and went to bed afterward, around ten. Again, only his family can corroborate that, and they have."

Culver asked, "Can you track down whoever the guest was and ask about that night?"

Shana nodded. "We're going back to re-interview Valdas."

Obed chimed in. "Find Elijah McCoy. Maybe he can vouch for Valdas. Let me know what you find out, lieutenant. Both of these men are patriots of the highest order. They did one hell of a job for our country over there."

The next day, Lieutenant Culver approached Shana and Marks at Marks's desk in the homicide bull pen. He tapped Marks on the shoulder. "Have you solved these murders yet?"

Marks smiled at him. "Very funny. We talked to a guy, Elroy, who was working at Buster's that morning. He said he remembered the visit from an officer who said there was a homicide down the block, but he didn't have any more information than that. All his customers pay in cash and he was alone with the cook that morning. The altercation was called in anonymously. Based on the CCTV in the area, there was some movement around the dumpster at that time, but not much."

Culver leaned in, examining all their reports spread out across the desk. Shana wrinkled her nose. He smelled like milk. "What do we know about the victim?"

Shana pulled up her notes. "He was a truck driver. Good record, no problems with his employer. He was involved in an incident about a year ago when he and another driver beat up a gay guy. He was charged with a hate crime of assault, but it was only a two thousand dollar fine and a year's probation. The judge said he had accepted responsibility for the crime and agreed to go to anger management. His partner got the same penalty."

"Where's the partner now?"

Marks tapped his pencil on the desk. "Living in Seattle with his new family. Hasn't been to California in months."

"So this guy was down in the port early in the morning, probably going to or coming from work. He was going to eat breakfast or get some coffee maybe . . . and then what?"

"We don't know," Shana said. "We've talked to the truck line and he was scheduled to drive about two hours after the incident occurred. He was probably down there for work and on his way to Buster's." Shana picked up her coffee mug so Marks could grab some paper. "No one has any information. When I looked at the interviews with his supervisors they said he had friends, but wouldn't be able to tell if he was with anyone on the day he died. We'll talk to his known friends later this week."

"Make it sooner." Culver turned to Marks. "Follow up on injuries to gay men on the day he was killed, through hospitals and emergency rooms. See if there was another fight that went against him this time. Maybe he attacked a gay green beret."

"I'll do that, lieutenant." Marks smiled.

Shana tried to not roll her eyes. These men were so intolerant.

Culver eyed the messy stacks of paper spread across Marks's desk. "So nothing. How about the people and officers involved with the biker death?"

Shana pulled out her notebook. "We talked to the officers who responded to the call from a neighbor, and we talked to the neighbor. We couldn't find anyone else passing by or in the parking lot that could give us a description of the event. The neighbor who called in the disturbance said she saw pretty much what the female victim reported, and it all matched with Mr. Valdas's statement. She was lucky to have Valdas passing by at the right time."

Culver frowned. "Yes, lucky . . . I need more information on his involvement. Why was he in the area? What does he drive? Go interview him directly, sergeant. Both of you. Give me a gut feeling about Valdas. We have damn few clues about any of the four deaths. We can't directly connect the truck driver to the other three, but the stalker could possibly be linked to Forester and Arias. That pair has a history of drug-related crimes."

"Didn't the stalker belong to Sons of Perdition?" Shana asked. "They've been controlling the Oakland drug market for years."

She'd seen past reports on their members, always in and out of prison. There was a rumor that when a member got his first confirmed kill, he'd be elevated to the title of Beast in a ceremony. Lovely people.

Marks held up a hand. "Wait a minute, if the stalker and the two men in the warehouse last Friday are related, then the arson on Valdas's warehouse could've been a revenge strike. Valdas might be in a one-man gang war—with the Sons of Perdition, no less."

Culver nodded. "And right after the fire, a major cog in the crime circuits shows up murdered on an empty pier. If Valdas is on a crusade, I want to know about it. If we're seeing the start of a war between the Sons of Perdition and Valdas, then we need to stop it. Now."

28

THE TEA DANCE

Elijah was nervous. He was never nervous. He paced around the condo, waiting for Phillip and Rick to pick him up for the group's night out. Elijah knew he didn't have any social skills—he didn't like large crowds or loud noises. But he did want to see his friends, and they had promised to show him a good time. So he waited, nervous.

Someone pounded on the door.

"Elijah, we're here! Open up!"

Elijah opened the door to find the whole gang crowded in the hallway—Phillip, Rick, Dillan, Ryan, and Chris. Most of the men were in skinny jeans with a variety of stylish shirts. Rick was wearing a silky shirt of some kind. Elijah didn't meet his eyes.

Phillip took one look at Elijah and shook his head. "No. Not in that."

"What's wrong with what I've got on?" Elijah looked down, embarrassed. He was wearing black jeans and a light, gray sweater.

"What are you, my grandma? Come on, I've got something I'm sure."

Phillip led Elijah by the wrist back to his closet. Elijah turned his head as he went, giving Rick a silent plea for help.

Rick only laughed. "We'll wait here."

Ten minutes later, Phillip managed to find Elijah a nice button down that was a little snug—no one complained about that—and they were on their way.

The White Horse was a bar downtown notorious for its live entertainment and excellent drinks. As soon as they arrived, the group found a corner booth and settled in, ordering Pomegranate Martinis, a white wine called Egalite, the Mexican beer Salamander for Elijah, a Cosmopolitan, a Sidecar, and Rick ordered a new popular cocktail called Apology. The group laughed at this. Dillan said, "What do you need to apologize for?"

Rick looked at Elijah. "Nothing, yet."

Elijah was squeezed in between Dillan and Rick. "Is this your first time here?" Dillan asked. Elijah nodded. "Welcome! Kick back and relax. You'll see how good you feel tomorrow."

Rick clasped a hand on Elijah's shoulder as he leaned across Elijah. He was warm. "Hey now," he shouted above the noise. "This is Elijah's first Tea Dance, so I'm in charge of his social calendar for the evening."

Dillan raised an eyebrow. "Are you his date for the night?"

Elijah looked between the two men, amused. He didn't know what to say.

Rick grinned. "No, I'm his host."

Despite the close distance, the music was so loud that Rick had to almost put his mouth on Elijah's ear in order for him to hear anything. "There's gonna be a pool tournament. You in?"

Elijah screwed up his face. "What?"

"A pool tournament. Come, play."

Elijah was not a pool shark. He and Rick were eliminated in the first round, leaving Phillip to rise in rank as Rick dragged Elijah to the dance room. Elijah was actually able to dance by just following Rick, once he got into a rhythm.

DJ Zombie Prince was performing that night. Rick moved with fluid motion to the EDM tracks pulsing from the DJ booth. The colorful lights washed across his tan face, highlighted by a slight shine of sweat from the heat of the room. Rick was beaming, laughing at the music and encouraging Elijah to find his stride.

The tight room kept the two of them close together. Elijah could feel the heat radiating off Rick's body, and occasionally would brush up against his silky shirt—now unbuttoned two more buttons.

"Let's take a break!" Elijah yelled over the music.

Rick nodded and motioned for him to follow. They each got a tall fruity drink with some ice in it and sat on a couple of stools along the wall to recover from the wild techno dancing.

"This is great." Elijah couldn't keep himself from smiling. "I'm actually having fun tonight."

The lights were pulsing; there was a little fog in the air that made the room feel very intimate.

"You thought you wouldn't?" Rick asked.

"I wasn't sure. I didn't know I could dance."

Rick made a motion, like he was going to put a hand on Elijah's shoulder, but stopped himself. "What are you talking about? You're an incredible dancer! With that muscle-bound body of yours, it's effortless. You'll have to come back with us again sometime."

Elijah watched Rick's mouth as he spoke. Without thinking, Elijah reached over and took hold of Rick's shirt, pulling him into a kiss. Rick's surprise lasted only a heartbeat before he melted into Elijah, their lips forming a perfect seal. After a minute of soft kissing, Elijah felt Rick's tongue slide into his mouth.

The tender exploration of soft tongues sent a strong message to Elijah's cock. It surprised him, but in an exciting, invigorating way. Rick melted and put his hands on Elijah's shirt, feeling his firm chest. Elijah had one hand around Rick's waist, the other knitted in Rick's soft hair, pulling him closer. The kiss lasted for almost ten minutes, and when Elijah finally released him, Rick almost slid off the stool. Elijah moved closer to Rick to balance him.

The Brazilian's dark eyes glittered in the hazy room. "Am I dreaming, or did that just happen? That was *wonderful*, Elijah."

A few men dancing nearby hooted and applauded their approval. Elijah shifted in his seat. His stomach fluttered at the sound of his name. He wasn't sure what had come over him, but he had liked it. It cleared up a few things about his feelings and interests.

He smiled. "You seduce everyone you meet, Rick?"

Rick gave a breathy laugh. "Fuck no. I haven't been kissed like that since . . . well, a long time."

"Are you and Phillip lovers?" Elijah had to ask.

Rick stared at him, taken aback. "No, we're not. God, Phillip is like . . . a brother, or something. Can I tell him you kissed me, and that it was wonderful?" He added slyly.

Elijah took Rick's hand and looked deep into his eyes. His blood was burning in his veins, and he was having trouble thinking straight. He didn't know what to do next. Did they tell people? What had just happened?

"I don't know how all this works, or what this means," he admitted. "But I'm so turned on right now, you better run for your life."

A visible shudder ran up Rick's frame. "I think we just see what happens next and tell people once we figure out what we feel. In our social circles, once you kiss a man like that you find a time and place to fuck his brains out—and vice versa."

Elijah blushed.

Rick leaned over and spoke in a sultry voice in Elijah's ear. "You're a strong man, Elijah. I'm guessing that you're a top, and I will be your willing slave. I've had fantasies about you since our talk in my kitchen, but I'd better get a lot more creative about them."

Elijah could feel Rick's lips curl into a smile against his ear. He shivered.

"I can hardly breathe right now," Rick whispered. "I hate to be so blunt, but I think my dick could fall off, it's so hard right now."

Elijah pulled away, trying his best to look alarmed. "We really can't let that happen, can we?"

Rick extended a hand and led Elijah back on the dance floor. The rest of the evening was a blur for them both. Phillip and the gang sat at their corner booth, talking and drinking. Occasionally one of them would join Rick and Elijah on the dance floor, but they were left alone for the most part, their friends giving them knowing smiles. During these times, Rick and Elijah would take turns stealing innocent kisses, never as consuming as their first.

Around ten, the party started to break up. People had to get home and go to work the next day. Chris, Dillan, and Ryan all waved goodbye as Phillip, Rick, and Elijah left the bar. When they got to the parking lot, Phillip gave the two of them a suspicious look, hands on his hips.

"Would you guys like to sit in the back together?" he asked.

Elijah exchanged grins with Rick. Without a word, Rick slid into the backseat following Elijah. Phillip's mouth fell open in a gape. "That's it, you two tell me what's going on right now. I'll get in an accident if you don't, I swear."

Rick squeezed Elijah's hand. "Elijah and I had a really good time tonight. We're not saying anything's happening, but we're . . . open to exploration." He turned to Elijah. "Is that fair?"

Elijah nodded. "I'd say so."

Phillip eyed their hands in the rearview mirror. "Oh come on you guys, tell me something juicy. What's going on?"

Elijah reached up and squeezed Phillip's neck from the back. "Rick stuck his tongue in my mouth."

Phillip whipped around, grabbing the headrest of his seat. "You're just teasing me!"

Rick hit Elijah on the shoulder. It was more of a pat. "Only about the part where I was the one doing the kissing. Elijah took advantage of me!"

Elijah started laughing. "But it was your tongue that snuck into my mouth first, right?"

"That part was true," Rick admitted.

They were all laughing as they drove back. Elijah asked, "Can you guys drive me back past Juno's warehouse? I want to take a look to see that it's OK and not a drug supermarket or anything yet."

"Sure." Phillip guided the car down toward the bay, driving out of their way to get a look at Elijah's unbeknownst home. They turned onto the last street.

"Stop the car," Elijah said. Phillip did so, flicking off the headlights. "Is there someone down there?"

Parked just outside the warehouse, hidden in the shadow of the building, was a Big Dog motorcycle.

29

THE RECON

The dark night was misty, a sparse orange glow from the streetlights cast on the burnt warehouse. The Big Dog Mastiff sat parked in a corner of the lot with no one in sight.

"What are we looking at, Elijah?" Phillip asked.

Elijah scanned the front of the building, looking for the silhouette of anyone inside or out. "The police have reason to believe the fire was set by bikers."

"The Sons of Perdition?" Rick asked. Elijah nodded.

"Bikers?" Phillip looked between Elijah and Rick, confused. "What bikers?"

Elijah briefly explained the night with Roxanna's stalker. Rick kept his eyes focused on the building, looking for intruders. He'd already heard this story once.

Phillip frowned. "So you beat up a biker and now they're burning down your friend's shop? That doesn't make sense."

Rick looked back at Elijah. "It doesn't, unless . . . Elijah, did you?"

Even in the dim light of the street, Elijah could see the meaning in Rick's eyes. He nodded.

"What?" Phillip was obviously frustrated now, left out of everything happening in the backseat. "What did he do?"

"Elijah killed him." Rick's eyes were sad, but he still held Elijah's hand. That was . . . comforting. Elijah didn't know how to process that. Rick wasn't scrambling to escape the monster.

"You killed the stalker? That was your assessment of the threat?" Phillip sort of blushed when he said that. "I'm trying to sound like a military guy, or police. How did that sound?"

Phillip wasn't going to run from him, either. Elijah smiled. "Very official, Phillip. Yes, that was my assessment of the situation. The man was going to kill Roxanna, no doubt about it."

Phillip shuddered. "That's awful. But what do you think's going on now?"

Elijah craned his head past Rick to examine the scene.

He smells nice. He shook himself. He had to focus.

"My first thought was that someone's planting a bomb. The arson didn't work the first time, and if they had wanted to shoot or stab Juno they would've come early in the morning when he'd be here alone."

"Let's call the police and see if they want to come by." Rick pulled out his phone.

Phillip said, "Elijah wants to go kill that bastard, don't you?"

Elijah laughed. "You're sounding like a badass tonight. Maybe we should send you in to take care of the threat."

Rick's tone was solemn. "Elijah, is that what you're planning?"

Elijah didn't answer. There was an immediate threat that needed to be addressed. This guy wasn't going to be talked down. He was going to kill Juno, somehow, and have an alibi by morning. Something had to be done. "I'm going in. I'm ending this fucker."

Elijah went to open the car door, but Rick clasped a hand on Elijah's shoulder, restraining him.

"Hello? 9-1-1? I want to report a break-in at a place of business."

Elijah turned around to see Rick with his phone up to his ear.

His eyes were latched onto Elijah, pleading him to stay put. "We're sitting down the block and can see an intruder. Yes ma'am, I'm aware of the fire. We'll keep a distance." He hung up the phone. "A cruiser will be here in a few."

Phillip grinned at him. "Protecting the boyfriend, huh?"

Rick rolled his eyes. "Oh shut up. What with you trying to be a badass, and Elijah actually being a badass, I could just picture the two of you going in to beat the shit out of a giant biker. It'd be a disaster."

Everyone laughed, more to ease the tension than because of the humor. In a few minutes, a patrol car slid up beside them. The patrolman rolled down his passenger-side window. Elijah did the same in the backseat.

The patrolman spoke in an even whisper. "Tell me what's going on, quietly."

Elijah explained what he saw and why he thought it might be a bomb. The officer nodded slowly. "How long have you been here?"

"Twenty minutes or less. We haven't seen anyone, inside or out."

"You're doing the right thing here. There's someone inside for sure."

"Is it the Sons of Perdition?" Rick asked.

"Yeah, we think so. I've got backup on the other side of the warehouse. Just sit tight while we go in and have a look."

"Do you want a backup?" Elijah asked. "I'm a veteran." He was acutely aware of some glitter residue on his cheek.

The patrolman shook his head. "Can't do that, sir. You're a civilian now, it's our job to protect you. Just sit here and watch your buddies."

The patrolman pulled his car across the road to block it, then got out. He keyed in some information to his dispatch and turned his dashboard camera toward the warehouse. Without looking back at the Audi, the officer pulled out his flashlight and quietly approached the warehouse, hand on his Glock.

The three men watched as the patrolman disappeared inside the building. Elijah stepped out of the vehicle, senses on full alert. A tense minute passed, then a second unit pulled up.

The second officer approached Elijah. "Where's Officer Jones?"

Elijah pointed to the building. "He's been in there for a few minutes."

The patrolman nodded and moved toward the burnt entrance. Elijah started to follow him but stopped when the officer looked back at him and gave a curt shake of the head. Rick and Phillip remained in the car.

"Elijah," Phillip hissed. "Get back here."

Elijah returned to the car. Another five minutes went by. Suddenly, there was a series of shots fired inside the structure. Elijah jumped out of the car and sped toward the building, determined to stop the biker if he was the one that emerged. He stopped within fifteen feet of the entrance, poised.

Nothing and no one emerged. A minute passed, then another. Then, there was another barrage of shots, this time at least a dozen separate shots. Rick jumped out of the car and ran over to the patrol car. Elijah heard him call in the shots over the squad car's radio while Phillip started the Audi. Elijah half-expected them to pull out of there; it's what they should do.

He himself was at the boarded-up door, ready to go in. There was motion at the entry point to the burned part of the building, and one of the police officers walked out. It was Officer Jones.

He looked at Elijah and shook his finger at him. "What were you going to do, civilian?"

Elijah exhaled, adrenaline rushing from his lungs. "Whatever needed to be done? I wasn't going to let anyone but you come out without stopping them."

The patrolman smiled. "You veterans all think you're Superman. Thanks for the backup, but please get back to your vehicle. We have the intruder down. He was hit several times in the last volley of shots and is wounded in at least three places. My partner has him restrained and I need to get an ambulance headed this way. Come on, walk back with me."

Elijah fell into step beside the officer. "Did you recognize the man? Was he Sons of Perdition?"

"Oh, we know Aryan, alright. It's been a while since he and I've had the chance to catch up." He smiled to himself.

Elijah shrugged it off. It had been one of bikers. That was all he needed to know.

The officer took down everyone's information and sent them on their way. "This is a crime scene now. Go home, and we'll give you a call to get further statements. Make sure you're available in the morning."

Once they were back on the highway, Elijah turned to Rick. "I would've gone in there if you hadn't taken over. You saved me. I . . . thanks."

Rick took his hand. "No problem. Let's take you home so we can all get some rest."

Phillip was almost bouncing in his seat. "I can't believe that we were involved in a police gun battle. Oh man! This is wild. I can tell that our life is gonna get a lot more intense now that we have Elijah in it." He pushed his asymmetric bob out of his eyes and signaled for their exit. "People say that gay guys are dramatic, but we have nothing on Elijah. I'm glad we waited for the police. I know you could've taken care of that guy, Elijah—I've seen it. But I'm glad you didn't."

Elijah agreed. He wanted nothing more than to get back at those bastards who burned down the warehouse, but that was probably what Lamb wanted. "Yeah, me too. I'd be even deeper in a hole with the law. Thanks for helping me, guys."

Rick squeezed his hand. "I'm keeping you for later."

Phillip made a disgusted noise. Elijah caught a glimpse of his eye roll in the rearview mirror. "You two better work out and not ruin the group. You're part of the family now, Elijah."

Elijah squeezed Rick's hand back, but his mind was suddenly

elsewhere, in another time and place. He was back in the warehouse on Pier 51, the body of Orville Forester sprawled before him, his lifeless limbs entangled in the building's shadows. He could feel Lamb standing behind him, feel the cold pricks of his laughter piercing his consciousness.

30

THE CHECK-IN

Shana Thomas hustled down to the break room in the station closest to the Homicide Department. She was finally doing *real* police work, and not only that—she was getting noticed. Well, sort of. Her ideas were being used, at least. Now she just had to get the white men above her to recognize the ideas' origins. But it was a start. A promising, wonderful start.

She slid around the corner doorframe and made a beeline for the coffee maker. In her haste, she ran straight into Lieutenant Culver. Some of his coffee splashed onto his tie.

"Oh for Christ's sake," he muttered.

"Sorry, lieutenant." Shana grabbed some napkins and offered them to her boss. He had a big folder under his arm, and it looked like he was going to try to get some work done away from his phone.

"It's fine, Thomas. Damn blind corners. I swear I run into an officer once a week coming in and out of this room." He dabbed at his tie. It was a dark blue one; the coffee was hardly noticeable. He motioned at the break table. "Join me for coffee."

"Oh, I don't want to interrupt your work." She had a lot to do today, and she didn't want to continue this embarrassing moment any longer.

"I want to talk to you about the cases you and your sergeant are working. Did you hear the latest?"

Well, that was worth staying for.

"A fire and now an attempted bombing." Shana poured herself a cup of steaming coffee and pulled up a chair across from Culver, savoring her coffee's aroma. "I think our suspicions about the gang war is right. The SOP are definitely targeting Valdas. I've looked into the gang. Penny Garlitz was one of their senior officers, a favorite amongst the men. It seems like all of the members are boiling over his death. Valdas isn't safe."

Culver opened his file and started to make a note inside. "Thomas, I've been watching you on this case. You're a serious, hardworking officer. I see the hours you keep. On time, often working late. You seem to be in for the duration. I like the way you're handling yourself. You're good with people, and you seem to be a good partner for Marks. He's had nothing but good things to say about you."

Shana smiled, trying to keep herself from reddening. It was high praise, coming from the lieutenant. "Thank you, sir. I'm just happy I can contribute." She sipped her coffee. It was strong, just the way she liked it.

"Where's Marks?"

"He should be here in fifteen."

"Good. I want you and Marks to go to Valdas's home this afternoon. Find out if this is all a business deal gone wrong or if we need to throw some protection around him and his family. And see if you can find out if Valdas is in contact with this McCoy guy. If two Rangers are involved, I want to know. You're good at reading people, Thomas. Find out what this guy's hiding."

Shana stood up. "I'm on it, sir. I'll go see if Sergeant Marks is in yet."

Culver smiled at her. "Go get 'em."

Shana was pumped. It took all of her self-control to remain calm as she left the break room. She had to be careful and really controlled around the men. But the lieutenant liked her work! She was ready to grab Marks and drag him out to the cruiser to go find these guys.

Shana was going to make sure this case was closed nice and tidy.

31

THE CROSS-CHECK

It was late morning, the day after the break-in. Elijah reclined along Phillip's pristine couch as he spoke on the phone with Juno. "This is really getting out of hand, man. They're leaving bombs now."

The living room of Phillip's condo glittered with natural light this time of morning. Everything was clean, orderly—it was perfect. This day was perfect. Sure, there were bombs in his safe house and a biker gang after his best friend, but he'd dealt with all that before. Today was a *new* day, a glorious day. A day he hoped included Rick.

"You stopped by to protect me again," Juno said, his words seeped in gratitude. "*I'm* supposed to be taking care of *you* these days. Why were you out so late?"

Elijah smiled. "You'd be proud of me. I decided to go hang out with the guys last night."

"You went to that bar?"

"Yup. It was fun. I'm starting to get the hang of having friends. You won't have to carry me all the time now. Speaking of carrying, do you think it's safe to go back to work this morning?"

"I'm meeting an officer down at the warehouse in an hour. They're searching the place for booby traps now. From what I heard, you actually called for the police's help this time. Am I supposed to believe that you didn't just go in and kill this motherfucker?"

"Yeah. Rick and Phillip talked me down. They probably saved my ass, calling the cops before I could get my hands on the bastard."

"They've been pretty good to you."

Elijah thought about that. He'd been really honest with these guys about who he was and what he'd done—Phillip had even seen some of it firsthand—but they cared about him, regardless. They took him out of the battle before he could get in trouble.

"Yeah, they have." He said.

"Sounds like we're turning the corner here."

Elijah nodded, even though Juno couldn't see. "I think so. But, what are we going to do about these bikers? It sounds like they're pretty hot for you."

"They're hot for you, they just don't know it." Juno sighed. "You picked the wrong biker to kill, man. They're out for revenge. So far they've tried to burn me out and blow the place up."

"They weren't trying to blow up the warehouse, they were planning to blow *you* up." Elijah got up from the couch and started to pace around the living room. "They're trying to kill you. We have to find a way to strike back. I can do some recon on them if you're ready to deal with this."

"Oh good. You get the lay of their headquarters and we'll go in and blow them up. Then we can track down whoever escapes and kill them one at a time in a really painful way to make a statement to other biker gangs."

Elijah could almost hear the eye roll. "You're making that sound like it's not a good idea."

Juno laughed. "Well, I don't. Let me talk to the cops this

morning and see what they recommend doing. We'll support whatever plan they have—legally. OK?"

"Fuck."

32

CLOSING ARGUMENTS

Elijah disconnected the call and flopped down on the couch. He shielded his eyes from the bright morning light as he thought about their plan. Leaving his friend's safety—and possibly his own—to the police was going to be hard. He rolled over to his side and opened his eyes.

A nice Italian leather shoe was inches from his face.

He jumped up, dropping into the power position, ready to fight. Mr. Lamb stood before him, wearing a heather-blue suit and his signature relaxed smile.

Elijah glared at him. "Damn you. Quit sneaking up on me. Get out."

Lamb didn't move. "I was going to tell you something, but I can go if you want."

"Please do."

No one moved. Lamb just stood there, as if waiting for something.

Elijah sighed. "You're just going to tell me anyway, aren't you? Fine. What is it?"

Lamb laced his fingers in front of him. "You were so impressive with Forester and his friend. I was surprised by what a baby you were last night."

"Fuck you. Get out."

"You're fucked."

Elijah blinked. "What?"

Lamb shrugged his shoulders. "You're fucked, is all. That's what I came to tell you. The police are investigating all the murders from the past week, and they think your friend Juno is the murderer. It's ironic, isn't it?" He laughed. "You've taken the one person who has always been good to you and let him take the fall for a murder you committed. You got him in trouble with one of the most dangerous gangs in the area. You got his warehouse trashed—he can't work. He's the suspect in four murders, but all you can say to me is 'damn you.'"

Lamb leaned closer. "Hell doesn't scare me, Elijah McCoy."

Anger built in Elijah, a seeping coldness in his chest.

"You were a good soldier, Elijah. You're a horrible civilian. Look at you." Lamb swept his hands over Elijah, encompassing his boxer shorts, T-shirt, and tired eyes. "You're not a very good friend, not to Juno or any of the new men in your life. You want to start a relationship? Now? You're just going to leave them—you always do. You know that."

The cold anger in Elijah stiffened, transforming into uncertain fear.

"Juno and his family are going to be ruined. The children are going to grow up with a father in jail. Believe me, Elijah, I love these kinds of situations, but you're fucked. If you'd just done what I asked, you'd be off on your own by now and rich. I would only give you seven or eight jobs a year. You'd have lots of free time. You could become a sugar daddy to those gay boys."

Elijah frowned, even more uncertain. He didn't want all of those things to happen to Juno. "If I just disappear, then Juno is still screwed, isn't he?"

Lamb put a finger to his temple, as if considering the possibility. "Go tell the bikers that you killed Penny. Kill as many of them as you can, then disappear. That would solve a lot of problems for the police. They will never solve the death of the trucker, but it will give the police their answer to who killed Forester and Arias. Juno would be free."

"That's your idea for how to fix things?"

Lamb gave another shrug. "It's the truth. A little messy, but a simple solution. Then you and I can start working together."

"Can I kill you?" Elijah took a step forward.

Mr. Lamb chuckled. "No. I've got to go. Just checking in, my friend." He walked out of the front door of the condo this time, still laughing heartily.

33

THE WALK

Rick took a final look around his office and out at Lake Merritt before leaving the office for the day. Life was going pretty well for him. He loved his job, working with smart people who cared about each other and the environment. He had a wonderful group of friends to support him and have fun with. His smile faded. But why did he feel so agitated? Like he was going to jump out of his skin if anyone touched him?

He descended the nine floors to the street and started off on his walk home. Living less than two miles from work had been a great move for him. He loved his daily commutes on foot to and from the office. Walking up Grand to San Pablo always made him feel his community. The mix of people in the area made him and his Brazilian face feel right at home. Only around ten percent of the people here were white, allowing for great diversity among the people and small businesses, all mixed with skyscrapers filled with big corporations and high-tech industries. The rich corporations up above and the people on the street. The smells of local eateries always put him in a good mood. There was a man outside a bakery drawing on the shop's sandwich board that looked a little like Elijah.

Elijah McCoy is the reason for my agitation.

Rick sighed. Elijah was a great guy, and he had to admit he was a hunk, but last night's kiss had complicated everything.

He kissed me—he did, not me. Elijah said he was unsure about his sexuality, and while he believed him, the kiss had solidified Rick's feelings toward this mysterious solider. *What a kiss.* Rick had actually felt his knees get weak at the touch of his soft lips. They'd fit so perfectly together. When their tongues had met, it was like Rick's life was draining out of him and into Elijah, only to suddenly feel Elijah's strength pouring into him.

He'd almost exploded right there. He stopped and took a breath.

He didn't think he'd ever climaxed just from a kiss before, but it had been pretty close.

I knew we liked each other. Elijah had been so willing to let Rick take over his dance card at the White Horse. He was fun as a dance partner, even if Elijah had been more working out than dancing. That was OK, he could learn. It just felt like the world had disappeared around them.

Whenever Elijah looked at Rick, Rick could see into him. It'd been that way ever since the first night they met. He still didn't know why he offered the internship right away, but it was a smart move. He'd have a chance to see Elijah almost daily for the next couple of years, with plenty of reasons to talk to him.

That's what I want, I think. To have him in my life and spend time with him.

Rick smiled at the neighborhood as he walked up San Pablo. It was beat up, but it was getting better. Most of the buildings, including his own Victorian home, were built in the 1920s or 1930s. Old and either ready to fall apart or be rebuilt. More and more of them were being fixed up, but the neighborhood still looked like it did for the last century. This was his home now.

He turned onto Thirty-Fourth Street and found Phillip waiting for him on the front porch, a tray of something iced and red sitting on the porch table.

"Hey," Phillip called from the porch. "You OK?"

Rick trudged up the steps and dropped his bag against the house. "Yeah, just got some stuff on my mind. How was your day?"

Phillip handed him a cranberry and Pellegrino cocktail. "Oh no you don't. We can talk about my boring day over dinner. I can tell something's up. Come on, spill. What's going on in that head of yours?"

Rick smiled inwardly at his friend's efforts as he sat on one of the two rocking chairs. *It's so nice having Phillip stay with me. Where would I be without him?*

It was tragic, how Phillip was too scared to go back to his own condo, but the company was nice.

Elijah had saved Phillip. Just another allure to the man.

He sighed. "I've been thinking about Elijah all the way home," he admitted. "He's really thrown me for a loop."

"Because of that kiss?"

Rick nodded.

"Do you love him?"

Rick sipped at his cocktail. "Do you?"

Phillip laughed. "No. I admire the man, but nothing like that. Answer the question."

I don't know, do I love Elijah? Rick had a deep affection and brotherly love for Phillip. He'd die for him—and right away, but with Elijah . . . they'd never be brothers.

"He's a hunk, and I want to play with him," Rick said, speaking slowly, thinking as he words flowed from his mouth. "Like other men. I've wanted to touch him since we met."

Phillip nodded. "And you generally get what you want, looking at your record."

"Right." Since Jason's death, Rick had gone through men faster than most women go through lipstick. "But there's something different about Elijah. I don't know. Why not just fuck him and spend a week in lust and then on to the next one?"

Rick gave a nervous laugh. It sounded hollow, even to him.

Phillip's face was serious. "Because that wouldn't be fair to Elijah. After everything he's been through, you can't just play with him like that."

"I know." Rick drained the rest of his cocktail. "And I don't want to. There's something that makes me want to get close to him, like, really close to him. Being gay can be a life of pain and loneliness for most of us—you know that. Elijah's already full of so much pain. It hurts me to be around him, feeling that with him. That's the crazy part—I can *feel* his pain, Phillip, and I want to do something. I want to help him. I think I do love him."

Phillip put his glass down. "Hold on a minute. I get that he's something different, and I could see how you feel, but Rick . . . it was just a kiss."

"A damn good kiss."

"Even so. But you've kissed lots of men. We were both rooting for Elijah, and it was nice to see him like that with you, but come on."

"Phillip, I'm swept away here. I can hardly wait to get my hands all over him, but this is something else. I want to pull him in and hold onto him and merge with him. Is that a thing? Can two men merge?"

Phillip was cautious as he spoke. "They can, but Elijah is a very rough man. A really good man, but he kills people. I don't know how much control he has over all that violence, and he seems so comfortable with it. You could be crushed easily here, emotionally or physically. You see that, don't you?"

Would he kill me? Elijah had killed people, apparently lots of people. *How do I feel about being around a man who kills others?*

That entire way of thinking was a mystery to Rick. How could anyone think that it was OK to take a life? He could see protecting yourself, though at that point why not just remove yourself from the danger in the first place? It seemed like Elijah was always looking at people around him in a threat-assessment way—he used that term, sometimes. He always seemed to be deciding how he would kill them if he needed to. *Do I want to be close to that?*

"He's dangerous," Rick said. "I just can't imagine him ever hurting me. I feel like he needs me—I'm needed, Phillip. For the first time in a long time."

Phillip gave him a small, sad smile. "I want you to feel that way. It's been so hard watching you lose Jason and live with his ghost. But I need you, too. I don't want you getting seriously hurt or killed because of your proximity to Elijah. Promise me you'll be careful as you explore these feelings."

Rick put down his empty glass and leaned over to take Phillip's hand. He squeezed it and looked into his friend's eyes. "I promise. I'm going to live a long, long life with you as my brother."

He released Phillip's hand and picked up his glass, turning the tumbler 'round and 'round in his hands. "I just feel like I've had this hole in me for so long, you know? I have lots of sex, sure, but you get to a point where you realize that hookup sex and heartfelt sex are different. One fades into a memory. You lose the names after a while. But heartfelt sex is like a tattoo on the soul; it can't be removed. I'll have Jason imprinted on my soul forever, but the color is fading." He looked up at Phillip, who was watching him intently. "I think I'm ready for a new tattoo. I just want to make sure I get the right one."

A tear rolled down Phillip's cheek. "Damn it, Rick." He got up and pulled Rick into a tight hug. "You know I'll always be there for you. Pursue your man, go find that new ink."

"You mean it?"

"Yeah, but keep me updated on everything. And *please* be careful. Now." He pulled away, smiling. "I've got a fabulous dinner planned tonight, and I'm not going to let heavy words ruin it. Come on, you can slice the veggies."

34

THE RIDE

Elijah stepped in from the balcony of Phillip's condo. He felt bad. The condo was beautiful, but the longer he stayed here the longer he suspected Phillip wasn't going to ask him to leave. He'd think it would jeopardize their friendship—that wasn't true. The warehouse was almost repaired; they'd have to talk about it soon. Sure, Phillip seemed to be enjoying staying at Rick's place, but he could be renting the condo out for three grand a month, at least. The place had an underground parking space for Christ's sake—who had those in the city?

After the fire, Elijah had told his new friends about his safe house in the warehouse. They had been really upset, insisting he stayed at the condo. How could he refuse? These guys were serious in their affection. Elijah had the dimmest idea of what a close family looked like, yet he knew these guys had adopted him and the Valdases into their family.

He'd been a little surprised they didn't ask him to move in with them at Rick's place. He had been hoping for that.

Elijah walked to the dining room and started to load up his Montague Paratrooper bike. He packed his backpack with a book and some food, pumped his tires, and checked the bike in general for the ride. He dressed in layers with his jeans and work boots. For some reason, the title song from the movie *Men in Tights* came to mind.

The movie was so absurd, but he laughed every time he thought of it. *I think I'll live as a man in pants instead.*

The morning air was wet that day. Knowing the bay area, the fog would burn off and the sun would come out over the next hour. Elijah rolled the bike out into the hall and locked up the condo, went to the stairs, and bumped down to street level. He was ready for a day out. He'd spent the past week working on the docks, but physical labor wasn't the cure for the heavy weight bearing down on him. No, a ride was the solution to so many of his stresses.

Elijah worked his way to the Embarcadero, just a couple of blocks from his fancy condo. He followed that to Twenty-Ninth Street and made a right on International Boulevard. Watching traffic and lights, he made a left on Lincoln Avenue uphill, crossed Highway 13 onto Joaquin Miller Park Road and entered the beautiful urban park.

Joaquin Miller Park was huge, nesting above the city in a haven of tall trees and winding paths. As Elijah entered the park, he really felt as if he was out in the country, minus the occasional glimpse through the tree gaps of the bay below. He was close to Lake Chabot, which was a good trail riding park. The road through the park was cool and quiet. People who drove into the park were pretty calm; the roads ended in the park and didn't go anywhere that would lure traffic.

Elijah parked his bike in a small clearing with only two tables. Sitting at his wooden picnic bench, he took out a book by Andrew Vachss and started to read. Vachss was a natural for Elijah. Vachss literally wrote about the life Elijah lived, from his characters to the themes of the book. His books seemed real to Elijah. Vachss had been on the police force, went to law school, served as a prosecutor, ran a prison, and now worked as a legal advocate for children to protect them from abuse and violence.

This book, *A Bomb Made in Hell*, was one of the first written by Vachss in the 1970s. Every publisher he contacted until 2012 rejected it. Vintage Books finally picked it up. It was roundly criticized as being too tough; the story was described as a "political horror story" and not realistic at all. But Elijah strongly identified with this story. Reading was a tool Elijah used to build a truth in which he could believe, since everything he'd been told before the war was now seen as a lie.

Elijah popped open his water bottle and took a sip. There were birds chirping in a nearby tree as he started to read.

The central character, Wesley, was the product of growing up with no parents or guidance. He spent lots of time in prison as society's idea of what he deserved for the fate pushed upon him, and he had become hardened as a result.

Elijah felt abandoned by his own family. They were always dismissive of him, happy to see him go as soon as they could. When Elijah went to war, he had been terrified. He'd had to pull himself together and connect with the warrior inside. He realized that he could destroy and kill, much like Wesley. His path may have been different from this fictional hero, but they had arrived at the same mental place.

I live in a world of shit now.

Elijah wanted to find a way out—a way to love, to have family, to be in a community. And he wanted to do it in a way that avoided violence. But he was too much like Vachss's character; violence was what he did best.

Wesley didn't have a Juno.

Elijah had carried the violence of the war back home, but this was the first time it had gotten to a level where it touched Juno. Elijah was violent; it was always a quick answer to big problems. But now . . . now this big problem had started a chain of events he couldn't control. It'd end up hurting Juno, Gabija, and the kids. Elijah refused to lose Juno now.

He'd been choosing to live in the darkness, cutting himself off from the people around him. No one except Juno knew about him, about his heart or soul. Elijah was so far disconnected from the world around him that he was overwhelmed, and no one knew. Now he had attracted that darkness.

I could kill the bikers, if that's what it came to. I know the enemy when I see them, and they're my enemies.

Elijah put the book down. The book brought up too many heavy thoughts for such a cool, breezy day. There was a nice water fountain near the tables, so he refilled his water bottle and sat down to eat lunch, pulling out his sandwich, apple, and a bag of nuts.

There was such a simple pleasure in this sunny day and natural surroundings. Life poured into him from the rustling leaves and drifting clouds, urging him to *live*. Where did this all come from?

He wasn't really living anymore. But more than that, he didn't care to go on living. He wasn't able to kill himself, but he could easily enough let himself be killed.

It would be even better if I were in the midst of a big battle with the Sons of Perdition.

That bloody mess would be washed away from the streets, as would any lingering threat to Juno and his family. He would no longer be a burden on Juno and everyone could just move on. Juno would be upset at first, but after a while he'd be relieved. *Besides, I look better in memory than I do in life.*

This was his commitment now. He just had to figure out a way to do this without letting Juno get involved and hurt.

The hair on the back of his neck stood up. He jumped up, looking around. No one was there.

The breeze picked up, gently guiding the trees around him in their rhythm. Elijah took a deep breath. He was alone. He pressed his palms on the table and turned his head to the sky, closing his eyes and letting the breeze wash over him.

In this position, he felt grounded yet open to the air and the sky above. He wanted to do something good, to take his place in the world. *Surely I must have other skills than killing. I'm not being the best man I could be. I'm so sorry, forgive me.*

He didn't know who he was apologizing to, he was just *sorry*. He was willing to turn away from his violent life, to seek cleansing and help. *I can't control what's happening around me, but I need a way out. A way out of the violence, the danger.*

Maybe the only way was through death.

He stood that way for a long time, feeling the air around him, the solid ground beneath him; he was a conduit of the raw power of the universe, a fragile wire in a massive machine. Suddenly, relief and peace washed over him. He sighed, thanking the unknown.

Elijah lay down on the table with his jacket rolled up under his head. *What if this is the last time I have a day like this? Under the open sky and free.* With that thought, he drifted into a doze.

Someone was speaking to him. He couldn't see them, or hear them—he only *felt* that there was someone speaking to him where he lay.

"You have alternatives, Elijah," the voice said. "Everyone does. You have to choose what you want and what you are willing to pay."

Elijah nodded to himself. *I want the danger to my friend and his family to go away. I'm willing to pay whatever it costs.*

"Are you willing to give up your connection to this earth and the life you are living? Do you really want to pay with your life?"

I am. Life hasn't been so good for me. I am alone except for Juno. I've never been in love, never had a job or a career, never been close to my family. No one seems to really care what happens to me. I can do this one last act of destruction to save Juno.

"What if you are killed before you finish destroying the threat?"

These men have no moral compass. If I get caught and killed first, that's that. I would die doing my best to save the only friend that I have.

"What about Phillip and Rick? What about the internship? What about Selma and the work you two are doing? And Juno himself. His family loves you, Elijah."

It doesn't matter. Those things haven't fixed me yet. They can't.

"It's your choice, but remember that there are alternatives. There is help available to you. There is a way to fight the darkness."

Elijah felt himself being shown his life and his present world. He saw the faces of his new friends and how they looked at him. They seemed to really care about him. Rick had a small, sad smile on his face, like he was pained by what he saw when looking at Elijah—but out of love, not pity.

Elijah woke from the dream. He sat up, agitated. He felt the strong need to pedal down to Juno's house. He wouldn't share his ultimate plans with him, but Elijah could work with him to find a way to stop the Sons of Perdition. It was turning into a life-or-death situation, and Elijah wanted to ensure that Juno walked out of this on the life side of the conflict.

35

JUNO'S HOUSE

Juno was working at home. The fire had taken out some of his inventory, but the only thing he truly lost was his office. That was OK, short term. His home PC and phone let him keep in contact with his vendors and clients no problem. He'd been spending the morning emailing and calling his contacts to explain his capacity problems while the warehouse was being rebuilt when the doorbell rang.

He quickly saved his spreadsheet and went down to answer it. It was the two cops from the biker case. Juno's stomach sank. He had initially felt comfortable around the officers because they shared his dark skin—but he was well aware of the problems in the OCPD and how they handled the public, particularly black men. If they were back again today, it could only mean trouble.

Juno nodded at the officers. The woman—Officer Thomas—removed her sunglasses. She was the only one smiling.

"Good day, Mr. Valdas," said Sergeant Marks. "Can we come in?"

"Good morning. Of course." Juno didn't move out of the doorway. "What's the occasion?" He kept his voice light, untroubled. He wasn't going to be bullied by these two.

"Just wanted to go over some details, ask a few questions. Just a chat. Got a few minutes?"

"Sure." Juno stepped aside and let the officers in, leading them to the dining room. "Coffee?"

"Yes, please," said Officer Thomas.

Sergeant Marks sat at the head of the table. "That'd be great."

Juno entered the kitchen to start a big pot of his favorite Blue Bottle Coffee. The officers were still in sight of him, something he was sure they appreciated. He sliced a Lithuanian potato babka and put it on a tray.

"It'll be ready in a few minutes," he said, putting the tray in front of the officers. "This is babka. Potatoes and onions in bread. Homemade. It usually has bacon in it, but my vegetarian friend is over so often I stopped adding it."

Officer Thomas took a slice. "That's very thoughtful of you."

"It's the least I can do. I want to thank you all for everything you're doing to help me. You and the fire department have really come to my aid. I appreciate it."

Sergeant Marks gestured for Juno to sit before folding his hands and leaning forward. "Mr. Valdas, we stopped by to talk about your involvement in the trouble between you and the Sons of Perdition."

Juno nodded slowly. He had been expecting this. "Do I need a lawyer for this conversation?"

Marks leaned back in his chair. "You always have a right to representation if you feel that you need it. Today's visit is just a fact-finding mission. I've got some questions and if at any time you are uncomfortable answering them, just tell us and we'll stop. If you feel you need a lawyer now or anytime during the conversation just say so."

Juno huffed, amused. *If I show any sign of discomfort with their questions, it'll only point to my guilt.* "Go ahead and ask your questions. Let me get the pot of coffee and some mugs and I'll be right back."

Juno got another tray and put a cheese babka on it—everyone loved his cheese babka—along with three mugs and the coffee pot. He set it all up and then sat back and waited. The officers seemed to be relaxed and enjoying the food and drink. He nodded at them to start.

Marks said, "We're able to say that it is likely that the fire at your warehouse was arson. We think it was an act of retribution by the SOP for you killing Penny Garlitz. Did you know Mr. Garlitz before the incident?"

Juno shook his head. "No, sergeant. I wasn't aware of the gang when I went to help. I told you, I was driving by the apartment complex the day of the attack. I know Roxanna through her brother, Hector. He's a longshoreman who works with a friend of mine. I was driving back from some chores and when I went past her complex, I saw a man attacking a woman. I didn't know it was Roxanna at the time, but I don't live in a world where it's OK to beat women."

Officer Thomas asked, "Excuse me, Mr. Valdas, but what did you do with your car? How far did you have to run?"

Juno handed her another slice of cheese babka. The young officer had already had two cups of coffee. "I pulled it over to the curb and jumped out. I had to run through a gate to get in the lot, but it was opened by a car coming out. I just wanted to tackle the man and break up the fight, but when I got close the attacker had Roxanna by the throat, her feet off the ground. When he saw me coming, he dropped her and put a knife to her throat. I didn't hesitate, I just dove into him."

Juno took a sip of his own coffee. Officer Thomas was taking notes. "I pushed the weapon out of the way and when he went to strike me I retaliated. I went to grab him with my right hand, but my fist snapped across his windpipe and crushed it. I was going to get my hand around his neck from behind and pull him to the ground. Hitting his throat was just something that happened in the confusion. He had started moving fast toward me with a lot of aggression. His weight added to mine had just caused a massive impact at his throat."

Marks nodded. "That's consistent with your initial statement. Ms. Ramirez said this guy had been stalking her and that she was afraid for her life. Did she tell you about that?"

"No. She and I had never talked before this. I've talked to her brother a couple of times, but never to her. I'm so glad I was there for her, but sorry that it turned out so bad." He added that last part quickly, though that's how he genuinely felt. Elijah wasn't supposed to have let that night end like that.

Marks nodded again, a small smile on his lips. "What kind of car did you say you were driving that day?"

36

THE INTERROGATION

Shana could see that Juno was getting hot. Marks was turning it into an interrogation. She half-expected Juno to stop and ask for a lawyer, but he didn't.

"My car?" Juno asked.

Marks leaned in. His coffee was untouched. "We're trying to develop a timeline of that night for our lieutenant. If you could just show us your car, that would fill in a chunk of time we're missing. It'd let us figure out how long it took you to cross the parking lot and reach the biker and your friend, Ms. Ramirez."

"She's not my friend," Juno said, a little too quickly.

Marks pulled out his laptop, where Shana knew he had the security footage from that night. "You see," Marks continued, "we have this footage from the CCTVs of the property, and we can't seem to get a glimpse of your car that night."

Juno sat up and smiled. "More coffee for either of you?" He turned to Shana. "Did you like the coffee?"

Shana nodded her head eagerly and held up her cup. "It was wonderful, thank you. What kind of coffee do you brew?"

Over the rim of her offered cup, Shana met Marks's furious

glare. She slouched a little in her chair. *Shit.* She'd just broken the interrogation, allowing Juno to wiggle out of the pressure Marks had been building.

She could feel the blush creeping up her neck. *Stop it. Officers don't blush.*

"Back home we put some ground acorns in the coffee blend," Juno said. "That's what you're tasting. I'll go make us all some more." He scooped up all the cups and pot onto the tray and was gone before anyone could object.

Marks said nothing. He leveled Shana with a cold glare.

"It was good coffee," Shana muttered, breaking his gaze. "We drink our fair share of shitty coffee at the station. The acorn touch is cool."

Marks took a deep breath, then another. He exhaled his anger and put his hand on her wrist. She flinched. "Shana, we're supposed to see if we can crack this guy, see if the biker walked into a premeditated trap made by Valdas. Maybe he would say something about an ongoing feud with the bikers. I was closing him into a logical box to get him to break. He was going to break. We don't know if he had a car that day. What if he rode over to the apartment with Ramirez? What if she dropped him on the sidewalk and then walked into the biker's trap just to draw the attack so Valdas could run in and kill him? What about that, Shana?"

The coffee pot in the kitchen started to gurgle, the hot water percolating through the fragrant grounds. Shana glanced over at Juno, who was busily making more babka.

"You could communicate better with me, sergeant. I'm sorry for not knowing what your secret plans were."

She immediately wished she could take that back. Secret plans? It was an interrogation. What a lame thing to say.

Marks blew out his cheeks. "I was this close, Shana. We could've moved this whole investigation forward. If the four murders are connected, we could've been a big part of solving one of the biggest mysteries our department's ever seen."

"Well, fuck then."

Marks just shrugged.

The kitchen's back door opened. A man had entered the house, talking quietly to Juno. Shana cocked her head. With a quick hand signal, Marks led the way into the kitchen to investigate.

37

JUNO'S FRIEND

There was a man in the kitchen with Juno shedding his bike gear. Not a motorcycle, but a cyclist.

The new man smiled when they entered the room, as if thinking of a joke. "Oh, I'm sorry for just walking in without calling first. I didn't know you were busy." He addressed Juno, though he continued to watch Shana and Marks. "Are you working on the warehouse troubles?"

Juno put his hand on the man's arm. "This is Sergeant Marks and Officer Thomas. We were discussing the root issue of the fire, in a way."

Marks crossed the room and reached out to shake hands with the man. "Come on in. You're welcome to stay. Are you a friend of Mr. Valdas?"

You're welcome to stay. Shana raised an eyebrow. *That's subtle.*

The man held Marks's hand firmly. He stared into the eyes of the sergeant, and Shana saw Marks blink in discomfort. "Yes, sir. We served together in the army and came home together. He's my best friend."

This must be McCoy. Shana resisted the urge to place her hand on her Glock. This soldier emanated danger. It was something in his eyes, a fierce disregard for consequence or greater power.

Shana quickly ran down the list of weapons they had with them. Glocks, Tasers, batons, handcuffs, pepper spray, SWAT knives, and ankle backups. It didn't feel like enough.

If they fucked with Valdas, McCoy would kill them. No doubt about it.

She took a step to the right to put a space in between her and Marks so that McCoy couldn't kill them both with one motion. He really did seem that dangerous. Valdas was a decorated Ranger, but she didn't really see him as a killer. Now they were in the presence of a man who was born to kill. He looked at them with no fear in his eyes, more ready than worried.

McCoy looked at the coffee pot, releasing some of the tension. "This is almost ready. Maybe I can sneak a small cup out of this, if that's OK?"

Shana almost jumped when she realized that Juno had stepped away so that the officers were between the two veterans. That was a mistake.

Shaking it off, she said, "We just heard that the good taste is from acorns. That's cool."

She edged her way out of the trap. McCoy smiled and nodded at her. So he knew.

Marks asked, "Didn't catch your name. You said you and Mr. Valdas served together?"

He hasn't figured it out yet. Marks was brilliant, but sometimes . . .

"Elijah McCoy, sir." He smiled.

Marks stiffened. "We've heard your name. We did a background check on Mr. Valdas when we were checking his story out and I think I heard a story that you may have saved Mr. Valdas's life in the war. Is that right?"

McCoy looked almost embarrassed. Why was that? "Juno and I fought together for six years. We saved each other's lives a hundred times."

Marks looked at each of them. "I think we heard a very dramatic story about you dragging Mr. Valdas off the field of fire and protecting him for four hours until help arrived. That true?"

McCoy shook his head. Juno asked, "Who did you hear that from?"

Shana made it to the other side of the kitchen, now in position to counter any attack from the two soldiers. She rested her hand on the top of her Glock; she was ready. McCoy glanced at her, but his body language didn't change. A chill ran down her. He was confident, unconcerned with her movements. That said something about a man.

Marks shrugged off the question. "Our lieutenant has asked us to find you, Mr. McCoy. We'd like to ask you to come down to the station with us so he can talk to you. Just some questions. Is there anything preventing you from coming along with us right now?"

Shana watched with interest as Juno and McCoy exchanged looks. Juno's lips were a thin line, a pleading look in his eye. McCoy gave a small nod—his chin hardly moved, but Shana had been watching for it—and said, "I can come with you."

"Excellent. You can ride with us." Marks turned and led the way to the front door. Shana lagged behind, intending to follow McCoy.

McCoy clasped a hand on Juno's shoulder as he passed his friend. "It's my turn to look out for you. Stand easy, brother."

38

THE MAN WITHOUT LIMITS

Shana was still shaking from the ride to the station with Elijah McCoy in the backseat. He didn't do anything, or say anything, really. His presence was just really unnerving.

McCoy now sat alone in Lieutenant Culver's office while Shana and Marks briefed the lieutenant about this chance pickup. She could see him through the open blinds of the office, sitting erect, breathing deeply. He looked oddly comfortable in the station.

Marks had just finished detailing their trip to Valdas's home to the lieutenant. Culver turned to Shana. "Anything to add, Thomas?"

"That's all correct, sir. McCoy gives off a weird feeling, if you ask me."

"How's that?"

Shana looked to Marks, who shrugged. He felt it too, but it was hard to explain. "Valdas seems like a normal guy. Nice home, loving family, good hospitality, excellent coffee."

"Thomas . . ." Culver warned. "To the point."

"McCoy's not like that." She shrugged. "He doesn't seem to know any limits."

Marks folded his arms. "When I shook hands with McCoy, he looked straight into me. No fear of the law, no worry of our presence. He just held onto my hand and stared me down, challenging me. Like he could kill me before Thomas could draw her weapon."

"He's a killer, sir." Shana nodded. "He still is."

"If there's a case to be made about the four murders," Marks said, "he's your guy. The idea of a man killing known criminals with his bare hands is very believable with him. I felt it. If we can find the evidence to convict him, the city would win the trial, no problem."

Marks put his laptop on the desk. "Check this out."

Shana followed the lieutenant around the desk to stand behind Marks. He pulled up the surveillance videos from the CCTV cameras. "I was just about to show these pictures to Mr. Valdas when McCoy showed up. That's a Ford Focus pulling up to the curb, after Valdas was done talking to the officers on scene." He clicked to a new picture. "He gets in the vehicle and drives off. If Valdas was driving home from errands, why did he get picked up?"

"Why didn't you press the question?" Culver asked.

Marks gave a quick glance at Thomas. "We were interrupted."

Culver nodded. Shana released a breath to herself. He obviously thought Marks was talking about McCoy's arrival, not anything she had done. Culver leaned over the laptop screen. "Who's the driver?"

Marks gestured behind him. "He's in your office."

Lieutenant Culver looked at the frozen image, a frown on his thoughtful face. "Do you have images of the attack itself?"

"No, there were parked cars blocking the attack. Valdas ran up from the other side of the vehicles, out of sight. If there was anyone with him, he'd be unseen as well. You can only see Garlitz hitting the ground when he was struck down."

Culver straightened, a groan escaping his lips. He had a hard time moving around these days, Shana noted. "Time to talk to this soldier. Marks, follow me to my office."

"Do you not want an interrogation room, sir?"

Culver shook his head. "I have some questions I don't want on public record."

"But sir," Shana protested. "If McCoy really did kill these four men, then he's extremely dangerous. The truck driver was dead before he hit the ground, the biker was armed and worked up but stopped breathing as soon as Elijah got within arm's reach, and the two men in the warehouse were trying to get away when they died. Do you think your office is the safest place?"

"Thomas, don't question my decisions again," Culver said sternly. "Yes, I'm aware. That's why I want you sitting outside the door, ready for anything. Got it?"

"Yes, sir. Sorry, sir." Shana did her best to stand straight. She was sure the lieutenant hadn't considered his safety, only his machismo. If she had to be scolded to save her lieutenant's life, then so be it.

Marks put his Taser in his pocket and handed Shana his Glock. "I don't want him to be able to get to it."

Culver led the way to his office, doggedly followed by Marks and Shana. A few other officers in the bull pen looked at them, curious, but they knew not to bother the lieutenant's work. Culver shook hands with McCoy when he entered his office, Marks settling in the back corner to take notes. "Nice to meet you, Mr. McCoy," Culver said. "Anything I can get you? Coffee? Water?"

"No," said Elijah. "Let's get started."

Culver closed the door behind him, leaving Shana in the quiet hallway. She took a position by the door to the outside, ready to respond. She had her Glock in her hand, Taser charged, ankle backup good to go. Her SWAT knife was in her pocket, and her pepper spray and baton were strapped to her belt. She had a direct line to the gun cabinet for a shotgun if needed. It was quiet so far in the lieutenant's office.

She was breathing like she'd run all the way back to the station.

39

THE CONFESSION

Elijah sat in the lieutenant's wooden desk chair, watching the large man settle in his own plush leather chair. The officer from Juno's house was sitting behind him, armed with some kind of weapon, no doubt. Did they think they were being clever?

"Thanks for coming in, Mr. McCoy. We're concerned about the safety of your friend Mr. Valdas. We have some theories on the events happening to him of late and wanted to see if you know anything about it. The stalker that attacked Roxanna Ramirez was a hardened criminal. He had been arrested several times for selling drugs, fighting, and general mayhem in the community. He was known as an enforcer for his club, the Sons of Perdition."

"You mean gang," Elijah said.

Culver sighed. "Yes. From what we've gathered, the gang really respected him. We believe that because Mr. Valdas killed this man, the Sons of Perdition tried to burn his warehouse to the ground. They aren't very good arsonists apparently, and we have an excellent fire department. They came back. I think you were one of the people who called that return visit in. Is that right?"

Elijah had his hands folded in his lap. He nodded. "I was one of the people who called that in. We were impressed with the quick response."

Culver looked at Marks and then again at Elijah. "The man we arrested that night was a known member of the Sons of Perdition. They call him Aryan. He had a bomb. That sounds like an escalation to me. It wasn't successful, and we believe there will be other actions taken until the Sons of Perdition are satisfied in their revenge. Do you understand?"

Elijah nodded and sat up straighter. "That can't happen, lieutenant. I owe my life to Juno and I can't allow anything bad to happen to him or his family."

Culver looked sternly at Elijah. "Can't, or won't?"

Elijah didn't answer.

"You called the police when you saw the bike outside the warehouse, as you should have. That was the right thing to do."

Elijah stared at the lieutenant. He knew he was making the man uncomfortable, but a part of him enjoyed the subtle power. He leaned forward and Culver leaned back. There was the scrambling sound of Marks pulling something out of his pocket—the hidden weapon, presumably.

"I know that it's very hard to be a police officer in this complicated legal world." Elijah spoke in a slow, calm voice. "You must be frustrated with all the rules sometimes. You're faced with known criminals doing bad things to good people, but you have to wait until they're done before you can move to arrest them. I don't know if I could have that restraint."

Elijah noticed the small sweat stains sprouting under Culver's arms. He smiled.

Culver wet his lips. His body was afraid, but his voice and face were calm. Elijah admired men like that. "You're right, Mr. McCoy, but that is our choice. In order for us to have any hope of living in a civilized city, we have to hold on to the legal process. Everyone has a right to live their lives until they do something illegal. We have to do it this way."

The tension in the room pressed upon Elijah like a humid summer's day. The hairs on the back of his neck were pricked, sensing Marks's fear more than anything else.

He's here to protect Culver. I'd have to kill Marks first and then use his body as a shield to move toward the lieutenant.

Elijah's heart was cold, hard. He would prevail here if that became necessary. Or he could let them kill him. Use this final act to find the release from his sad and lonely life, the life that he felt would never get any better. He'd have to give them a reason to justify killing him. He had to give them a real fear for their lives.

But that would have to wait for now.

He had one more job to do before he could make his exit from this battlefield. He held himself still so that everyone would stay in position. He looked at the lieutenant. "This has gone far enough, lieutenant. I've got something important to tell you, so listen up."

Elijah heard Marks stand behind him.

Culver said, "Go ahead and tell me."

"I've gotten information about the gang and Juno, information that I've acted on. I think you know that I was there with Juno at the stalker attack." He paused a moment to gauge their reactions. Yes, they'd known that. "There was another man, Orville Forester, who had a contract out on Juno. I say 'was' because I know he's dead. He and his bodyguard."

Culver and Marks exchanged looks. "How do you know this?"

"Because I killed them. In a warehouse at the end of Pier 51 last Friday. Hold on lieutenant, just sit there for another minute." Culver had started to rise from his chair. "Forester was an intermediary for the bikers. He asked me to be the hit man to kill Juno. That turned out to be a bad choice for them."

Culver frowned, his eyes alert. "Are you a hit man, Mr. McCoy?"

Elijah let out a bark of a laugh. Marks had taken a step toward Elijah, setting himself and the lieutenant up for a horrible crossfire mistake. Elijah gestured a hand behind him. "Have Marks sit back down before you two hurt each other. No, I'm not a hit man, but I was invited to become a permanent partner in that field."

Culver looked a little speechless. He rustled with his paperwork for a bit, then cleared his throat. "In order to verify what you just said about Forester and his bodyguard, let me ask you how you killed them."

Elijah leaned forward and laid his hands on the desk. "I reached out my hands and took their lives away from them. The bodyguard died from a head injury and had a badly broken knee. Mr. Forester died as a result of a choke hold."

Culver was staring at Elijah's hands. "Are you going to fight your way out of here, Mr. McCoy?"

"No, sir. I'm hoping that I can work with you to kill the Sons of Perdition before they hurt my friend. I could do it alone, but I want to stop this war that won't let me go. I want to come home, even if it's to a prison. I have information for you and I'm willing to work with you as a plant if you want."

Culver stood up very carefully. Elijah mimicked him. Culver said, "I think it's time that we moved into an interrogation room where we can record the rest of this conversation. Will you come with us?"

Elijah was a torrent of emotion. He was relieved to share his crimes, the ultimate dedication to his brother Juno in his eyes. But he was also worried about going to jail. He was electrified with emotion and close to shedding a tear.

Once Culver, Marks, and Thomas were settled in the interrogation room with Elijah and everything was recording, they started in again with the lieutenant listing the people in the room, the time and date, and then proceeding.

Culver said, "We are treating the death of Garlitz, Forester, and his bodyguard Arias as connected. Should we go back further than that? Are there any other incidents that are connected to these three deaths, Mr. McCoy?"

The interrogation room was well lit, nothing like the ones in the movies. It was Spartan, with only the table, chairs, and recording devices between the four walls, but the room itself wasn't menacing. It was like a bachelor's first apartment, in a way. There was a water cup for each of them.

"Not that I know of, sir. I was aware that Roxanna Ramirez was being stalked. Her brother told me about it." That wasn't true. Roxanna had hired Elijah to confront Garlitz, but Elijah didn't want to get her in trouble. "Hector and I work together sometimes. We've become friends of a sort. When he told me about the situation with his sister I just couldn't allow a lowlife to have any power over a good person like Roxanna. She was very worried. We went to her home on the day he was waiting for her and the rest is, well, you know."

"Who did what during the altercation with Garlitz?" Culver asked.

Elijah explained the sequence of events as honestly as he could, including a few hand demonstrations.

Marks nodded. "That's what we've seen on the CCTV. Did you know about the fire at the warehouse before it happened?"

Elijah said he didn't. "We didn't know anything about the bike gang until after the fire. We just thought we were dealing with an asshole."

Culver crossed his arms and leaned back in his chair. "What happened after the fire that drew you into confrontation with Forester and Arias?"

Elijah scratched his cheek. He was beginning to get some stubble. He'd need to shave soon. "I was approached by a man who said he knew Forester and had been asked to find a hit man to kill Juno. Forester ran drugs and prostitution. He used the bike club for delivery and other work."

"Why use Forester? The gang's done plenty of hits themselves."

Elijah shook his head. "The gang was too angry, they were getting reckless. Too many bikers taken out by the police would've been bad for Forester's business. He volunteered to help."

The three officers exchanged looks. Elijah couldn't tell if this was something they had already known or not.

"Mr. McCoy." The female officer spoke up. "Who wanted Forester dead? That doesn't make sense. If Forester had approached you directly because he heard you were a killer, and you killed *him* when he told you about Juno, that's one thing. But Forester was his own man. How does this other person relate to all this?"

Elijah shrugged. He wasn't being aloof, it was just difficult trying to describe a person like Lamb. "I don't have much more than a name for you. B. A. Lamb. No first name, just initials. He's over six feet tall, Caucasian, around two hundred pounds. He's always dressed in expensive-looking clothes. He's very good at covering himself—I haven't been able to track him. He first found me at a Peet's Coffee, then again at my gym. He knew everything about me. I've tried to get him to leave me alone, but when he told me the hit was on Juno I had to deal with it."

"So you took the job." Culver spoke. It wasn't a question.

"No. I went on my own, unbeknownst to him." *Though he met me there anyway.* "I wasn't paid, wasn't contracted. It was a personal threat to a friend, that's all."

Marks asked, "How'd he find you in the first place?"

"I'm pretty good at sensing when I'm being followed, and I felt something for a few days before he walked into the Peet's. He said he'd been watching me and that he wanted to start a long-term, professional relationship with me as a hit man."

"And what'd you say to that?"

"I told him to fuck off in every language I know—still do, whenever I see him."

Culver leaned across the table. "But why you? Did he give a reason?"

"No, sir. But I'm glad they asked me and not someone else. It saved Juno's life."

Culver sighed, rubbing his temples with his right hand. "McCoy, you could've come to us and worked with us to entrap Forester—maybe even Lamb. This isn't a one-man battle."

"I know." Elijah wet his lips. "That's why I want to work together. To save Juno and his family."

"As a plant, yes. It seems like this Lamb guy is our key to breaking the Sons of Perdition. Do you think you could see him again?"

"Sure." That would be easy enough. It seemed like all Elijah had to do was think about him and he showed up.

"Good." Culver stood up, as did the other officers. "Work him for information. I want to know what the Sons of Perdition are up to and see if we can nail them. Find out what their operations are. A few dozen arrests would be good for this city."

"Or maybe we could get lucky and end up in a huge shoot-out where you and I kill most of them—legally." Elijah smiled. It was a fun thought.

Culver took a deep breath. Apparently not so funny to him. "Fuck, McCoy. This isn't a game. Follow the law. We're going to let you go today. You run, we'll arrest Juno and charge him for your crimes. You fail to check in with me daily, we'll put Juno behind bars. Gather information and bring it to me directly. My people, not you, will be involved in any and all contact with the Sons of Perdition. If there is any battle it will involve us. Got that?"

If I run, Juno's life is ruined. No, he wouldn't let that happen. He'd see this out to the end. "Yes, sir. Understood."

Culver turned to leave the interrogation room, his officers flanking him. "And McCoy? We're not done with you."

40

B. A. LAMB

Elijah walked out of the police station alone. He stood for a moment in the cool night air, letting the darkness wash over him. Soothe him.

I could easily fade into the night and disappear. I don't need Lamb's help to do that. If he wanted to be an executioner, he could manage all the details himself. *Maybe when all this is over. After Juno is safe.*

He walked down to the corner where a little twenty-four-hour coffee shop called On Duty sat. He went to a booth in a dark corner to sit and think, ordering a cup of coffee, a fried egg sandwich, and some hash browns. He was alone when he sat down, but wasn't surprised to look up after ordering and find Lamb sitting quietly in the booth next to him.

Perfect.

Elijah allowed himself to put an arm on the seat back and turn to smile at this specter of the night.

Lamb returned the smile. "Boy, you walked right into the police's hands when you went to visit Juno. What an awful surprise, hmm?"

Elijah shrugged. "Nothing I couldn't handle."

"Did you see how the police were scared of you? Oh." Lamb put a hand to his chest. "It moves me. This is what I'm talking about, Elijah—you're a natural! There are lots of people who do activities that society labels as bad behavior, things like burglary, rape—even murder. Most of those people are just visiting the realms in which I operate. We're happy to have them, but they are, and always will be, just visitors. You, on the other hand, are . . ."

"A resident?" Elijah frowned. "Are you saying that I'm actually a part of the 'realms' in which you operate? Just call it the under-world like a normal criminal."

The back corner of the diner seemed to recede into the dark night, the line between night and diner blurring.

"You know you are." Lamb took a sip of his coffee. Elijah hadn't even seen a waitress deliver it to him. "We're talking about what is already true about you, not asking you to make a decision to come visit. So how did the visit to the station work out? You told Juno you had this under control. What's your plan?"

"The police have rules that bind them. Anything they do is going to take a long time. All I have to do is sit quietly and not give any real answers, information, or acknowledge anything. I don't think they can manage the details here. They're showing CCTV videos and stuff, but they don't know what they're looking at or for. They had a picture of my Focus, but didn't even realize it's my car. They haven't gotten to asking Juno about the truck driver or the warehouse deaths. I don't think they have him in their crosshairs for those. It really seems like they don't want to catch Juno for anything. It'll blow over."

A lot of that was true, to an extent.

Lamb's smile faded into a serious grimace. "But what's *your* plan, Elijah McCoy?"

Elijah sipped his coffee. "I'm not worried about the police. But I am worried about the Sons of Perdition and their plans for Juno. It'd be nice if I could get the police to blow up that club."

Lamb nodded. He was weighing Elijah's words, he could see.

Trying to figure out how genuine the soldier was being. "There's plenty of room for destruction and sadness here in this city. I'm impressed with your ability to bluff. You're coldhearted, my friend. It's a shame you couldn't be a part of the Sons of Perdition. I don't know how we would fix that up now, but you would've been a great replacement for the two men you took out of their ranks."

That's it. That's why I hate them so much.

Elijah had a personal hatred to this gang, holding it closer to him than any other hate he'd experienced. It wasn't just because of Juno, it was more personal than that. And Lamb had just connected the pieces. He was afraid of how similar he was to them.

Elijah didn't naturally gravitate to groups or clubs, but he had their mindset on many things. He went out looking for trouble; he was able to cause real harm and kill people. He was not going to be limited by the laws of the city. In fact, he felt superior to the bikers in that he was a more dangerous entity than they were. He was trained better and more experienced. He wasn't squandering his health on drugs and alcohol.

He looked at Lamb, sitting all smug in his dark booth. *I might even be more dangerous than him, mobster or demon.*

"I'm feeling like some mayhem and destruction is due here," Elijah said. "Not to offend you"—he smirked—"but I'm thinking about killing all of the Sons of Perdition. It would be a good use of my skills. That wouldn't rob you of personnel, would it?"

Lamb looked surprised. "Oh, I never worry about running out of bad people. I've helped this club a good deal over the years but I owe them nothing. It might be fun for you and I to work together to kill this group just to show them never to trust anyone—especially me. I could help you, but then I would own you. You would become my executioner. You and I could build another malevolent force here. We could do so much harm, spread so much sadness, and create a deep loneliness in this city. Are you ready to join me? To admit your true nature?"

"It would be that or get a job." Elijah frowned. It was a

tempting offer. Being a good man was a nice thought, but fighting himself was so hard. If he lived through everything with Juno and the gang, he could embrace his talents. But work with Lamb? "I don't need your help to take this gang down, though."

"Oh, but you will do so much better with my help. I know everything, have eyes everywhere. You need to do this carefully, without drawing attention to yourself. I can help you there. We can take care of this gang, free Juno, and walk away from it all. I've done it before."

Elijah let out a slow, deep breath. There was truth to Lamb's words. Elijah was in over his head, and he didn't trust the police to do a good job. "What do you suggest?"

"There is never a better strategy than to be devious. Lies and false promises are so effective. People want to believe in the goodness of others. They misjudge their own intelligence and experience, which causes them to be so vulnerable. The police don't seem to suspect you—you walked free tonight, after all. I have some information about the gang's next plan that I think the police would love to hear. Take it to them, and make sure they turn it into a firefight. I'd love to see the looks in the bikers' eyes when they realize I betrayed them to the police—so satisfying."

Elijah stared at Lamb. Did he just hear what he thought he did? He wanted Elijah to be a plant in the police station, just as the police wanted him to be a plant with Lamb. Who was he really working with? And what kind of man gets excited about betraying his own people?

"You're interesting, to say the least." Elijah said. "The police are looking for any excuse to take down the gang. I can feed them any kind of lie, but I don't have anything they'd be interested in."

"Oh, what I have isn't a lie." Balaam took another sip of coffee. "I've introduced the gang to some very effective 'henchmen,' as we might call them, in Mexico. This project isn't drugs, not prostitution, not money laundering. This is a new level of success for me. I am so pleased with myself. You know, I knew you'd kill Forester and that it'd create chaos with the Sons of Perdition. It was just the boost I needed to move them into a new area of crime."

"What area?" Elijah had an uneasy feeling about this.

"The Mexican henchmen deal in black market organ sales. They kidnap children and put them in refrigerated truck trailers until they freeze to death, then harvest the organs. It's a booming market with a high demand and oh-so-expensive supply."

Elijah blinked. That wasn't the area of crime he'd imagined for a Californian biker gang. "And you think I'm dark. But won't missing children draw too much attention?"

"Don't think their parents care about what happens to their children. That is not universal, you know. Especially for children of impoverished, drug-addicted parents who see their children as more of a liability than a blessing."

This news was perfect. The police would work with Elijah as he fed them just enough information at a time to keep them moving forward. "There will be hell to pay."

Lamb shuddered. "Isn't it exciting?"

"What kind of a timeline are we talking about?"

"The Mexican gang is bringing trucks up here in three weeks for the pickup. It'll be a mass kidnapping, all in one day. The bikers are already tracking down potential victims. Once the trucks leave Oakland for the harvest, the bikers will scatter. It'll be the last you'll see of them for several months. This is going to be beautiful. When the media goes to the parents to get their grieving response, they'll get apathy half the time. What a marvelous kicker to all the saps following this story. No one cares about these children."

Elijah held up his hands. "Stop. I'm not getting myself involved in killing a large number of innocent children. That's not me."

"Of course not. You're going to make sure the innocent children are safe by killing a large group of malevolent bastards. Still, lots of death and sadness." Lamb smiled.

Elijah nodded, distracted. It was a lot to take in. "I've got my source, and I've got my information. We're done here."

Lamb stood, dusting the front of his pants. "You remind me of one of my favorite accomplices, Antoine Rasseneux. Heard of him? No? He was active from 1855 to 1871 in Algeria. What a wonderful place, Algeria. One of my boss's favorite vacation spots. Rasseneux was one of the most famous executioners in history, and such a wonderful technician. You're in that mold. I look forward to working with you, Elijah."

Lamb turned and walked down the dark hallway to the back of the diner. There were no exits that way. As he left, the heavy atmosphere receded and Elijah saw the waiter coming with his food. He had forgotten how hungry he was.

The food was cold. As Elijah chewed on the rubbery eggs, he thought about everything that'd happened that day. It was overwhelming. There was so much to digest, so much to do. He wanted to talk to someone about it, but who? Juno wasn't the right man, not this time. Not when so much of it all revolved around him. And he'd left his bike at Juno's house. Fuck. How was he getting home at this hour? It was almost ten.

Elijah pulled out his phone and dialed. "Hey, Rick? It's Elijah. I know it's kind of late, but I'm stranded by the police station and need a ride. No, I'm fine, but could you come pick me up? I . . . I need you."

41

THE SHOWER

E lijah brought two drinks out to the condo balcony. Rick accepted his gin and tonic with a nod of thanks. He was in a white button-down tonight, casual but complementary.

"So the police want you to try and infiltrate a gang?" Rick asked. It was the third time he'd asked that question since picking Elijah up.

Elijah settled himself into the patio chair next to him. "Not the gang, just this loose cannon calling the shots."

"Do you really think you should be doing this? It could be dangerous."

Elijah sipped his Bulleit Bourbon. *Danger is the point.* "I know."

"Elijah." Rick put a tentative hand on Elijah's knee. Elijah looked at his concerned face. "Are you OK? You seem upset."

"You can tell?"

Rick smiled. "Of course I can tell. I know when you're happy, and when you're troubled. You look *very* troubled. What's wrong?"

"Nothing." Elijah looked out over the balcony's view of Jack London Square. The well-lit palm trees were rustling in the night air, and the faint voices of late-night shoppers drifted on the breeze along with the melodic lapping of the bay. He'd miss nights like these, if he went away.

Rick squeezed his knee. "Elijah," he whispered.

"It's just . . . I have a hard time justifying my existence." As he spoke, Elijah kept his eyes fixed on the square below. He could feel Rick's stare boring into him. "What am I doing with my life? I've killed people, I've broken the law—and to be honest, Rick, I don't feel bad about it. It was all necessary. But I can't even feel remorse like a normal civilian. And now I've endangered my best friend. I'm always more trouble than I'm worth."

Tears were starting to prick his eyes and the warm lights below blurred. "I can't come home, Rick. I can't leave the theater of war. I was a soldier, a piece of a larger machine. But here, in Oakland, I feel like a piece removed from a machine. I can't function alone. I can't do anything, except kill. I look at my life and the things I've done and I realize that no one would miss me if I was gone. No one cares about me."

The tears spilled over. Elijah looked down and Rick pulled him into an embrace. He buried his head in Rick's chest, breathing deeply through Rick's warm shirt. Rick's smell was comforting. It soothed Elijah's soul like a masculine aromatherapy oil. Rick stroked his hair, allowing Elijah to regain composure.

After a quiet moment, Rick said, "I care about you."

Elijah took a deep breath. "I know." He sat up and looked at Rick. Rick's eyes sparkled, his bronze skin glowing in the city's night-light. His lips were curved in a small smile. They looked as soft as they felt. Elijah put his hand behind Rick's head and pulled him in for a kiss. It lasted for several minutes, and when Elijah pulled away it felt like he was floating on the balcony.

Rick looked elated. It was as if something had changed for him, like he had finally solved a long-elusive riddle. He stood and offered his hand. "Follow me."

Elijah took it and got up from his chair. "Where are we going?"

Rick gave a sultry smile. "To go shower."

With that, Rick turned around and led Elijah into the bathroom. Rick had been to the condo before plenty of times to visit Phillip; he didn't need to be told where to go. Once in the bathroom, Rick closed the door and stepped up to Elijah. Elijah's heart was racing in his chest. He was so close. One deep breath would push his chest against Rick's.

Elijah held Rick's gaze as Rick began to unbutton his shirt. He was completely undressed in under a minute, his pants and shirt folded and his pocket things placed neatly on the counter. He didn't look at Elijah, he just walked into the bath and started the shower.

Elijah smiled. He was really turned on.

This was good, almost too good to be true. He really wanted this to happen, but he wasn't sure what to do now.

For starters, get in the shower.

Elijah undressed and stood for a moment, staring at Rick in the shower. He'd had fantasies of Rick before, but this was better than anything he'd imagined. Elijah stepped in behind him.

Rick was well soaked by now, ready for a wash. He stepped out of the way, gesturing for Elijah to get under the water. He did. Rick put his arms around Elijah in a tight embrace from behind. Elijah pushed back into it. Rick bent over and started nuzzling and kissing Elijah's neck. Elijah felt a tingle go down his spine. It helped to relieve some of the tension about what was going to happen.

Rick let go of Elijah and leaned down and pumped some soap into his hands.

"OK, step out of the water," Rick murmured.

Elijah complied. Rick started to wash Elijah's shoulders and back. Elijah couldn't remember anyone ever washing his back before. Rick took his time, exploring Elijah's body with his hands. The soap felt nice on his skin. He paid close attention to Rick's movements, noting the care he took on Elijah's chest, his navel, his thighs. Everything but the one standing beacon of Elijah's passion. It was driving him crazy.

"Make sure you do a good job below the waist," Elijah said. He was short of breath, barely able to focus. "You know that boys can be stinky."

They both laughed. It helped ease some of Elijah's tension, but the anticipation was still building for him, pressing against his skin.

Rick slid his hand down Elijah's abdomen, cradling Elijah's delicates in his soapy hands. Elijah gasped. He was tight, sensitive. Rick's adroit fingers sent a shock of pleasure, almost painful, throughout Elijah's body. He found Rick's mouth with his own and kissed him, allowing the energy buzzing in him to transfer to Rick.

When they separated, both men were gasping.

"My turn," breathed Elijah.

Elijah was burning with desire, but he didn't want to go too fast. He lathered his hands in soap, trying to devise a plan through his drunken thoughts. That's what this feeling was: intoxicating. He wanted to devour Rick with his eyes and hands, to do for him what he'd just done for Elijah.

Rick was facing the stream of hot water, his glorious back exposed to Elijah. He loved the curve from Rick's shoulder to his neck. He washed down to Rick's somewhat soft—but very cute—butt and worked his way up the back of his thighs and calves. Elijah's excitement continued to build.

"Turn around," he said. Rick turned and looked at Elijah with his soft brown eyes. They were both breathing deeply.

Elijah reloaded some soap on his hand and started to massage Rick's chest, over his shoulders and down each arm, under them, rejoining on Rick's firm chest. He took his time, partly to let the passion build and partly because he really wanted to remember each detail of this first intimacy. Elijah washed his way down to Rick's abdomen. Rick had a very prominent indicator that he was enjoying the experience. Elijah washed that indicator really well, not teasing Rick the way he'd been teased. He washed the front of his thighs and shins. Elijah looked up at Rick from where he knelt, noting with pleasure how flushed his face was. With Elijah bent to wash his legs, Rick's indicator was brushing Elijah's face.

They were both so close to just exploding. Somehow, they made it through the rest of the shower. When they were done washing, Rick and Elijah dried each other. They brushed their teeth and walked hand in hand to the bedroom.

Rick slid into the bed first, laying on his side as he watched Elijah. Elijah was watching him, too. Rick looked so good to Elijah. He was looking forward to taking the time to explore to his heart's content. As his mind raced over all the things he wanted to do, his confidence in this night grew.

Rick smiled. "What?"

"You'll stay over tonight, won't you?" Elijah asked.

Rick grinned. "Of course."

Elijah allowed himself to fall on Rick. They started one of their long, sensuous kisses while their bodies entwined from mouth to toe. Elijah felt safe. He trusted Rick and followed his lead, innovating moments as the inspiration came. He allowed his body and mind to do what they wanted. Rick helped where needed to make the evening smooth and beautiful.

It was after midnight when Rick asked, "Can I back into you?"

Their embrace lasted into their dreams.

42

THE SURVEILLANCE

Officer Shana Thomas was in her Crown Vic down the street from McCoy's condominium. The night had been cold, but not very, and she had a blanket in the car for the surveillance. She was going to be fine. The sun was peeking over the high-rises now, and she only had to wait until nine or ten that morning for Sergeant Jamel Marks to relieve her. They'd get a third partner by tomorrow to divide up the shifts while they kept an eye on everything that McCoy did. The third partner would stay out of sight and roam, just to backup the work she and Marks were doing. They still needed to put in the hours so McCoy wouldn't wonder why there were gaps in coverage.

The night had been really quiet. She'd spent most of it using her book light to read her copy of *Debbie Doesn't Do It Anymore* by Walter Moseley. She loved this book. All of Moseley's books were brilliant in her eyes, but this one seemed to touch her more than the others.

I'd love to meet Mr. Moseley someday.

She sighed. Part of her felt bad for spending the night reading, but she'd spent most of her afternoon yesterday digging through the homicide database at Culver's request, searching for any hand-to-hand combat cold cases over the past two years. The lieutenant wanted to see if McCoy could've been responsible for any other deaths in the area.

She got her first call from Sergeant Marks around seven. "You survive the night, Thomas?"

"I'm OK. McCoy's in the condo, and he's not alone."

"Anything dangerous? Is it the Sons of Perdition?"

"No." Shana smiled. "He's up there with someone who spent the night. I don't think they're up yet. The friend's car is still parked in front of the building. It's a one bedroom, isn't it, Marks? Maybe two?"

Marks laughed. "What are you saying, Thomas? You think this guy confesses to murder and then goes home to fuck someone?"

"I saw the light come on a couple different times during the night, so, yes—I think that's exactly what they're doing."

"Well this isn't going to be totally boring, at least. What's she look like? Scary? Gorgeous? Tell me."

Shana looked back up at the balcony. "I got a good look when McCoy got picked up at On Duty, and again when they went in the building. In my opinion, he's gorgeous."

"I don't care what you think about McCoy. What about the girl?"

Shana laughed. "The girl is a he and *he* is the gorgeous one."

Marks sucked in a deep breath. "Get the fuck out of here, Shana Thomas. Stop fucking with me." Shana could hear car doors closing on his end of the line. "I know the night shift is tough, but you're the junior partner here. So tell me about the girl sleeping with McCoy and stop pretending you have a scoop."

Thomas was laughing harder now. "The girl is a *boy*. No shit. I'm telling you, McCoy is upstairs, right now, locked in his condo with another man. Now this fellow could be sleeping in the living room or something, but they hugged real tight when the man picked him up by our station, and they were holding hands when they walked into the building. I wish my husband was so nice to me."

"OK Thomas, I know you have pictures. I'm coming down to sit with you. Get some pictures of this man if he comes out. I'll kick your ass if this is a joke. Shit. Elijah McCoy? The killer? Get the fuck out."

Shana slugged Marks pretty hard in the shoulder when McCoy and the other man came walking out of the building together. They were holding hands, and when they got in the friend's car they kissed. Shana had seen them both out on the balcony earlier with cups of coffee, but that had been before Marks showed up. She didn't want to ruin the surprise.

"Holy fuck." Marks swore, shaking his head. Shana laughed.

The Audi started up and the two men drove off. It was pretty easy to figure out they were on their way to Valdas's house after a few minutes of trailing them.

"I bet he has this guy drop him off a block away," Marks said. "He won't want his Ranger buddy to see this shit."

43

MEET RICK VARGAS

Juno was home alone. Gabija had taken the children to school on their cargo bike then rode to her job. The sound of a powerful car rolled up his street. Juno peered out the kitchen window, curious. A beautiful Audi sat parked in his driveway. Whose car was that?

Elijah stepped out of the passenger side, just as a tall Brazilian man got out of the driver's side. Juno smiled.

Rick—it must be Rick—smiled at Elijah before casting a worried glance up at the house. Elijah shook his head and said something Juno couldn't hear. He rounded the hood of the car to put a hand on Rick's shoulder and together the two men walked up the drive.

Juno jumped back to the coffee pot right before the kitchen door swung open. Rick came through the door first. Juno was careful to do a double take in surprise. Elijah came in close behind. His friend was glowing, absolutely glowing.

Juno couldn't help himself. He went right over and hugged Rick and then grabbed Elijah and shook him.

"Thanks for letting me know you had a ride home last night," Juno said to Elijah, "and that you were out and OK."

Elijah reddened a little. "I'm sorry. I was busy."

Juno glanced at Rick. *I'm sure you were.*

"Well, come on." Juno showed the two men in to his kitchen table. "Hungry?"

"We ate, thank you," said Rick.

"It's nice to see you two this morning." Juno poured a second cup of coffee. "Rick, we've been back from Afghanistan for two years and I've never seen Elijah come walking in to anywhere with another person—especially not first thing in the morning. And I hear he's been out partying recently?" Juno playfully pushed Elijah. "You're having quite the effect on this old soldier. We love having him over, but he can't spend all his time with a first- and third-grader." He grinned. "So, thanks."

Rick blushed. "Phillip and I just adore Elijah. I've been happy to chauffeur him around. We want to help you two with anything—anything at all. You just tell us."

Just chauffeur? Judging from the glow in both their eyes, Juno would say it was little more than driving a car around. He'd pound Elijah for details later. Rick was a good-looking guy.

"I mean, everything that's happening is just terrible," Rick continued. "First the incident with Phillip, and now the police are asking Elijah to be a plant in that gang—"

Juno snapped to focus. "They're what?"

Elijah's face went white.

Yeah, you forgot to mention that, didn't you?

"Well he had to, after confessing to those three murders—which weren't even murders at all, just self-defense. Right, Elijah?"

You could've heard a pin drop in that room.

Juno stared at Elijah, disbelief robbing him of words. He'd confessed to murder? To *three* murders?

Rick must have sensed something was wrong. He stood from

the table. "I'm going to be late for work. I'll talk to you later, Elijah?"

Elijah stood as well. He kissed Rick on the cheek. "Yes. Tonight."

"Pleasure meeting you, Juno." Rick hurried from the kitchen. A moment later, the Audi pulled out of the drive.

Juno was devastated. His stomach had turned to stone and he was boiling. "*Three* murders? What have you done, man?"

Elijah ran his fingers along the groove of the wood table. "I'm fixing my mistakes."

"Elijah, you're throwing your life away!" Juno paced around the kitchen. "This isn't going to save you from anything. I've really tried to help you get things turned around. I want to see you be happy and to live as normal of a life as possible. All you had to do was to sit and not talk. But you *confessed*? What about us, man? What about your new job, your new friends—Rick? You're gonna go to jail, and just throw that all away."

Elijah put his hands up, trying to stop Juno from rampaging. "Hold on, Juno. Let me explain. The police told me they were starting to build a case on you." Juno's eyes popped open. "They had enough information to show that you lied about the biker. They're investigating other cases and think that you might be involved because of the similarities in the manner of death. I'm not going to let my self-destructive actions ruin your life—or your family."

"Did the police tell you all this?"

Elijah looked down. "No. It was Lamb. He said the four murders were all connected by manner of death, and they were looking at you as number one."

"You mean *Balaam*? Damn it, Elijah, you know everything he says is a lie." Juno was fuming, frustration and anger boiling into his words. He couldn't remember the last time he'd been this angry.

"But he's right. You know that if the police go back over any part of the last two years, they could find another dozen similar cases. You know about them. When I talked to them at the station, to the lieutenant, I realized that they were connecting the biker and the two deaths in the warehouse and starting to look at you. So, I told them what I knew about the recent murders."

Juno went to get the coffee pot to have a chance to breathe. He didn't need the extra caffeine, but he served each of them another cup anyway. "What did you tell them? And what the fuck is this about you killing another man?"

"Two men, actually." Elijah accepted the cup from Juno. "The police don't suspect the guy who attacked Phillip. Not yet at least."

"Explain."

Elijah told Juno about the Sons of Perdition and the murderous encounter on Pier 51. He explained the planted bomb, Forester, and the looming threat now hanging over Juno's home.

When he finished, Juno was nodding his head slowly, his eyes unfocused. "Why didn't you tell me this before?"

Elijah frowned. "I just . . . didn't."

Juno sighed. He felt tired—so tired, despite all the coffee. "The police know all this, yes? What was that Rick said about you being a plant?"

Elijah sipped his coffee. "We have to get this gang, Juno. I volunteered to help them get the bikers by using me as a plant with Lamb. They let me go on the condition that I check in every day. They're tailing me even now. When they get the Sons of Perdition, then they'll decide what to do with me."

"You know what they're going to do with you. They're going to put you in jail, but be nice and not give you the death penalty. Then you'll be able to live the next fifty years of your life in a hard-ass prison. This is going to be the end of your freedom. I'll visit you in prison, and bring pictures of the family, and we can pretend you have a life. Fuck, damn, damn, dammit."

Elijah nodded. "The alternative is for you and I to start killing the biker gang. I would love to go in together and blow these fuckers up, but I just can't see us doing it without both of us going down. I have to get rid of the biker gang, and this is the only way I can do that. I need the police to help me, they have a bigger gang."

"And Balaam?"

"I'm using Mr. Lamb, not the other way around. Come on, work with me, Juno."

Juno rubbed his temples. How did Elijah always manage to get into these situations? Everywhere he went, he found himself in impossible scenarios. "This is fucked up."

Elijah moved around to the end of the table to be closer to Juno, who leaned toward him. "But that's not all. Lamb has something else he's up to." He proceeded to detail a horrific kidnap-murder plan. Juno's stomach knotted as he listened, thoughts of his children stuck in a refrigerated truck haunting his mind.

"Oh man, that's horrible." Juno winced. He couldn't help himself. "Shit, I can't stand to even hear that. Fuck, let's go kill those bastards together. Is there any way the police would let us kill those motherfuckers? We'd be money savers for them and the rest of us taxpayers."

"I haven't told the police about it yet. I will this afternoon when I go to check in. You know the Mexican gang and the bikers are going to fight like hell. Hopefully lots of them get killed. We just need to work with the police to get this done."

"Then the police will decide what to do with you." The thought saddened Juno.

"Not just the police. Lamb expects me to be his executioner after this."

Impossible scenarios, every time. "It seemed like we were starting to make improvements for you. How'd we get into this mess?"

Elijah put a hand on Juno's shoulder. "I did this. I was doing bad things and attracted a bad result. The police are nothing. Lamb is our biggest concern, now. He can get me away from the police, but I'd be his executioner from then on."

"Then what, just come home to Rick at the end of the day?"

Elijah smiled at him. "Have some faith, brother. We'll find a way out of this."

Juno smiled a little. "I have faith, but I'm surprised to hear you say that. I'll pray for you, my friend. Actually, this is a situation where only God could help us, I think."

"Sure." Elijah leaned in conspiratorially, a stupid grin plastered on his face. "So, do you want to hear about Rick?"

44

AN EXCHANGE OF TRUST

Sergeant Marks was waiting in the Crown Vic outside. Thomas had taken a cab home when they'd arrived at the house. The overnight visitor had left in his Audi over an hour ago. Finally, McCoy came out of the garage on his Montague Paratrooper folding mountain bike.

How'd he get a military bike home with him? It seemed pretty cool, to be honest.

McCoy put a foot on the pedal and swung himself onto the bike as it rolled down the driveway. He sped down the street from Valdas's house, heading south. Marks started up the cruiser and followed.

When McCoy got to the end of the street, he made a quick left and disappeared into a stairway that dropped down a long block to connect to the street below. Marks stepped on the accelerator and pushed his heavy car down the street, making a hard-right turn and curving quickly down with the road that would bring him to the bottom of the stairs. He should be able to see which way McCoy had gone if he was quick.

Following a bicycle in a city was no easy deal.

The road leading down was narrow and cut into the hillside, so there was a wall on both sides. Marks really couldn't see either way on the street below more than a few feet. He slid the Crown Vic to a stop at the bottom of the decline and leaned around the corner to see if he could catch a glimpse of McCoy. He looked right, and as he scanned across to look left he saw McCoy riding up to him.

McCoy waved and Marks lowered the window. "Hey sergeant, how're you doing?"

Marks frowned, suspicious. "I'm fine."

"I know you guys are following me. Makes sense. Want it to be easier?"

Marks raised his eyebrows. "It's always nice to have help. What do you have in mind?"

McCoy reached out his hand. "Give me your phone, and I'll put my number in."

Marks considered this. McCoy probably wanted to be in charge of his own security detail—he was that kind of veteran. Marks wasn't sure if that was the best idea, but McCoy had been pretty up front with them up to this point. Besides, if he ran, they'd arrest Juno. That'd bring the veteran running back to the station faster than anything.

He consented and handed over his phone. McCoy entered the data and sent himself a text message. "Send me Officer Thomas and Lieutenant Culver's information as well."

That request made Marks hesitate. What would Culver think of Elijah McCoy having his number? *Eh, it's a work number. It's made for these kinds of things.* He went ahead and called out the numbers to McCoy.

"Great." McCoy handed him back the phone. "I'll text you when I move around so you can keep up with me. I don't want either of us to get hurt. Did you guys get a third to split shifts with?"

Marks shook his head. "Not yet. We're supposed to, but if the lieutenant likes this plan better, we might be able to do this with the two of us."

"Sure, just let me know." McCoy smiled and pedaled off. "I'm going to my gym, God's Gym on Broadway at Twenty-Fifth Street. I'll see the lieutenant at four."

Marks wasn't surprised this Ranger was on to him. *I sure hope he's not pulling one on us.* He punched in the gym's address on his navigator started off down the street.

45

INFORMANT

Shana Thomas sat next to Sergeant Marks in Lieutenant Culver's office. She was frowning. "McCoy asked for you to meet him for a drink? At the Misericord? What the hell is that?"

Culver sat with his hands folded on his desk. He was in his characteristic dark grey suit, pristinely pressed as always. "An underground bar. He said he had information for us he wanted to share in private."

Shana raised an eyebrow. "At a bar?"

Culver smiled. "He said he's buying. He obviously knows how this station works. Free drinks work all the time."

Marks and Culver laughed. Shana smiled. She felt like she was finally part of the team.

Marks said, "OK, that's racist—or some other kind of -ist."

"But it works all of the time, right?" Shana asked. She turned to Culver. "Where's this bar? I've never heard of it."

"You're not alone. We're the fucking police and most of us apparently don't know about it." Culver chuckled. "I asked around our detectives with dependable CIs, and only a few had heard of it before. You know the Brick House Condos over in the produce section near Jack London Square?"

"No," Marks said.

Shana nodded. "I do, lieutenant. It's only a couple of blocks from McCoy and his boyfriend's condo."

Marks winced. "That just sounds like a way to get McCoy to drop you like a sack of sand when you say that."

"Only if you mean it cruelly," she replied.

Culver didn't address it. "That's where it is. It's been open for eleven years and is literally underground—very secret."

"Misericord." Marks rolled the word around his tongue. "Is that Latin?"

Culver nodded. "I looked it up. It's the name for a place in medieval monasteries where they took monks to be disciplined. It's also a long slender knife that was used to deliver a deathblow to a fallen knight who was going to die, but not soon. It was slender enough to slide into the eyehole of the helmet, or down the neck of their armor to the heart, or under the arm to the heart."

Shana took a deep breath. As Culver spoke, the image of a fiery gate came to her mind, smoking in darkness, tendrils of anguish intermingling with the ash of eternal damnation. *An underground gate to hell.* Sweat coated Shana's neck and palms.

"Wonderful associations." Marks said dryly. "I don't know if this is a dungeon, a sex club, a bar, a joke, or what. You OK, Thomas?"

Shana shook herself. "It sounds like a gate to hell. How is it that in eleven years, no one has started a brawl, had a complaint about being kept out, or not paid for a drink?"

Marks huffed, amused.

Culver eyed her, concern in his eyes. "It's part of the under-world, Thomas. I'm sure they have other ways of dealing with trouble than going to the law. You and Marks will be out on the street for backup."

"So you're going?" Shana asked, feeling foolish.

Culver looked surprised. "Kidding? This is too strange not to go."

Sergeant Marks patted his belt and said, "I hope you're carrying tonight. Whenever I'm anywhere near McCoy, I feel like I need to have as many weapons as possible."

Shana nodded. She carried extra ammunition with her at all times now.

Culver pulled up his pant leg and showed his ankle holster and his Glock 27 Standard 40 compact handgun, with 9 mm rounds inside. "I have a Taser and a pepper spray on the back of the belt under the jacket. Be listening for any calls from me for additional backup."

Shana started to talk but Marks bumped her shoulder. "Got it, lieutenant. Just watch what you drink."

Shana spoke up. "How does a loner veteran end up with access to a place like this? He's making money in some way that isn't on our books. He's associated with bad people, sir. He's a part of the underground here in the city—I mean, this bar is actually underground."

Culver checked his pepper spray on his belt. "He's associated with a criminal we don't have on the books and who we can't seem to lay eyes on. This contact of his knows all about the biker gang and might even be directing what they do. That's why he's our plant, Thomas."

"What kind of info do you think he's got?" Marks asked.

"Who knows." Culver stood. "Ready?"

Shana and Marks stood. As they followed the lieutenant out, Marks asked, "Which detective told you about the bar?"

"Can't tell you," Culver said, "or his cover would be blown. But he's the best of the best. He knew right away what I was talking about."

"Has he ever gone in there?"

"No."

"Did he say anyone ever came out of there?"

"No."

46

THE TRUTH

Elijah walked into the condo's living room, where Rick had set up his office for the day. Laptop, legal pad, an assortment of pens, and a hot cup of coffee were spread out across the side table. Rick sat on the sofa, his bare feet propped up on the coffee table.

Elijah shook his head in wonder. *Modern work is so flexible.* Elijah was used to going in to Sten's office down by the docks and getting put on a list. He'd show up to work, do the work, go home. It was old-fashioned, apparently. *The way Rick works is kind of like my old role in the Rangers. Work where you're needed and figure out all the details along the way.*

Elijah rounded the edge of the couch. "Rick, will you tell me if I look OK?"

Rick looked up from his laptop. "Well sure, if you're going to hang out at a truck stop."

"Come on, seriously. I have to go soon."

Rick shrugged. "How can I tell you if you look OK if I don't know the place you're going?"

"I told you, it's a secret bar."

Rick took Elijah's hand and pulled him down onto the couch. "I still don't understand why you can't talk in the cop's office. Come on, Elijah. Be honest with me."

Elijah gripped Rick's hand. His palms were smooth in Elijah's rough ones. "Are you ready for the truth?"

"You sound like Tom Cruise in *A Few Good Men*." Rick sat up and in his best Jack Nicholson said, "You can't handle the truth! You telling me that?"

Elijah smiled at him. "You're adorable. Fine, but you may not like it. The Sons of Perdition are planning to kidnap a lot of children soon, turn them over to a gang from Mexico, and sell their organs to the black market."

Rick turned to him, shocked. "What?"

"It's what I've been talking to the police about. It's what makes it possible for me to get closer to closing down the gang. My . . . contact offered me a table at this exclusive bar for the evening. It's not something I could refuse. But he didn't say I couldn't bring someone with me."

Elijah smiled to himself at that. He wished he could see Lamb's face when he realized he brought the police lieutenant into his club. "I'm going to try to get the lieutenant to let me go with them on the bust. I'm hoping that by talking privately we can bond a little."

"And you *want* to be there?" Rick stood with a shudder. "Why?"

"I have to be there. I've put Juno and his family at risk and I have to get them out. This situation I've caused is too big for me to do alone. I have to use the police as a bigger gang."

"But Juno's not in trouble with this kidnapping scheme, is he?" Rick was pacing around the living room, agitated. "Are his children at risk? You don't have to go—I'm not even sure you're allowed to go. First you cancel on Selma this week, then our dinner with Phillip, and now you want to get into a firefight? You're backsliding, Elijah. Please don't ask to attend what could very well be your funeral."

A lump formed in Elijah's throat. He needed to steady himself, but his voice told more than his words. "It's my chance to make sure no one in the gang survives to go after Juno ever again. If you were in trouble, Rick, I'd raise holy hell to save you." He thought about his choice of words. "Please just back me up here."

Rick stopped. "No. I can't 'back you up' if it means letting you die. You feel invincible, but that's only true until you get yourself killed. Call me selfish, but I'm not willing to let you do that."

Elijah pulled Rick into a tight embrace. He felt a tear tickle his neck. *Is Rick crying . . . for me?*

Elijah murmured into Rick's soft hair. "If I don't stop this now, they'll never stop hunting Juno. One last battle. I promise."

Elijah had decided not to tell Rick about his deal with the devil —real or not, Lamb was without a doubt the devil, as Juno kept saying—and possibly becoming a full-time executioner. It was too dark, too ridiculous sounding. Elijah longed to be strong enough to share everything, really everything, with Rick. He wanted to open up all the way, but he was afraid to expose his innerself that he hated. He was still afraid, like many veterans, that if Rick really knew all about him, he would leave.

After all, if Elijah had the choice, he'd leave himself too.

Rick nodded. Elijah pulled away, wiped a tear from Rick's cheek. "I'll be back tonight. I'll tell you everything that happens."

"I'll be here."

Those simple words warmed Elijah's heart.

47

MISERICORD

It was almost eight. The setting sun had already tucked the alley in darkness. Culver waited with his hands in his pockets. Marks and Thomas sat in an unmarked car half a block from the corner, listening to Culver's concealed mic in case he needed assistance. Elijah melted out of the shadows.

"Evening, lieutenant."

Culver jumped. "Shit, McCoy. You're late."

"Sorry, I got caught up in a conversation. Ready for that drink?"

Culver nodded. *And some critical information.* "That's why I'm here."

Elijah led the way down the alley to a shed. It was a much more substantial building than Culver had initially thought. The veteran approached the shed and slapped his hand on door.

"Discipline," he growled.

The door swung open noiselessly. There was nothing in the small room but a stairway with metal railings on each side leading down into a dimly lit pass, not unlike a subway entrance. They descended what could have been twenty or more feet before they entered a short tunnel, finally emerging into a cool, dark room.

The room had stone walls and floors with dark wooden fixtures stationed along the walls, like a medieval dungeon. It looked like a gentleman's club, a rich man's club, and Culver was happy that McCoy was paying. He remembered the caution about watching his drink.

Elijah found a corner and signaled for Culver to follow him. They sat on a firm, green leather couch that had a beautiful, polished dark cherry coffee table flanking its whole length. The leather couch looked Italian and was very comfortable, with shoulder-high ends that added to the privacy. This place was designed to have its clients sit for a long time and talk safely in private. There was a soft light around the seating arrangement, but not much on the actual sofa. Every seating area in the bar was like this, creating islands of dark for conversations with the soft light acting like a curtain between. You couldn't make out anyone else sitting in the bar. That was the idea. You could tell there were other people in the room, but it was clearly not your business that they were or what they were doing.

"I half-expect to see the mayor or district attorney in here," Culver whispered.

Elijah looked around. "Who says he isn't?"

As soon as they got settled, a waiter appeared. He must have been in his seventies. He stood there and looked at the two with cold, focused eyes.

Elijah said, "I've been told that the Armagnac is excellent here. Can you bring us each four fingers in square glasses?"

The waiter turned and disappeared into the dark room. With the plush carpets and the angles of the seating areas, sound was deadened. There were other conversations going on, but it was impossible to hear any part of them. Culver thought of Thomas's words, that the Misericord could be a gate to hell, and found himself glad it was cool in the bar.

The pair waited in the dark silence. The waiter reappeared soon after and set down a tray with a Waterford cut-glass decanter full of beautiful amber liquid and two Waterford Lismore Diamond tumblers, sparkling as if a jeweler's light shone down on them. The tumblers were empty and the matching decanter was full. Apparently, it was up to them to decide how they wanted to drink. A second waiter, probably a junior study and just in his fifties, was right behind with a cigar tray: torpedoes from Dunhill, a cut-glass ashtray, a sterling silver cutter, and a torch lighter. Both waiters disappeared.

Culver had never seen such extravagance at a bar or club. "What the fuck is all this?"

Elijah looked as astonished as Culver felt. "I know. This isn't my club. I'm just as amazed as you are. This is fancy, and certainly not a place I could ever afford. Mr. Lamb is the member here. He asked me to come tonight and I thought I would bring a guest. I figured, secret, expensive, underground club? It's probably one of the most secure places in the city to talk privately. Looks like I'm right."

"B. A. Lamb is no joke, then." Culver let out a low whistle. It had an odd, muffled sound in the quiet room.

Elijah nodded. "We're guests tonight. One of the reasons I offered to pay is that we aren't going to be charged. No money is exchanged here. The members pay an annual fee. So, drink up."

"He has to be connected to some big underworld power."

"Some big underworld power? That's probably accurate, but I can't give you a name for the organization. I've never met any of his associates or detected them following me, but they seem to be all the time now. Look at this place, for example." Elijah gestured around them. "Apparently, no information ever gets out of here. Drink?"

Culver shook his head. "No, not yet. What's the information, McCoy?"

"I talked to Lamb last night. He found me at the diner."

Culver raised an eyebrow. "Oh?"

"He knew I'd come in to the station, somehow, and wanted to

know what I did. I told him that I just bluffed my way through and that you were suspicious of me but didn't have anything to nail me."

"So you omitted your confession?" Culver asked.

Elijah nodded and looked sharply to let Culver know they could be watched. "He had a plan to wipe out the bikers and wanted to run it by me."

Culver looked worried and held up a hand. "McCoy, I warned you. We're supposed to take care of any conflicts, remember?"

Elijah met Culver's eyes with a steady gaze. "I'm here telling you, aren't I? Calm down. He wants me to tell you the bikers' plans. Hopes to see lots of people on both sides get killed. He's pretty excited about it. I think we're each going to get what we want out of this."

"What plan?"

Over the next hour and a half, the two men discussed all the details they had on the Sons of Perdition. Their past activity, known movements, possible network. Culver tried to dig into Mr. Lamb's background and how exactly Elijah knew him, but Elijah repeated the same answer every time. "He found me."

Culver pulled a hand over his face. It felt much later than it was, the heaviness of the conversation tiring him. "I've got a lot of work to do before this Organ Concert starts."

Elijah raised an eyebrow. "That's what you're calling it? You've got a bit of a dark side yourself."

"I'll take that drink now." Culver rapped his knuckles on the table.

Elijah reached for the decanter and poured each of them a good three fingers of the amber liquid. Culver took a sip and pulled the glass back, surprised. "That's the best brandy I've had."

"It's Armagnac, actually, not brandy." Elijah swirled the drink in his glass, watching the amber legs slide down the glass with a frown. "I'm not much of a liquor enthusiast. I just know that Lamb's favorite is the '79. I'm sure that's what we got."

Elijah reached over and picked up two of the perfect Dunhill torpedoes, took the silver clipper, and snipped off the points. Culver accepted one and lit it with the torch. Elijah borrowed the torch with a nod and lit his own cigar. Several moments passed, both men absorbed in their own thoughts. Children murdered for their organs . . . it was a strange world they lived in. There'd be a lot of paperwork if this lead turned out true.

"We're going to hell for this, you know," Culver said. "If we're not already there."

Elijah nodded. "Lamb's just like that. Bad to be bad. I'd love to kill him, but he's too careful. And, I dunno." Elijah pulled on his cigar. "Maybe it's bad luck to kill a guy like that."

I could be sitting in the entrance of hell with a deadly killer. What would my priest say if he saw me now? Culver's palms began to sweat. He was nervous.

Culver was never nervous.

"Are you a religious guy?" he asked.

Elijah poured Culver some more Armagnac. "Nah, I'm not. Juno is. His family goes to church and prays and everything. He thinks Lamb sold his soul to Satan, like the actual devil. He keeps saying, 'Elijah, go talk to God. Ask him for help.' But . . ." He made an indifferent grunt and took a sip of the amber liquid. "I turned to you instead."

"Well, I'm certainly not God, but I'll take that as a compliment. Why is Juno so important to you?" Culver tried to gauge Elijah's eyes in the gloom, but his face was covered in shadow. "Why risk jail for this friend?"

"Because he'd do the same for me." It was matter-of-fact, simple. Culver didn't feel like there was much room for argument in the soldier's words.

"Are you carrying tonight?" Culver asked.

Elijah just showed him his hands. Culver's own hands were drenched with sweat, itching to retrieve his concealed Glock. This place gave him the creeps.

"So Marks and Thomas told me about a nice-looking young man you're keeping in your condo," he said nonchalantly, changing the topic. "Are you guys fucking?"

Elijah actually snorted and coughed a little. He smiled at Culver and leaned over to him, staring deep into his eyes. Culver leaned away. There was a coldness pouring into Culver from that gaze; he couldn't see anything in Elijah's eyes. He felt as if a machine was analyzing him. Elijah picked up the lieutenant's tumbler and straightened, refilling both. He handed back the tumbler and Culver took a big swig.

Elijah kept his cigar going. "Well, that takes the pressure off how I was going to come out to you. Yeah, we're fucking. Really, men are so much more diverse than women, and there are so many types for the choosing. It was easy to get physical with him, but I'm sure you know about all that."

Culver was nodding yes but said, "No, really I can't imagine that at all. This does seem kind of like a bad time to start a romance." He frowned. In spite of all the intensity, Elijah was really so young. It was hard to remember that, sometimes. He sighed. "If you were my son, and you were in all the mess you're in, I would tell you to wait and see how things turn out. Doesn't this just complicate your situation?"

"It's only been a couple of weeks since I was the most anonymous person in the city. Now it seems like suddenly I have friends, a counselor, and a lover. And I'm up to my armpits in trouble." Elijah's smile faded, the steel returning to his eyes. "Lieutenant, I have to be present at the Organ Concert. I have to be able to see the destruction of my friend's enemies. Do you understand my need here? You know I'm a good soldier. I won't cause trouble. But if something goes wrong, I want to be able to fight."

Culver shook his head. "Absolutely not. It's a liability for the city and illegal."

"But I can fight."

"Maybe with your team, but not with ours, not as a civilian.

You know how tight your team was in the Rangers? You guys trained hundreds of hours to be able to anticipate each other's needs, their moves. I'm sure you were terrified that the new guys who joined late would make a mistake and get you all killed. Yes?"

Elijah gave a tight nod. Culver continued. "We may not be the Rangers, or Special Ops, but we're a tight-knit team. We're going to do everything we can to subdue, arrest, or kill these bastards. Trust me, Elijah, we want them. But if we even think you're going to try to sneak in, we'll have you arrested for obstructing justice. Read me, soldier?"

Elijah didn't move. He stared at Culver, a flicker of defiance dancing in the dim light of their seating area.

Culver groaned. This night was more than he'd been ready for. Secret hellish bars, a dangerous killer sharing drinks with him, talking about black market organs and gay life. He might be getting too old for this job.

"You like baseball, son?" Culver asked.

The two men launched into a good talk about baseball with an analysis of the A's and the Giants, as well as the blue-collar, white-collar differences of the two teams. No consensus was reached, but the game was a shared passion for both men. Culver told Elijah about life on the police force and they did a comparison to the military. They talked about the need for political skills as you move up, and Elijah said that was part of his decision to get out and come home. He was at the end of his allotment for combat. The military will only let you spend so much time in combat before you have to cycle out and do something else. He'd been offered a security job at an embassy of his choice, as a reward for his time in battle. He just couldn't see himself in his full dress uniform every day, watching high ranking officers interacting with politicians and going to social events. It sounded horrible to him. They relaxed into the easy conversation of two teammates as the night wore on.

Finally, Elijah said, "Well, it's time to see if we can fight our way out of here."

Culver reached for his Glock, but stopped when Elijah started to laugh. Slightly embarrassed, Culver followed the soldier to the tunnel, up the stairs, and through the shed's door.

The men came out just about arm in arm, both looking like old friends. Elijah followed Culver back to the Crown Vic and opened the back door for him.

"Evening, officers," Elijah said, waving at Marks and Thomas.

"Hey, McCoy." Marks nodded. "Thanks for returning our lieutenant."

"Anytime. I'm walking home. Text me if you need any thing."

Culver closed the car door and watched Elijah walk away, disappearing into the darkness.

48

THE PARTNERSHIP

Elijah walked down toward the produce section of the waterfront on his way home. The Misericord was only a few blocks from the condo, an easy stroll. Rick was waiting for him at home. After the strange bar, a night of light-hearted, normal fun was well in order.

He turned down the street and saw someone sitting on a bench in a little park just back from the street.

Lamb.

He slowed and turned into the park. Officer Thomas wasn't behind him yet, still dropping off the lieutenant and Marks at the station. If he left the road, she'd wonder where he went. The park was not lit for her to see.

Lamb smiled as Elijah strolled up to him. "How'd you enjoy the bar? Did you like the Armagnac?"

"It was nothing I'd ever seen before." Elijah rested a foot on the end of the bench. He didn't plan on staying long.

"Or tasted, I hope." Lamb was dressed in a black sweater this evening, marked with a clothing brand Elijah had never seen before. Its silver thread glowed in the dim park light. "So, you're

239

directing the whole circus now? You've got them waiting for your texts, devising plans in secret bars . . . I have to admit, I didn't suspect this side of you. But then you were a natural leader in the Rangers, weren't you?"

Elijah shrugged. He'd often planned and led the ops for his team when they were required to move into a situation on a moment's notice. The gang bust wasn't too different from that.

"How'd the planning go? Any frustrations?"

Elijah let out a sigh. Of course Lamb would know about Culver's refusal to let him go to the bust. He wouldn't let this smug man lord that over him. He'd find a way to convince Culver to bring him along. "No, no frustrations. They'll be present on the big night in full force. It's on now. It's hard, not really being in charge. It's also hard to be unable to call in an air strike."

Lamb nodded. "You seem to be doing well managing the *politics* of this situation." His emphasis on the word *politics* confirmed for Elijah that Lamb knew he wasn't allowed to fight. Elijah found his hands in tight fists. Lamb laughed. "Don't worry, we'll get you there."

"I can figure it out myself."

"Of course."

There was a pause. Then Elijah asked, "Have you talked to the Sons?"

"The Sons, the police, rats on the street—I talk to all. The Sons believe this deal with the Mexicans will give them a new push, restoring confidence in their leaders and securing a position of power in the city. Everyone from the head of the club on down to the newest rider will be on this run. They'll have their war wagon, the crash wagon, and they'll all be wearing their FTW patches."

Elijah raised an eyebrow.

"Fuck The World patches. It's their name for this operation." Lamb waved a hand, dismissive. "Not nearly as creative as Organ Concert. It's going to be a grand night, my friend. Almost forty bikers, over a hundred police, eighty kidnapped children, and an entire city in chaos."

Elijah frowned. How could Lamb already have soft numbers for the police? He'd just left the bar with Culver. *He has spies higher up in the department than I'd imagined.*

"There's so much potential for destruction. Families, children, social workers, educators, friends—all will be drawn into the sadness. The police are going to sustain casualties, the Sons of Perdition and the gang from Mexico will both sustain casualties. The children are going to suffer, and then, after the event, the parents who were so disconnected or incapable will be exposed. Isn't it glorious?"

"Death is not glorious, Lamb."

Lamb raised a knowing finger. "But you're excited, nonetheless. Just as I am. There are a lot of people who are attracted to the darkness, Elijah. It's usually because the people who attach themselves to the light are arrogant, mean. It's such a help to me in my recruiting efforts. But you, you are different than most. You are very dark, and you feel very comfortable with it. Don't you?"

Elijah was comfortable with his darkness, it was true. But there was a small part of him, ever-growing of late, that wanted to leave that darkness. To find release.

"I'm going to find my way into this battle, and I don't plan on making it out alive." Saying the words aloud made the thought real for Elijah. He didn't want to live in this darkness, and death was looking to be the only way he could escape Lamb's grasp.

Lamb tsked. "You were born to be an executioner, Elijah. It's your skill, your forte, your modus vivendi. Death is not your release. *Fatum mors est, quae timetur in tenebris.* Oh—forgive my lapse into a beautiful language. Causing death is your destiny, for you are to be that which is feared in the dark."

Elijah felt a coldness grip his innards. Something powerful resided in those words, and that terrified him.

"Besides, there's an ever-increasing list of people who would miss you if you left," Lamb said. "You use your natural talents to remove bad people from the world. You didn't do anything wrong. But Culver doesn't see that, does he? He and his little team would feel safer knowing the bad man killing criminals was locked up."

Elijah felt a drop of adrenaline fall into his system, anger polluting his hot blood. Culver wished he was locked up, and that angered him. No amount of car talk, swapped stories, or tactical cooperation would change who Culver saw Elijah to be. They would use him, then betray him.

Lamb stood from the bench. "You have a lot of blood on your hands, Elijah McCoy. Do you think anyone who claims to follow light would forgive that?"

Rick is waiting for me.

Elijah turned and walked away. He didn't look back over his shoulder. Lamb would already be gone.

The waterfront closed down after dark, leaving the streets empty in this part of town. Elijah walked toward the condo, his mind racing with Lamb's words. He'd said causing death was his destiny.

He'd also said that people would miss him, and he felt that they would. No one would miss him if he was a deliverer of death— surely that meant it wasn't truly his destiny. Didn't it?

That night in the shower had been amazing. He'd loved following the nice curve at the top of Rick's neck, right behind his ear, down the neck to the shoulder. He liked the curve of Rick's soft bottom. He liked Rick's hands. He liked the whole package. He was amazed as they'd caressed and fondled each other how easy it was, how right it felt. It was a beautiful, sensuous dance, and the music had yet to fade.

It was like his soul was opening and a light was pouring into a void that had never been filled in his life. *I could let myself fall in love with Rick, dedicate the rest of my life to him. But it could all be over in three weeks.*

He walked a block toward Jack London Square before he went

up to see Rick. He needed to calm down. He didn't know what was going to happen. There was a chance he would survive and the police would find a way to get him off. It was a slight chance, but he had to believe it existed. He just had to drive ahead and give happiness a chance.

He turned back toward the condo again. He just wanted to be with Rick. He wanted to hug him when he saw him, to make dinner together and eat on the balcony. He wanted them to clean up and shower together, just as much as he wanted to make love to Rick.

Now that he was in a romantic relationship, Elijah saw the intimacy of day-to-day chores shared with Rick that were otherwise mundane when alone, like shopping and doing laundry. Love was more than romance. How much more, Elijah wanted to find out for himself. He wanted for them to be able to hold onto each other while they slept. He wanted the morning to come and find them together.

Stop this, Elijah. These thoughts were useless to him. The more he saw what their relationship could be, the more he realized that he would probably never have it.

Elijah wanted a partnership with Rick, feared he was pretending to have a partnership with the police, and suspected that he might actually have a partnership with Lamb.

By the time he arrived at the condo, a black and white was sitting on the curb with a very pissed Officer Thomas inside. He patted the roof of the cruiser and stopped by the driver's window.

"Where the hell have you been, soldier?" demanded Thomas. "You're not supposed to be out on your own."

"Calm down. I had a lot to think about and added a couple of blocks to my route. Sorry if I worried you—I've got to get up to Rick. See you."

"I know you do." Thomas shook her head. "I can't believe I'm saying it, but you're pretty damn romantic, McCoy."

49

THE TASK FORCE

Culver found out that while there was a lot of talk about protecting children, there was also a lot of resistance to spending time or money actually doing it. In a world of limited resources, kidnapping was often given a lower priority by law enforcement agencies. It was always an emotional and challenging case, and not many people were willing to take it on.

The upcoming kidnapping plot was bad, real bad. Added to it the additional allure of jailing two gangs, and Culver thought he might actually have a chance at getting some support to prepare for it. Drugs were the main focus for the OCPD, and the Sons of Perdition were one of the biggest distributors of contraband in the city.

Culver had taken McCoy's tip to his captain, who took it to the commissioner, who then took it to the mayor and city council. The FBI got involved, working closely with the OCPD and their officers. Facts were run down and information from Mexico, border police, and other agencies were combined to answer the simple, terrifying question on everyone's mind: Was such a crime plausible?

Added surveillance on the Sons of Perdition and one detective's snitch from the club provided some pretty damning evidence. It wasn't just plausible, it was happening.

Despite the department and FBI's best efforts, it looked like the only way this was going to end was in a battle. The problem of trying to protect the general populace without giving away the FBI's intel was heavily discussed, planned, and re-planned.

Culver walked over to Sergeant Jamel Marks's desk, where the man was busy typing up a report. "Pull your head out of that computer and talk to me."

Marks looked up, his eyes still unfocused in deep thought. "I'm just getting our journal on McCoy up to date. He's keeping us informed about his movements, but I'm running into one problem with our surveillance method."

"What?"

"There are times when we lose sight of him. He always shows up where he says he will, but—"

"Are you telling me you're allowing McCoy to disappear?" Culver growled. "And you're not looking into that?"

Marks looked ashamed. "I've talked to Thomas about it. She thinks—and I agree—that he dips off radar to talk to his source. We've never seen him talk to this Mr. Lamb before, have we?"

Culver frowned. After his visit to the Misericord, he wasn't surprised his officers weren't able to get an eye on McCoy's source. "No, we haven't. And I don't think we will."

Marks looked around, then leaned toward Culver. "This whole thing's got Thomas spooked, lieutenant. She seems to agree with Valdas. It's all she could talk about while you were in the Misericord."

Culver snorted. "What? That Lamb is the devil? Tell your partner to pull herself together."

Marks nodded. "I mean, I have. But you can't blame her. After that bar, and the way he seems to always know the exact moments we won't have an eye on McCoy . . . it's a little weird, right?"

"Marks, don't fall for Thomas's superstitions." Culver scolded.

"Just watch for McCoy doing any form of a drop-off. There's no ghosts on this case, only intelligent, malevolent bastards."

Marks raised his hands, passive. "It's weird, that's all I'm saying."

Culver rubbed the back of his neck. Everything was "weird" with this case, no denying it. He sat down next to Marks. "I've thought about McCoy being the source for all this information."

Marks raised an eyebrow. "Like working for another agency maybe?"

Culver shrugged. "He's a military hard ass that fits the FBI, DEA, NSA, and other agencies' profiles." He sighed. "I don't know how we'd ever find out."

"I don't know. I don't think someone running the show would beg to go with us to the bust. And when he confessed, he seemed honest enough."

Culver laughed. "That's a word for it. When he confessed to killing everybody, I felt like saying no shit."

Marks tapped his pen on the desk. "What're you going to do with him when this is over? You know he killed that truck driver, even if we don't have the evidence yet. Thomas has found nine murders with the same hand-to-hand combat modus operandi. She's not done. McCoy may have killed a dozen or more people. He seems to kill only criminals, people outside the law, outcasts, and assholes. You'd think that if he were in cahoots with a gang or something he'd help them, not hurt them. It seems like he's someone's executioner. So, maybe he is working for some agency."

A shudder ran up Culver's spine. "Yeah, I've had those thoughts. Shit, just give me a good old drug addict or bank robber. At least we can understand them and they understand us."

"Maybe he's the angel of death, the ultimate executioner." Marks grinned.

"Working with the devil?" Culver raised an eyebrow. "As far as what are we going to do with him . . ." He shrugged again. "Not our decision. It's in the FBI's hands now."

Marks stopped his tapping. "Speaking of, do you think the FBI will let Thomas and I go in on the bust? That Dodson guy won't give me a firm answer."

"Agent Dodson's just like that. Everyone involved in this case from the department will be there. We've got the best context for the gang and the victims involved. I'm telling you, it's maddening, knowing we'll have to watch the bikers stalk children and be unable to step in until the last moment."

"Yeah." Marks grimaced. "These kids aren't going to be picked up from the rich white neighborhoods. They're already in danger just from their own families. I wonder which kids in our beat will get snatched."

Culver sighed, his words and thoughts heavy. "We'll find out next Thursday."

50

THE VOW

Elijah had looked in every room of the condo at least ten times while he waited. Rick was doing a transportation interface presentation in the neighboring city of Walnut Creek and had been gone all day. Elijah stopped pacing and sat down on the balcony with the view he loved—and was about to lose, maybe forever.

That was not the only thing he was about to lose.

He was angry at the situation. He finally found someone worth spending his life with, someone who loved him in a way he had never been loved before, and now Elijah faced a future without him or anyone else like him. His breathing wanted to accelerate, his body temperature was ready to rise. He was ready to explode.

Elijah made himself sit still and controlled his breathing. He could see his own complicity in the events that had brought him to this point. But why him? Really, why? He felt a tear in the corner of his eye and was surprised by it. He didn't cry—there was no value to that in his life. He had been put in the situation of having to deal with everything that happened with no help, no possibility of help.

Rick wants to help me.

Elijah's anger was mitigated by his sudden sense of right and wrong. He felt so deeply about Rick, about being with him, caring about him. He needed to be responsible with Rick. He knew that whatever had pushed him into this situation had not yet reached into Rick's life. Was Elijah willing to drag him into this darkness? Rick had had to go through the loss of a loved one already, and he still hurt from it. It hurt Elijah to feel Rick in pain. Without knowing how he knew it, he knew that he couldn't hurt Rick any more.

Elijah gripped the edge of the balcony. No. He was determined to find a way to let Rick go, before it got worse.

Would it be better for Rick to think he had been rejected, or for him to feel loss again? To think he'd allowed himself to fall in love again just to have that love torn from his grasp. There was a strong possibility that, if Elijah continued on his path, he'd leave Rick to bury him. Elijah wanted to spend his life with Rick, to hold him and kiss him and tell him every thought that passed through his head. He wanted to caress Rick through his actions and words and comfort him.

But that didn't seem possible anymore.

Elijah was pain, and violence, and death. He felt hopeless. He knew he was in a situation he couldn't control, in way over his head and unable to do what he wanted. His violence, anger, and frustration had filled him to the point that it had spilled out and affected the life of his only true friend, Juno. He had created a situation that put Juno and his family in mortal danger. Did he want to do that to Rick? Could he interact with any human being without causing pain and doing intense damage?

He felt hopeless.

Then he heard the door to the condo open and the most beautiful sound. Rick's voice.

"Hey, Elijah, I'm home."

Could there be a more beautiful message from a more beautiful voice?

"Elijah, are you here?"

A shudder ran up Elijah's spine. "I'm out on the balcony. I'm coming in."

Rick met Elijah just inside the door to the balcony and they wrapped their arms around each other, pressing their cheeks up against one another. Elijah took a minute to breathe in Rick's warm, alluring scent before releasing him. He sat on the long black leather couch and patted it to indicate that Rick should sit next to him. Rick sat, but Elijah didn't adjust himself, leaning neither toward nor away from Rick. It was clear he was just going to talk.

Rick looked at Elijah like he had expected a kiss. He shrugged, then started talking at a rapid pace. "I had a very good meeting today. With our success here in Oakland City, I think the surrounding cities realize they need to be able to connect to the new transportation system if they want to draw business to their sites. This is going to be a deal." He smiled that beautiful smile at Elijah.

Elijah returned the smile. "Super! Congratulations, Rick. You're so good at speaking to people. I'm happy about this and really want you to be successful."

"Thanks." Rick leaned over and put his hand on Elijah's knee. Elijah tensed. "But? You seem preoccupied. What's up?"

Elijah took a deep breath. "You know the upcoming confrontation between the OCPD and the Sons? The date is getting close, and I think it's time for me to pull out of here and prepare for what I need to do."

Rick blanched. "Out of here? What're you talking about?"

"This is a big deal, Rick. It's going to be dangerous—violent—and everyone involved is going to be after me. I prepare for battle in a certain way, and need to do that. I'm going to have to fight hard in a few days."

"Which is why you need to rest and spend time with me." Rick put his hands on his knees, palms up, offering them to Elijah.

"Rick, listen to me. This is going to be very hard, very violent, and everyone is going to end up being after me."

"I thought the police said you couldn't go. Did they change their minds?"

Elijah hesitated. "No, not yet."

Rick balled his fists. All traces of his smile were gone. "Then why are you going? I asked you not to go, the police *tell* you not to go, and you're still going! I understand how important Juno is to you, but don't you think the police can handle this?"

"No." It was a flat answer. "I have to go, Rick. I am going."

"But do you plan on coming back?"

Elijah didn't answer, didn't look him in the eye. Rick nodded slowly, understanding. "Come back, Elijah. Just, plan on it, OK? Once you're there, *if* you go, can't you just watch from a safe distance? I'm sure the police will handle everything, and when it's over, you'll be happy. They want to rid Oakland of the Sons of Perdition, and they're not going to let this chance get away from them. So they'll surround and arrest the bikers and take them away to jail, and you'll come home. Right?"

"Oh, Rick, I wish that was what's going to happen. I've been in so many bad situations that I just don't see that happening here. I've turned the tide in lots of horrible situations, and I can change it here when needed."

Rick tensed. "What are you planning to do?"

"What I always do. I'm going to kill people if I have to; I'm going to get a result that will be definitive in making Juno safe. I can do this." Elijah was confident, more confident than he had felt on the balcony. He could win this, he could change the tide for the OCPD. For Juno.

"Elijah, why can't you just let the police take care of this? You're providing them with all the information they need. When they're done, they'll be happy and may go light on you. If you go in all crazy, they'll want to lock you up and throw away the key."

"That's probably going to happen. I may not survive." Elijah looked down at his twisting hands. "That's why I think it's time to pull away and get into the mental state of a warrior before the battle begins."

Rick stood up and seemed to hover over Elijah. "Pull away from me? From us? Are you trying to tell me that I'm in the way? Of you going ballistic? Is that what you want?" He was on the balls of his feet, in a position that would allow him to jump on Elijah.

"Rick, stop for a minute." Elijah put his hands up, staring into Rick's eyes.

"I'm coming Elijah, that's that." Rick threw down his arms and stood planted.

Elijah's eyes widened. What?

"What? Rick, you can't come. It's too dangerous. You'll get hurt. And I . . . I don't want to hurt you anymore. That's all I ever seem to do. I don't want you to get hurt."

Rick's voice was thick with emotion. "It would hurt if you pull away at a dangerous time like this. What good are we if I can't help you when you're in danger?"

Rick sat back down on the couch next to Elijah, touching Elijah's knee.

"What good are we if I can't protect you?" Elijah whispered.

Rick sat looking at Elijah, eyes moist.

"Let me just say it, Rick. I'm not a good person, and I don't think I'm good for you."

Rick put his hand on Elijah's thigh. "You're not bad, Elijah. You're stupid."

"What the fuck?" Elijah pulled away from Rick.

"You're stupid, Elijah, if you can't see that there is no alternative for me that doesn't involve being with you."

Elijah took a deep breath. He was losing control of this conversation. "Rick, you are the best person I've ever met. I only know how to hurt. I don't want to hurt you."

"Too late." Rick's hands were moving with nowhere to go. He was agitated and needed a hug. Elijah's heart constricted.

"Just to be sure you understand what's happening here." Elijah finally leaned in toward Rick, putting a hand on his shoulder. "I'm going to observe a confrontation between fifty hardened criminals and almost a hundred police officers. They're going to fight to the death, probably. That's more emotional than you can imagine, 'til you've experience it. *And—*"

Elijah raised his hand, cutting off Rick's objection. Rick closed his mouth. "If things don't go in a way that'll prevent the bikers from hurting Juno, then I'm going to engage and do whatever it takes to make sure he stays safe. The police have told me not to attend. They have charges against me already. I may be killed and will probably be jailed for a long time if I survive. Your future is brighter than that, and I refuse to let you get involved. Do you understand?"

"Yeah." Rick sniffed. "It really sucks." A tear rolled down his cheek and fell onto his chest. "I hate this, Elijah. I can't tell you why, but I can't turn away from you or your life, period."

"Why?"

Rick swallowed, and his voice was more sure of itself. "Because I can't. Something happened to me over the last month. I see you like you're glowing. Everything you say burns into my mind and heart. I have to know where you are exactly, and I have to be able to talk to you. I told you all the horrible details of losing Jason, and you heard me, understood me, and accepted me. I told you that I wished I'd never met him at times, even though I waited with him for his death. I don't have those thoughts with you. I have to see you, talk to you, be with you." Rick's eyes were full of fire.

Now a tear appeared in Elijah's eye, but it didn't fall over the edge and run down his cheek. That made it twice in one afternoon.

Rick stood and walked over to the door of the balcony and looked out. Elijah remained where he was and stared at his back.

Rick kept looking out, but softly said, "Damn it, Elijah."

"Is there any way I can absorb all the pain here?" Elijah was leaning toward Rick, but didn't seem to be able to stand.

"Why would you want to do that?"

Elijah stared at the back of Rick's head. "Because I have to know where you are exactly, and I have to be able to talk to you. I told you the horrible things I had to do in battle, and you heard me and understood me and accepted me. I'm unable to continue living without being able to hold you, kiss you, talk to you."

Rick turned around. "You're not leaving here. You're going to talk to me about everything, and no matter what happens you and I are going to face it together. I can get a ride with Juno to come visit you in prison; we can make a day of it each time. What he can't do, and what I can't do, is ignore or forget about you. That's not on the table here."

Now tears were rolling down Elijah's cheeks. Rick was the most open, honest person Elijah had ever met. He was so open and honest with him, and Elijah still held one last secret. "Rick . . . I have one more thing to tell you, and this could be the thing that causes you to shoot me."

Rick rolled his eyes. "Oh great, one more thing. How bad could it be? I don't think you're going to marry Roxanna, so what is it?"

"I may be working for the devil." Elijah's heart was pounding with his fear that it was true.

Rick frowned. "Just tell me, Elijah. Don't try to be funny when we're being serious."

"I may be working for the devil." Now Elijah's hands were solid fists, and he really wished he could murder Lamb.

Rick shuddered. Elijah watched his shoulders tense. Rick balled his hands into fists and turned back to the balcony, looking out at the street below.

"I told you about the source for the police. He called himself B.

A. Lamb when we first met. He's been able to find me whenever he wants, he can get into any room I'm in. He knew that I've committed murder since I came home from the war. He's the one who asked me to kill the men in the warehouse. He's also the advisor to the Sons of Perdition, and he's encouraging me to kill them by whatever means necessary, including the police. He likes me. He wants me to be his executioner after this is done. He says he can get me out after the Organ Concert."

"Shit," Rick whispered. It seemed like he was collapsing into his own soul.

"Rick, look at me. Talk to me." Elijah stood, but couldn't walk over to Rick.

"Can you choose not to be an executioner? I was thinking the internship would be a good fit for you . . ." Rick's voice was distant, disconnected.

"I don't want to be an executioner. I want to be with you."

Rick turned and took a half-step forward. "Elijah, look at me and tell me what's going to happen here."

Elijah walked over to Rick. He put his hand flat on Rick's chest. "I don't know."

"What do you know?" Rick's eyes drilled into Elijah.

"I only know that I love you, Rick."

It was the first time he had said it. Rick put his hand gently on Elijah's, the one on his chest. He looked into Elijah, and they stood engaged in each other for a full minute.

"I love you so much, Elijah," Rick said. "I'm connected to you, and that's never going to change."

Elijah felt a flush of heat rising through his body. They leaned into each other and pressed their lips into a perfect seal, breathing into each other's souls. They melted into each other, wrapping their arms around each other.

Elijah pulled Rick in hard. "Me too, Rick. Everything else will have to work itself out."

51

THE MASTIFF AND THE FAT BOY

Later that evening, Elijah paced the condo with frantic energy. Rick was gone, hard at work reporting on his day's appointments. He couldn't say why, but Elijah felt like he needed to go to Juno's home. His sickening urgency was aggravated by something like a pat on the back of his head, several times, even after he donned his helmet. He took off down the slick streets of the rainy city.

Elijah had rolled his bike out through the garage without passing by the cruiser. He'd texted Marks where he was going. It left Elijah free to use the short cuts only a bike could navigate.

At a red light, he texted Juno. RIDING OVER NOW.

Juno didn't respond.

~

Sergeant Marks stood in line at World Coffee. There was a cute punk girl behind the counter and he couldn't keep his eyes off her.

She smiled at him. "What can I get you this evening?"

"One medium black coffee to go, please." Marks pulled out his wallet to find cash.

"Is that all you want?" There was a coquettish lilt to her voice. He looked up from his wallet. He was attractive, no shame in knowing that about yourself.

It's always a surprise which ones like the uniform.

He leaned over the counter. "And a chocolate croissant. What's your name?"

"Sarah. Sarah Rose."

"What are you doing this Friday, Sarah Rose?" He smiled at her as she pulled on a strand of bottle-black hair.

"Ab-so-lutely nothing. Why? Got any ideas?"

The buzzing in Marks's pocket went unnoticed.

~

Elijah felt inexplicitly frustrated. Everything was moving too slow. A cold, deadly focus was building within him as he felt himself slide into battle mode. He loved the feeling, his heart rate elevating, pushing blood through his brain.

Riding was a therapy as well as a healthy transport for Elijah. *This could be my whole life,* he thought. *I could live in battle mode. Not be responsible to anyone.*

Not even Rick.

He loved Rick, more than he had loved anyone before. That terrified him. He'd rather fight a thousand battles than venture into this unknown, where the stakes were so much higher for him. *I'd miss the sex, but I could always buy that.* Even the thought made his stomach twist. No, he loved Rick too much to do that to him. Fucking conflicts.

He pedaled harder.

As Elijah turned into the Adams Point neighborhood, a sudden calm hit him, like passing into the eye of a storm. His battle state settled in. He was riding up with Lake Merritt off his right shoulder. It was getting dark, but as he neared his friend's home, he turned off his headlight. As he approached the house, he saw two big motorcycles parked about four houses down the street. One was a Big Dog Mastiff, the other a Harley Fat Boy.

Elijah stopped just short of the motorcycles and scanned the area. Nothing to see, nothing to hear.

Where the hell is Marks?

Elijah texted him again. There was no time to waste sitting around for the cruiser; Elijah was too agitated. He got off his Montague and pushed it out of sight into a tall hedge. The drab, matte olive paint paid off here. He peeled off his bike jacket, gloves, and helmet and pushed them into the hedge, leaving him in his customary black garb. He walked past the motorcycles. There was a Sons of Perdition gang mark on the seat of the Mastiff.

~

Marks had to say, he was really attracted to coffee shop punk girls. It was like there was a punk girl agency that sent out workers all over town. Many of these women were really done out in their punkness. Sarah Rose had the requisite asymmetric bob with some tendrils curling around one ear and down her lovely neck. She had some tattoos showing and wore glasses with thick black frames. She was slender and looked delicious.

Sergeant Marks was still breathing deeply when he got back in the cruiser, Sarah Rose's number scribbled on his croissant's napkin. It would be nice to spend some quiet time alone while he 'watched' Elijah. He heard a tone and pulled his phone awkwardly out of his front pants pocket to see who it was.

I hope it's Thomas. I know she'd want to hear about my date with Sarah. He was smiling.

Shit. It was from Elijah. WHERE ARE YOU? I CAN'T SEE THE CRUISER.

He texted back, I'M OUT FRONT OF YOUR CONDO, WHERE ELSE WOULD I BE?

The response was almost immediate. CHECK YOUR TEXTS, MAN. I'M ON THE STREET WALKING TOWARD JUNO'S. TWO SOP BIKES PARKED ABOUT FOUR HOUSES SOUTH OF THE HOUSE. I'M WORKING MY WAY UP TO GET A LOOK. GOING IN. GET HERE ASAP.

Damn it.

ROLLING. COMING WITH NO LIGHTS AND NO SIRENS. MOVING FAST. WAIT FOR ME.

Marks grabbed his radio. "This is Sergeant Jamel Marks. I got a call on suspicious activity at the Valdas home, going there now."

Marks hoped there was no real threat—he'd have to admit to the lieutenant that his dick caused Elijah to not only break surveillance, but put himself and Juno in danger. He slammed his car in gear and was off, almost running over a couple and their dog.

～

Elijah maneuvered along the street, careful to not trip any of the houses' front yard security. *I could really use a weapon right about now. I'll be carrying from now on.*

A quartermaster sergeant back in Afghanistan had hooked him and Juno up with a couple of powerful handguns and rifles when they returned stateside, along with plenty of ammunition. It was time Elijah pulled them out of storage.

Elijah felt the coldness settle in around his heart and abdomen. He felt late, like he should have felt this premonition sooner. How long had it been nagging him?

Elijah was one house away from Juno's. He couldn't see anyone on the street, the lawn, or in the shrubs in the front. There was an alley on the other side of the house that split the block and went down the side of Juno's house and backyard. That was the way

Elijah usually approached the house; it led to the kitchen. He made his way to the alley.

In the backyard, there was a gazebo and a small patio attached to the kitchen door with two steps down to the yard and one step up to the house. From the backyard, you could see through a small window into the kitchen and a large window into the family room.

Elijah knelt at the alley's entrance and put his head around the corner, quiet as death. Something rustled in the darkening lane. To his horror, the gate was not fully closed.

His threat-analysis training kicked in, his mind running over the possibilities of guns, bombs, arson, kidnap, execution. He was dealing with two men—there were only two bikes, after all, and bikers didn't ride passenger—but he couldn't rule out any backup that may have arrived in a war van. There weren't any suspicious-looking cars in the alley, or the street. Probably just two men.

The Sons of Perdition probably still didn't know about him, but that wouldn't mean they'd hesitate to blow him up. These guys weren't going to go back and say that they didn't get their target. They would be in to the death. It was on.

Elijah realized that he was happy, in a way. He was in full battle mode; the mission was to protect Juno and his family. He was all in. The enemy would be jumpy—they weren't trained and didn't have enough experience to be any good at battle. They'd start shooting as soon as they detected someone coming through the gate, and in their enthusiasm and blundering aggression might actually hit him. Dead wouldn't save Juno, but it might warn him. Juno had weapons in the house. He was a Ranger, after all. Elijah was counting on Juno jumping to his aid as soon as he engaged the enemy.

Elijah moved to the gate, keeping his head on a swivel and looking for any motion. It was getting darker. The gate was open an inch, so he didn't have to risk a squeak to peer in. The shadows of two men knelt by the garage door, looking into the house. One was holding a shotgun. It looked like a Mossberg 590. That would have nine rounds in it. The other man held what looked like a Glock in his hand. There were sure to be hidden backups on their persons. He couldn't see grenades or any other explosive device. They wouldn't have pepper spray or a Taser, or a baton. They were almost guaranteed to have a knife each.

Where was Marks? He hadn't heard any cars pass by or drive up. Not even a neighbor coming home from work. It was quiet. It was probably the dinner hour for most of the families on the block.

The two men gestured to the house, nodding and adjusting their stances. Elijah would have to take the nearest man first and kill him on contact so he could use that body to absorb the first shots from his partner. He knew that within thirty seconds of the first shots or shouts, Juno would be coming out guns blazing. It'd be great to be in a battle with Juno again.

There was a box attached to the outside of the fence that Juno had built to hold his trash cans. Elijah moved over to it. Stepping onto it, he was able to peer over the fence under the tree to get a better view of what the bikers were looking at. It was Juno, playing in the kitchen with his children. They were chasing each other and laughing.

The biker with the shotgun stood up. It was time to move.

At the same moment, he sensed a motion behind him. Elijah snapped his head around and found Marks standing in the ready position next to the box, his shotgun across his chest.

Elijah motioned for Marks to jump onto the box before jumping the fence himself and running quietly toward the bikers. His feet had just hit the ground when the biker fired four rounds of the shotgun into the kitchen, one after the other.

In the thundering noise, Elijah crashed into the back of the rear biker with the handgun. He snapped the biker's spine with a forceful move, winding the man. Elijah planted his feet and smashed the man's face into the patio, cracking his skull and bloodying the stained wood.

Elijah pushed himself up into the ready position, breathing

hard. The forward biker was laying facedown, blood pooling from several gun wounds to the back. Marks stood at the back of the yard, his gun still trained on the motionless biker. Elijah's target had stopped breathing as well, sprawled on the patio. There was a quiet moment in Elijah's mind as his brain caught up with the time passed. Two men lay dead at his feet, and he was the cause. This was wrong, so, so wrong . . .

Something at the back of his mind registered his remorse with surprise, but the realization was drowned out by screams from inside the house.

The window glass was still dropping with a crash to the floor, the sound smothered by the woe rolling from the kitchen. Elijah stood up and stepped over the dead biker as Marks rushed to check the bodies, pulling the weapons out of the corpses' reach.

Elijah froze, unable to move, as he took in the scene before him.

Juno was bleeding heavily from his back, but he was forcing himself to crawl across the kitchen floor to his daughter. Austeja sprawled across the tile floor, her limbs folded awkwardly beneath her. Blood trickled from the side of her head, and she made no movement. Matas sat in the corner, screaming at his sister. Gabija had run in from the dining room and was kneeling over her daughter's body, sobbing.

Her body.

Elijah uttered a deep, animalistic moan of pain. Juno's eyes flashed in his direction at the sound, then continued to grip Austeja in his arms. He had failed. Elijah had failed to protect Juno.

52

THE BOTTOM

Elijah moved like a ghost through the kitchen door as Marks called in the attack. An ambulance was on its way.

"Police! I'm coming in!" Marks announced his entrance, following Elijah into the building. Marks grabbed a kitchen towel from the oven and rushed to Juno's side, trying to staunch the bleeding. Gabija now held Austeja, trembling, her hands covered in her daughter's blood. Elijah tentatively put his hands on Gabija's back. She whipped around, striking Elijah across the face.

"Leave us alone!" she screamed, her voice breaking into hysterics.

Elijah had let the blow touch him, his own grief numbing the impact. He felt the sticky blood left on his cheek from her hands. Austeja's blood.

Gabija leaned over her daughter and continued sobbing.

Elijah's eyes found Juno's. His failure washed over him as he took in Juno's brokenness: his labored, troubled breathing, his outpouring of loss.

The five minutes it took for the ambulances and squad cars to arrive seemed to be the loneliest hours Elijah had ever experienced. The arrival of police backup was the usual flashing lights, shouting, clearing the property, and closing the alley and surrounding area to preserve the crime scene. Juno's family was taken to the nearest hospital. As the police gathered what they could and made the necessary calls, Marks led Elijah to the front of the house.

"Where's your bike?"

They gathered Elijah's stashed bike and gear and put it in the squad car. Marks drove them back downtown to the station, but stopped halfway to pull into an empty parking lot.

Elijah stared out the window, not saying anything. He felt more than saw Marks examining him by the dim streetlight glow. "How're you doing?"

Elijah growled. "Fuck you, Marks. They hit Juno and killed his daughter. How the fuck do you think I'm doing?"

His voice was rising. Marks grabbed his wrist. "Stop."

Marks released him. No one spoke as Elijah gathered himself. Then, in a quiet voice, "Are we going to their meeting hall now?"

Marks knew whose hall he was talking about. "No. It's only a few days 'til they come to us. When they do, we're all gonna be sure there's such a battle that there'll be very little need for prosecution afterwards. I've had it, you've had it, and, believe me, the officers at the station will be more than happy to make that dream come true. I was thinking we could go to the hospital now, instead."

Elijah stared into the darkness. Juno had taken care of him since they'd gotten back. He'd made sure Elijah stayed healthy, eating and exercising. He'd talked Elijah down over and over, always there to listen to his night terrors and dark thoughts. Elijah would've killed himself by now had it not been for Juno. He'd included him in his family, and look how Elijah repaid him.

"We fucked up, Marks. Where the hell were you? I got all the way up to Juno's house and you weren't there. What the fuck were you doing?"

Elijah turned to look at him, but Marks avoided his gaze. "I went to get some coffee and missed your first text. When I got back to the car, it didn't occur to me to look at the fucking phone. I knew I'd fucked up when you texted me the second time. I missed it, man. I hauled my ass up to the house as soon as I could. You were over the fence before I could react. We didn't yell out that we were police. We didn't give them a chance to surrender. We violated fucking procedure."

"We did what we had to do."

"I know, but how am I going to explain that you got to the bikers before I did?" Marks groaned. "I'm calling Culver in a minute. He'll bring us in for a debrief in the morning. Do you need to call anyone while I call Culver?

Elijah realized that he did have someone to call. At that moment, he wanted to hear Rick's voice more than anything.

53

THE HOSPITAL

Gabija sat in the uncomfortable chair—the only chair—of Juno's hospital room. Her hands were folded under her chin, her elbows propped against her knees. She was probably stiff from sitting like that for so long. She didn't know. Didn't care to know.

Her daughter was in the morgue. They had pronounced her dead in the ambulance.

Her husband would be fine, physically. He needed surgery, and he'd lost a significant amount of blood, but his organs were fine, the pellets removed. His mental state was another matter. They'd been doing so well. Their family had been whole, growing . . .

Hot, fresh tears rolled down her cheeks. Gabija didn't move to wipe them away.

Matas was with Gabija's cousin, Kajus Okunis. He'd arrived at the hospital within an hour of them, handling the paperwork and questions Gabija couldn't bear to answer herself. He'd taken Matas home with him when her son had been released, a decision she hadn't fought. She didn't have the energy to care for her son, didn't have the strength to comfort him. Not this night. Her daughter was in the morgue.

And it was all Elijah's fault.

Where she had grown up in Lithuania, she was taught that each person was assigned a specific death, at a certain time and in a certain manner. At that time, the angel of death would collect her souls and take them to paradise. Austeja should not be in the hands of the angel of death. She was snatched because of the stupidity of Elijah McCoy.

All that man did was take from her. He may have saved her husband once, but he had since taken her husband's patience, his reputation, her family's safety, and now her daughter. He was a heartless, selfish man. She wanted to snatch her daughter from the hands of the angel of death and tell her to take Elijah instead. She wished she could do to Elijah what he had done to her daughter. She knew that Juno loved Elijah as a brother and would still love him. But it was over between her and Mr. McCoy.

Juno moaned in his sleep. Gabija's eyes focused on his bandaged form for a moment, but when he resumed his deep, medicated slumber, she let her focus slip away.

Austeja needed a funeral. The thought was sour, foreign, and difficult for her to comprehend. Lithuanian culture demanded a quick arrangement, but Gabija didn't have the strength to coordinate one. Her cousin was taking care of that, too.

"A funeral will be sad at first, but a happy occasion, ultimately," her cousin had said to her in the hall some hours before. "Austeja is in celestial paradise now. She walks along in God's gardens."

Gabija remembered going to her mother's funeral as a small girl. Mother had been covered in the traditional funeral shroud, hiding her kind face from the light of day forever. She had been laid out like that for three days, feet facing the door, welcoming all visitors seeking closure. That was how it should be, a daughter burying a mother. Not this way.

The death process was a time of forgiveness and reconciliation. Gabija could not see how this was going to be possible, not when this horrible mistake had been made. The entire Lithuanian community through their church would come to pay respects and show solidarity with the family. Gabija was not prepared to be so forgiving.

Kajus had offered for someone in his family to stay with her at all hours until *this*—whatever "this" was—passed from her family. She wondered idly if they knew she desired revenge and were trying to stop her.

Elijah entered the hospital room with a police officer at his side. Gabija lifted her head from her hands, her neck protesting at the long-awaited motion. She'd never seen Elijah look this way. He was pale, his eyes bloodshot, face dirty. Nausea flooded her stomach when she realized what the small specks of brown were on his cheek.

"Gabija, I . . ." His voice was hoarse. "I don't know what to say. What to do."

"You could leave."

"Elijah?" They both turned to the bed. Juno was waking up, groggy from the medicine. Gabija rushed to his side.

"How do you feel?"

"Empty."

A lump formed in her throat. It was all she could do to nod.

Juno turned slowly to Elijah. "Brother." He held up his hand for Elijah to hold. Elijah just looked down, unable to face his friend.

Elijah started to sob. Gabija didn't know that man could cry. He grabbed his friend's hand and bowed his head to Juno's chest. Juno patted Elijah's head. "You risked your life to save me."

Elijah sniffed. "I drew this hate to your family and then I hesitated."

"It's the evil hearts of the bikers that brought this darkness to my family. We have been through so much, Elijah, and there is no end to us. We are brothers. Period."

Gabija stood. "I'll leave you two." She glanced at the officer, who stood with hands folded before him against the wall. "I'm down the hall if you need me."

She stormed from the room, anger and grief blurring her vision.

54

THE DEBRIEFING

It was 8 a.m. Elijah sat in the lobby of the police station waiting for Culver to call him in. He'd had close to no sleep the night before, and his mind throbbed like a bad hangover. Lying in bed, watching the black night turn to gray dawn and listening to Rick's soft breathing had given Elijah plenty of time to think about what had happened. Why it had happened. He'd hesitated, it was his fault. But why had Juno been hit in the first place? The bikers should've been too preoccupied with Operation FTW, the Organ Concert, to bother with him. It had to be Lamb.

After hours of wrestling with the idea, Elijah had come to the conclusion that it was the only explanation that made sense. Lamb wanted Juno out of the equation so it'd be easier for Elijah to walk away.

Officer Thomas settled into the seat next to him, offering him a cup of coffee. "It's from that place near your condo, I thought it would taste better than what we brew here."

Elijah held the cup with both hands, letting it warm his hands. "Thanks."

"I ran into someone interesting at the coffee shop," Thomas continued.

"Oh?" Elijah didn't look up from his warm cup.

"Mm-hm. A young barista. Apparently, she's got a date with Marks this Friday. She met him last night. Thought he was a real charmer."

Elijah turned to her, a cold fury stirring within him. "Last night? Are you telling me the sergeant's dick put his phone on Do Not Disturb?"

Thomas gave a careful nod. "I think that might be true."

"Damn it!" Elijah pounded his fist on his knee. "It was his delay that cost me the jump on those rat bastards. I started to move on them just when he showed up. When I turned to be sure there wasn't another biker sneaking up on me, that delay allowed those bastards to shoot. Austeja is dead because of it."

Thomas clamped her hand on Elijah's wrist. "I know. This could cost the sergeant his job. Do we want to do that? There's no justification for what he did when he was on duty. Are you going to share this with anyone other than me?"

Elijah huffed. "I don't know. When I see him, I'll know what I'll do to him."

"Do what you gotta do, man. But use your head. If you rat Marks out, do it calmly and with facts. Don't blow up and attack him in a police station. That'll only hurt both of you."

The front door to the station opened, spilling bright sunlight and an exhausted Marks into the lobby.

Shana greeted her partner. "Good morning, sergeant. You OK?"

Marks looked like he had spent the night pacing. There was still the smell of alcohol on his breath. He turned to Elijah. "How you doing, McCoy?"

"Fuck you, Marks."

"I won't have that talk in my station." Lieutenant Culver walked out of his office, hands on his hips. "I want all of you in here. Come on."

Elijah followed the two officers into the cluttered office. He and Marks sat in the chairs opposite Culver's desk. Thomas leaned against the wall, her right elbow resting on her left arm wrapped around her torso, coffee in hand.

Culver settled into his desk. "McCoy, you were not to engage the bikers under any circumstance. Sergeant Marks was on his way to help. He didn't call it in as a possible shooting because he didn't know the details based on your texts. You chose instead to act on your own. How the hell did this happen?"

Elijah looked at Thomas, who looked at Marks. Marks shrugged and let out a slow breath. "If McCoy had given me more details, I would've had all available units rolling toward Valdas's house. We would've gotten there in time."

Marks looked at Elijah, but flinched when he met Elijah's death stare. He turned to Culver. "Oh shit. Lieutenant, McCoy was waiting outside the fence in the alley for me to show, but by the time I arrived they opened fire and he was over the fence. It happened. There's no changing it now."

"*It?*" Elijah stood and rounded on Marks. Thomas pushed herself between the two, forcing Elijah to take a step back. "*It* being a dead child, you fuckhead."

"McCoy!" Culver barked. "Control yourself."

Elijah met Culver's eyes, but his words were directed at Marks. "Juno's daughter is dead. Juno is injured, and he and Gabija are crazy with grief. Their son watched his sister die, and you want me to *control* myself?"

Tears stung Elijah's eyes, from grief or anger he didn't know. Tears were a new experience for him. Gabija's cousin, Kajus Okunis, had always told Juno that Elijah was trouble, to not let him get close. Gabija was staying with Okunis while Juno stayed in the hospital, and Elijah knew he'd never get a chance to speak to her, to apologize. Hell, he felt too guilty to even go see Juno again.

Culver turned to Marks with a sense of dread. "Tell me,

sergeant, how did McCoy get to the Valdas home before you? And how did he have time to identify the problem and track it to the backyard of the house? From your report and what you just said, McCoy was at the fence in the alley when you arrived. Is that accurate?"

Marks looked down at the desk. "It is, lieutenant."

Culver leaned over his desk. "How does a man, a man *you* were supposed to be watching, get halfway across town on a bike before you noticed?"

Marks didn't respond. Elijah saw that his hands were slightly trembling. Culver looked at Elijah. "Tell me the truth here, McCoy. What the fuck happened?"

Thomas walked over to Marks and put a gentle hand on his shoulder. "Tell him, Jamel. Go on."

Marks shrugged off Thomas's hand. "I took a break and went to get coffee. I started talking to a girl, and I didn't hear the first text come in. McCoy rode out without seeing that I wasn't in the car. I didn't realize he'd gone until I got the second text asking me where I was."

Culver ran a hand down his face. "You didn't hear the text in the coffee shop. Did you check your phone when you walked out of the coffee shop? Did you check it when you got back in the car? Tell me that you did. Blame the phone. Do something to help me out here, sergeant."

"I didn't look at my damn phone."

Culver stood. "Marks, turn in your guns and badge and go home. You're on administrative leave until we complete this investigation. You will give this statement to IA before you leave. McCoy." Culver looked him square in the eye. "We're a few days out from the bust. Everything's in place here, and I don't want to hear anything about you hunting down bikers or meddling with our operation. Understood?"

Elijah felt the kind of calm, dead calm, that he often experienced in the midst of a battle when there was a gap in the action. He was composed, ready to act. He was sharp and cold, the person-ification of violence.

"Understood."

55

EXIT STRATEGY

Elijah had Officer Thomas drop him at the condo. He was exhausted, the past few hours finally catching up with him. When she pulled up in front of the condo, she turned and held Elijah by the wrist. "Hey. Call me if you need anything, OK? I'm always here to talk."

Elijah nodded and got out of the cruiser. When he got to his floor of the building, he wasn't surprised to see the door hanging ajar. Rick was too careful in this part of town to not double-check the locks as he left.

Elijah walked up to the door and called, "Hello, Lamb."

Lamb was sitting on the living room sofa, some kind of clear drink in his hand. Elijah doubted it was water.

Lamb smiled. "Last night was an opera for me. You provide the best entertainment I've had in a long time. Look at you!" He stood, sweeping his cocktail-armed hand over Elijah's stiff frame. "You sent two more people out of this sphere for good. Well, maybe not *good*."

"I didn't kill two people. You're slipping."

"Oh, I know that officer shot one of them, but you get the

credit. When you went over the fence you scared the pants right off the sergeant—it was great. I just love to watch you work. And once again, you're the only one that comes out unscathed. Juno and his family are scarred for life. Wow. Just think, it will never end for that family."

A blackness filled Elijah, its chilled fingers gripping his heart. He could see Juno's family, always changed and always with the pain of Austeja's death. He could see them marking holidays and landmarks in life by wondering what Austeja would have done, or how she would have reacted. "Fuck you, Lamb. Juno said you were the devil, but I didn't believe him. Didn't buy into that kind of thing. But you are, aren't you?"

They were supposed to be working together, but he killed Austeja. An opera, he'd said. A beautiful night at the opera. Elijah stepped forward, his aggressive stride pushing Lamb further into the apartment.

"I want to see you torn open with a shotgun shell," Elijah snarled. "I want to see your organs torn to shreds, to hear you cry out in pain. You motherfucker. All your time and energy is spent on sadness, destruction. God damn you."

Lamb raised his hands, a hint of fear in his eyes. "Watch it, soldier. Careful what you say and bring into this conversation. I'm helping you. I'm not the one who's killed a dozen men in the last two years—that's serial killer numbers, you realize. You were the one who killed the truck driver in cold blood, instead of scaring him off. You *choose* violence, Elijah McCoy, as if you have the right to kill whomever you want. You think you get to make the death decision about people you don't even know. Now this destructive addiction of yours has caused your best friend to lose his only daughter. You did this, Elijah. Not me. And that truth just kills you, doesn't it?"

Elijah formed a fist. He could hit this creature, couldn't he? "You're a bastard."

"Always the poet, Elijah. I know suicide has crossed your mind. You're thinking about it right now, aren't you?"

Elijah blinked. He'd been thinking about that on the drive home, just now. Lamb smiled.

"I'll be happy to take you, if you do that, but what a waste of talent. Give your new life a chance. Try it for a while. You can always get desperate later and kill yourself."

"I could die this Thursday. I could die in prison."

"You're not going to prison, my dear. Let's just say you have a . . . different life waiting for you. Money, weapons, women—I guess men, now, eh?" Lamb gave a wicked grin. "All that and more, as soon as the time comes for me to retrieve you from your iron bed. You just have to be willing to give up all connections to your past. You hurt people all the time, it's how you are. You kill people. The best thing you can do for people you like is to leave them alone. It's safer for them."

Elijah thought about living without love or friendship, without a real connection to anyone. There'd be no Juno, no Phillip, no Rick.

No Rick . . . The thought was a stab to his heart, but a part of him knew Rick deserved better. Elijah would only bring pain to his life, the way he'd brought pain to Juno's.

Elijah released the tension in his fist, allowing his muscles to relax with an inward sigh. "I have to get away from Juno. I'll never be able to forgive myself for Austeja's death."

But I'm preparing a large group of children for death and injury, just like Austeja in her innocence and vulnerability.

Like earthworms wriggling to the muddy surface in a rainstorm, the pain of all he had endured and caused over the past eight years surfaced in his heart. There were so many children that would live without their fathers, brothers, or uncles because of him. *They will never be able to forgive me, either. None of them.*

"When I go with you, I want it to look like I was killed," Elijah said, decided. "I want Juno to be able to accept my separation."

And Rick, too, but he wanted to keep Rick as far from Lamb's thoughts as he could.

Lamb looked thoughtful. He backed away from Elijah and lowered himself slowly onto the sofa. "Of course. You will be given a way to escape at the end. All you have to do is get to Pier 51 and someone will help you get out of the area. Apropos, no? All you will have to do is make the decision to walk away. That's the rule."

Elijah raised an eyebrow. "There's a rule? Really? Who makes the rules *you* have to follow?"

Lamb looked directly at him. "It's better if you don't know. No need to frighten you. You've met my boss once, at your old safe house, and he's not the one."

Elijah sunk into a chair, palms sweaty. He remembered that night. He hadn't been able to process it, what with everything happening. It was easier to shove the whole memory to the back of his mind. "So, I have to either walk away with you, or from you."

"It's as simple as that, my *budelis*. Have you decided how you're joining the fight?"

A shiver ran down Elijah's spine. He'd heard Juno say that word before, whenever he slipped into Lithuanian while talking to Elijah, normally when he was really upset. It meant *executioner*. Why had Lamb chosen to use that language?

He tried to shake it off. "I'll go over and set up a forward observer post. But I'll need you to give me as much lead time as possible. I have to get in and settled with no one knowing. I want to make sure that the birds and rats and anything else in the area are comfortable with me being there. I don't want anything to give me away. When the bikers start to win, I'll kill them all."

Lamb stood. "You'll have the information by the morning. I'll be nearby the day of. When the time comes, and you will know when that is, I'll provide you with a way out. Have fun. Kill some cops as well, if you want."

Then Lamb was gone.

Elijah stood, a little shaken, and walked out to the balcony.

Gripping the rail, he looked out over the neighborhood and the afternoon bustle down on the streets. He liked this neighborhood, it was nice. In a few days, he'd never see it again.

He'd never see Rick again.

Rick, with his warm heart and selfless passion. He loved him, he loved him with as much of his heart as he could bear, and he was going to lose him. Their long nights together. The internship. The patio breakfasts and evening talks. Gone.

Elijah's heart cracked with pain, and he had to put his hand over it, pushing hard, to get it to stop. There was love and dancing and romance in the world, but not for him.

He thought about Phillip and the group he'd introduced him to. He had gone to at least one party and danced. It would never happen again, though. Why not? Why couldn't he fall in love and get married and have a long happy life with Rick? How had he gotten here? Eight years spent with Juno in and out of the military, eight years of intense brotherly love, over.

It would be kinder for Elijah to walk away from the people he cared about, but it'd be more painful, too. Leaving was the only way to survive. The other alternative was to stay and fight, only to go through a heartbreaking trial and off to jail to fight for his life there. He was trapped. There was no good alternative; there was no one to turn to. Was there?

56

A SLENDER THREAD

Rick's sore back woke him. He exhaled a breath, his sleepy mind acknowledging the pain. Soft light filtered through the bedroom window, the city's glow highlighting Elijah's shoulder beside him.

Rick smiled as his heart filled. He rolled over on his side to face Elijah, his back straightening and the pain subsiding. He was careful not to bump Elijah. It was hard for the soldier to sleep through a night, and Rick didn't want to disturb his partner's still slumber. He got close enough to smell Elijah and let himself slide back into his peaceful sleep.

$\sim$

This was not like any helicopter Elijah had ever ridden in before. He had been called back—he always knew he would be. The equipment was more advanced than what he was used to, far surpassing the technology he had worked with before returning to the States. It was a helicopter and it was taking him to a mission, that's all he needed to know.

The flight was so much higher than any he'd ever taken, the trees below a green haze through the patchy fog. One of the helicopter's large side doors was open, but there was no rushing wind or prop gurgles. A nice improvement. He could tell they were moving faster than he was used to, but that would get them to the drop site earlier and could help with any element of surprise.

Lining the opposite side of the copter were his men, a dozen soldiers decked in more of the strange equipment. Elijah wasn't a small man, but he seemed to always be placed in these units that were staffed with giants. It didn't bother him, not when he knew they'd be on his side in battle.

Elijah knew his orders for this mission: obliterate a small village in the mountains. The orders were specific. It was important that every human being they found in the village be killed in a way that would make identification difficult. There were no forensic labs in the mountains, and dragging parts of dead people long distances would be tough. But that was not his concern. He was supposed to ensure the buildings were rendered useless—an easy task by the looks of the explosives his team carried.

There shouldn't be any confusion about what exactly was to be destroyed—the mountains were fairly remote. In his experience, he'd handled unclear orders by making sure he damaged everything and killed everyone he could find. He'd always wondered if he was supposed to kill any animals he found. Sometimes he did, sometimes he didn't.

One of the men yelled something Elijah didn't make out. "What was that?"

The man repeated himself, but he wasn't speaking English. Elijah frowned. "Did anyone catch that?"

Several of the other men then spoke as if to answer him, their faces calm, but none of them spoke English. That was odd. Concerning, even. No point worrying about it. He was sure he had the right men for the mission and that they knew just what was expected of them.

The red light over the door clicked to yellow. They were close to the target. Elijah started to pull his gear together, sliding on weapons, ammunition, and supplies. He turned to the men and motioned at the yellow light, hefting his gear suggestively. As one, they began to prepare for the strike.

The village loomed through the mist, only a few minutes away. Elijah looked away from the open door and noticed the three men farthest from him. They were bleeding heavily, one holding his hand over his gouged stomach. What had happened? He looked around the cabin of the chopper but didn't see any reason for the wounds. The other men didn't seem to be interested. They all just turned their backs on the wounded men and moved toward the door. There was blood on the floor, and it smelled like death in the chopper. Why wasn't the open door dragging away the smell? It was stifling.

The men lined up for a quick exit, but without warning, the first man stepped out into the void. These men were not paratroopers. The mission was designed for them to jump down from a few feet above the ground as the chopper hovered.

"What are you doing?" Elijah yelled. The second soldier followed the first. One by one, each solider quietly turned to look at Elijah before stepping out into the mist.

"Stop!" Elijah wanted to scream, but no sound came out. Elijah tried to move, to stop at least some of the men, but his limbs were heavy. He couldn't reach them in time.

The village was almost under him. The last man stepped out just as Elijah reached the edge of the helicopter. Elijah watched in horror as the soldier hit the hard ground, his head bursting on impact. The soldier's body flailed for a brief moment before becoming still in a pool of blood. And then he was out of view.

The chopper stopped over the village, Elijah the last passenger on board. There were over thirty armed village men waiting on the ground looking up at him. Elijah knew that he was expected to fight. That was what he did.

A green light started flashing over the door, even though they were still thirty feet up. The chopper seemed to be set there with no move to descend. He looked at the cable by the door. He'd been picked up and dropped with a cable like this many times before.

The cable was much more slender than normal, but it must be some modern material. All these types of cables were set up with a leather strap at the end that was wrapped under your arms and connected to an open hook at the top of the strap. Only the fact that you closed your arms across your body kept you in, and when you were close to the ground, you'd just open your arms and slide out. Elijah reached over and hit the button and the cable started to unroll. He hooked himself onto the cable and approached the edge of the helicopter—and the leering faces below.

Elijah was certain he was going to be shot as he descended from the helicopter, but he had a job to do.

He stood there for a moment, taking deep breaths, then pulled his M16 around and fired into the crowd below. A handful of men fell to their knees, badly wounded. The rest of the men yelled at him, telling him to stop being a coward and to come down and fight like a man. This, like so much he had been through, seemed stupid and dangerous. He stepped to the door, shouldered the M16, gripped his SRK knife, and stepped out.

Elijah swung for a few seconds before the cable engaged and started to lower him. As he descended, Elijah knew that a static electricity charge was building within him. When he got close enough, he kicked out at one of the men, shocking him with enough electricity to send the man to the ground shaking and moaning. Everyone stepped back.

Elijah let go of the strap when he landed and pulled his M16 around. The men of the village were enraged, moving toward him with machetes and knives raised. Elijah pulled the trigger of his gun, but nothing happened. He frowned. He took care of his weapons, and it had fired just a few minutes ago. He let the gun swing back to his side and pulled out his SRK.

This'll make things messier.

Elijah was ready to throw himself into the oncoming villagers. He crouched, ready to engage a man with a stained bandage wrapped around his neck, and raised his knife to—suddenly, something pulled him back, lifting him high into the air faster than anyone could reach him.

Elijah . . .

Rick? What was he doing here? Elijah didn't want him to get hurt. He felt arms wrap around him, replacing the cable that hung from the helicopter. Elijah tried to get away from Rick, to save him, but Rick wouldn't let go.

Elijah, wake up. Elijah. Rick called his name, over and over, as Elijah dangled over the mountains. Someone touched his cheek. Elijah was in Afghanistan, he *knew* he was, but he turned to find Rick holding him, the bedroom wall his backdrop. He recognized that wall; there was the picture of the Northern California coast they had purchased together.

Elijah tried to push Rick away, intent on keeping Rick out of the battlefield. *I can't lose you.* He struggled harder against the arms, but Rick jumped on Elijah, keeping a firm but gentle hold on him as he continued to say his name.

Elijah stopped moving. It was quiet. No chopper, no angry villagers or guns. The only sound was Rick's intent voice, calling to him. Rick's soft hand stroked his cheek. Elijah's heart squeezed, his breathing calming.

Elijah wrapped his arms around Rick and breathed in his familiar smell. It felt so good to have him in his arms. In a minute, the mountains disappeared completely and Elijah found himself again rooted in their bed, in their bedroom. It was night, and they were in bed together.

Rick was kissing Elijah on the cheeks and holding him. He sat up, pulling Elijah with him. "Are you back? Are you OK?"

Elijah looked into Rick's soft brown eyes, there in the half-light of the Oakland night, and whispered, "You came back for me. You saved me."

Rick kissed away a tear from Elijah's cheek. "Always."

They settled back into bed, their bodies sliding together from toe to chest. Rick reached down and hooked a corner of the comforter and pulled it up over them before putting his arms back around Elijah.

"I was called back to Afghanistan," Elijah whispered into the darkness. "I was being sent to my death. Until you saved me."

Rick was stroking Elijah's back, still kissing his cheek. "You were moving around quite a bit. It woke me up."

"I'm sorry."

Rick chuckled softly. "Don't be. You were moaning a little, but it sounded more sad than scared. I didn't know where you were, but I knew you were under attack from something. I wanted you back here with me."

Elijah had never been held, not until he met Rick. He had never snuggled with anyone in his life. He had never had affection or tenderness, never had peaceful sleep. "I hate this fucking war, Rick."

"It's OK. We'll just keep fighting it until we win. If you need to fight, then take me with you. If you want to talk, then talk to me. If you need help, then let me give it to you. I just want you, Elijah. All of you."

Elijah couldn't talk without wanting to cry for a long time after that. It was a thought he didn't dare form completely, but maybe—just maybe—he'd be able to come back from the war someday. He had someone to come back to now, if he came back. When he fell asleep again, Rick was still holding him.

Outside, the darkness caressed the window, trying to get in.

57

THE COFFEE SHOP

Officer Thomas was waiting for him outside World Coffee. Elijah waved at her as he rolled his bike to a pole and locked it up. It'd been difficult to convince her to meet him like this, but Elijah knew the rookie didn't have much of a choice. She was babysitting him solo now, with Marks on suspension after his fuck-up at Juno's house. If she hadn't agreed to sit down to talk, he would've just climbed into her cruiser.

"Coffee?" Elijah offered, holding the door open for her.

Shana looked nervous, glancing around as she entered the café. "Yes, please. Black."

Elijah smiled. "Coming up."

He ordered their coffees and Thomas found them a table by the big windows. Elijah sat across from her. He tried to keep his composure, but his leg kept ticking. He folded his hands on the table. "It's almost time for the big day."

Thomas sighed. "Elijah—"

Elijah put his hands up, stopping her. "I know, I know. I'm not a part of this. But you know I love a good battle. I'm just curious how you're all doing. Are you all organized? You know what's important to me here."

Shana sipped the hot coffee and smiled a little with pleasure. The coffee shop babble hid their words from unwelcome patrons—not that anyone was sitting close to the cop and veteran. "We have agencies from around the country logged on for the operation. No one likes child murderers. We've all had bad encounters with the Sons of Perdition, and everyone in the station is hyped to finally do something about it. FBI's been working with us around the clock since you gave us the tip-off. The lieutenant was telling Lieutenant Cho—"

"Who?" Elijah leaned forward.

"Benson Cho. The SWAT commander. He was telling him about our informant, but Cho was suspicious that you may tip off the gang. Lieutenant Culver was adamant about defending you. He really trusts you."

Elijah frowned, the compliment rolling past him. There were a lot of moving parts to this operation. Hopefully not too many. Oversaturate a mission with too many commanders and it could easily topple.

"The fact that you came to us so willingly," Thomas continued, "and that you're close to this Mr. Lamb guy is pretty amazing. We couldn't have pulled this off without you."

"It's not pulled off yet," Elijah reminded her. "As a soldier, I can't imagine giving up your troops to anyone. You know, I tried tricking Lamb into giving up his troops, but then he just offered their lives to me—and he was enthusiastic to do it."

Thomas's eyes narrowed, concerned. "He's disturbed."

Elijah nodded. "At least."

There was a short silence. Thomas drummed her unpolished nails against her paper coffee cup. "Why have we never seen this man? Is the source really you, Elijah?"

Elijah put his hand on top of hers. She looked surprised, but didn't remove it. "It's not me. You might think I'm crazy, but I trust you, and I trust that you understand that I completely mean what I'm about to say."

He took a breath. "I think Mr. Lamb is a servant of the devil. B. A. Lamb—Balaam. He seems to know everything, knows where I am all the time. I've never seen him use a door, and sometimes I think I'm the only one who can see him. This isn't the first time my mind's played tricks on me. I didn't think he was a spirit for a long time. It was Juno's idea. Something I just chalked up to his religion. But I get a really bad feeling from him. I see no love or kindness or truth in him. I just . . . thought that if you were going to fight him, and if I'm right, then you should know this. I know I'm not the sanest person you know, but Juno's the sanest man I know, and if he believes it, then so do I."

Elijah waited for her to laugh, but Thomas was silent. She stared at his hand for a moment longer, then turned her hand over and wrapped her fingers around Elijah's strong hand and squeezed. "Juno's right."

Elijah gasped. "Really?"

"Mm-hm. And I think Lieutenant Culver might believe that as well. It's not the kind of thing you ever say out loud in a police station. Do you think that something supernatural is going to happen Thursday night?"

Elijah spoke slowly, trying to speak to the woman before him while convincing his own self of reality of his words. Thoughts of a darkness in his safe house floated across his mind. "The fight will be horrible, with or without the supernatural. Death will roam between the two sides at will. Any battle like this is supernatural; there's no human sense in fighting like this. All you can do is survive."

Thomas's hand trembled. "Fuck, Elijah. I—I have to say I'm scared."

Elijah put his other hand on top of their joined hands and stilled her. "Then you might survive. Be scared. There is something you can do to make sure you survive."

"Tell me."

Elijah met her eyes. They were brown with flecks of gold that complemented her rich, umber-brown skin. He'd never cared to look that closely before. He was surprised to see a bit of himself in her eyes, the wild panic he'd once felt before a first battle many years ago.

"Thomas, feel your fear. Just be mechanical about your preparation. We'd travel to our mission in helicopters and not a single man would speak on the way there. It's better that way. Travel without distraction, without talking. Once the operation gets underway, you'll see bad men and helpless children moving around with weapons and cold hearts. Don't be afraid. Be outraged. Let your sense of right throw you into the battle. Have the attitude that they cannot shoot at you and try to harm you without having to pay the ultimate price. Use your skills and training. They will kick in for you, I promise.

"Take the weapons and your outrage to the fight. See the enemy as dead as you approach them. When they attack, you just tell yourself, 'oh no you don't, not with me motherfucker.' You don't have to worry about getting hurt or killed, you just have to worry about fighting. Go beyond that and don't think of yourself as fighting. You're killing. Injuries and death either happen or not—that's for after the battle. It's surprisingly easy to pull a man's life out of his body. Let them be afraid of you."

Elijah exhaled a breath he hadn't realized he'd been holding as he spoke. His blood stirred at the memories of past battles in the deserts and mountains of a distant country.

Thomas's eyes shimmered, the cold fear replaced with a burning.

"Shit, McCoy," she breathed. "You think I can be that tough? Me, a rookie detective?"

"Stop thinking that way. Doubt often becomes a self-fulfilling prophecy. You'll have to think of yourself as the agent of death, or . . ."

He dropped her gaze and pulled away from her, his agitation returning.

"Or? Or what? Tell me."

"Take me," he whispered. "I'm death to any enemy I encounter. I can help you get through this."

Thomas pursed her lips. "You know that isn't up to me. I'd have you right next to me if I could, but that isn't going to happen. Don't try to come, you'll be so fucked if you do. It's not like you're in a very good position with the force. Don't make it worse."

He knew this was coming, knew Thomas couldn't give him some free pass into the operation, but hearing it out loud from his last hope made Culver's decision somehow more final. Juno, Gabija, Austeja . . . how could he ensure their vengeance if he wasn't able to fight for them?

"I have to go. Please."

Thomas sat up, her old resolve returned. "What about Rick, huh? What the hell have you two been doing that you're trying to get killed in a battle?"

Elijah took a drink from his coffee. "I tried to leave him, to hurt him enough to make him leave."

Thomas raised an eyebrow. "That's terrible."

Elijah held his hands up, stopping her once more. "Hold on. He wouldn't let me. I told him everything—the deaths, the devil, all of it, but he won't let me just walk away. He doesn't understand, I *have* to avenge Juno's family. It's my responsibility. But if I die in battle, then Rick . . . fuck."

Thomas smiled. "Love's a bitch sometimes, huh?"

Elijah nodded weakly. Thomas laughed. "It's good to feel this way. It's called feelings, having a heart. You weren't like that when I first met you. Welcome home."

Elijah fidgeted in his seat. He felt so exposed at that table. "So, what's the mission look like for Thursday? What's the plan?"

Thomas was quiet, an awkward tilt to her posture. "I can't say. It's confidential. You know that, Elijah."

Elijah sighed. "I do. Thanks for hearing me out, Shana. You're a good soldier."

Thomas choked on her coffee. "I think that's the first time you've ever called me by my first name."

Elijah smiled and stood. "A moment of weakness. Be careful out there, but be bold. Trying to hide or hesitating will get you killed."

Like when I hesitated at Juno's. His heart cracked open.

Shana walked Elijah out of World Coffee and got back in her cruiser. She followed his bike all the way back to the condo, parking in her usual surveillance spot and watching him enter the building.

An hour later, Elijah exited through a side door, speeding away undetected.

58

FINAL BRIEFING

Magnus Carlson hated these meetings. To distance himself from his guest, he stood and walked away from his desk to the small coffee bar along the far wall. "I still don't like this. We'll have to see what my sergeant at arms and road captain say this afternoon. I don't feel like we're totally ready for this." He poured himself a cup, then, on second thought, pulled out a second mug. "Coffee?"

"Please," said Mr. Lamb. "This is simpler than you're making it out to be, Magnus. You have the element of surprise. Thank you."

Lamb accepted the cup of coffee and had a small sip, then set it down on the end table and laced his long arm over the back of the blood-red leather couch. "From what I hear, the police are focusing on money laundering operations—yours and others—that they know about. Between that and all the prostitution busts they've been making, the OCPD is delightfully distracted."

Carlson returned to his desk with a grunt. Mr. Lamb seemed to hear a lot of things most folk didn't. He wondered just how high up Lamb's sources were in the police station, and how much they cost him. "And you think that's all enough to keep them busy this week?"

"I do. How are the personnel plans? Do you have a final number?"

Carlson gave a rough laugh. He was never much of a planner. That was what that damned Forester was for, before he got himself killed. Planning this operation virtually alone had been a nightmare for him. "I will soon. Each of my men have been tracking at least two children and have plans to pick them up."

Lamb made a face. "In a dependable vehicle, I hope? I can't imagine children going unnoticed on the backs of bikes."

"Yes, yes. The bikes are just for the getaway." Carlson caught himself smiling at the thought. Things were developing smoothly, after all.

"See, this is not that complicated, is it? Relax, my friend. It's business as usual. Where are you going after the drop-off?"

"I haven't decided for sure, but I'm leaning toward Morenci, Arizona. A favorite oasis of mine."

Mr. Lamb raised his mug in salute. "Go get rich. Things are good right now."

Carlson walked Mr. Lamb out not long after that, holding the door open for him. After he was gone, Carlson reviewed the logistics for Operation Fuck the World while he waited for his two designated leaders to arrive for their final briefing. A soft knock at the door announced their arrival.

"Come in," he called.

Tito and Yuri sat with their notes across from him at his desk. Even Carlson found humor in the contrast between the men's grungy clothes and crisp, white notepaper.

"The trucks are rolling toward us right now," Tito said. "They'll be in Oakland City this afternoon and will sit overnight in the yard."

Carlson nodded. "Send out a message to the men that the operation starts mid-afternoon tomorrow. I don't want any side hustles going on while the Coyotes are here. Yuri? How many riders did you manage to gather?"

"There are thirty-nine ready to work tomorrow. We could've had a few more with more notice."

"It is what it is. Thirty-nine plus the three of us?"

"Thirty-nine includes us, but not you. So, forty with you. I'm so happy you're riding with us, boss."

"Like I'm going to be sitting here twiddling my thumbs after all this. Tito, are you sure everyone's got a couple of kids ready to pick up?"

Tito nodded, thumbing his eyebrow before ducking down to pick up a large white binder. "Right here, boss. I've got every man's plan written down, from where his abduction is now to where he'll stash himself and his bike after he hightails it outta here."

Tito handed the binder to Carlson. He had put each plan in a clear plastic sleeve. It was . . . well organized, for sure. "And where will this binder be lying around for the next few weeks?"

"It rides with me. You've got my number if you need any of the info in it."

Yuri grinned. "This is so good. We're gonna to kick ass on this."

Carlson agreed. It was the best plan he'd ever hatched. It was a very good plan, except the police knew all the details. "You guys have done great. Today, talk to each man again. Have them in over the course of the day so there isn't some big ride in or nothing. Make sure they're ready to start picking up kids as school ends, that's the prime time. Make sure they've something to do from the time they pick 'em up 'til around the drop-off time. Give 'em a rough order of delivery. I don't want no big group of vehicles pouring into the lot. OK?"

Yuri nodded. "I'll be sure that happens, Magnus."

Carlson slapped his shoulder. "Good. Take each man to the vault and let him pick something from the stash. Let's get them started on their celebration for once they've gotten out of town. Anything else?"

Yuri held up his hand. "Several of the men have asked what they can do to the kids once they pick them up. You know, they're asking if they can fuck the little bastards."

Magnus raised an eyebrow in surprise. "Oh."

He hadn't thought of that. They're taking the kids to harvest their organs, nothing else. He didn't see how it'd be a problem to rough them up a bit first, they were just going to be thrown in a freezer truck anyway.

"Fine. Just make it clear that heavy beatings or anything that would affect their organs is out. Dead or severely injured property means no deal with the Coyotes. Comprende?"

Tito stood up, and Yuri followed. "Sí. We'll be the kings of Oakland City after this. So cool. Yuri, you good?"

"I'm good. We done here?"

Carlson stood as well. "Don't tell the men, but I have a surprise for the po-po. I'm taking all our C-4 in my trunk. Any sign of the cops, and I'll blow the whole city block. We're gonna leave a mark one way or the other, got me?"

Yuri slammed his fists together. "Fuck yeah, things just keep getting better. Penny and all our brothers are gonna be avenged, the city will get a kick in the ass, and we'll be living the high life."

Tito slapped Yuri on the back to get him moving. "High is for sure."

Carlson went back over to his desk. He looked at the operation's designated lot, circled on the map that Mr. Lamb had given him. He had to acknowledge that the man was an amazing planner. Mr. Lamb always made Carlson look good.

Acorn Industrial Area. West of the city, Mr. Lamb said he picked it because as a neighborhood it was rated "barely livable." But it wasn't really a neighborhood, it was an industrial area. Warehouses, heavy industry, and the commercial seaport. One report even said there was really no reason for the general public to visit the area. It was all gritty depots and storage supply centers with ugly business parks surrounded by chain-link fencing. There were loading docks for the transportation of goods and machinery, a few abandoned buildings with bars on the windows, and business-based trucks parked outside.

Carlson, with the help of Mr. Lamb, had arranged for the Coyote gang to set up their trucks in a large dirt lot filled with shipping containers. The Coyotes were bringing two trucks, even though one would be adequate for the size of the load. When the time came, they'd roll out the short distance to the Embarcadero and go in opposite directions, one truck carrying the load and the other serving as a decoy.

If they pulled this off . . . well, maybe Carlson wouldn't have to deal in the drug market ever again. This could be the start of a beautiful partnership.

59

OPERATION FUCK THE WORLD

Janette hurried to catch up with her big sister, grabbing the older girl by the corner of her pink and orange jacket. "Where we going now?"

DuSharme slowed her fast walk and smiled at her. "Same place we go every day after school. The clubhouse. Do you want some water and chips or somethin' from the store?"

Janette hopped up and down. "Yes!"

Her big sister always had the best ideas. Janette was in the third grade, but DuSharme was all the way in seventh—that meant she knew everything.

"How long you think we gonna be able to hang there?" Janette slipped her hand through DuSharme's elbow and DuSharme led the way to the corner store.

"Nobody's ever gonna buy that ratty old house. We'll hang out there 'til they come to tear it down. Who would care?"

The sliding door of Friendly Market dinged as Janette walked through. "We never going to the apartment again, are we?"

"Not while Mom is dating that unhappy George." DuSharme squinted at the bright bottles of soda behind the clear doors.

Janette wished they could get a Dr. Pepper, but DuSharme had only been able to snag a ten-dollar bill from their mom's boyfriend's wallet while he was asleep this morning. "He's just too big, and we lose whenever he wants to play with us."

Janette shivered at the thought. DuSharme put a hand on her shoulder. "It's OK, we've got the clubhouse."

They each got a bottle of water, an apple, and some chips before heading out down Twenty-Ninth Street. DuSharme talked about her friend Ranae as Janette munched on her apple, happy to listen. Once they got to the clubhouse, they sat on the stoop of the abandoned house and ate their chips, waiting for someone to notice them. When no one did, the two girls picked up their backpacks and started to go around the back.

"What you got for homework tonight?" Janette asked, her mouth full of chips. "We starting time problems. Teacher told us that even though there are fewer and fewer clocks with hands, they still gonna teach us on using them. What 'bout you? DuSharme?"

Janette turned around, surprised to see a look of fear on her sister's face.

"What—?"

Just then, a giant man lunged from the house's overgrown bushes, grabbing DuSharme by her pink and orange jacket and yanking her up off the ground. Janette tried to scramble out of the man's reach, but he quickly grabbed her before she could get away.

The man pulled two filthy socks from inside his leather jacket and crammed one into Janette's mouth before doing the same to her sister. Janette tried to look around, to see if anyone had noticed them, if anyone would come help, but a hood was tossed over her head and all she could see was darkness.

The van rumbled to a stop, but Janette's shaking continued. She could hear the all-too-familiar sounds of a bar outside. Beside her, DuSharme squirmed and rolled, but Janette guessed her sister was tied just as tightly as she was. After what felt like hours, the van doors opened and the she heard more than one person get in. The strangers were chuckling quietly in rough voices, their presence accompanied by the smell of cigarettes and beer.

What happened after that was worse than anything George had done to them.

~

Raimondi Park was a short ride from school for Ronnie. Mom wanted him in soccer to keep him busy until she got home in the afternoons. Ronnie liked the big green space, but he never stayed for stupid soccer practice. It was fine. None of the guys liked him much anyway. Today, he had a nice, big fat juicy joint in his backpack that he'd gotten from Steven Barninski. Once he slipped away, he'd have a hell of an afternoon to himself.

Coach Wilson called, "Ronnie, do you have your shirt this time?" The coach stood several yards away on the soccer field, his arms crossed before him.

"Hey, coach," Ronnie yelled back from the sidewalk. "I have it, but I have to get a quick assignment done, then I'll be over to practice. Just going to ride over to the tables and do it."

"You're here for soccer, Ronnie, not homework."

"Come on coach, I'll be there. Lighten up."

Coach was a loud man, but he never tracked Ronnie down once he disappeared. He was swamped with two assistant coaches and almost fifty kids to worry about. It was the same at school; the adults all talked a good game, but it wasn't that hard to just slide.

In the middle of the expansive park was a shallow ravine. There was always a breeze in Oakland City, excellent for blowing away the sweet stench of weed. Once a kid was out of sight, he was out of mind—and smell.

Ronnie reached the tables and looked around. No one was looking at him, not even Coach. They were all busy doing their own thing. He smiled and rode over the grass and down the sharp, short hill into the ravine.

Ronnie was halfway to the bottom when he realized he wasn't alone. Amongst the rotting logs and weeds crouched a man. He wore tattered jeans shoved into steel-toed boots and a leather vest over a white T-shirt that read "SOP."

Ronnie couldn't stop himself in time on the steep slope, his bike unresponsive on the wet dirt. The man jumped up and had a hold on Ronnie's handlebars before Ronnie could think of what else to do. The man's eyes were bloodshot, kind of like how Steven Barninski's eyes got after he ate his paper goods.

"Get off my bike, man." Ronnie said.

The strange man grabbed Ronnie by the neck in a vice grip and slipped a pillowcase over his head. There was a ripping sound followed by rough tape circling around Ronnie's mouth. Ronnie struggled, falling off his bike, but a heavy boot hit his side, pinning him to the ground. His backpack was yanked from his shoulders and he listened as the man rifled through his stuff.

The man hooted with glee. "Oh shit, a joint! Good omens today."

The pressure on Ronnie's side lessened as the man stepped off him, only to hoist the boy over his shoulder. Ronnie was shaking so hard by the time he was thrown in the trunk of a car that he could hardly breathe, not even caring to wonder what had happened to his nice bike.

~

Thiago had always hated his name. What had his mama been thinking when she named him that? She must've known it was a mistake, because his whole life Thiago had been called every name in the book except his own. But that had changed recently.

Ever since his dad got shot, walking by a bar one night after putting in his hours for the family at a second job, Mama started calling him Thiago more often. She treated him like he was the man of the family now. It all seemed so heavy. Sixth grade suddenly felt like kindergarten to him. He wanted to help out, but how was a kid like him supposed to get a job? He liked being treated like a man, like his mama needed him. He was determined to figure something out.

So, after school each day, Thiago walked the neighborhood before coming home to get to know the city and see what men do. He liked the guys that worked in construction. The neighborhood was changing so much, there seemed to be plenty of that kind of work going on. They did such cool stuff, and Thiago wanted nothing more than to join them. But he had to be eighteen to get a job like that, and six years seemed like a hundred to him.

Anything he could do at his age would only pay him like a dollar or something. It wasn't enough, but Thiago had a promise of money waiting for him on the outskirts of his neighborhood. He had the hundred-dollar bill in his pocket to prove it.

Yesterday, Thiago had been sitting outside a coffee shop, watching the shop boy across the street sweep the awnings, when a guy in a big, fancy car pulled up. It was dark blue and shiny, bulky like a car from an old movie. He'd stared, his eyes wide.

A man got out of the car and, seeing the boy on the curb, smiled at Thiago.

"Whatchya doing, son?" he asked. "You look down."

"I'm trying to find a job," Thiago replied. "But it's hard for someone small like me."

The man leaned against the car, listening. "Why's a kid like you need a job? Don't you have school?"

"I do, but after Dad . . ." Thiago swallowed. "After Dad died, Mama says I need to be the man of the house. I wanna help, I do, but most folks say I need to be eighteen to work."

The man nodded, thoughtful. "I've got a clubhouse with a few friends that always needs some little helpers like you. Ever heard of the Untouchables? No? That's 'cause we're secret." He'd winked, then rummaged in his pockets, pulling out the hundred-dollar bill Thiago now carried in his pocket. "Come find us tomorrow. We'll put you to work."

Thiago hurried down the lonely streets, searching for the address the man with the fancy car had given him. He had time before Mama got home from work to do a little something. He could start helping now.

Thiago heard boxes being stacked and looked down an alley. There was a guy putting some boxes in his van. The man smiled and waved to him.

"Over here," he said. The man smiled and said to come down.

Thiago wondered if he was an Untouchable, or knew about them, so he went over. The man pointed into the van. Thiago turned to look, but the man dropped a bag over his head. It really hurt as the man slipped some plastic wire-feeling things around his wrists and feet, then tightened them a lot more than he needed to. It was when the door clicked shut that Thiago realized he wasn't going to be home when his mama got there.

60

ORGAN CONCERT

Shana woke early Thursday morning, not well rested but unable to sleep any longer. She got up in the dark and dressed, keeping her movements methodical and under direction. She had to be mechanical today. Elijah had told her it was the best way to survive. Mechanical was fine by her. It was that or panic.

The people involved in that night's operation were told to come in a little late, as it was expected to be a long day, but Shana was at her desk and filing busywork by 7 a.m. At eleven, she went to the briefing with the Federal Agency Task Force on Missing and Exploited Children, the Child Exploitation Investigation Unit (ICE), the FBI, SWAT, and Lieutenant Culver. Details were given; descriptions, goals, strategies, and specific assignments were discussed. Questions were taken, and everyone was sent to prepare their weapons and equipment before being called into action.

Shana had received her orders over a week ago, but she'd listened intently through the meeting anyway, taking notes. She wished Marks was going to be here with her, he always had something to say that made her feel better.

But Elijah said not to talk to anyone. Maybe it's better this way.

Shana was working directly under the SWAT commander Lieutenant Benson Cho as the first contact with each recovered child. He had had her attend three separate training sessions with his team during the week preceding. She was given SWAT equipment to wear, including a Glock 27 in an ankle holster in addition to her personal Glock 40. She also carried a baton, knife, and all the protective layers of her teammates for the operation.

After the Mexican gang Los Coyotes had dropped off the freezer trucks in the Acorn Industrial Area, several SWAT members had driven into the lot undercover to set up their base. They, along with actual longshoremen, had replaced some real shipping containers with decoy containers that were equipped as medical shelters, child protective quarters, and temporary holding jails. The entire replacement operation was done in less than ninety minutes.

Shana was ready at 1500 hours to get in the armored vehicle with Lieutenant Cho. The truck moved to one of the police rendezvous points near the Acorn Industrial Area. Lieutenant Cho's team was to lead the first wave of interception when the first drop-off car was positively identified. The interception of the child in the first drop was going to be critical. Shana knew there was no room for practice; she had to get in and protect the children, every one.

Shana sat in the back of the command truck with her small team, practicing the plan over and over again in her mind as they bounced along the road. She imagined herself doing the work, steeling herself to the chance of injury or death. She was determined to be the best team member possible.

"Hey, kid, you OK?" asked the man next to her, Officer Herman "Homey" Munoz.

Shana tried to look tough. "Yeah, I'm good."

"You sure?" asked Cho. "I don't like vomit in my truck."

Shana laughed. "I'm good, promise. You know, I've got a veteran friend who told me there's never any talking on the way to a mission. He said he'd fly into combat in a helicopter and no one talked, because, it was only on the way back that anyone had something worth saying." She laughed, but even to her it sounded forced. "Can you tell this is my first time?"

Munoz smiled. "Yeah. Lieutenant told us to keep an eye on you, but he must think you're tough if he's gonna have you be the runner. We're just maintaining and protecting the safety container. So." He raised an eyebrow. "Are there gonna be any problems?"

"Nope." Shana shook her head. "I've got this, Munoz."

I'm going to fight hard and just see what happens, she thought. *I don't know where Elijah is, but I'm going to channel him tonight.*

2100 hours. The truck sat parked a little ways from the Coyote drop-off zone, waiting.

Shana thought she understood a little better what Elijah meant about the helicopter rides. She was tense, but it was more of a hold on her nerves, something she could manage. Munoz sat next to her and appeared to be asleep. Was that a stress thing?

She went over her instructions again and again, walking herself through the various scenarios she may encounter on the field.

Lieutenant Cho's radio crackled to life in the front seat. "Concert One, this is Concert Leader. We are watching a vehicle approaching from the north and turning on to Middle Harbor Road. Driver seems to be headed right for the trucks. Roll to the perimeter and watch. All units, stand by to move in behind Concert One, on my command."

Shana clenched every muscle in her body. *Relax, remember the game days on the basketball team.* Relaxed and alert at the same time was the best way to perform.

Munoz's eyes were open, alert. Shana turned to say something to him, but he held up a finger to his mouth to quiet her. He pointed. Two more cars were turning off the road and heading toward the trucks. Their headlights were off. About a dozen

Coyotes moved warily out from the freezer trucks as the three cars rolled to a halt about thirty feet away.

The SOP drivers got out of their cars and slapped hands with one another. They turned to the gang and motioned for them to help unload. The bikers opened their cars and pulled a total of five children out onto the ground.

Five? There wasn't supposed to be that many. How was Shana supposed to get five children out of there by herself—and alive?

Lieutenant Cho hit the radioman on the shoulder, and he transmitted, "Close the road. Backup, start rolling."

The driver of the command vehicle hit the ignition and barreled toward the trucks, totally ignoring the bound children. The criminals started toward the trucks as soon as they realized what was happening. The SWAT driver managed to slide to a halt between the pile of children and the retreating criminals just as Munoz threw open the door and jumped out, leading the initial assault team.

Munoz made it to the stack of shipping containers with his partner right behind him. They were going to unlock the protection containers and then the temporary jail containers. Paramedics would be in the second group rolling in.

"Get on the ground!" an officer screamed, holding up his rifle. "On the ground! We *will* shoot if you move. Ground!"

Don't worry about the team going after the bikers and Coyotes. Shana was having trouble breathing. *Just get to those kids. Move.*

All five of the children were tied and hooded. She couldn't carry five. There were two girls closer than the rest, one wearing a pink and orange jacket, the other with a small red stain on the back of her pants. Anger flared in Shana. She could grab those two first.

"Get down! We will—" A gunshot cut the officer's words short.

Shana risked a glance up just in time to see one of the Coyotes raise his gun before another officer shot him through the chest. One of the kids screamed.

Shana had to keep moving. She grabbed the first two girls and ran, keeping low to the ground as she sped toward the first row of shipping containers. She needed to find the end, get around the corner, out of the line of fire, then get back as fast as she could.

Both sides were now firing, the remaining three children in the cross fire of the battle. Shana ran as fast as she could, using one of the biker's trucks as cover as much as possible. She managed to find a waiting Munoz and handed off the kids. She turned and ran back.

The small lot was chaos, the bikers and gangsters distracted from the five other vehicles sliding to a halt around the SWAT assault truck. Backup had arrived. Soon, all six groups of SWAT and feds were engaged.

Shana dove toward the remaining children, grabbing two by the ankles and pulling them toward her under the firing range. The kids were kicking and screaming, trying to get away from what they were sure was another attack. Shana was struggling to keep her grip on them, but suddenly one of the children went limp, a small pool of blood forming on the dirt ground. Shana cursed and let go of that child, using both hands to pull the other one under her arm.

Three black and white units from the OCPD drove right past the conflict to behind the shipping containers, setting up protection and paramedics.

Shana deposited her load and went back for the last two children. Neither resisted her touch, the one's back sticky with blood and the other bleeding from the head. By this time, the criminals had all been apprehended, either surrendered or shot down. A cleanup crew was busy moving bodies and driving the bikers' cars to the piers. Within a quarter hour, the site was ready to present itself as a child drop once again, several FBI agents staged as Coyote members out by the trucks.

Shana sat leaning against a shipping container, hidden from the drop-off zone. Her knuckles were bloody, but she didn't notice the sting. Munoz dropped to the ground next to her with a grunt. He peeled off his gloves and handed them to her, indicating she should put them on.

"Hey, kid. How you holding up?"

"Two died." Shana's voice rasped. She cleared her throat. "I had him. I had him in my grip and he just . . . and I was too slow for the girl . . . fuck."

"But you got three out of there. That's three more lives you saved tonight, and there's a lot more to come. Come on." He lightly punched her shoulder. "You did your job. Take a breath and push it all down for now. You've got to focus."

Tears blurred Shana's vision. "We followed the plan exactly, and my children are dead. I want to do my job, but . . ."

"We never save everyone, officer. This is about doing a job and doing it right."

Shana crossed her arms. She wished Marks was there to talk to about this, not Munoz. "This is bullshit. I need help pulling these children off the field."

What the fuck had Cho been thinking, leaving all the children to one officer to secure?

The radio called in three approaching cars to the site. Munoz stood. "Go see if there're any OCPD nearby and grab one of them to go out with you. Do it now, the cars are on Middle Harbor. Move."

Shana moved out and saw Officer Azadyar Nazari. "Azzie, come here. I need help." She explained the assignment and asked if the officer would be able to assist her.

Nazari checked her bulletproof vest and nodded. "On it. We have more than enough backup here."

"Hurry. There's three cars coming in." Shana jogged off to the shipping container closest to the lot's clearing, pressing herself against the cool metal siding next to Munoz.

"Nazari's a good choice," he whispered as the trucks came to a stop.

Three new bikers got out of the trucks, clasping hands and

laughing jovially. They ignored the "Coyotes" sitting by the trucks, instead talking to each other about how their pickups had gone and how many children they had in tow. They all wanted to know who had some fun with the kids. They were laughing.

Nazari silently joined Shana, her SWAT knife held at her side. She'd slice the children's leg ties so Shana could grab them and run. That first group had shown that her original plan had several issues that needed to be addressed. Children being able to run was one of them.

The FBI Coyotes shouted at the bikers. "Ay! We got beer over here. You hombres want some or no, man?"

The bikers exchanged looks, shrugged, and went to collect their children. Each had grabbed two; that made six for Nazari and Shana to retrieve.

Shana nudged Nazari and gave the hand signal to prepare to move.

The bikers were too far for Shana to hear their words. They were laughing about something as they approached the fake Coyotes and the hidden agents. As soon as the bikers were within reach of the beer, the SWAT stepped out from the surrounding containers and the "Coyotes" pulled their weapons.

"Drop to your knees! Hands on your heads!" barked the Coyote who had offered the beer.

As the first one went down, Shana smacked Nazari and both took off toward the children. Nazari quickly cut the children's feet free and Shana got them up. The two officers were able to usher them off the field without incident.

Shana felt a little better. When she handed them off to Munoz, he gave her a look that seemed to say, "See?"

61

THE NEST

Elijah closed his backpack, careful to keep the zipper silent. He sat nestled in a quiet corner of a warehouse attic, next to a large air vent that looked out over the Acorn Industrial Area. Lamb had told Elijah where the Los Coyotes gang intended to park their trucks, so Elijah had brought his essential supplies and broke into the warehouse the previous day to set up his nest.

Elijah had gotten a lot out of his training to be a spotter for a sniper unit eight years ago. It wasn't Elijah's favorite detail: too much watching and not enough action. It took a lot of patience and dedication to be a good sniper. Elijah admired all the men in service who chose this day in and day out. Over the course of the night, and all throughout the day, Elijah sat quietly in the attic, allowing the local wildlife and warehouse workers to accept his presence, even his secret presence.

Rick had not been happy with Elijah when he'd told him where he was going. Elijah had called Rick while packing his things in the condo, before he'd given Shana the slip.

"That's it?" Rick had said. "You're just going to join the battle anyway? I thought we'd decided you were going to listen to the cops and stay out of it."

Elijah paused. "I never said I'd stay. I won't engage unless I have to, I promise. I'll be safe, and . . . and I'll come home to you." He swallowed, hoping his words sounded like he believed them. "I love you."

Rick's voice was choked with emotion. "I love you, too. I won't see you before you leave, will I?"

"No."

"Then, I guess I'll see you at home tomorrow."

Elijah was numb. He'd never had to deal with something like this before. "Yeah, at home. Friday. Hey, Rick?"

"Yes?"

"Don't stay home alone tonight. Please. Stay with Phillip, or Juno. Just . . ."

"Come back." Rick's words had followed Elijah the rest of the day, an echoing command Elijah was afraid he might disobey. For Rick, he'd do anything—after this score was settled.

This particular warehouse sat next to a dirt lot filled with shipping containers. The freezer trucks had arrived yesterday around 1630, just as Lamb promised. The Mexican gang parked the trucks and left in a couple of vans, just as if they were going to rest and would be back to work the trucks later. It was a smooth, flawless operation. No one would have suspected anything unless they knew about Operation Fuck the World.

At 2330, one of the men had snuck back into the lot. Elijah watched as the man climbed a shipping container and jumped onto the low rooftop of the warehouse across from where Elijah hid. He'd be watching the trucks overnight, just as Elijah was.

It was 0100 when the police arrived. They came undercover, dressed as longshoremen, but Elijah recognized some of the men from the station. He also recognized some of the guys from his union down at the docks. Hector Ramirez was one of them. Elijah doubted he knew what was going on as the police moved shipping containers around. They removed some containers and put in some new ones Elijah was sure were filled with equipment for the battle. As he watched them work, Elijah was proud of the longshoremen as if they were his men. It'd been too long since he'd been down to the docks. He missed working with these guys.

The police left as quickly as they'd come. The whole operation had looked like any other job you'd see in the docks. The hidden Coyote had watched the whole procedure as well, but since the police had completely ignored the sitting freezer trucks, the man appeared unconcerned.

Since then, Elijah had just sat. The longer he waited, the more his anger brewed into his heart, steeping his thoughts of what was to come. He watched the empty dirt lot for hours. This was where the children of Oakland City will be brought to be sacrificed to the god of greed and darkness, by the same men who murdered Austeja Valdas. Elijah hated these men. If it weren't for their murder, for how they'd ripped apart his dearest friend's life, he may have been out of the war by now. He'd be home with Rick, now. But the threat they posed to Juno was too high for him to not address. It was his duty to be here, to witness the end of the Sons of Perdition—and to cause it, if necessary.

He was so motivated to ensure that this police operation went smoothly, Elijah decided it was appropriate for him to remove the sniper threat.

Elijah stepped out from the large vent on the pier side of the building. He easily climbed down and went to the blind side of the building that supported the Coyote sniper, climbing the wall using the drain pipe. Slowly, he raised an eye under his black cap to see if the sniper could see him.

When nothing happened, Elijah pulled himself up silently to the roof and moved over the low hump in the middle of the building. It was easy for Elijah to move silently after all his training and battle experience. When he crested the hump, he saw the sniper with his rifle next to him. The sniper was asleep on watch. When he was close enough, Elijah heard the regular breathing of dreamland. Elijah frowned. It was a shame the man wouldn't be awake to put up a fight.

Elijah stepped next to the Coyote and softly placed a foot over the man to straddle him. He reached for his SRK knife, a practiced and familiar move. After Elijah separated his life from the body, this man would be sent to a different sphere. Wherever that place was.

He leaned forward, judging the bottom of the ribcage, and readied to drop a knee just below the diaphragm to keep the man immobilized. The man didn't even have a protective vest. So little training.

Elijah dropped his knee, clamping the neck of the enemy as his SRK knife pierced the man's clothing. The knife slid perfectly under the bottom rib, slicing the diaphragm and sliding up into the chest cavity, into the heart. He drove the knife deep into the heart, then twisted the knife to do maximum damage to the internal organs.

The man gasped and a tremor ran through his body, but fear had overridden the Coyote's ability to fight back. Elijah pulled out the knife and considered decapitating the fallen man, but he did not. He knelt beside the man, putting weight on his back and keeping the grip around his throat. He waited until he'd bled out enough so that Elijah was sure he was dead. Elijah was careful not to be covered in blood from this murder.

This was one thing that he'd done to help avenge Juno and Austeja. He pushed himself up and silently retraced his path back to his nest. Something Lamb had once said came back to him. He was not afraid of the dark, he was what you should fear in the dark.

The day ticked by, and Elijah watched with a keen eye as first the FBI arrived at 1500 hours, then the first batch of bikers at 2100. The sun had already set, but between a full moon, the lot's bright security light, and the city's streetlights, Elijah had no trouble making out the people below. After the confrontation initialized, Elijah noticed a seventy-foot semi rig on Inner Harbor Road stop to maneuver a tight U-turn. That was good. The FBI must have set up this traffic block to give them some time while securing the perpetrators and remanning the truck with under-cover officers. No other bikers or Coyotes could reach the drop-off spot with the entrance road closed like that. The FBI had really done their homework.

Gunshots brought his attention back to the dirt lot. The approach was on, fast and crushing. Elijah watched as Shana darted out toward the small pile of children. Right away, she had to prioritize human lives, one of the many impossible decisions in a crazy activity like war. One of the children was shot, then another. Shana didn't pause but continued to pull the victims out of the line of fire. Elijah gave a grim nod of approval, even though the metal vent kept him hidden from his friend below. She was a good solider, not letting her emotions get in the way of duty.

But she's got a good chance of getting hit, the way she's moving out there. I need to work with her on that sometime.

The semitruck conveniently finished its U-turn just after the FBI finished clearing the battleground. Elijah had to grudgingly admit that the operation was well organized. Too organized, in fact. The FBI were bogged down with laws and standard operating procedures, while the Sons of Perdition had none. The law versus the lawless. In a war, the focus was on killing and destruction with no limits.

He sighed as he watched the second delivery truck roll up the gravel road. He didn't come here to kill, only to watch and assist if needed. He'd helped already, and if it came to it, he was ready. He stroked his Cold Steel SRK knife in his idle hands.

Elijah had carried this knife through all the battles he'd fought in the Rangers. It magically transformed soldiers into carcasses. With its great Krafton grip, the seven-inch, black matte knife was a thing of beauty. It didn't reflect light: all darkness. Long enough to destroy internal organs, the point was shaped so that it first stretched the skin of the enemy before puncturing it with a pleasing *snap*. Once the point was in, the elegant curves of the blade and the incredibly sharp edge allowed this knife to slice deep into skin, muscle, and deep tissue. Elijah had always been able to inflict a deep wound with plenty of directive control for specific damage. He had mastered the wound, the puncture, the penetration, and the precise incision that would end the life and the hope of life in the enemy. It had been a long time since he'd used this knife in battle, a true battle, yet it felt so familiar.

The second group of bikers was apprehended, Shana and all the children safe. She had a helper now, that was good. It was suicide sending one woman out into the field to gather all the victims.

Elijah gripped the knife harder. The operation's plan didn't have contingencies for the irregular deliveries of children. He should help. They needed his help. He'd promised himself and Rick that he would only fight if it became necessary, and now was the time. The police were trying to adjust as they went but, their oversights in planning were now resulting in deadly mistakes. Innocent children were dying. Shana was smart, but she wasn't safe. Not under leadership like that. Elijah itched with anticipation. He had given up his freedom after this attack to be sure that Juno and his family would be safe for once and for all. Kids were dying down there, and he'd be damned if he would allow any bikers to leave this battlefield.

He quickly gathered his belongings and made his way to the warehouse's pier side to scale down once again unnoticed. He found a void space in the foundation of the warehouse for his backpack, pulled out the equipment he wanted to use and secured them tightly to his body. Then, he moved toward the fight.

62

ACORN INDUSTRIAL AREA

S hana was beginning to feel grateful for all the long nights spent in the cruiser while watching Elijah. It had thrown her religious sleep schedule off just enough to keep the long day from gnawing at her. She had the feeling she wouldn't have felt tired now, anyway. The adrenaline-filled night sang through her veins, more potent than any type of coffee.

Although Shana felt more alive than she'd ever felt before, her faith in the operation was beginning to waver. She wondered what other mistakes were being made like the failure to anticipate clumps of children arriving amid gunfire.

It was now midnight. The previous hour had seen another three vehicles come in, one pair traveling together and a single delivery, all with two children each. The arrest process had gone pretty smooth for the pair of vintage cars that arrived together. The surprise was sufficient enough to simply freeze the bikers involved. However, when the single car arrived shortly after the first two were packed off, the biker had gotten out of his vehicle already visibly on edge.

Shana suspected he was on something that had him paranoid.

He dragged his two children out and pulled his gun from its holster, holding it high. The biker had several clips in leather pouches on his belt, and a second gun stuck out from his boot. He pushed the children toward the truck and motioned for the truck gang in a quick, impatient manner.

He approached the back of the nearest truck, but when two SWAT team members stepped out from the right side of the truck to tell him to drop, he immediately started to fire. Shana and Nazari had already started running toward the truck when they heard the first shot. Shana didn't care, her eyes were fixed on the two struggling children. Nazari hesitated before following Shana.

The biker was distracted by the returning fire, not noticing Shana and Nazari sliding in under him to grab the children. He was able to stand his ground for several seconds, getting a fair number of shots off. One hit an undercover Coyote in the head, the man who traditionally offered the beer.

An agent approached the biker from behind and put his gun to the man's head. He fired, ending the threat and covering Shana in organic debris.

Shana realized one of the children was hit. She clutched the bleeding boy to her own body. He still had a heartbeat. He could make it. She shouldered the child and took off at a run, leaving Nazari with the little girl. A medic team rushed out to meet her and took the boy from her arms. Around her, activity flourished as the crew worked to reset the battleground back into a drop-off spot. It was good that the ground was dirt; it absorbed the blood better. In the dark, it could even be mistaken for mud.

Shana went to one of the holding containers and found some water to wash the boy's blood off her gloved hands. Later, when she looked back over this horror of a night, she would realize what true hatred felt like. For tonight, it steeled her, helped her do her job. But she could see the anguish tearing away at Nazari, who got quieter and quieter as the evening wore on.

She was drying her gloved hands on her stained pants when Munoz entered the container grinning. "Hey, did you hear?"

Shana raised an eyebrow. "No, what? Did the Sons all surrender?"

Munoz's grin widened. "Basically. Culver's team just reported from his team's raid on the clubhouse. They caught a rat and got a copy of their operational plan."

Shana was confused. "What?"

"When they got in there, one of the Sons was in a vault full of contraband, filling his pockets with coke. Stealing from his own gang." Munoz shook his head. "And, get this, the bastard had on him a fucking binder detailing the whole operation!"

Shana's mouth dropped open. "A binder? Of their plan? Are they stupid?"

"That or cocky as shit. It has everything, the names of the bikers, where they're going, how they're getting there . . . all of it. It's the outline for the charging document when we get them all back to the jail."

Shana frowned. "Yeah, clever." A thought occurred to her. "Munoz, if the binder has a list of all the bikers, then how many are left to come?"

"Culver says the plan was for thirty-nine plus the leader. We've got the one from the vault, plus the ones we have so far . . . That leaves about thirty."

Thirty? Shana's head swam. So many. They'd already lost three men tonight, another four injured, including the man shot by the last biker. How long was this battle going to go on for?

A light flashed in the container, signaling that another delivery was coming down the road. Shana and Munoz rushed to their positions. When the car rolled into the delivery area, the team was a little more proactive and moved out to the vehicle to gain the advantage when the biker got out.

The man wore ragged jeans and a stained white shirt. In the yellow yard light, the stains looked purple. Shana growled. He didn't stop the engine, just hopped out and opened the trunk of his car, revealing his bound children. He smiled at the Coyote nearest him. "There ya go. Hurry up so I can get outta here."

One of the kids started to squirm. The biker looked down, and as soon as his face was turned away the Coyote slid a cuff around the man's wrist. Shana and Nazari started to move toward the children.

This biker was over six feet tall and at least two hundred thirty pounds. He yanked his wrist up toward his head, pulling the undercover officer off balance.

"What the fuck?" The biker roared. "You gonna take my load and not pay for it?"

He pulled the officer into a choke hold before the smaller man was able to regain his balance. The officer was starting to turn blue. Shana was running, quickly closing the distance between herself and the biker. She was torn—save the officer, or grab the children? Before she could get any closer, another officer reached the biker and put his Glock to the right side of the man's head and pulled the trigger.

The bullet tore through the man's brain and exploded out the back of the skull, spraying bits of bone and brain matter across the yard. The anger of the SWAT team had been building all night, and it was burning now.

Shana looked away from the destroyed head and gathered up the children—also now splattered with blood—and took them to the medic's container.

The medic containers held small cots for the children as well as basic first aid, supplies for stitching up any bad cuts, and blankets for the children to wrap themselves in. Every child was given an initial examination for any serious injuries before getting a bottle of water, some fruit, and a sandwich. The children with the more serious injuries were kept in a separate container so their suffering wouldn't further frighten the others.

Shana set the little girl she was carrying down on a small cot and gently removed her bindings. "You're OK now, sweetie."

The girl started to cry. Shana hugged her. "Shh, you're fine now. This is Officer Munoz. He's going to patch you up and give you some food, OK?"

Munoz crouched down in front of the girl, some alcohol wipes in his hand. "Anything hurt, angel?"

A short while later, a 1947 Plymouth pulled into the lot. Before Shana and the team could go out and meet him, a white Chevy work van pulled in behind him.

"Chuck!" The biker in the work van called. "I thought that was you!"

The short, pudgy biker in the Plymouth got out of his car. "Carlos, my man. I'm good and ready to hit the road."

"Totally. Hey, you, is that beer?" He waved at the Coyote holding cold beer—a different officer, now. "Yeah, I just got a call from the boss. You were on my call tree, but here you are. You, this applies to you too."

He pointed to the Coyotes. The lead officer behind the containers with Shana held up a hand, signaling for the team to hang back until the biker finished speaking.

"Magnus wants to wrap this operation up. He's calling everyone in and the rest of the deliveries should be made in the next half hour. Get ready for the rush."

63

ELIJAH MOVES

E lijah was able to climb down the side of the warehouse, smooth and quiet. That side faced the bay and wasn't lit. Getting out of the warehouse was one thing, but making his way into the fenced dirt lot with potential FBI snipers was a whole new challenge.

Elijah moved like darkness through the shipping containers, adorned in shadow and stealth. He heard a few more gunshots as he worked his way into the lot, but he focused on his own movements. He slipped past a few patrolling officers. While he was sure that, under different circumstances, he could pull off the persona of a SWAT member and just waltz into the base, he wasn't sure if Culver had shown the team his face or not. It would be just like Culver to make sure everyone knew he was to stay away.

Elijah peered around a corner, spying a medic tending to three wounded bikers sitting on the ground. The medic looked up at the echoing boom of a gunshot. Must've come from the trucks. She returned to cleaning one man's bleeding arm when another officer ran up to her.

"Cho wants everyone on the field, now. Emergency."

The medic dropped her bandages and followed the officer deeper into the container maze. Emergency? Elijah wondered what kind of emergency would pull a medic from her wards.

Silence settled in the darkness. The bikers lolled on the ground, unable to escape, injured and unable to move while cuffed with plastic ties at the wrists and ankles.

Elijah slid over to them and knelt by the first one. He put his left hand over the man's nose and mouth and pressed the man's head back, hard, against the cool metal of the container with a soft thump. With his right hand, Elijah reached down and placed his palm against the biker's xiphoid process, the little bone at the base of the sternum.

All I have to do is push to break the bone and ram it up to puncture the diaphragm.

It was so easy to do, like performing CPR. His breathing would be interrupted, the chest would start to fill with blood. One of his enemies could be dead in just a few minutes, long before anyone would notice.

Elijah started to apply the pressure, but then he hesitated. The second man had noticed his presence and was staring at Elijah, horrified. Elijah saw the fear in his eyes, the wild panic of a man who knew he was going to die. The third man was groggy, possibly from some sedative in his system, and didn't notice the danger. He might be dying already. But the second biker Elijah stared at, looking deep into the man while he controlled his first victim. Something tapped his head, and he twitched.

These men are already captured, something whispered in his mind. *This is murder, not vengeance.*

Suddenly uncomfortable, Elijah let go of the man and backed away. The man's chest heaved, gasping for breath through his gagged mouth. Both men stared at him in terror, and for once the look of terror in his enemies didn't fill Elijah with elation, but shame.

He slipped away, back into the darkness. *I have a battle to finish.*

64

THE RUSH

Shana's stomach clenched. The rest of the gang was coming in a rush. What if ten, or even twenty cars showed up at the same time? How many were left? They had been managing, but just barely. Having two or three vehicles come in together made it tough for Shana and Nazari. What if they were trying to separate out a dozen children when another six arrived?

The SWAT crew moved in on the two bikers. Chuck and Carlos pulled their weapons and fired. Each hit an officer, one falling to his knees and then over forward, the other knocked backwards when a chest shot connected with his Kevlar vest. The police opened fire.

Shana and Nazari ran for the vehicles. Two of the four children were bleeding from gun wounds, their breathing shallow. Shana pulled out a living child and handed it to Nazari, who took the child with a numb expression, her movements mechanical as she took off back toward the containers. Shana pulled another child from the car and turned just in time to see Nazari get hit in her Kevlar vest and fall, her body shielding the child from the firefight.

The accumulating fury from a night of horror had clicked in for the SWAT, and Chuck and Carlos went down, their faces and chests mutilated by numerous rounds. The police were finally at rage level after this horrible, surreal night, but Shana's own anger was mixed.

If we fight like they do, does that make us any better?

When Shana reached the containers, she handed the child off to one of the OCPD officers and pointed at the fallen Nazari. The officer headed to the protective container and Shana ran back to Nazari. The child under her was fine, but Nazari needed attention. Shana heaved Nazari over her shoulder in a fireman's carry and with her free hand tucked the child under her arm. An officer ran to help her, but Shana shook him off.

"There's two more in the trunk who need a medic. Go."

The breeze from the nearby bay helped to move the smells out of the battlefield, pushing away the stench of blood and excrement.

Shana delivered Nazari to a medic container and returned to the main stage of the operation. What she saw coming made her dizzy.

~

Magnus Carlson felt very satisfied as he drove his 1956 Cadillac toward the waterfront. The operation was a success, he'd land a mountain of money off these organs, and the Sons of Perdition would forever be a force to reckon with in their community—and the police had no idea.

The message he'd sent out to the men was simple: bring in the hostages, hit the road, and no contact for at least three weeks. He'd also sent along his congratulations.

Other members of the club fell in behind his car as he headed toward the Acorn Industrial Area, and soon he had ten cars trailing him down the road. Most of the Sons preferred old vehicles like his

Cadillac—some for the classic beauty, others because they had money needing laundering. To an onlooker, they looked like a car club out on an all-night ride—or a *very* early morning ride.

Carlson followed his iPhone to the truck rendezvous location. He slowed as he turned off on Industrial Road and then Middle Harbor Road, looking for the dirt lot. His clubmen slowed and turned in right behind him. Carlson saw the trucks, but there was also a swarm of men in the lot, bustling with activity. Carlson frowned, his mind racing.

The Los Coyotes seemed to be cleaning up the area with what seemed to be another gang. Carlson didn't recognize anyone under the dim streetlight, but all were decked out in fighter gear. He didn't get this.

He recognized two of his men's vehicles being driven off toward the piers, a pair of bodies lying at the feet of a few Coyotes. The fuck was this? Were the Coyotes running a double cross on the gang, trying to take the children and not pay? How many of his gang had already met a similar fate?

Carlson looked harder, turning on his brights and flooding the lot with light. Most of those men didn't look Mexican, and they were too organized, too coordinated for a random rival gang. They seemed to be working a plan, and—

We've been sold out.

He imagined a pile of dead friends somewhere behind the shipping containers and a truck full of unpaid-for children. He gripped the steering wheel in rage. There would be hell to pay for this.

Carlson flashed his lights and honked his horn. He stuck an arm out, signaling the cars behind him to circle up. He stomped on the gas, tearing down the gravel road and swerving around the edge of the lot. Soon, all eleven cars were in a tight circle in front of the freezer trucks.

The men pulled out their weapons. Carlson slid across the bench of his car and got out the passenger side. He waved his gun high above his head to alert the men to scan the tops of the huge shipping container stacks for possible snipers. Others got out of their cars and trucks, using the heavy doors as shields, just as more armed men slid out from the shipping containers across the lot. Some wore official SWAT uniforms.

With a yell, Carlson fired into the crowd of officers around his fallen brothers. He hit the Coyote standing closest to the body of Carlos. He recognized the biker's bloody face lying in the dirt. His shot was the catalyst, setting the rest of his men into action as the bikers fired at police.

~

"Lieutenant Culver!" Shana ran through the containers, pushing medics and officers out of the way. "Culver!"

She found him with Lieutenant Cho. He waved her over without a word, and Shana fell into step with him and Cho as they hustled to the freezer trucks. Nazari was still in the medic container, and Shana didn't want to be alone in this fight. She was scared, she couldn't help it.

Everything they had accomplished could turn to shit. And if it did, she wanted to be with her lieutenant.

Lieutenant Cho was speaking urgently into his radio, asking for backup and directing the officers locked in the melee. They were pressed up against a container, the fight just on the other side.

Shana checked her Glock as another officer rounded the corner of the container, his gun raised to engage the enemy. But soon as he cleared the container he was struck down. Blood flowed from his neck as he slid to his knees.

Culver dove for the man, dragging him out of harm's way.

"Medic!" he screamed. He tried to staunch the wounds by pulling the man's jacket up to his neck and pressing down hard. Shana leaned in to help him.

There was a rumble in the distance, like thunder. Cho's radio went wild, but Shana knew what was happening before the transmission had finished.

"There are seven more vehicles pulling up. Repeat, seven more armed perps coming down the road."

Even as Shana's team was dropping, the Sons got reinforcement.

~

Elijah stood in the shadow of one of the large forklifts used for moving the shipping containers. He watched as seven trucks barreled across the dirt into the lot. They rolled out and started to engage.

Elijah watched this all, but didn't move. He was crouched near the battlefield, ready to spring into action, but he was waiting for the right moment. He hoped beyond hope that the police could pull it together, to finish these bastards without his help. He was surprised, however, that after all their preparation and planning, the police were just pouring rounds into the gang with no real plan of action. He would've moved men and weapons to contain and constrict the ability of the gang to fight.

This wasn't effective. He might have to enter the field, and soon.

~

Shana didn't have a plan for retrieving the children from the bikers' cars. With eighteen vehicles, there could be over thirty children in harm's way, but it'd be suicide to try to get to them in this firefight. Their presence was foremost in her mind, but she could tell the focus had shifted to an all-out firefight for her commander.

Shana, Culver, and Cho had worked their way to the freezer trucks, exchanging fire with the enemy. The lot reeked of blood and death, but most of all Shana felt like she could smell the fear of the children on the breeze.

She shook herself. *Stop it. You're imagining things.*

The fight had been going for almost ten minutes, and three more officers had fallen. Only two gang members had dropped.

In this kind of all-out battle, there was no room for emotions among the police to allow them to begin the mourning process for their fallen teammates. They were, however, driven to avenge what they saw.

Shana hit a bearded man shielding himself behind a classic DeSoto in the shoulder and smiled in satisfaction as he screamed. It was enough of a distraction for another officer to aim and strike him in the head.

Shana remembered her talk with Elijah in the coffee shop. She was not here to fight the gangs, she was here to kill. She was doing her best and realized all the police on the scene weren't going to back down, either.

How am I supposed to get to the children?

Rage ignited as both sides poured every ounce of energy into killing the other group. A helicopter appeared overhead with its searchlight illuminating the dark lot. It looked like reinforcements were on their way.

～

Elijah watched the battle proceed. The lot was littered with the wounded, dead, or dying. It was hard to tell which side suffered more. He spotted Culver and Shana, a couple hundred feet from him dug in beside the freezer trucks. There were bodies on the ground from both sides. Elijah scanned the gang members, looking for a leader. Take down the leader, and maybe the rest would crumble in resolve.

Elijah found him. A Nordic giant in club colors. The man was scanning his fellow bikers and seemed to come to a decision. He straightened and started yelling at his men. It didn't sound like orders—the tone wasn't harsh enough—but Elijah was too far and the night too loud for him to understand.

The leader reached up and had something in his hand. There was a lull in the gunfire and Elijah knew what was going to happen next. The lives of the children filled his mind and heart. He broke out in a dead run, pointing at the biker and shouting, "Bomb!"

65

THE GATE

Elijah was sprinting, pushing himself as hard as he could to cross the lot. At his shout, Lieutenant Culver located the man with the detonator and started to run right toward the bikers. What did he think he was going to do, disarm a heavily armed, hardened criminal who was surrounded by other heavily armed, hardened criminals? That was Elijah's plan.

Elijah realized that he and Culver were going to intersect. He barreled toward the police officer.

Shana had reached for Culver when he took off and watched him run toward the biker with what was probably a detonator. Then she saw Elijah powering toward Culver on a line to the same destination.

Everyone seemed to be aware of what was happening. From the corner of his eye, Elijah saw Benson Cho and two of his men start to fire at the opposite flank of the gang to provide cover. Those men turned and started to return fire, but Elijah focused on the closing gap between Culver and the biker leader.

Elijah caught Culver about a hundred feet from the line of enemy vehicles and tackled him hard to the ground, pressing him into a depression in the lot. There was a satisfying *whoosh* from Culver, telling Elijah he'd winded him. Good. He hoped he'd knocked Culver out.

"Stay," Elijah growled as he rolled over on top of him. As soon as Culver was down, Elijah was up and moving toward the container side of the gang circle.

The biker raised his hand and shouted, "Fuck the World!" as he squeezed his fist closed.

The explosion sent out a tremendous shock wave in all directions, throwing Elijah back through the air. The oxygen was sucked from the area and the force of the explosion toppled some of the shipping containers and trucks. Loose dirt rose in a cloud mixed with the metal, car detritus, and body parts and fluids. This was buffeted and supplemented by the eighteen smaller explosions from each of the bikers' gas tanks. Elijah soared through the air, carried by the force of the blast.

Elijah was still alive, somehow. The explosion had obliterated all the bodies of the Sons, each vehicle destroyed along with the children inside. Something heavy had struck Elijah in the blast. He rolled over with a groan and saw that it was the lead biker's head. He remembered how the heads of bombers in Afghanistan were often found intact after an explosion.

He pushed himself up on his elbows. There was a pair of shoes standing before him.

Elijah looked up to find Lamb smiling at him, hands clasped before him and dressed in his usual perfect dark blue suit with a vest and a soft green tie. His presence would've startled Elijah, but another, larger figure stole his focus.

It was same figure from his safe house. A pulse of shadow cloaked his silhouette, absorbing the firelight and blurring the man's details, but Elijah recognized him. This form had been burned into his memory forever that night, all those weeks ago.

Lamb was dwarfed in this man's aura of power, but he was smiling proudly, his teeth gleaming in the flickering flames.

"See," Lamb said, "here he is." Elijah was not sure that Lamb had actually spoken, but he heard him. Lamb turned to Elijah. "Just as we talked about, here you are, and here I am to help you get out of here." Lamb stretched out his hand, palm up.

Elijah took the hand and pulled himself up. He had landed in a spot that was miraculously clear of debris and shrapnel. He was hurt, but able to move. All of the tendons and connective tissue in his body had taken a massive blow and were registering the pain of having been almost separated.

"Come," Lamb said, gesturing behind him. There was a gate out of the dirt lot behind him at the end of a row of shipping containers. The metal posts holding the gate were glowing red from the reflection of the fires.

Elijah surveyed the lot itself. The debris of the explosion—a mix of blood, bits of flesh, pieces of machines, broken glass, rubber —seemed to be suspended in the air. The breeze had stilled as well, stagnating the air with the smells of the battleground, and somehow that comforted him.

Elijah turned back to Lamb, carefully avoiding the silent figure beside him. "Balaam?"

Lamb grinned. "Now there's a familiar name."

Elijah nodded, more to himself than to the man—or whatever— and faced the gate. That confirmed it for him.

So, Lamb had done everything he said he would so he could escape. Elijah smiled at the gate caught in the red glow of the fire. *How bad am I really if the devil's keeping promises to me?*

The other spoke, the familiar voice haunting Elijah's mind like a remembered nightmare. "You are my servant. I saved you, and now I claim your life as mine. You will be a strong force for the work to which we are dedicated. Come through the gate with me."

Elijah's thoughts flashed like a high-speed train. Going with Lamb was to escape prison. People would think he was dead because of his proximity to the blast. He hoped that if he went with Lamb, he would be remembered kindly. He felt a stab in his heart for Juno and Rick.

Walking back out to the battlefield was surrendering to the police. That meant time in prison, but he could still have Juno and may even still have Rick and his friends.

"Do you really want to go to prison, Elijah?" Lamb asked, his voice like smooth silk. He was standing next to the gate, his master beside him. "A man in prison is a burden to everyone. You'll lose all your friends."

"Not Juno." Never Juno. But what about Rick?

"Rick wouldn't love a man in prison. He's too good for the likes of them, for the likes of you. He won't stay, friend. Don't make this choice for a passing pleasure like him."

Lamb's words stung Elijah's heart. They stroked his deepest fears, like an alcohol swab on a bloody wound. Was it possible that Rick didn't love him, didn't want him?

The dark form stepped in front of Lamb and raised a hand. "Submit and follow orders, soldier. Come."

Elijah's chest constricted in similar way to how it had the night he first met this Satan-like creature. Elijah's memories washed over him, his inner violence and battle fury burning through his veins. Every death, every fight, every moment of stealth and victory. The memories exhilarated him, fused with his being. This was what he was good at, this was what he was meant to do.

Another, smaller memory flashed through his mind. It was gone almost before it had fully developed, like it wasn't supposed to be there. Elijah, soaring back over the misty mountains of an imagined village. Rick's voice calling to him, his kind smile in the soft light of the bedroom.

The fire in his blood cooled. Elijah wasn't sure exactly what life was all about, but choosing the darkness and becoming an executioner for what he had come to believe was the devil couldn't be it.

Just to live from one battle to the next called to him, but fighting to the death would lead to . . . what?

It was time to decide. Elijah stepped forward, joining Lamb at the gate. Lamb stepped back and opened the gate to let Elijah pass through first. The king of darkness seemed to demand that Elijah come through, he could feel that command in his bones. Lamb seemed to want to reach out and grab him, but for some reason did not.

If they wanted this so badly, why didn't they just force him? Elijah remembered something Lamb had once said in the condo, something about the rules.

Elijah walked up to Lamb, then turned to his master and looked into where he thought he would find the eyes. "You told me that I had to make my own decision about what I was going to do at the end of the battle. You kept your part of the bargain—you actually kept your promise to me."

The figure was silent. Lamb leaned in, peering around his king. "We're going to be very effective together. I'm always so impressed by how comfortable you are with death and destruction. You've made an excellent choice, friend."

Elijah nodded. "Thanks, but I actually came over here to tell you goodbye."

Lamb blinked. "You're . . . what?"

"I don't know what's going to happen to me when I walk out to the battlefield. I'm not very optimistic of the probabilities. But I have a pretty good idea about what'll happen if I go with you. And frankly, I've been made for more than that. Fuck you, Balaam."

There was an intense increase in the pressure around Elijah's head, and he thought he was going to pass out from the pain. Lamb and the other were gone, though the gate remained open to the darkness beyond. Elijah thought he heard Lamb moan, but then Elijah's pain increased and he fell to the ground.

A sudden rush of air blasted through the lot. The vacuum created by the explosion had released, like the world had been holding its breath. Elijah realized that his encounter with Balaam and Satan had lasted for only a second or two, and now all the airborne debris began to settle back to the earth.

Elijah got to his feet and looked down. There, in the dirt, was a pin of the sort you'd stick in a lapel or on a jacket. It was probably the one worn by the gang's leader, the one with the bomb. In large letters, the pin proclaimed, "FUCK THE WORLD," the name the Sons of Perdition had called this operation. Elijah picked it up and put it in his pocket.

66

FINDING CULVER

The air was still vibrating from the explosion when Shana opened her eyes, almost afraid to look. She had dived behind a forklift parked near the trucks, but the force of the blast had pushed the machine up against a container. Luckily, it had only forced her knees up tight to her chest. Other than that, she seemed to be OK.

Shana wiggled out of the tight space and carefully looked at herself. Fingers, arms, toes, legs, torso. She moved everything. It all worked. She was covered with whatever it was that was floating back to earth—she didn't want to think about what (or who) it was.

People were calling out around her, their voices warped from her damaged ears. Everything sounded like it was underwater, far away.

Lieutenant Cho shook her shoulder. "Are you OK?"

Shana nodded. "Where's the lieutenant?"

"We're looking."

She looked around. The whole area was now covered with human and mechanical debris. After the bright flash of the explosion, the burning vehicles took on a dark, menacing glow in the lot. The power in the surrounding warehouses and streetlights were out. The emergency fleet of vehicles on the way would set up lights.

This is a nightmare. Her head ached. Where was Elijah? She should've known he'd come anyway. The roof to one of the older cars, one with a soft top, collapsed on itself in flames. It didn't matter that the soldier came now. He was dead, wherever he was.

Culver. She had to find her lieutenant. Even if—no, she wouldn't consider it.

She stumbled to her feet and walked toward his last known location. A hand stuck out from under a pile of debris. She rushed to him, frantically throwing off the dirt and who knew what else.

"Lieutenant, can you hear me?"

Shana knelt on one knee and saw him emerge as she pulled away the dirt. She put her hands on his back and grabbed his jacket through the dirt and shook him. He was lying in a depression facing down—that might have saved his life. He moved, just a little. Shana ran her hands over his body looking for serious injury, and when she didn't find any protruding bones, she rolled him over gently.

When he was facing up, he opened his eyes and looked at her, his face covered with dirt except for the eyes. "What the fuck happened? I've such a ringing in my ears."

Shana put her hand on his chest to feel his breathing and heartbeat. Regular—nothing was punctured. "We all have a ringing in our ears. Do you remember running toward the bomber?"

Culver put his hand on top of Shana's. "There were children in those cars. I had to try to save them. But . . . who the hell tackled me?"

Shana gave a choked laugh, tears running down her face. "Elijah McCoy, of course. He took off after he tackled you and ran toward the bomber himself."

"Elijah? That son of a bitch . . . but then again, here we are talking about it. I mean . . ."

Shana understood. The "we" didn't include Elijah. She turned and raised her arm.

"I have a man down here and need help," she yelled.

Shana helped the first responders dig Culver out of the ground before allowing herself to be checked out. Within a few minutes, the lot was swarming with people from just about every department in the city. A few newscasters were arriving and tried to bring cameras onto the scene, but Lieutenant Cho brusquely turned them away.

It was over. Not the operation, no. There were bodies to identify, families to call, perps to book, and reports to write. But the battle was over. She had survived, for the most part. They had won, but lost at the same time. She couldn't bring herself to look at the burning cars, to think about what lay ashen within.

Triage was quick and effective; the most serious were treated first. As more police arrived, Benson Cho became the communications and site command officer. He gave Shana three sergeants who had just arrived on site and told her to take them to the personnel containers to check on the status of the children and bikers. He clapped a hand on Shana's shoulder as she passed, stopping her.

"You did good," he said. "We've work to do now, but don't go home just yet when you're done, OK? Come with the rest of us to the bar. It'll help. You don't have to talk, if you don't feel like it."

Shana nodded numbly and started toward the last known location of the special containers to do her inventory. There were people moving around now as well as they could, being careful not to walk too much on the evidence of the very complex crime scene. Two officers parted to walk past her and the three sergeants, and Shana was surprised at how glad she was to see Elijah walking toward her.

67

ABSENT WITHOUT LEAVE

There was a group of bikers who, during the course of their pickups, found themselves too drunk or high to be able to follow any plan. They were scattered across the city, finding themselves each in different bars and abandoned apartments the following morning. But they all experienced the same sense of horror when they realized that they'd never gone to the drop-off.

They didn't need to listen to a newscast or make any phone calls to know they were fucked. They all realized that they needed to get the hell out of town and try to remember the intended locations they'd given the gang and make sure they went somewhere else. Three of them went to the place they said they would and were found within a month by friends of the gang.

Before they departed the Oakland City area, they knew they had to do something with the children. All but one of them realized that transporting a minor across any state line made them a target of the FBI. The one who thought it would be a blast to take the kids along to his favorite hiding place in Idaho was picked up two days after arriving, when one of the kids started screaming in front of a liquor store. People in the parking lot had interceded, and soon a police cruiser arrived and the officer was questioning the biker and the children.

The other eight were smarter than this, and so they did the next best thing. Three of them took their children to run-down parts of the city, each finding an underpass with booming traffic rumbling above. They had the exhausted, dehydrated children get down on their knees and executed them. To the bikers, these children were not part of families, just liabilities.

Two of the bikers had contacts in prostitution, and they took their four children and sold them to the pimps for a nice payday. Ronnie and another girl were sold together, the girl destined to star in a series of adult films while Ronnie was designated to star in a snuff film. The other two were going into regular daily service as prostitutes. There's always a market for children.

The final three bikers all made a decision, independently and early in the morning, to drive to a church that had fed them when they were down and out at some point in their lives. They dropped the last six children off on the church steps, tied and hooded, before they departed the city under a rising sun.

68

THE RELEASE

Seven weeks later, on a Tuesday morning, Elijah stepped out of Glenn Dyer Detention Facility into a crisp afternoon and drove away in Juno's car. The drive was quiet. Elijah stared out the window, marveling at how . . . how *free* he felt. He knew he deserved to be in jail.

When he had returned to the station after the Organ Concert, he thought he'd go to trial and then on to a bigger prison, but Culver had worked something out with the feds. Juno wouldn't tell him much detail, only that he was to be Elijah's accountability point of contact for the station, Elijah had to maintain a full-time job—easy to do with his internship at Rick's work—and he had to continue regular counseling at Solace. Elijah tried to imagine what kind of strings had to be pulled and promises made by the OCPD to swing this kind of a deal.

Juno got on the 80 South to head down to his warehouse. He broke the silence first. "How's it feel?"

"Unbelievable. You know, I made a decision, during the battle, that I intend to uphold. I thought I'd have to make my peace with it in jail, but things seem to have aligned in my favor."

"Tell me about that decision, brother."

The car slowed as it fell into traffic. City traffic was never an issue when Elijah was on his bike. He tore his gaze from the grid-lock and looked at Juno. "After the big explosion, I could've walked away into the darkness, fully commit myself to the life of violence and loneliness I had been living. Remember the darkness I saw in my safe house?"

"You mean when I found you sleeping in my office?"

"Yeah." Elijah grimaced. "I'd forgotten about that. He was there that night. He and Balaam—"

"So you've taken my opinion on that bastard! Glad to see jail knocked some sense into you."

Elijah slugged him. "Will you listen or not?"

"Sorry, man. I've just missed you."

"I missed you too. Anyway," he gave a pointed glare, "Balaam and that form of whatever it was, were there, standing next to a gate right by where I'd landed. I had a vision of what life would look like serving them, and what I was giving up. I would've never seen you again, never make up with Gabija or see Matas grow up. I would've given up my counseling and any chance of getting better. Most of all, I would've given up Rick. That brought me back. I didn't want to get away from all that. I wanted to be free. So, I told Balaam and his master to fuck off."

Juno clasped a hand on Elijah's shoulder, his eyes on the road. "I'm glad you came out and turned yourself in."

"And I'm going home today!" Elijah grinned. "I can't believe I have this deal, it's amazing."

"No, my brother, it's a miracle."

The sky was turning pink when the Nissan Leaf pulled up to the old warehouse. Elijah got out and stretched. It was strange, standing at the entrance to his safe house again. He hadn't been here in almost four months. It seemed like a different life.

Juno pulled out his keys and locked the car. "Phillip and Rick came and moved most of your stuff out. We just need to grab the last few bits. They were amazed at its existence and, by the way, thought it was pretty nice. So, a vote for my decorative ability."

Elijah followed Juno past the shed where they parked their cars and up to the door. "They're right. It's really nice in there. Maybe you can rent it out to some deserving millennial."

Juno laughed. "Maybe. I'm saving it for when Matas is an unruly teenager."

He got the door open and went inside. Elijah flipped on the lights behind him. Most of the furniture was still there, but the shelves were empty and the TV was gone. Someone had gone through the kitchen and packed away all the canisters and utensils.

Elijah had never been attached to his material things, but seeing the empty house like this—knowing that his stuff now belonged somewhere else, outside this oasis of privacy and out in the public world—made him realize just how different his life was now. How broken his life had been, hidden away from the world in this den.

"Juno, what you did for me by giving me this space . . . thank you." Elijah's voice was thick with emotion. "You are so good to me. You made me feel safe to be back. I did a lot of healing here, in spite of the horrible things I was doing. I really appreciate it, and know that it wasn't deserved."

Juno wasn't facing Elijah. His back was turned toward a box he was filling with bed sheets. "If you make me blush, you'll have to walk to Phillip's party." He looked up at the clock still hanging on the wall. "Let's not take too long. Phillip has killed himself to get this party organized. Every friend they have will be there, and my family's already at the house helping him set up. And I'm sure Rick is nervously awaiting your arrival."

Elijah's stomach knotted at Rick's name. "What do we need to pack?"

"Not much, especially since you're leaving the furniture to

Matas." Juno sat in one of the chairs by the table, grinning. "Take a look around and put anything you want that Rick and Phillip missed into the box. Those guys are so helpful. They were at our house on the night of the battle. Phillip is magic with Gabija. She just can't be mad at you when he's around. You picked some great friends."

Elijah walked the length of the safe house, searching for any lost objects. His steps were light and full of hope—he couldn't remember the last time he'd felt this way.

"I've been stuck in a cell for almost two months, you know." He grabbed a smooth rock from his bedside table he'd found on the beach and put it in the box. "Catch me up. Did all the Sons die in the explosion?"

"Did Shana not tell you all that?" Juno sounded surprised. "The Sons of Perdition are no more. Thanks to that binder, the police knew all the men involved. Nine men who failed to show at the drop-off point altogether are now either dead or being tracked."

Elijah pulled the clock from the wall and put it in the box. He didn't need the clock, but he'd rather donate it somewhere than let it tick away in an empty room. "What about the kids? Did Shana say anything about them?"

"She doesn't like to talk about it." Juno sounded sad. "But that part of the story is all over the news. It's common knowledge. The bodies of the murdered children have been recovered to the extent that was possible. DNA ID for some of them. Not all are accounted for and probably never will be. The men who were arrested from the Mexican gang and the bike gang were all arraigned. The police estimate that the eighteen cars involved in the bomb blast probably had around thirty-six children, all of whom were lost."

They were quiet for a minute. Elijah knew Juno was thinking of another child lost to the Sons. "What about the others?"

"The children in the shipping containers were knocked around but survived the blast. The office also yielded good information about the rest of the Mexican gang, and they're being pursued. The truck crew members that survived the big night weren't providing information, but there was information developed from them."

"Good," said Elijah. Served them right.

"The police have plenty of red meat to chew on after all this." Juno sighed. "Identifying the children who died in the blast is proving to be difficult. There's talk about a public monument built as a Tomb for the Unknown Children."

"Do you think I've done enough to correct the fucked-up situation I created?" Elijah sat on the other chair, staring at his friend. "Are you and the family safe now?"

Juno nodded. "I am, Elijah. It's over, so just let it go. You're getting another chance and I want to focus on that, OK? Changing topics, your girlfriend Roxanna is dating a guy she met at Fog Lifters. She started hanging out there after you two talked. Apparently, he heard her say she needed batteries for her vibrator and told her when he saw her again. She said they both laughed and it started them talking. So, they're a thing. Too late for you now."

"I will kick your ass, Juno."

"Just saying." Juno tapped his fingers on the table. "So, you haven't talked to Shana at all in the past few weeks?"

"No, why? What's up with Officer Thomas?"

"You mean *Sergeant* Thomas, now. She got promoted. Culver too. He's now Captain Culver."

Elijah grinned. "That's awesome! They deserve that. I think Culver will make an even better captain after going through something like this. And Shana was really brave, a hell of a fighter. We'll put her on our strike team."

"We're going to put the team on hold for the present." Juno was stern, but only slightly. "I don't know if you were told or not, but Marks was busted to buck private, but kept his job. He was only suspended for six weeks. Last week he came back to start some additional training, and then he'll be out on traffic duty for a year or so. You good with that?"

Why was Juno asking Elijah if he was good with that? Elijah wasn't the one hurt from Marks's mistake.

He shrugged. "He couldn't've fucked up if I hadn't fucked up. We wouldn't have been out there to protect you if I hadn't killed that biker in the first place." A lump formed in his throat. "I am so sorry, Juno. I can't stand what happened to Austeja because of me. I hurt you and Gabija so much . . . and all you have ever done was help me." Elijah covered his face with his hands.

A chair scraped against the floor, then Juno was pulling Elijah to his feet and in for a hug. Elijah put his head on Juno's massive chest and let his hot tears fall free. Juno's own tears slid down his face, splashing against Elijah's cheek.

When Elijah's sobs subsided, Juno released him. "It hurts me too, Elijah, but it's over. We've avenged her—*you* avenged her. I give you permission to forgive yourself."

Elijah smiled at him and wiped his face on his sleeve. "Thanks."

"We've got to live differently now, brother. We have to keep everyone safe, but that includes you and me. No more redeemer work, OK? Focus on the six of us here to take care of."

Elijah nodded. He found some tape and closed up the single box of items. He had a lot to learn about how to live in the light, but between Juno, Rick, and Phillip, Elijah felt he had a good shot at making it.

Juno checked the time on his phone. "Speaking of family, we better get our asses in gear and get over to your new home. You can't miss your own welcome home party."

Elijah hefted the box into his arms and followed Juno to the door. "You know I usually run screaming from a party, but I'm actually looking forward to this."

"Screaming? That's a picture I'll think about. Ready?" Juno stood in the doorframe, waiting for Elijah.

"Yeah." Elijah gave one last look at his old home, then flipped off the light.

They didn't talk at all on the way to the party. The closer they got to the house, the more nervous Elijah became. The streetlights painted the neighborhood trees with a warm amber glow, the houses lit like a Thomas Kinkade painting. Juno pulled into the driveway and Elijah stepped out into the nippy air with some hesitation. The door to the house was already open, and someone was waiting for them on the front porch. Elijah's heart skipped a beat when he looked upon the most beautiful smile he'd ever seen.

69

EPILOGUE

I t was just after eleven at night when Elijah pulled the Audi into the driveway of Rick's house in the Hoover-Foster neighborhood. *Their* house. He had to keep reminding himself of that. This was just another Thursday night of classes for him in his internship's college education program. Even after months of college, the long evening classes left him feeling filled to bursting with information. It was a tiring but happy feeling.

He stood in the dark drive and took a deep breath. There was a light on in an upstairs window. He liked the night. He didn't need much light to see or move. He was happy not to be seen as he went quietly in through the side door.

Elijah went around checking the first floor and making sure the front, side, and back doors were secure. No sound greeted him. He went quietly up the stairs and into the bedroom. There was a soft bamboo light on in the corner, and he went to turn it off. As he crossed the room, he could see Rick's face framed by the big, soft white duvet on their big, white platform bed. Elijah's heart swelled looking at him. He was beautiful.

Rick stirred and an eye slipped open. "Is that you, Elijah?"

"Yes. Why are you sleeping with the lights on?"

"It just makes me feel safer."

Elijah smiled as he kicked off his clothes. In a war, sleeping with a light on just made you a better target, but he didn't want to scare Rick by saying it aloud. He stepped over to his side of the bed and slipped in under the duvet. Rick scooted toward him. Elijah slid one arm under Rick's neck, his other arm wrapped around his lover, pulling him against Rick from head to foot.

Rick was still half asleep. "Did your class go well?"

"It did. I think I can do this. I'm finally catching on to everything, and all the new stuff keeps my mind busy. It gives me something to think about other than my past."

"We'll talk through the past as many times as you need." Rick yawned. "We're the future for each other, the past can't touch us. I'm yours and you are mine. No matter what comes up, we will deal with it together."

Elijah smiled. "I love you, Rick. I'm happy with you. I just can't seem to get enough of this affection."

"Remember, we read that is called—called—" Rick yawned again. "Skin hunger. We both need to be fed."

"You smell good." Elijah wrapped his arms tighter around Rick. Rick pushed back into him. Elijah could feel Rick start to let go and fall back to sleep.

"You don't need the light to feel safe, Rick. I'm home now." Elijah reached over and clicked off the light next to the bed.

As they slipped into the darkness, Elijah held Rick and knew he would always be comfortable in the dark. But so long as he felt comfortable there, others were sure to be out there as well, and constant vigilance would be required.

The darkness pressed against the window, not as hard as before, but it remained nonetheless.

ACKNOWLEDGMENTS

Until you heal the wounds of your past, you are going to bleed.
You can bandage the bleeding with food, with alcohol, with drugs,
with work, with cigarettes, with sex; but eventually, it will all ooze
through and stain your life. You must find the strength to open the
wounds, stick your hands inside, pull out the core of the pain that
is holding you in your past, the memories, and make peace
with them.

– IYANLA VANZANT

This book is part of my healing process. Those that have been on
this journey with me are compassionate, talented, and dedicated to
their work. They took the time to understand my story.

Over many evenings at the beginning of our relationship, I
read-aloud the draft of my first novel, *The Arena of God*, to Michelle
on the patio of her condo. Through this read aloud process, I
unveiled my war story. And she loved me anyway. It was a full
confession. She decided to leap onto my platform and our journey
began.

While on one of our stops in Marin County, I was fortunate to attend *A Pathway to Publishing* weekend workshop at the famous Book Passage bookstore in Corte Madera, CA. I was connected to a successful published author, screenwriter, filmmaker, and TV and radio host, Phil Cousineau. His consultation and encouragement with the *Arena of God* helped me draft the seven-book series titled the *Gideon Jones Chronicles*, which is still in the revision process. Phil later provided input on *The Consequence of War*, and urged me to get it published as soon as possible.

The cover artist, Allen Gilliland, a UK illustrator, took the time to understand what this story was and created a disturbing image of the tormented soul that lives inside all combat veterans.

A young, talented editor in Texas, Amber Helt of *Rooted in Writing*, worked on a long developmental edit with me over several months. When she told me her writing peers responded to the story with, "I would read the hell out that book," I knew that I was making a connection with younger readers as well as veterans like myself.

Thanks to this team, I am already publishing my next novel. Writing can heal the spirit, and through my work I hope that veterans and their families and friends will acknowledge and understand the pain and damage war can cause on your spirit, not just your body. I will continue to write and to heal my spirit, and perhaps others in the process.

ABOUT THE AUTHOR

Brian Oldham's life was forever changed when the mailman read the draft notice to him on the front porch of his Fullerton, CA home in 1966. Oldham served five years in combat in Vietnam and the war has never left him. He was not able to integrate back into college life and struggled with failed relationships. He had difficulty holding down a job that required him to take direction and work with a team.

After wandering the country for several years and caring for his dying father at home, he settled in New Mexico and found solace in his ability to use his fitness and combat skills in marathon running and extreme fitness events, eventually leading to a successful coaching career.

Post Traumatic Stress Disorder (PTSD) was being studied in the early 1970s but not fully understood or treated until veterans started returning from the Middle East conflicts of the 1990s. Oldham eventually moved into the financial services industry where he could work independently and earn a living for his family. The gift of fatherhood changed his life and began the steps of healing and reconnecting with humanity.

Today, he devotes himself to advocacy work in his community and he writes fictional stories with culturally relevant topics, always with a veteran protagonist, to help people understand the struggles all veterans face. He lives with his partner in many places around California, until she retires. He credits his healing to finally having someone in his life that would listen to his war story without judgment or condemnation. He speaks to service clubs and veteran's groups about his PTSD and how important it is for veterans to have a safe listener to tell their story to, so they can begin to heal and move past the horror, guilt, and shame that damages veterans for life.

CPSIA information can be obtained
at www.ICGtesting.com
Printed in the USA
FSOW02n0156181117
41238FS